PRAISE FOR

BEST AMERICAN GAY FICTION 1

Edited by Brian Bouldrey

"An annual series that promises to take gay belles lettres out of its literary ghetto. . . . The fiction gathered here is united more by its quality than its queerness. . . . The word *best* is entirely accurate."   —*Out* magazine

"This collection is filled with wonderful surprises that totally break up the stereotypes. The writing is always richly, provocatively, inspiringly individual, and on such a high level I want to cry out to the world: Watch out, writing by gay writers is a force to be contended with!"

—*David Plante*

"The high quality of the prose in this anthology comes as no surprise; for the last decade (and well before) gay men have been consistently producing some of the best writing in America. The greatest pleasure comes from reading the wealth of stories by new names. *Best American Gay Fiction 1* offers the opportunity to re-encounter well-known favorites and discover superlative work by new voices."   —*Fenton Johnson*

"Proof of another very good year for gay writers is in this anthology, with its mix of subtle voices, its hints of varying proclivities, and its musculature formed of so much palpable and poetic language. I felt younger, happier, and more dangerous after reading it."   —*Brad Gooch*

BEST AMERICAN GAY FICTION 2

Edited by Brian Bouldrey
Foreword by Bernard Cooper

"A highly readable collection. . . . From the elations of first love to the emptiness of a partnerless old age, *Best American Gay Fiction 2* explores the full range of human emotion."   —*Swing*

"A savvy, lively overview of current gay fiction."   —*Kirkus Reviews*

3 BEST AMERICAN GAY FICTION

Edited by Brian Bouldrey

Best American Gay Fiction 2

Best American Gay Fiction 1

Wrestling with the Angel:
Faith and Religion in the Lives of Gay Men

By Brian Bouldrey

Genius of Desire

3 BEST AMERICAN GAY FICTION

Edited by Brian Bouldrey

Foreword by Jim Grimsley

1 d0G-90-
520

Withdrawn

LITTLE, BROWN AND COMPANY

Boston New York Toronto London

ISBN 0-316-10236-9

ISSN 1088-5501

10 9 8 7 6 5 4 3 2 1

MV-NY

Book design by Julia Sedykh

Published simultaneously in Canada by Little, Brown & Company (Canada) Limited
Printed in the United States of America

140 6.99.520

This book is for Brad Craft,

the Queen of Hearts.

CONTENTS

FOREWORD

by Jim Grimsley

Sitting here, keyboard poised, computer spinning and humming, I am ready to begin work for the day. I want to write, but what shall I write? Shall I make some gay fiction? Or should I make some Southern fiction? Or maybe mix it up, just for variety's sake, and write some Southern gay fiction. Or, for a real change of pace, maybe I'll write some science fiction (although some would say this is more fantasy than science fiction—what I'm working on, I mean). Or maybe I'll simply shuck all the categories and write for the sake of literature itself, embracing that most refined of all the genres, literary fiction. Heavy with the need for this decision, changing my thinking this way and that, I wonder what to do, what to do, until at last it is sunset and clearly too late to do anything. I have spent so much time wondering what kind of writing to do that I have written nothing at all.

The practice of attaching a label to types of literature serves the needs of the marketplace, which requires a neat package for each product, and this is as true of the term "gay writing" as it is of any other label, like "romance writing" or "science fiction." Examine any of these labels too closely and it dissolves like the chimera it is, for these terms are useful only as long as we agree not to define them. We postulate that there is something called "gay writing" and that we can agree that certain pieces of writing could be grouped together under that category in a useful way. Implicit in that agreement is the fact that we do not attempt to define what gay writing is, and we avoid this for a very good reason: we cannot succeed at creating a successful definition.

The simplest case, and the writing that we clearly recognize as gay, is a story in which gay sex occurs, or may be about to occur, between gay men, the story being written by a known gay male. Most of us would agree that this would fall squarely into the box labeled "gay." Change any one of those conditions, however, and we are not so sure. A man wrote the story, and sure, there's gay sex in it, but the writer—is he out of the closet? Is he openly gay? If we call his writing "gay," will he be offended? If he turns out to be heterosexual, can his story be called gay at all? Do lesbians write gay fiction or lesbian fiction or what? Does the term "gay" include men of color or are we really talking about white guys? Should we switch to the term "queer writing?"

The questions accrue without end, layer upon layer. If a lesbian writes a lesbian novel with some gay men in it, and gay men buy it, is that a crossover novel? Are there any conditions under which a heterosexual could write a gay novel? Could a bisexual write one? Do bisexuals actually exist? Are gay people and homosexuals the same thing?

I myself am gay twenty-four hours a day, seven days a week, even when I am not masturbating or having sex, but when I write, am I writing gay fiction if I write a novel that has no central gay characters in it?

It is an open question as to exactly what function sexuality plays in the writing of anything. Sex contributes to the writing precisely as much as sexuality contributes to the life of the writer, I would guess, and the answer to that question then becomes, there is no answer. People grapple with sex in their own way, and writers deal with it in their writing in their own way, and what gets written may have the ring of truth or it may not, for reasons that have nothing to do with anybody's sexual credentials.

For me, sitting here in front of my computer, more important than any theory I have about what I am writing is the fact that I am sitting here at all. Any obsession, any compulsion that I have managed to collect can contribute to the work that I do. No idea of what my writing should be can be allowed to interfere with what the writing becomes, in actuality, as I make the words take shape.

But for you, sitting there with a book in your hand with what's called "the best gay writing of 1997," do any of these questions have any meaning for you? Probably not. Probably it's enough for you that Brian Bouldrey has some idea of what gay writing is and that he has given you a selection of gay fiction that he thinks is worthy of being called the best of the year. I expect that's a healthy attitude, and one with which you can proceed, with pleasure, to turn the page and read.

INTRODUCTION

*"There are no new stories,
there is only the rhythm of the times."*

— *Ezra Pound*

As the century and the millennium wind down, there's a kind of bewilderment in the collective psyche: what is going on here and now? It's an artificial pivot point, but artifice can often seem more real, in terms of what it can reveal to us, than reality.

In the writing classes I teach, all of my students are creating two kinds of stories: ones that take place more than a hundred years ago, or ones that take place ten minutes into the future. It's too troubling to write about the here and now, for there is no apparent movement, just a stasis, a fog.

All the movements are running out of energy: grunge in music, new narrative in literature, the Kate Moss waif look in fashion. We recycle things so quickly now that seven-year-old music is played at retro dance clubs.

What's left is a grab bag of broken-down pieces. They call it mannerism in art, the self-conscious exaggeration of what was once genuine. We are tapping our toes impatiently, as if we can resume our creative lives only after the ball drops and ends the century. Well, we tap one toe, anyway, because it feels like the other one is nailed to the floor and we're capable only of walking in circles—pivoting, at best, in this direction and that.

Gay men, especially, feel the pivoting. We are turning about but not, apparently, moving assuredly in any particular direction: protease inhibitors help some HIV-positive men live longer, but not all, and they're not a cure. Born-again queers such as Gabriel Rotello and Larry Kramer think gay men should start behaving like heterosexual couples and settle down, while younger gay men feel they have the right to sow their wild oats just as Rotello and Kramer did. Legal issues such as gay marriage and partner benefits get caught in internal debate. Rather than presenting a united front, gays are discovering that they have the luxury of disagreeing.

Gay-rights groups such as ACT-UP and Queer Nation—and all sorts of other previously strong coalitions—have drifted even as they have succeeded in making real progress in gay rights. There's infighting, even scandal and misuse of funds, in some of the most prominent philanthropic organizations. Things fall apart.

Maybe "fall apart" is too harsh a description. "Become porous," perhaps, is more accurate. After years of huddling in groups, gay men are going back into the world, living side by side with heterosexuals of every flavor. The wounds of homophobia heal, and we discover that on top of all the pitfalls of being gay in America, we are also prey to all the pitfalls of being American in America.

Like all other Americans, for instance, we crave privacy. It was once a fact that the iconic American household had a wraparound porch with a big front door where people met one another and talked. Now we have back patios protected by high fences, and architects build houses with huge, hideous garages in front, the symbolic opening to the house being a windowless, locked-down garage door that can be opened only by the owner with a remote control clipped to the sun visor of his or her car.

We are tremendously private, but we bottle it up; when we finally do see people, we are confessional. We divulge our secrets to utter strangers in therapy and on talk shows. The whole world is ours to study, in our private rooms, and the only way we can describe the world is in the way it shows how it affects us. Our stories are told too often in the "I" point of view; how can that be anything but self-absorbed?

Well, it can be a lot of other things, actually. Look at how Allan Gurganus climbs into the head of a widowed preservationist in "Preservation News"; how Tom House splits the "I" into two (very) different characters when a self-described blueblood meets a decided blue-collar at an art museum; how Dennis Cooper's "I" is so distorted by mind-altering substances and desire that it seems egoless, or else nothing *but* ego. And the others in this collection using the "I" are more interested in what others are thinking: the "I" of Robert Glück's consideration of his father, Eric Gabriel Lehman's "I" that looks with a kind of wonder and sympathy on a man who seems worse off than he. We are looking out into the world, and it's ours, once again, to "make queer."

What other pitfalls do we face as gay Americans? Like other Americans, we are waiting for our lives to become *perfect*, whatever that means. And because human life is not perfectible, it creates great disappointments among us. Perhaps one of the real atrocities of what is called pornography (besides its lame misuse of language) is that it portrays sex in perfectly choreographed ballets of bodies.

How does a really good writer talk about sex—or anything else—without slipping into the tired language of porn? Some of the best writing here, such as J Eigo's "Nomads," almost bruised in its purpleness, takes on the stuff of smut and turns it into a spiritual experience, one not void of humor and a relish for all that is imperfect and fumbling in sex, rather than for what is blandly (and incorrectly) laid out as a perfect moment. Eigo raises a bathhouse into the realm of myth, and he does so by avoiding cliché. The language is clean, but the bathhouse isn't. There are false starts, hurdles to jump, enemies to confront.

Life is not tidy, nor is the good fiction that depicts it. Keith Banner's characters bide their time in crummy jobs; Matt Sycamore's queens have to dodge the bashers; people die; relationships end. Everything falls apart. Rather, everything is made porous.

Even in the literature category.

In a bleak mood, readers like you and me can feel as if entropy has sucked the heat energy out of the literary world, or that our writers have worked the material far too much. It's all pie dough that's been overhandled; a child has mixed too many tempera paints into one big gray muck, and she has to wait for her birthday to get a new set.

Look at all the true-confession biographies. Writers have turned to nonfiction as if in an ever-escalating competition to outdo each other in horrific experience:

"I had sex with my dad!"

"I had sex with my dog!"

Another writing teacher I know offers a course in "creative non-fiction." His waiting list is a mile long: everybody is discovering that fictional constructions and forms both afford for more room to tell some kind of truth that is more important than facts, and give a reader an enjoyable way to receive this truth.

Writers subtitle their works unabashedly with words that seem, at first glance, a kind of waffling: "A Novel in the Form of a Memoir," or vice versa. Fictional biography, biographical novels.

Where does all this come from?

The line between fiction and nonfiction has been crossed and recrossed so many times that even Truman Capote might raise an eyebrow at the numbers of fictional memoirs and autobiographical novels being pumped into bookstores.

No, there's nothing wrong with it—there's nothing that brings writing more vividly and emotionally to life than personal experience, whether dressed up or understated. But it doesn't always have to be in the first-person point of view, and the best writers are discovering that there's more than one way to spill one's guts.

That's what makes the stories in this collection different, what marks them as something new and part of this strange, murky time.

Don't worry, it's all here: the big names, the new names, the rediscoveries, the confessionals, the comings-of-age, the erotica, the multicultural diversity, the drag queen's campy bitchery and the sorrows of AIDS, the families that understand and the ones that don't, the sex, the drugs, the rock and roll.

The stories, in general, never do really change, as Pound put it; only the rhythm of the times does. You can see the 1920s in the fiction of F. Scott Fitzgerald. You can see Hollywood in the '60s when you watch Elizabeth Taylor play Cleopatra. And you can hear the great gong of the late '90s sound when you read stories of puzzlement and conflict in this collection and elsewhere. Fiction today is doing one of two things: either breaking down into smaller and smaller special-interest genres or raising its head, seeking outside of itself commonalities and sympathies.

Yet this anthology is more than just a time capsule or a dusty archive to show what we were thinking about as the new millennium approached. There are great movements afoot, signs that gay men have grown tired of navel-gazing and are beginning to integrate themselves into the culture at large. Much as we sometimes hate it, we are American as well as gay.

But what's really exciting, what's really new and not muddy and not tapping its toes impatiently, is the number of authors who are using formal innovation to find new ways of expressing the truth. There are stories in this volume that give voice to heretofore inexplicable emotional states. Thomas Glave's "Whose Song?" is set up and told like stream-of-consciousness crossed with African-American skaz, while Dennis Cooper's "The Freed Weed" is written in the stripped-down, drugged-up style of somebody trying to get at the truth through sex, drugs, and rock and roll. Allan Gurganus's "Preservation News" begins in the form of a historic preservation newsletter.

Here is a way that queer writing is queered in a more subtle way: not just in showing gay men in gay sexual situations, but in providing a means of looking at the whole world through pink-colored glasses.

What makes a story gay—the author or the content? Is there a queer language? Is there something that is inherently "queered" about the books gay men bring into the English language? Yes, and in an exquisitely subtle way, a way that can teach anybody, gay or straight, how to speak that language.

Any good writer, after all, teaches the reader a new way of reading within the course of the storytelling. Some of the classic American novels—Toni Morrison's *Beloved,* for example—have early chapters that resemble a kind of schooling. You must read slowly at first, as you learn the story's alphabet, then its grammar, then its vocabulary, and then you're up and running, you never want that language to become silent.

Each and every writer has her or his own language to teach a reader, and maybe that's what we call style, or originality, or genius. A writer who describes panty hose as "itchy fickle leg jails" is somebody who has spent a lot of time wearing panty hose. Those of us who have *not* worn panty hose can learn what it's like to wear them, even if we've never put them on.

In the same way, great writers can give new insight into the most exotic, impossible-for-others-to-experience things, such as lesbian sex or giving birth or dying of AIDS, as well as put a new spin on ordinary objects we deal with every day. That's what queer writers can do, too—make the world new through our own, original desires.

Some of my favorite writers have written thoroughly queer

books that have few or no gay characters in them. Jeanette Winterson's *Gut Symmetries*, for instance, or *Art and Lies*, in which Winterson defamiliarizes heterosexual relationships by familiarizing them to the queer sensibility.

Similarly, Dale Peck's *Law of Enclosure* makes but minor references to gay themes as it maps the rise and fall (and fall and rise) of a heterosexual relationship of many years. And yet I'd call this, too, out-and-out gay fiction.

William Haywood Henderson's *The Rest of the Earth*, excerpted in this volume, is a novel that follows a man from a starting place in San Francisco as he travels east into the Wind River Range of America's heartland during the great migrations of the 1800s. Henderson's book is queer from tip to toe, though the word *queer* is never uttered (or not, at least, in the way we use it). Walker Avery, the hero of the novel, heads east against the general "Westward ho!"; he is a silent man taking his knowledge from women he meets along the way, yet he feels such an intense attraction to men he encounters that he trembles—as does the story's narrative style—when they appear naked before him. I would even suggest, though I can't quickly say how he does it, that the way Henderson has written about terrain, landscape, and geography is bent, queer, gay original style.

And once again, a queer author has taken a genre, in this case the Western (arguably a hackneyed form with a tired language, like that of pornography), and revitalized it by looking at it through new, queer eyes.

You can also see this in "The Future of the Flynns," a story by Andrew Sean Greer. First published in *Esquire*, a magazine that tends to panic around homosexual material (as it did when it pulled David Leavitt's blow job–ridden novella during the same year), Greer's story may be the most subversive of all, hiding its obvious queer content behind something only a little subversive—who is that quiet little boy at the dinner table? Imagine all those rugged straight men reading and loving that story and then finding out the truth of it—it's like finding out that the chef served you muskrat when you thought you were eating chicken.

What I'm trying to say is that gay men write inherently gay stories, which may never have to have a queer character in them.

What makes a story gay, then—the author or the content? If it is indeed the content, then the content is much bigger than what we may think it is. The whole world is a rather queer place.

Brian Bouldrey
San Francisco, March 1998

3 BEST
AMERICAN
GAY FICTION

J Eigo

NOMADS

ALL UP AND DOWN the corridor, door after door opens and shuts. Rectangles of light shuttle back and forth across the darkness. Bodies come forth, and shadows flee. Some are swallowed up. Others go on display, traders at their stations.

A door ajar is a frame. The ill-lit figures that traverse it become suddenly, almost painfully, overreal. Those who settle into poses in the glare remain that way. Situated in semishade at the end of a bathhouse hallway, I survey the whole illuminating relay. Every guy whose path I cross I imagine in my grip.

Although no one in this drafty, windowless hallway knows for sure, outside it likely snows—this, after all, is a city of snow. But every private room has its own small heater, and this establishment's four corners (shower room, steam room, porn lounge, sauna) range from warm to torrid.

At the opposite end of the passage, a man moves into the light, muscles stretching visibly over his broad, lean frame, an arresting figure. The wide spans of chest and hand narrow to slender waist and wrist. This effortless differential confers on him automatic graciousness. The stark-white towel around his middle is only slightly whiter than he. The pallor of his skin clashes with the black of his hair, brows, and lashes.

He flashes cheekbones so high you'd think they'd interfere with his sight. But his eyes are large and wide-set, and they make it clear that he's taking all of the scene in, including me. Although we each catch the other looking his way, we each eye the other back.

A shadow of a beard enables the observer to read all the big and little bones of his lower face when he speaks, which is what he does once he's closed the distance between us: "Hi, I'm Dane."

"I'm charmed, I'm sure." The opposite of blond: is this Dane not a paradox? I try not to blink. "Beyond that, just who I'll be tonight is still negotiable."

"Me, too." He smirks. "So why don't we do it together? We might be the two hottest guys here tonight. Justice decrees that before we leave, we come together. How 'bout it?"

"Are you inviting me back to your room?"

"Tonight I've only rented a locker. You could invite me back to yours."

"Like you, tonight I didn't rent a room."

"I never do. I never seem to need to." He didn't need to add, My body and bearing assure my entry to any room I please. Vagabond by propensity, the cock of the walk interjects his inimitable energy wherever it's needed. When he flashes his teeth, he lights our end of the corridor. "Good luck." He turns on a heel. With a swagger that comes naturally to one who is beautiful, brilliant, and built, he retraces his path to the end of the hallway, turns a corner, disappears. I'm frozen in place.

Into the vacated space in the spotlight, one of this venue's stream of refugees springs from the shadows. This slender guy of composite gender misreads my visible distress at losing sight of Dane as shock at his own outrageousness. He throws one willowy arm over his head and lets the other fall to the mound his towel insufficiently conceals. Once he's sure he's grabbed my eyes, he raises both arms, snaps his fingers. His incisive voice vaults the distance between us. The way he shakes his head as he talks sets off invisible quotation marks.

"Drapery is an art that few of the newer boys have mastered." The towel he's knotted at his hips highlights what it doesn't quite hide. I gawk despite myself, then drop my eyes to the floor as I walk. Soon the feet I'm looking down on are his. Now when he speaks it's intimate. "Welcome to the cities of the plain. Or what remains of them. We are neither bar nor brothel, sir, though we offer a bit of what both provide."

"Just because I'm from elsewhere doesn't mean I'm not a native, thanks. Are you a visiting angel, too?"

"Among the common nomads here I am the Gypsy Prince. I surf the hallways in search of the perfect big one."

"And when you find him?"

"I steer him to that man who, among all the men here tonight, will do him the most good."

"And if he disregards your advice?"

"I toss him back into the pond."

"Why not take him for yourself?"

"I think of bodies not as objects but as paths. The city of Sodom today is not any one spot but the road there. It's up to us, titular citizens of the plain, to take its pleasures and pains and rename it."

I don't pretend to understand him. "A lot of men here tonight are from out of town."

"Don't kid yourself: we all are." His eyes for the first time fix on me. "Some of us wander by choice; some are condemned to. Which are you?"

"Tonight I'm going home with no one. I'll go back to my hotel room alone. Any sex I have, I'll have here on the premises."

"You're the kind who tries to conduct what there is of his love life elsewhere, am I right? If I find another cute boy who blows as hot and cool as you, I'll send him your way."

"Tonight, after what I've just seen, cute won't do."

"You've heard of the classic hunter-gatherers? Here we queer that a bit." He mimes a laying-on of hands. "A fugitive and a vagabond shalt thou be."

"And I aim to enjoy it."

Now that my migrant eyes have caught a bit of the local color, I'd like to capture some regional flavor. The corner porn lounge emanates promise of warmth. So I duck inside: a lot of bodies in a small space, arrayed around the video hearth. By local decree, no sex is permitted in public, so in fact there is none here now. The air sits thick with the anonymous prospect of something coming.

Who enforces this hush if not the lounge's denizens themselves? Silent before a soundless video monitor, men in a row, wrapped in towels, sit on a padded bench. Ghostly in the cathode glow, the room's sole illumination, they are themselves its primary source of heat. Reading my intention to sit among them, a few of them shift to facilitate that; all settle.

This aesthetic draping of genitalia can advance the erotic as well. We spectators compose a picture just shy of the pornographic— until a boy who sits in the dead middle perceptibly stiffens, tipping the softcore over into the arguably hard, rending the occasion's fabric of semicivility.

Before the climax of the porn flick's ultimate scene, guys with some degree of stealth begin to grope each other. When the tape goes off, the screen goes blue; when the screen goes dark, so does the whole room. It's like a sudden plunge into the brush; intensity of sensation all but swamps me. Singly and in small groups, the room's inhabitants come to life, a hushed rub and grunt of men about the work of discovery. Initial dumb fumblings increasingly take aim.

When you fire all the senses, turn up the juice, and turn out the lights, some sort of disordering of the faculties occurs. I've a brief, strong whiff of two men, one on either side of me, each unambiguously male, each emphatically himself. If aroma is Eros suffused, touch is Eros telescoped, Eros localized. So fingers follow to confirm what an advance scent has reported lies on either side.

Each of the boys has a lean, muscular frame, with narrow hips and hard ass. The one with the longer torso has a lower waist, the one with the longer legs a higher butt. Oh, this tyranny of choices! Why not both? And even as I explore, each explores me.

I induce one guy to flex an arm, and work my face into the sweaty nest underneath. I stroke the other guy's slender haunches and hips: when he tenses, it's revelation. Just at the spot where the lower back becomes the upper buttocks, both of the boys I'm touching touch me; they trigger involuntary shudder up my vertebrae, jerking my head back.

When I sense yet a third boy before me, I reach out to confirm, touch his hairy torso, and marvel that flesh so firm can be so pliant. Rubbing it I wonder if it gives him even half the thrill that rubbing it gives me. It must, for now he reciprocates. We four are a warm, moist blur of bodies interlocked; we pulse.

"You think you see me because my skin is hot," I hiss into the newest (nearest) ear. I tongue it, then suck the full of the shell of it into my mouth. If potato chips were pliant, this is it. I imagine that the darkness must emphasize the thunder of my tongue, and that my simple breath must approach the storied voice in the desert.

It's dwarfed though by the thunder that follows. This boy pulls my mouth from his ear to his own. Although the kiss is blind, I know this boy: the pale, dark Dane. By the fresh shock that I think I can taste on his tongue, I gauge he now knows me too. Our teeth click together harder than either of us mean. Immediately the guys at our sides fall away; two mouths go to work on our peripheral flesh. Our own mashed lips remain central.

The video monitor kicks back on, a fresh tape in progress. Past the head of the boy I kiss, I can see it all. Except for a placid Gypsy

Prince who beams benignly over the scene, the men around us make like the movie more or less; make like us. In the hallway a passing bathhouse attendant carries an armful of fresh linen. He pokes his head through the doorway, smirks, and chirps: "There is no sex in the porn lounge, gentlemen. You will have to conduct your business in private or leave the premises."

Dane and I break. "I guess I was just passing through." Between us a smile of recognition flickers; who mimics whom? Using exits at either end of the lounge, our company for now disbands, disperses.

In the one well-lit facility of the entire club, a few coals keep the sauna warm (if not quite hot). Here every nomad between rounds, his hunt temporarily suspended, finds a temporary home. In this desert no cactus flowers: it's become the community chat room where the Gypsy Prince holds court.

In the incomparably hotter steam room, by contrast, all is quiet. Amid the completely tiled whiteness I remove the towel from my waist, drape it around my shoulders, and sit. Slowly the empty cubicle fills with steam and, soon after, swirling specters of flesh. A few lounge on the benches, a few lean against the walls; the rest mill about, as restless as the thickening haze. The midnight lizards steam. A liminal libido leaks everywhere in; soon it impinges. A row of cocks like hothouse flowers blossom. Soon formerly pendulous genitals stand. Eyes labor the fruited plain. Here the wages of sin like ours go untaxed: the whole tribe bends the same way.

In the democracy of the steam bath, is there no one dreamboat? Now entering, fresh from the shower, shaking the water from his shapely frame, Dane is a wet dream come to visit the wide-awake. It's the first time I've seen him naked, and he me. He advances into the room, slings his towel around his shoulders as if in mock homage to me. Through the thick fog his more-than-horizontal cock precedes him by several inches. He sits a few feet to my right.

Sideways I see Dane studies my sweat-slick chest and gut. For these few moments his eyes strike hotter than a sun. Oh, have I got the hots for you, his eyes say, and so, I fear, do mine. He himself seems to have tailored his body to the steam room, where, streaming perspiration, his superior definition appears that much more extreme. I got a boner for the best-honed boy I know. Between us some steam-bathers move into action. The players dissolve and reconstitute recurringly. Although their faces may change, they operate largely the same. Fog like a swath of gauze rises to wrap the overhead light. In shards we are all refracted to odd points on the dripping walls. To this spectral world Dane and I are peripheral, catching the other's eye from either side of the blurry action when the swirl momentarily thins.

From a cloud: a sudden head. Before my eyes fog fully over at a fresh blast of steam, I've abandoned myself to the pull of anonymous mouth, wetter and warmer than the air that swarms around my head. All of my body goes limp with the heat except my cock, grown so hard it borders on discomfort. If I had my head about me, I'd be frightened. Lifted to my feet (and away from the mouth at my crotch), I'm kissed and I kiss back: clearly it's Dane. We entwine.

"Welcome to Testosterama!" someone hisses from the side-lines—the Gypsy Prince? Whoever was sucking my cock returns; another mouth moves to my butthole. When the steam clears I can see the boy who's been sucking my cock now moving to suck Dane, who is also being rimmed.

We are confections of sweat and flesh, as palpably evanescent as sex. Now that we can't swap fluids, melt is the closest we come to mingle. All the moisture that beads on Dane's upper back comes rolling down to puddle now in the cleft of his butt.

Odor is to aura as weather to climate: we carry about us an entire atmosphere. "You can smell a man's experience from the sweat of his balls," claims the Gypsy Prince; taking heed, a man begins to lap at mine in earnest. "Suck enough sweat from that

armpit, kid, you'll one day be a man." With his lips, a boy traces
a vein around Dane's biceps to the trench. "He's so well built he
pulses almost as strong as he tastes, huh, boy?"

Dane and I alone are left standing, the steamsuckers. Through
my nose I take the hot, damp air down into my lungs; I expel it
into his mouth. Soon he's doing the same, and I think I'm going
to faint. I'm so steam-cleaned by now I'm see-through. What is the
temperature of flesh at flashpoint? Will we pop or fizzle?

Only our holding each other up prevents our slumping to the
floor. When the fingers of his steadying hand graze my anus, I brush
them away. So he wraps his legs around my waist and straddles
instead my rib cage, lays his erection deep into the cleft between
my pectoral muscles, and rubs furiously, as if this were a quicker
route to my heart than any more natural orifice. I hope he makes
it before we all burn off like a morning fog, never to return.

On his progress through his uncontested subjects, the Gypsy
Prince of Sodom stops before us and smiles his blessing. Like an
animate boa a plume of steam curls over his shoulders. How is it
his makeup doesn't run? The density of this chamber approaches
pressure cooker. I cover over the topside of Dane's hard-thrusting
cock with hand and hand. I foresee he'll hump until he comes all
over my chin and neck and nose and forehead, but my vision's
preempted.

The steam-room door opens. Framed in black a passing bathhouse attendant, dragging a bagful of soiled towels, scowls and
barks, "There is no sex in the steam room, gentlemen. You will have
to conduct your business in private or else leave our establishment."

Freshly scattered outcasts flee the steam room. I turn to see it's the
Gypsy Prince who's grabbed a handful of my butt, see he's also
grabbing at Dane, who also looks to see it's the Prince. Now he
turns to me. The Prince tugs the towels from our shoulders. "Better
cover up before someone steals you away; I'm about to find you

boys a room." Will prince prove fairy godmother? He steps between us and takes the lead. I whisper to Dane, "At this point I've a better idea of how you taste than what your taste is." When my fingers graze his anus he brushes them away, even as his lips nip at my newly naked shoulder.

"Only beefier boys than I get to boff me, and rarely then."

The Gypsy Prince lets out a hoot. We both ourselves have to laugh. I finish knotting my towel around Dane's waist; he, his around mine.

We three traverse the shuttle of shadow and light that constitutes passage here. At intermittent intervals, from up and down the hallway, behind shut doors and thin walls, over the roofless cubicles, there come the muffled sounds of men in the clutch of climax too intense to successfully muzzle. Others might find it distracting; me, it fuels.

When our itinerant Prince stops we stop too. Just opposite us in the open doorway of a private room stands a tall young man, backlit in dramatic semisilhouette, his arms above his head. His hands press out against the frame, as if he were some biblical figure trying to hold the temple up, or bring it down. Traversing this vital turnstile, Dane and I enter his room, ducking under either arm. When the boy spins around to monitor our advance, the Prince supplants him in the doorframe. Whether this boy is fair or dark or in between, I'll never learn. He's shaved and branded and pierced and ringed; when he moves I halfway expect him to jingle. Albeit lean, he appears uncommonly sturdy, and cuter than he's fierce, despite the tattoos. There's the crude name of a woman on his arm; her name is MOM. The rest appear more professional and memorialize males. His room is little bigger than the cot it has to accommodate. Is the semen that streaks the floor someone else's or his own?

His calm and guileless eyes make an offer: Be my body's marauders. His words, when they come, are hardly more civil. "Have either of you guys fucked butt yet tonight?" Dane's eyes go wide; despite himself he smiles, shakes his head no. "Would you like to, dudes?" I nod. We've reached the night's destination; he in turn reaches for each of our towels and tears them away.

We'll fuck a road to nowhere. It may be no one's home, but nowhere's home like here is. Let's dub this boy with a buzz cut sprawled on the bed now stroking a boner: conduit for our impossible union. Now let's anoint him such.

Even in the dim light, when he puts his arms behind his head, I can see he's had tongues of flame tattooed along his flanks. When he lifts his legs to his shoulders he proffers a butt, smooth as marble, white as bone, that has never been inked. What was utterly white soon glows as ruddy as Babylon's blushing bride. I smack it again.

When he rolls over onto his stomach, the better to greet my open hand with the full of his fleshy ass, he's confronted with Dane at the head of the bed, the head of his cock aquiver on its rigid staff. This savage knows it will take a tongue to tell him what he wants to know about this organ in all its specificity. After he slobbers over the knob, he ingests it as easily as air.

Where's a true man of the plains like me to zero in on Eros? Anus, as ever. More than the boy spread out around it, seat of affection, site of my meaning, eternal point of no return, and, if I look at it, just not there—and this one is shaved. Still, it's where I *would* be. My abode tonight is you, boy, but don't worry, it won't be forever. My thumb detects a butthole's involuntary tug; I touch a tidal pulse. Does the cock lodged in the boy's gullet throb in rhythm with it?

Still in position, Dane by sleight-of-hand produces a bright-red condom (a specialty of the house). He leans over to draw it down over my shaft. He pumps it with his fist; it plumps in his grip till it fairly shines by the light of electric heater. In nipple-tipped rubber its silhouette mimics a fire hydrant's. Extinguish me, guy, I dare you to try. Dane, rather, sets it free: my cue to enter.

Spread out like this, our fuckboy feels his whole being as an extension of his asshole. "And tonight you too will emanate from my buttcrack, bud!" growls the hungry mouth. "Render your maker its due regard." Aimed at this unutterable bull's-eye, I push my way through to my private steam room.

As if in recoil, the boy inches automatically toward the wall Dane leans against, inexorably gobbling cock. This boy at our core is, for the duration, nothing but what we make him. And this, for an indeterminate span of time, is what we do, rearing back and driving forth to take his measure repeatedly, and to take ours. Only when Dane speaks does my concentration break.

"We may each inhabit an orifice, but I'd be more at home in you."

"Quit bitchin' and let me feel you hump."

"In another life we might have loved."

"So what is this we're in?" All scrutiny is cruel; so long as it's that and no more, it isn't much fun. As I look Dane in the eye, I reach out. Like black smoke, wisps of hair hover above the pale mounds of chest, a contrast as much in texture as color. I twirl it; he yelps, I growl. Newly alive to the mutual fools we are, we're free to move beyond pure function and explore. From the series of displacements that is every sex act, the trick is to string together a sequence. After one last thrust we each pull out.

This suddenly yawning asshole is almost appalling. Were this plainly a parable, would the anus be death? a framer of absence? a placeholder? But I love the way our angel spreads his buttcheeks like they're wings, love how he swims the wind. Eros at the crossroads, in a crucifixion of limbs, a monstrous shock: like a monstrance raised in benediction and found to hold nothing. But the soft flesh of our fuckboy's inner thighs and butt bears faint impression of our recent encounter, not quite as red as the condom that our ever-solicitous Gypsy Prince, moving from his post in the doorway, now presses into my hand.

As Dane has done to mine, I bag his erection in latex. In either hand I grip us both at the base: now at least we're dicktwins (if not quite soul mates). In these luminescent condoms our cocks glow like x-rayed bones. Chimeric shimmer. From my hand he flops like a fish—and he's not even greased yet. I tug him into position: Dane's now set to explore the channel I've opened.

He wastes no time. As Dane begins to fuck our declared Mom's Boy from behind, I resume his former station at the head of the bed so the boy can suck me. The fucker fucks like he's playing percussion, knowing that the fiercer he fucks, the greater the chance he'll reach me. Thinking he's seeing double, our target shakes his dizzy head; now he knows for sure he is.

Once the boy, like some nameless amphibian, slithers into missionary position, draping his legs over Dane's shoulders, he can manage only to lick me. So ferocious does the fucking soon become that the fucked boy has to abandon even that. His loose tongue indiscriminately laves: scrotum perineum anus. He rubs his buzz cut up and down his erstwhile fuckbuddy's fuzzy balls and lower butt; his hardware chafes. I vibrate.

To provide him with a little direction, I, a thigh on either side of his torso, draw my raw butthole roughly over his open mouth. Jabbing at my pubic bone, his chin exerts such force that it's almost like being screwed myself, fuck's faithful reproduction: I absorb all reverberation. Likewise, the friction his skull exerts against my dick-shaft, being direct, is like I'm fucking.

Needing it still more direct, I throw my legs over the head of the boy getting fucked to fuck his face as I face his fucker. Astride his neck, I angle my butt till it winks at the sky; now I plunge. The latex he tastes is universal; the butthole? His own. Dane and I stroke each other's torso, punch chests. In the heated air above the action, the fucker's head and mine float closer, his wide eyes blank but for me. High over the upper gut of our ostensible suck-and-fuckboy I cover Dane's mouth with my mouth. The stubble that rings his lips pricks mine. We eat each other up.

The mouth is as big a nowhere as the eye of the anus is. Let climax reach beyond time. Like a mirror on the back of a bathhouse door, impact at orgasm granulates glass like sand. At such extremities even the self-possessed are untenanted. For fear the tremor may shake him free, I hold Dane's head in place; before I let go again I will know his cranium's bones like my own. Flashes now come so fast we verge on whiteout. Heat pouring off our bodies rivals the warmth of the corner heater we now outshine. Fearing suffocation, I yank the condom from my cock.

I spill my distillation across the belly below me, an extensive but discontinuous script of no explicit meaning, more odor than innuendo and of no intrinsic potential, shot under the star of Onan, safely out of ovum's range. Strange language that no race will claim: I'll say it translates the tongue that once again plays at my anus.

Now across the shaven torso that strains beneath us, my opposite number, free of orifice, spurts as well. Tattoos' eclipse is as partial as it's provisional. Into the gully between the muscles, the jism slowly runs, down the ridges of gut until it puddles. There our dual strains mingle, our rival brands cancel. Who'll untangle the claims? Not us. Now our fuckboy comes as well. His stream writes over ours as if to say: even on his back he's his own man. Who would argue?

"What does it say that the guy with the biggest sex has the least determinate gender? Call me Puck, I guess." Arms lifted in consecration, the Gypsy Prince, stationed still in the doorframe, comes like a fairy might spray his wand, spontaneously, over the rutted beasts he's brought into being. "You haven't, till you've seen a man's semen, seen him—and often not even then."

Soon I will unseat myself and Dane dismount. This home then too will have proved provisional, but no less home for so being. Our unraveling rubbers flutter like butterfly nets as they fall to the wastebasket. On the towels with which we wipe our cocks we leave imperfect imprint. Dane and I and the Prince leave the boy to his room. One by one we wash, dry off. We rub so much we glow. After Dane and I dress we exchange slips of paper. The Gypsy Prince dismisses us, out into the other domain. Warm, we exit to a blizzard, thick as a sandstorm but soft.

Tom House

PLEASE DO NOT TOUCH THE WORKS OF ART

THERE IS A PROVERB out here in the East End, popular with our year-round customers at the Dune Road Restaurant and Bar, that one never finds love after Labor Day. Certainly I can offer no evidence to the contrary, but neither am I ready to trade my cottage in the woods for some cramped downtown apartment. Once a country mouse, I suppose. I am not entirely averse, however, to occasional excursions into Manhattan for affairs of culture, and so come that chilling exodus with the first fallen leaf, when again one discovers one has his choice of parking spaces in the village, his pick of machines at the fitness center, I find it best to keep an up-to-date train schedule in the first photograph flap of my *portefeuille*— though I have not often found cause to journey much beyond the doors of the Museum of Modern Art.

As of late, I have developed a theory regarding the museum's second floor: one can conduct his latest gentleman caller through the painting and sculpture galleries there and, by the time he reaches Magritte's *Menaced Assassin*—that disturbing, misogynistic scene with those mistrustful lavender walls hanging, like a banner of scorn, before the exit—he will have the measure of the fellow's mind. Paintings from the modern period, more than any other, require their viewers to react; they sail at one, grapple and gore for one's soul. Take note of your suitor's sudden, consecutive cries—where the cries of horror, awe, or delight; where the hot, stifled cries of bewilderment—eventually they will tell you all you need to know.

I trust you recognize the name Alfred H. Barr, Jr.; he was, of course, the founding director of this museum and, as his words inscribed on a silver plaque beside the galleries' entrance will attest, a wise man. "He once defined his task," the plaque reads, "as 'the conscientious, continuous, resolute distinction of quality from mediocrity.' " We are birds of a feather, Mr. Barr and I, but while he was a connoisseur of art, I, on the other hand, am one of men. And though Mr. Barr's efforts have thus far proved more fruitful than my own—he found many examples to which he could point and claim, "Quality," whereas I am still wandering about very much alone through empty rooms—I share his persistence, and, on one particular occasion not too long ago, met with a striking, raven-haired man named Stanley Cartlin.

As a rule, expectations are mistakes. One should expect little or nothing of anyone, and thereby never be disappointed again. But to be aware of a problem is not necessarily to conquer it—problems are rarely, if ever, conquered—and I, knowing all too well the pitfalls expectations bring, nevertheless had them. You see, as far as biography and vital statistics were concerned—which I had been able to compile, for the most part, from our two rather short but incisive telephone conversations—Stanley measured up quite well: mid-thirties; non smoker, with no history of drug or alcohol abuse; had tested repeatedly negative for HIV antibodies; was inclined, he avowed, toward monogamy; and, to my delight, possessed of a virtually flawless set of gleaming white teeth. (Try as I may, I have never been able to consider anyone with crooked or discolored teeth, owing, perhaps, to the fact that through most of my formative years, my dear-departed mother was employed as a dental hygienist. The value of good, shapely dentition was impressed upon us continually and, in time, came to represent a mirror in which a person's character and worth were reflected. "Just like a horse." Who said that? Jimmy, my little Sancho Panza from Amagansett, full of all that . . . folklore. *Like a horse;* nothing of the sort. It was a sign, just like any other: the body is a temple; what transpires in the interior is bound to appear, sooner or later, upon the facade.)

All well and good, but to be perfectly honest, what I found most appealing about Stanley was that he owned an advertising concern in the city, something about the design and reproduction of logos and an account with one of the major cable networks, all admirably understated, it would seem, for judging from his addresses alone— apartment on the Upper West Side, weekend house in Southampton—his work was quite lucrative. Not, please understand, that it is primarily *money* that interests me, but I will say I find a certain amount of competence and self-sufficiency prepossessing. One grows tired finally of the darling boyish types, forever floundering about, looking for occupation. Invariably they show up twenty minutes late for the first encounter, or reveal, over the course of the evening, that they have a "friend" in West Hollywood or Palm Beach. No more, no more, I said; here at last was an established man, just a little older than myself, who had work he cared about and did well, a man whose very style and bearing betrayed an air of greater purpose and self-assurance—I noticed it the moment I saw him. Or rather, the moment my little Sancho saw him and pointed him out to me; as I recall, it was upon a Tuesday night in late August, and we had been sitting, as is our wont, at the corner of the bar closest to the entrance, reserved for staff.

"Uh-oh," he had exclaimed, at once nudging me and gesturing without subtlety to the dining room. "Admirers."

"What? Where?" I said, swatting at his pink, stub-like forefinger with mortification; yet I could not keep my heart from racing on ahead of myself: he was rarely wrong in these matters. "Control yourself," I insisted, glaring down at his ample-cheeked countenance, whereupon he slid back in his stool, mouthing the word *eight* with juvenile exaggeration. I nodded and, pausing to contemplate the dark wood grain of the bar, savored those seconds of pre-knowledge, bloated so suddenly, so *recklessly* with anticipation and resurgent hope:

You will turn, I informed myself, and gaze for the first time upon *ton âme soeur*. Here now the moment when that fair, mutable figment haunting the chambers of your mind takes on the semblance of an actual *person*. It will be as you have heard it described: at eyes' meeting, recognition—deep, unquestionable recognition; you will know you have found him; your inmost soul will vibrate like a stricken gong, the very ground beneath your feet will vibrate, as if the whole of the earth had joined into one resounding chorus, "Bone of thy bones! Flesh of thy flesh!"

Well, something to that effect, anyway. Sancho, of course, scolded me, as any good squire would: "What are you doin', chief? Look back, for Chris'sake; you're gonna miss your chance."

"Does he continue to look this way?"

"Yeah, he's lookin'. There's a few of 'em lookin', a whole section of 'em."

"Describe him to me."

"Describe 'em to you? Which one? You got a brunette, a blond, a strawberry blond . . . nope, now, see, you waited too long, you lost 'em."

At that, I raised my head and turned to the southwest corner of the dining room; there, my eyes were drawn, as it were, into the field of a slender, dark-haired figure at the center of a large party sprawled across tables eight and nine. The gentleman in question was pressing a palm to his heart while leaning to confer with a friend at his left—much, I thought, in the attitude of a little Christ presiding over a Little Supper. And I remember, in turn, that when he

finally did look up again, his gaze held me for such an extraordi-
narily long time that my breath suddenly caught beneath it, as if it
had just then extended across the room and touched me with a kind
of hand.

The ensuing half-hour was a fairly unbearable ordeal of suspense
and anxiety; I must say I remember none of the conversation at the
bar. I suppose there was conversation; I cannot imagine that Jimmy
would have stopped chattering for that long, or that Sonny Waterson and Clark Rogers—those two tireless ruminators always fore-
most in the klatch of elderly customers to our right—could have;
indeed, I was most exclusively preoccupied with the question of
whether or not the dark-haired figure would approach the bar as he
exited the restaurant, the particular outcome of which had become
suddenly and inextricably bound to the prospects of my future happiness.

Yes, well, I suppose I might not have fretted quite so much: he
did eventually accost me, though in the briefest of ways; in fact,
our exchange was so fleeting—one moment he was upon me, tapping my shoulder, the next he was drifting out the door again with
the rest of the group—that had it not been for the business card he
slipped into my hand (or should I say, dropped, like a lover's glove?),
I would have said it had never happened.

I do distinctly recall, however, his words, whispered discreetly
over his shoulder: *"Call me when things quiet down."* Of course,
there was, in his wake, ample time to recall them—time, even, to
mull them over and to commit them forever to memory. At length,
I found the words quite moving: clearly, I expounded, they were
not the standard salacious overtures, not the first turns of a romantic
maelstrom that would commence immediately with a profusion of
torrid, impulsive embraces; incessant, interminable telephone conversations—no, none of that, just, *"Call me when things quiet
down."* A sign of patience, I thought, of maturity, which the raised
black lettering on his card seemed to confirm:

S. F. Cartlin, Inc.
Design Consultants
Stanley Cartlin, President

"President?" Jimmy squawked, his chin fairly lodged on my shoulder; and at once I slipped the card into the breast pocket of my blazer, away from his vulturine inspection. "He's like some hotshot Madison Avenue executive," he informed the elderly klatch, upon which a somewhat vexed smile crossed my lips—for I must admit that, though I felt immensely flattered at having attracted the attentions of a man of such caliber, I instantly regretted his name; it brought to mind a misshapen, pustulated boy I had known in elementary school and impressed me as just my good fortune that when I finally did happen upon my other half, he would possess a forename I detested, like Stanley or Dudley or Arnold.

"Be nice if you went for something besides bar trash for a change."

"I beg your pardon?" I reeled in my stool. "Who said that?"

Sancho, of course, grinning into his ever-brimming mug of ale. No doubt his allusion was lost on no one: Bernard, the existentialist motorcycle salesman from Washington, D.C., who had approached me on the patio some weeks before. Of course, he was not at all the type to sustain my interest (I have always abhorred leather garments of any sort, really, particularly trousers), but there are nights—and perhaps you have experienced some yourself—when in lieu of a prince, a wolf may have a few things to offer. One cannot only wait.

"I vote for the executive, whaddaya say?"

"Hear, hear," Sonny Waterson said.

Still I was taken aback. *Bar trash.* As if it were a sordid selection process on my part, as if I deliberately sought out just the type of wayward men who would prove incapable of any genuine, lasting liaison. I assure you that nothing could be further from the truth.

To be in love is the only thing I have always wanted. I can recall dreaming as early as five years of age of the man who would prove my kindred soul; I have dreamed of him these twenty-five since. And though there have been times I thought him near—thought, even, that I had procured his acquaintance—in each instance I have discovered quite soon that was not the case; he had yet to show. The Lord has seen fit, for reasons not entirely revealed to me, that I should go without so long. There are days when I have detested that hoary-haired autocrat; periods, even, when I have refused to invoke His name. Brief periods. I do not have the courage of a Nietzsche. But let me find myself alone one night, confronting the long, dark wall of despair, and my lips shall be forming, before the hour is out, those studied syllables of the Our Father: *Oh give us this day! oh deliver us!*

"And don't be so picky for once."

"Picky?" What a vile word. "One moment I am chasing *bar trash,* the next I am too picky?"

"You eliminate people too fast; you have to give them a chance. No one's perfect. Sometimes you have to settle for what's least repulsive."

"*Least repulsive?*" I recoiled at the horrific implications of his off-handed statement. "Love is not something one *settles for,*" I said.

Jimmy laughed, interminably, but I, feeling just then for the business card in the breast pocket of my blazer, remained upright amid his cackles, once again envisioning that unimaginably different day when I would at last discover, for the both of us—nay, for the lot of us—what love actually was.

I meet them in the sculpture garden, weather permitting, Thursdays at five-thirty. Since Thursday is the one day the museum is open in the evening, it is a sound logistical arrangement: most of them reside in the city and, of course, are employed there, virtually always until five—which allows me an hour or two in the early afternoon for paperwork and placing orders before handing over the fort to Jimmy and taking the long sally in.

That September day in question, Stanley himself was running late, or perhaps I was a few minutes early and he arrived nearly on time; I am not sure; there is no public clock outside, thank goodness, and I have never worn a watch. I would rather be the one to arrive first anyway, so as not to have to ask them to move to another section of the garden—they invariably choose a seat close to the doors by that Picasso goat, which is one of the most heavily trafficked, wide-open areas. I much prefer a spot just opposite that, facing the far side of the English beech, its lowest, outermost branches a leafy screen blotting out New York. There, two can sit in relative privacy—their backs to the Matisse relief mounted on the brick wall, a view of Moore's *Animal Form* to the left, Maillol's *The River* to the right, the meditative splashing and bubbling from the jets of the pool just yards away—while wading through a repertoire of first-encounter queries or, in the pauses, allowing their eyes to follow the weaving and tangling of the ivy in the garden at their feet.

"Where did you get your degree?"

"Did I say I had a dagree?" He masticated inelegantly upon a piece of chicle gum.

"Perhaps I presumed."

"I went ta a community college on the island fa two years."

"So you have an associate's, then."

He worked the toe of a worn tennis shoe into a crevice between the long, dull slabs of gray and white marble. Or was it faux marble?

"I believe I'm like a credit away from an associate's—I ovalooked a gym or a lab or sumthin'. You, on tha otha hand, have a couple, I'm sure."

"A couple of what?"

"Dagrees." He cleared his throat and, tapping the brim of his navy-blue baseball cap, slouched down in the black-wire patio chair. "Not the most comf'table chairs in the world." He smiled, flirtatiously revealing his faultless teeth, white as a newly-painted picket fence. The smile lingered while the tennis shoe tapped in close proximity to my own polished loafer, and I noticed that just beyond the sparkling left canine lurked a section of the mashed, sputum-coated wad, like a ruinous pink mortar. I looked away, my eyes coming to rest, as they can never help but do, upon that annoying little gray sign on a small metal post, rising from the ivy: *Please do not sit or stand on sculpture pedestals, or touch the works of art.* There are many more like it, planted strategically throughout the garden, disruptive reminders that there are people who need to be told those things. They always catch me, as this one did then, between indignation and an elementary-school fear of chastisement.

"I have only one," I informed him, not seeing the need then of alluding to the many minors I had also completed during my extended stay at university, among them French Studies and Medieval History, "a Bachelor of Arts."

"In?"

"Philosophy."

His left eyebrow rose—whether in mockery or in interest, I could not discern. "Which is very helpful in the food-service business, I'm sure." Ah.

In moments of disappointment, I look to the Maillol for validation—to that large lead woman lying on her side, the tips of her bunchy hair touching the dark, foam-spotted water of the pool. She looks just-fallen, almost thrown, her palms raised against the threat of some descending object. As if the business of my life could be summed up in the phrase *food service.*

"Well, if one's criterion for a degree's usefulness is how much it prepares one for employment, then I would agree with you, there is a little discrepancy." I leaned back in my chair, arms crossed, and refused to look at him during those moments he gazed up into the branches of the beech tree, idly masticating. Silence ensued, and I was in the midst of rehearsing a polite exit from what I was certain would prove an entirely disastrous encounter, when a sudden noise, much like the discharge of a child's cap gun, took me unaware. I rose from my seat with momentary dread, looking left, right, heavenward, before realizing, with some chagrin, that Stanley had simply snapped his gum.

He squinted up at me with curiosity.

"Excuse me," I said, reseating myself.

"Sumthin' wrong?"

"Not at all," I said, inhaling deeply to moderate my quickened pulse.

Yet what I thought was brewing into antagonism took a surprising turn when he said, "You're right," albeit a bit cavalierly, and glanced up the left thigh of my trousers. "But on the same token, college isn't the only place ya learn things."

"Of course not." I leaned forward with guarded interest.

"In fact, I've met some people with dagrees up their ass—up their eyeballs—don't know the first thing about themselves, 'bout people, or the world, even. My brotha. Got six or more years of college unda his belt, the other day he calls me, he wants ta know what a deductible is. See, he's never paid for anything in his life before, right, and so now he's got a copy of an insurance policy in fron'a him he can't make heads or tails out of it. So you know what I said to him? I said, 'You are, asshole, you're a—' "

I felt my face jerk backward at the word, much against my will, as if a little dart had hit it.

"Whoops!" he said, eyes wide and fingers to his lips, as if I were the Virgin Mother.

I leaned back. It worries me how protective people become of their vernaculars in my presence. On the other hand, the word *was* decidedly out of place: we were not alone, or in some type of saloon or locker-room atmosphere. Here was the kind of person, I noted, who insisted on informality as the universal decorum: life was an occasion that did not require much more than a pair of tennis shoes, several shades of denims, some T-shirts and hooded sweatshirts.

It was not necessarily a *bad* quality, but it did indicate a certain earthy stubbornness, a singleness of expression that could grow rather dull. "I *have* heard the word before."

"Good. So I said, 'You are, asshole. For the last twenty-four years you been mommy and daddy's little fucken deductible.' "

Again my face jerked backward. A singleness of expression, I qualified, bordering on solipsism; instinctively, I looked about me. Several yards to our left, a mild, middle-aged couple sat peaceably conversing. "And where do you find you learn most?" I asked quickly, hoping to change the subject from the apparently rousing one of the brother.

"Where does anyone learn most? From watchin' people. Every minute of the day there's sumthin' happ'nin' you can learn from, all ya have ta do is open your f—"

"Stop it, will you?" I whispered hotly. "Can you not just say, 'Open your eyes'? Just 'Open your eyes.' There is no need to modify it."

"You said you didn't mind."

"Yes, but I—once, twice, perhaps, but I was not prepared for a—a—fusillade of vulgarities."

"A *what?*"

"Especially here, at an art museum, devoted to beauty, to aesthetics. . . ." Oh, but I had little patience for reprimands! You see, it was as if he had just ungloved the signet ring of a secret brotherhood, and I, weary, suspecting traveler, knew that beneath his vagrant rags the marrow of him was to be trusted. His theory, the gist of what he had said—I saw it immediately—was nothing more than a restatement of my own! Put in exceedingly pedestrian terms, but my theory nonetheless. Here was another anxiously collecting the signs the world flashed before him, busy with the subtleties of classification and interpretation, with the formulation of rules of behavior and speculations upon the nature of the universe. "So you think you are a good judge of character?"

I waited while he blew a pale-pink bubble, which, upon completion, he reingested with a sudden, deft snap of his lingua; there followed a muffled *pop,* whereupon his masticating resumed, and he spoke: "I'm a fairly good judge a characta, sure."

"What would you say, then, from your experience, if a person were to show up twenty minutes late for a first encounter? What would that be an indication of?"

"Encounta?"

"An engagement, appointment. Rendezvous."

"A date, you mean?"

"Precisely."

"Show up twenty minutes late here? For a date like this?"

"Exactly like this."

He leaned forward, brow wrinkling. "Was I *that* late?"

"You? Not at all. Several minutes, perhaps. No, you were not very late at all."

He sat back. "Oh. Well, let's see. I guess I'd say eitha sumthin' unexpected came up, which I'm sure they'd tell ya right away—oh, but I don't know, though, twenty minutes is a long time to keep someone waitin', 'specially someone you don't know very well. I'd say they were a person that was chronically late for just about everything they ever did, or that they just didn' give a—didn' care."

" '*Didn' care.*' That is exactly right. Do you like cats?"

"Cats? Yes, I like them very much."

"And how about fish?"

"Pet fish, you mean, in a aquarium?"

"Yes."

"Oh, I love them."

"And what is your middle name?"

"Fred."

"Fred?" Stanley Frederick. Doubly unfortunate; the product of a spiteful parentage, no doubt. But I was not to be daunted. "Excellent," I said, and stood up. "Shall we go in?" He rose, and as we made our way over the little bridge that traverses the rectangular pool, several of the fingers of his left hand respectfully grazed my forearm, as if to guide the way. The pool, of course, could not have been more than several inches deep, but the protective gesture was well-taken, a symbol of our new confidence.

––––––––––

You know, I probably would never have bothered with a guy like that in the first place, it's just that he was so fucking handsome. And I'm not just saying that the way some people throw that word around; I mean *exceptional,* one of the three or four best-looking men I've ever seen. Something like the humpy blond in *Room with a View,* big and tall and waspy-looking, with that kind of straight, English hair that bobs down in front—I love that shit. Kind of reminded me, too, of a guy in *Stryker Force,* if you've ever seen that one; calls himself Mark Hammer or something—he's busy doing the one little blond in the first part, then at the end him and Jeff get together and he just lays down on his belly and says, "I always wanted to know what that felt like." He looks the most beautiful when he says that, his eyes all nice and closed.

And I'm not joking, either, when I say that this guy had just as nice a body, if not better, than those two. In fact, his body was even more of an asset than his face, if you can imagine. I first saw it on the beach a couple of weeks before Labor Day, and my jaw just dropped, all our jaws did. I mean, just this long, perfect, preppy body, every little stomach square showing, every little obscure muscle, buffed and toned and tanned. It was enough to make you cry, it really was; I just grabbed my T-shirt and put it on. I know that's why we ate out at that place that night; I think that's half the reason anyone goes there, especially those old geezers, crowing and drooling all around him. One of my housemates, Todd, caught me staring at him during dinner and warned me privately to stay away, said he was supposed to be promiscuous, that he'd been seen recently sucking off some leather queen in the parking lot; then Bill, a different housemate of mine, must've heard who we were talking about, because he started glancing over at the bar and saying how crazy he thought the guy was, that he talked like he was from the eighteenth century, or some shit. But I couldn't listen to any of that, I had to at least slip him my work number as we were getting out the door. I tried to do it so nobody would see; I thought that if I could just get my hands on him once or twice, without anyone finding out; whisk him up to the apartment in September while Ed was away and give it to him good in the living room. I knew Ed wouldn't care too much, really, so long as I used a bag; we have that understanding, sort of—at least while he's in California, which is half the year, practically—but mostly I just wouldn't have wanted that to get around, fucking with the manager of a gay bar. I have a business to run. I mean, it's not much of one yet, but I would like it to be; I would like to live off my own money one day.

Then, of course, he insisted on meeting at the fucking MOMA, of all places, and it had to be in the sculpture garden, at five-thirty. Talk about anal. I said, "Well, what do you want to do it that way for, why don't you just come over around eight or nine and we'll order Thai or something?" But he started whining about "neutral territory," and how he liked to make a day of it when he came to town. "It's just Manhattan," I said, "it's not like you're going overseas." "Still," he said, and stayed pretty stubborn about it. He was like a woman that way, that was gonna make you take her out first.

So I went a little incognito—wore one of Ed's baseball caps, and dressed really down, in jeans and sneakers; I looked for the dirtiest pair of sneakers we had around, and came up with some ancient Adidas tennis shoes. Then just to finish it off, I bought some gum at the Korean deli on the corner. The real kid stuff, Bazooka, five cents a stick. I hadn't had a Bazooka in years. Oh, and you know, I really got into it, sitting out there with him, chomping like crazy and copping a heavy Long Island accent; I figured that was what he wanted, I figured someone so prissy and fastidious must love to be appalled. I could hear him saying that to me, very loud, between each line: *Horrify me; really offend me in some way.*

To tell you the truth, that was almost all I heard; I was finding it hard to concentrate. On the one hand, the conversation wasn't interesting—school, he wanted to talk about, and what I thought about some guy showing up late for an "encounter"—but on the other, I just couldn't keep my eyes from roaming all over him. He caught me once when I was checking out his legs, long crew-boy legs, you could just see the perfect preppy shape of them through the light-brown cotton pants he was wearing—oow, God, I loved those pants—and then, oh yes, Jesus Christ, there was that monstrosity of his, creeping down his left thigh. That was pretty shocking to me, when I first discovered it. I don't normally zoom for a guy's crotch the way a lot of queens do, but you would've had to have been a blind nun to miss a thing like that; it looked like you could've fed a few peanuts to it. And that wasn't even the most interesting part; what truly captivated me was what occurred to me next: he wasn't wearing any underwear. This Little Miss Prude that got offended by the words *fuck* and *asshole* was letting her big dick flap all around New York.

Mm-mmm. It was all I could do not to get erect right there; I could have really gotten erect over a beautiful little hill of contradictions like that. And so after he stood up suddenly, and I followed him across the little bridge, I couldn't help myself, I copped a little feel of his shoulder, and of his long lean arm, and I swear I could hear it then, too, even louder: *Horrify me; please horrify me.* I tried hard to figure out how, because I knew if I did, this guy would lay right down for me, like a little dog; he'd say, "I always wanted to know what that felt like."

Ascending to the second floor and alighting before that unornate portal to my endless petition, we entered the first gallery—Cézannes, mostly. And I must admit, with due shame, that as he loitered before *Boy in a Red Waistcoat,* his large, able left hand cupping his chin, I felt what I can only describe as a sudden invasion of a whole host of fluttering, brushing, bouncing little wings rising up some dark, cavernous portion of my interior. Clichés alone come to mind in the service of such silliness: "butterflies," "breathlessness," a "thrill," the likes of which I would not have believed myself still capable; yet I found I was going so far as to think that this Stanley might very well be one of the most promising men I had ever led through those rooms, when suddenly I detected an alarm—some distance off, but still quite audible and disconcerting, reminding me of just the type of incessant *ding ding ding ding* that had announced the fire drills at St. Anthony's.

"Do you hear that?"

He did not acknowledge me.

"Stanley?" I said skeptically. It was the first time I had called him by name, and for an instant, I doubted that it was truly his; perhaps I stood beside a Richard, I feared, or a Brian.

But indeed he answered, "Hm?"

"Do you hear that bell?"

"Sure."

"What do you think is happening?"

He shrugged, and as he passed on to *Still Life with Apples,* the alarm ceased. Upon perusal of the gallery, I discovered that no one seemed at all disturbed: people were absorbed in the paintings, or sauntering about, and even the rather stern-looking guard—a short, dark-skinned man with a protruding bottom lip that reminded me, quite exactly, of Alfred Hitchcock's—seemed, to the best of his ability, at ease. Crossing the room, I pondered what could have caused the alarm, while vaguely contemplating the outlines of the Lautrec pastel, or Stanley's enrapture in the Cézanne across the way. And I believe I had nearly succeeded in forgetting about it, and all but quelled the further uneasiness it had engendered in my midriff when, in the next instant, I saw Stanley look up from the painting and start at something he spied in the next gallery—he literally took a step backward, eyes magnificently wide.

"Did something frighten you?" I asked, joining him before the archway.

"Frighten me?"

"You looked up and something startled you; what was it?"

He shook his head distractedly.

"Nothing startled you?"

Again he shook his head and, masticating with renewed, methodical vigor, walked, without so much as a nod to Rousseau's *Sleeping Gypsy,* Gauguin's *Moon and Earth,* directly to the foot of *The Starry Night;* we made our obligatory pause.

Yes, yes, the cluster of blue and green flame-like cypress trees to the left, the sleepy little town down on the right, the church steeple piercing the blue hills, the swirling sky, the eleven stars, the crescent moon . . . I have seen this painting in so many books, over so many sofas, I have been given it so many times in the form of a Christmas card or calendar, that whenever I come across it actually hanging upon the wall, I suspect its authenticity. Surely this must also be a reproduction, I say, the original in a fortressed vault somewhere; or perhaps it has been removed from the planet altogether, like the Holy Grail. In any case, I can no longer see it. Like the visage of an old encounter, whatever ardencies it might enkindle behind a fresh eye are lost to me forever.

A capital masterpiece.

A powerful example of proto-Expressionist art.

One of the most beloved paintings in the world.

Let us move on.

I noticed that Stanley had arrived at an impasse of his own; he could not seem to look at it, but rather cocked his head to the right, shielding his eyes with his hand.

"How many million you think this one's worth?" A matronly woman poked her bespectacled head between us, the gold initials *N. R.* at the bottom of the large right lens. I breathed out, a patronizing half-laugh; Stanley made no response, as if he did not see her. "Tsh," she said, shaking her head at the painting, and walked on.

"Is anything wrong?" I asked Stanley.

"I forgot this was here."

"Why do you refuse to look at it?"

He shook his head.

"Look at it; do not be ridiculous."

"I guess I *am* bein' stupid," he said, hesitantly unveiling his eyes, upon which his lips parted and he inhaled fitfully, deeply, then slowly expelled the large quantity of air. And I noticed, as behind us a passing gentleman hummed a bar of "Starry, Starry Night," that his eyes did not move at all, but merely stared, fixedly, into the center of the painting; finally they fluttered and crossed; his entire body swayed; then he quickly straightened up, resuming the un-focused stare—an attitude, it seemed to me, of such sublime ap-preciation and reverence that you can imagine my astonishment when, several seconds after an almost unintelligible mumble had issued from his lips, the sentence he had uttered formed itself in my mind: *I have to touch it.*

At once I thought it the machinations of Sancho, insisting so suddenly and boldly from some lurid quarter of my mind that it appeared to be egressing from a source outside myself. Surely Stan-ley had said nothing of the sort; surely Stanley had said nothing at all.

To our left, leaning within the archway that led to the third gallery, was another blue-jacketed guard, younger, slim, with thin-ning flaxen hair and a prominent nose shaped like a capital *D;* he was sketching with ballpoint pen in a little green-covered memo pad, precisely the type of pad we were once required to carry to copy down homework assignments at St. Anthony's. I thought it best to move on, and was just about to suggest so to Stanley when, oh my, his voice rose to a whisper, and said, with unquestionable clarity, "I have to touch it."

Behind us, the elder guard with the Hitchcock countenance stood with his hands folded, his left foot out before him, tapping repeatedly. Could he have heard?

"Touch *what?*" I whispered back.

He did not respond.

"You do not mean the painting, of course."

Again no response.

"Stanley," I said anxiously, "you do not—"

He nodded.

"Touch it with your hand?"

"Distract those guards for me, will ya?"

The elder had joined the younger in the archway, who had shut his pad. I leaned closer. "So you can touch it? One of the great masterworks of the late nineteenth century, distract the security guards so you can touch it with your hand? Do you think I would be an accomplice to that kind of *sacrilege?*"

"Ask them the time."

"You want me—"

"A fraction of a second, that's all I need. One little touch. I can't leave until I do it."

"You will never get away with it. The instant your hand reaches out, those—" The northern sectors of his thighs pressed against the white guardrail, the only one of its kind in the entire museum; his upper torso leaned dangerously close to the canvas, his face not a foot from the bright, raised swirls, his respiration upon them already.

I struck out, despite myself, and tugged on his seedy sweatshirt. "Step back, will you? They are looking this way."

He shook my hand off callously.

"*Please* do not do this."

"I never leave a museum till I touch the van Goghs."

Van *Goghs!* A plural construction. He had done this before. And what of *Joseph Roulin,* would he have to touch that as well? *Saint Rémy?* I had no intention of finding out.

"I will not stand here," I said, and walked directly out through the archway, my back stiffening, heart palpitating, as if it were I who was summoning courage, I who was raising my hand, stretching my fingers toward the hard . . . lumpy . . . paint. MAN TOUCHES VAN GOGH IN MOMA. I stumbled blindly through the next two rooms, listening for alarms to sound, voices to raise. Instinctively, I turned left for Monet's *Water Lilies,* avoiding the further confusion of the Cubist galleries, and seated myself upon one of the gray vinyl benches that look out over the sculpture garden. There, a prickling scuttled up the back of my neck as the slow, sullen weight of truth descended: Stanley was a fool. Every man was, of course, I knew that, but I had agreed to be tricked, to be veiled with that delicate delusion that allows for the possibility of love. I had thought perhaps Stanley could sustain it—for several months, a year, four. Instead he had shattered it instantly. How could I feign blindness now? There was no return to ignorance.

I thought of Bernard from Washington, D.C.—the unpleasant odor about him, his doughy, pale anatomy. In my rarely doubly occupied full-size bed, I had tossed and turned into the morning hours: what we had just completed had been so narrowly defined, and yet he slept soundly enough. Time and again I had attempted to curl up behind him and drape my arm about his bosom, but then it would seem such mimicry, to be embracing a stranger so tenderly, and I would recoil to clutch at my pillow on the far edge of the mattress. Finally I rose for the shower; in the mirror my person looked blotched, handled. Then all in a dark moment, beneath the hot lashing jets, a quiet of seemingly infinite magnitude came over me: perhaps there would even be no making do, but only periods of yearning, followed by spells of nausea, yearning or nausea. Well, if one could accept that, what would he have left to fear?

Below me I now saw the raised, pleading palms of Maillol's thrown woman, and for an instant I imagined myself the weight she anticipated: hurled from the huge window in a wide, gravity-defying arc, limbs spread, taut abdomen impaled upon her wrist.

"Here you are."

I started, sensing a fast-moving presence closing in on my right: it was Stanley, already. Glaring up at him, I saw none of that unfocused, fluttering mania I had witnessed just moments earlier. Instead he stood before me, exhilarated, quelled. "Ya mad at me, aren'cha?" he said, smiling his snow-white, faultless smile. "I'm sorry; it was so thick and chunky I couldn' help myself." He attempted to touch my hand, but I quickly stood up and made for the next gallery, in awe of the transparency of his words; yet they served only to validate what I had already ascertained.

We walked on without speaking, then I broke off ahead of him, hardly caring, I told myself, if he were to turn around and leave. He followed me, however, doggedly, and at a measured distance, past the expressionists, the futurists, the constructivists. And it was not until the Matisse gallery, before the imposing *Dance,* that he stepped up beside me and, after a lengthy silence, I spoke to him: "Well?"

"Hm?"

"Did you do it?"

"Do what?"

"The painting."

"Did I touch *The Starry Night?*"

"Shhh. Yes. Did you?"

He grinned. "Uh-huh."

"Good Lord." I crossed the gallery, pausing before *Piano Lesson;* again he followed. There, in my distracted attempt to examine the painting, my eyes were drawn, as they so often are, to that green triangulation down the left side of the canvas, the insinuation of nature into the gray room. I noticed that Stanley, however, was preoccupied with the boy at the piano to the right, and I took the opportunity to glance briefly at his left hand—the hand I presumed to have accomplished the lawless deed—the thumb of which he pressed just then to his teeth: its knuckles were large and red, the veins bluely prominent; at the base of each finger, and across his wrist, was a tuft of black, brutish hair. "So?"

"So what?"

"So what happened? Did anything happen?"

"What could of happened?"

"No type of alarm went off?"

He shook his head.

"No one saw you?"

He nodded. "Someone did see me."

"I knew it. I knew you could not get away with it." I looked left and right, but the few people nearby did not appear to be in any kind of pursuit. "Who? Who saw you?"

"A woman did. She was standin' bahin' me."

"How do you know?"

"I heard 'er; she went, '*Goodness!*' "

"Oh God, and did she say anything else? Where is she now?"

"I don't know."

"Well, do you know if she told anyone? Did anyone hear her?"

"No. Nothin' like that. She just said, '*Goodness!*' and that was it. What did you go to Catholic school or sumthin'?"

"Now what would that have to do with anything?"

"Why are you so afraid of gettin' in trouble?"

"Why are you so insistent upon breaking every rule?"

"What rule did I break? Whose rule?"

"Why have you no respect?"

"I got plen'y of respect."

"No. No, I do not think you do. Not when you go pawing at one of the most valuable works in this entire museum on the least little whim; I can think of nothing more selfish."

"*Selfish?*"

"What else could it be, Stanley? You wanted to touch it, and so you did. Without a thought as to how anyone else might feel about it. What about the people who value that painting, the people who value it tremendously? Do you think they want your hands all over it? Your oily hands?" He would have nothing to say to that, I knew, so I returned to the Matisse, imagining, for an instant, the very tips of his fingers fleshing over the hard, hundred-year-old ridges of paint: he pulls his hand away, leaving several ever-so-imperceptible trails of moisture upon the night sky; they evaporate, and he discovers a particle adhering to his forefinger, like a piece of eggshell.

"Which part did you touch?"

He looked at me quickly. "Which part would you of touched?"

"I would never have considered touching it in the first place."

"Then why are you so interested?"

"You are quite right. Actually, I am not interested at all; I think it is absolutely infantile and selfish. You could have damaged it, for all you know—with the oils in your hand, with the pressure on the canvas."

"It was tight as a drum."

"What was?"

"The canvas. It didn' give one bit."

"Huh. Well, you could have cracked it, then."

"How'm I gonna—?"

"The paint. You could have chipped it."

"It didn't chip."

"It is old, Stanley, one hundred years old, a one-hundred-year-old chef-d'oeuvre of inestimable—"

"He couldn't trade that thing for a loaf a bread in his day."

"Oh, I see. So because—"

"This whole thing stinks like a lot a pretentious bullshit, you ask me."

"I beg your—"

"Personally, I don't think he woulda minded me touching it one bit; I think he woulda let me touch it all I wanted if I asked him to."

"Well, that is a facile claim, is it not, now that the fellow has been interred for more than a century? You think he had no respect for his work? He cherished that painting."

"So I like it, too."

"Then you should respect it."

"I touched it *because* I respect it."

"Now how does that follow?"

He sputtered.

"How does that follow, Stanley?"

"It wanted touching."

"What wanted touching? The painting?"

He nodded.

I laughed, incredulously. "How does a painting want? What did it do, did it speak to you? Did it say, 'Touch me, Stanley; I need you now'?" I watched his eyes narrow at the boy musician. "Is that what it said?"

"Nothin' happened. You can be as sarcastic as you want. I touched it, and nothin' happened."

That hardly seemed a justification, I thought, upon which another silence followed, and I pondered whether he was merely defending a puerile impulse. Perhaps it was he who was nothing more than a lapsed Catholic, one who after years of being threatened into submission with yardsticks and pointers now felt compelled to walk wherever he discovered a NO TRESPASSING sign. Or perhaps his words did arise from some theoretical perspective he could not skillfully articulate—one, undoubtedly, that had not been thought through very thoroughly, and which, at its kernel, would most likely be concluded unsound. How much did he believe, I wondered, of what he said?

But the next instant, before I was able to settle the matter to my satisfaction, he raised his lips within inches of my right ear and whispered, "I touched the crescent moon."

"The moon?" I nodded automatically; then, upon further reflection, wrinkled my nose.

"What's wrong with that? It's the best part of the painting; it's chunkiest there."

"That is such an obvious choice; anyone would have touched

the moon. Did you ever look closely at the lowest star, right above the smaller cypress trees? The paint is very thick and extruded at the center of it, like the tip of a ni—" But here I stopped myself.

"Tip of a what?" he said.

"Of nothing. Of a papilla."

"A what?"

"Teat, pap, the small protuberance through which milk is drawn from the breast."

"Nipple, you mean? 'Tip of a nipple,' you can't say that?"

"No. You said it."

"Why can't you say 'tip of a nipple'?"

"I—"

"Say, 'Tip of a nipple.' "

"Why?"

"Say it."

"I do not wish to say it."

"You better say it."

"I do not see any reason why—"

"Then there's something very wrong with you if you can't—"

"Why?"

"Say it."

"No."

"Say it."

"*Ni*—"

"All of it."

"*Nip*—"

"More."

"*Nipple.*" I scarcely breathed the word, taken aback, as I was, by the forceful entry into my mind of the image of a man—perhaps it was Stanley, or some equally uncouth thug with a similar, navy-blue baseball cap—his thighs pressing rudely against the white guardrail, his plump, moistened lips closing around the protruding star; he suckled it like a newborn babe, whimpered and writhed as he drew off the primitive saps and juices, as dribbles of primary yellow, primary blue, ran down his chin; and for an instant, it was as if I felt that tugging *upon my own breast,* the scraping of teeth across the hardened and reddened tip of skin. "Oh," I said, looking over at him, "did you ever feel that?"

"What?"

"Did you ever notice that?"

"The nipple star?"

"Yes."

"No, I didn't."

"I see." I exhaled. "Perhaps next time."

But his brow furrowed. "What next time?" he said and, without further comment, cupped his chin again and looked to the Matisse.

I did not know how to interpret his remark. Did he mean to say there would be no future appointment? Of course, I would never have wanted one, either; in fact, I had been hoping just previously that he would simply fade somehow, back into the squalid city air. And would that not be further evidence of his degeneracy anyway, that he would reject someone like myself? I should think any gum-snapping, expletive-spewing art molester would lose interest in a person with actual principles and tastes; I should think that would be very typical.

I turned slightly, squinting sideways at his profile, a not-unattractive one. The little wave of black hair that hung from his cap was stippled with strands of silver; his nose was well shaped, strong, Romanesque. And I thought then, for one depraved instant, that however selfish his act, it had been rather bold. That this man beside me, through the agency of his own foolish courage, had joined the ranks of the presumably few people to ever have touched *The Starry Night.* And I here shamefully admit that the action distinguished him in my mind, and that I had even begun to wonder about the others, others who might have touched it, when suddenly I found myself asking, "What did it feel like?"—the words racing from my mouth before I could stop them. Immediately my cheeks flushed with heat; surely I had betrayed my thoughts with their utterance; he would have every right to chuckle now, triumphantly.

But he did not chuckle, he merely stared into the center of the Matisse.

"Stanley?"

"It's hard ta explain."

"Try."

"You'll laugh," he said, turning to me with a seriousness I would have thought uncharacteristic.

"No, I will not. Try."

He looked ahead again. "I've been thinking about this, 'bout how I would describe it."

"Yes, and . . . ?"

"It felt like a soul."

"Like a *what? A soul?*" I believe I recoiled, physically. That such a simile should tumble so freely from his lips, that it should engender in my mind an image of such clarity, such enormity, I . . . *saw the paint moving:* smoky white wisps appearing, disappearing, tumbling, swirling, trafficking, endlessly, within the waves of the sky; transposed, under all that paint, the artist—just as I had felt the words of poems and stories betray their authors' being, as if there, within the ink, within the paper itself, dwelled the living, breathing thing: he *was* the paint! he *was* the page! "Are you mocking me?"

"I'm not mocking you," I heard him say.

And so, might it not be worth it, then, I wondered, if just for one second, really to feel one's soul pour out of oneself; if just for one second, really to be filled by another's? Might it not be worth it? And if that was the best this existence had to offer, then must one not be ready to die for it? Must one not go rushing gladly toward that death? Oh yes, I answered, oh flow: yellow, orange, green, white; suck in through the grooves of his teeth. Come blue, come indigo, come red and violet; run over his tongue, seep down his throat. For I have been too rash, I have been much too rash.

With new urgency, I looked to the senseless green insistence at the left of the canvas—senseless, and yet when I tried to imagine the painting without it, an uninterrupted gray room, a claustrophobia came over me. Yes! It would have failed, failed miserably— yes! yes!—and as I turned to say something anything, to Stanley that would have communicated my understanding of his words, I discovered he was no longer beside me. He had stepped back a yard or two and was engaged, to my surprise, in the contemplation of a young man on the other side of the gallery, fair-haired, sporting a black polo shirt and a pair of khaki walking shorts. His legs were tanned, though he wore yellow socks, and as he walked quickly from painting to painting, he held his hands behind his back, clutching a newspaper.

When Stanley broke his stare, he turned into my own— "Whoops!"—his eyes widening again in a chilling caricature of a schoolboy caught red-handed at some latest mischief. "Never forget to admire the works of art that are walkin' around," he added lightly, though I thought I detected more of a scarlet color to his cheeks than before. I must have glared; his eyes narrowed. "That doesn' botha you, does it?"

Botha me? Not greatly. And if several months from now I had the misfortune to stop by the apartment unexpectedly and happen upon an attractive blond in the bedroom adjusting his trousers, it would still not *botha me* greatly. Resiliency is a woman's ability, I have heard it said. Or perhaps it is a curse, this stubborn picking up of oneself, this dusting off and straightening up, this readying for the next blow, and the next blow. All because I cannot keep myself from needing, because all that I have always wanted is to be in love. You must believe me when I say that. *I'm sorry; it was so thick and chunky I couldn' help myself.* Indeed.

His eyes held me an instant longer, and I looked deeper into their golds and grays, down to the darker, spongelike recesses, down to the vast depths of the pupils, intricate and inexplicable. He was a terribly attractive man. "Museums make me horny," he admitted at last, and with a bright flash of teeth bowed his head in mock shame.

"Unnh!" The sound escaped from my throat. I had hoped not to entertain him with any reaction at all, but what did it matter now? I was free to turn, to walk briskly past the Klees, the Picassos, the Mirós, coming at last to the surrealists. Ahead lurked the final Magritte.

All the character, I remember reading, *of one of those psychological games in which one is supposed to make up one's own story from the image.* Exposed and bleeding from her mouth on the bed, the woman is love; the hatless equivocal man gazing into the gramophone, her latest assassin; others await their turn outside the room, one with a club, the second a net. Although the men-in-waiting always look the same, weekly their weapons change: a rope, a cleaver, a hammer. The woman's revivifications are brief, just long enough for her to re-dress while the men exchange places, long enough for the molestation, the disposal; I would imagine them quick, precise affairs.

And then one week, oh yes, one week I am walking toward that last gallery, that final canvas, ready to stand in the face of its pessimism, my arm linked to the one who will invalidate it, only to discover that the painting has changed completely. The walls are the blue of affirmation; a couple sits peaceably upon the sofa, the antechamber empty, the view from the window pastoral, green. It will always have been that way.

Where is he, mother? How much longer until I am free?

A hand touched my shoulder. Turning, there again were the grays, the golds—such captivating eyes. They were Stanley's. A sinking renewed in my interior at the thought of the circles I had yet to make through those galleries, the signs I had yet to interpret, theories I had yet to formulate. At best, we would dine at a mediocre restaurant, perhaps share a bottle of mediocre wine; I would follow him to his apartment on the Upper West Side. In an hour, we would finish, and the nausea that physical sensation can no longer postpone would claim me. I would dress and excuse myself in time for the twelve-forty train, a time of failure, of disappointment, perhaps, but as I settled onto one of the cracked vinyl seats, as the bell rang for the car doors to close and the train jerked and pulled out of this dirty city, a relief would come over me: a shedding of worries at the realization that Stanley had not been love, that love, when it finally did arrive—

"*Come*. In an hour, we would *come*. Blow our fucken loads to Kingdom Come, come, come—"

Enough. Vulgar thing. Love, when it finally did arrive, would be something far grander.

You could see the little war he was having with himself, should I or shouldn't I, all the while he was looking down at it. Then he mumbled something he thought I didn't hear: "You were not lying when you said you did not have HIV, were you?" I swear he mumbled that, and laughed this light, little crazy laugh. Poor guy; another second, and his little devil got the best of him: he fell right to his knees and gobbled me down whole. And I mean whole; he just went *at it*, whining and grunting like a little starving animal, clutching up against my thighs so tight I thought he was gonna try to climb inside them somehow. I gushed all over him, big creamy load. And when I finally was able to pry his mouth off me, he just did whatever I asked him to: lay on his belly across the couch, his right knee on the floor; said the line on cue. "Thata way," I told him. "Now smile, Cinderella."

Robert Glück

ON THE BOARDWALK

MY FATHER AND I rarely spend time together, even in my imagination, so it's strange that this day and story are ours. He's almost eighty, discouraged, and he dislikes to walk, so it's strange to find ourselves on the boardwalk with the rest of the people. Even his cane seems to wince as it steps. I'm impatient as a demigod who slows to a human pace; I feel ferociously expansive for no special reason other than I'm walking with my fragile father in the sunlight.

We drift away from a band playing too loudly. It's what guys do as a rite of passage: "Like, I have to be *heard!* No one's *listening* to me!" The sky is thin, the sand glares, and a salty breeze carries the scent of rotting watermelons. Two shirtless young men toss a mango back and forth, self-consciously winsome. My dad is drawn to a group in a huddle. They crowd around a con artist who slides shells across a TV tray. My dad and I hang back but also want to be part of the excitement. The con is good-looking, gathering people to him with a gesture. He shoves a bill away. "No bets under twenty." His hands fly over shells that replace each other furiously and then come to rest in a row. The bettors guess which shell hides the bead, and when the young man pockets their twenties, they share sick smiles.

The con is all face, a young Alain Delon—lavishly knowing features perched on a body without shoulders or hips. I have a mild aversion for the perverse man/boy. Even though he invites us to close in, my dad and I are afraid of making contact with a stranger who is after something. There's great refinement in his routine: he catches people looking at him, anyone would, then turns their interest into an invitation. He has an open manner, relaxed, not furtive or sly. The size of the group illustrates his allure (if I have to prove it), except to women.

And it's weird, but as I stand there with my father, my distaste for the con dismantles itself. I mentally draw his waist to me so fiercely that the two halves of his body fall backward. I wonder if my father is excited—that's possible. I'm so aroused I'm panting next to my dad. It tweaks me into the arbitrary. Why this body and not the table, the tree, the human standing beside it?

This configuration of father and son is an incitement: you kill your mother, and your dad fucks you. That's not logical, but violence speaks in correspondence. I think, Huh, Dennis Cooper. I'm not sure how I mean it—what would homosexuality be without Mom? My nostrils dilate—I can smell the con's sweat, and the fact that it's sweet means he's ready.

What is the desire to penetrate? It takes shape as an empty shell. It clangs like bright brass: so that's what that sound is. The con's too empty and that makes me too full—no way to break the tension except at the breaking point.

The offshore wind is exasperating. The two losers continue betting. From the way they are dressed and from their wallets full of bills, I guess they are professors who have drifted down from the university. The con collects their money graciously. A bee drifts into the game; it looks stationary compared to the whirling hands and shells. The Hiring Committee debates: the right one, no the middle one, the right. I call them the Hiring Committee because they confer, confer, then make the wrong decision.

The young white man provides ever-renewable hope; the older African-American calls the shots even though he doesn't say much. He's handsome and somber, not a man who puts his business in the street. That's why he looks so uneasy, more dismayed by the exposure than by the loss of money. The young man has the energy of a silent movie actor. He expresses: surprise, humor, thought, dismay. After listening carefully, averted and nodding, the black man prevails without effort and places their money on the wrong candidate.

Why aren't I attracted to the tree instead, or to the bike? I stagger a little, suddenly clumsy. I keep slapping my neck to kill a mosquito. As though responding to a request, the con empties himself of past and future. There's no difference between the con and what I feel for him. It somehow makes me angry and the thought of squeezing this random matter out of existence occurs to me, under the eye of my father. I remind myself to think about it later.

It starts with my hands, wanting to steady him. There's a sound built on hollowness, the clanging of cymbals. It's strange because you never get there—he's hollow. Or do you touch him everywhere if it's from his inside? His body is not reached except through the show he makes of the intensity inside him, and what's that? How does that secure him? Why hammer a nail into a hole already drilled?

A pale wraith roams through the crowd, too close to people, attending every conversation as though we were all on an outing together. He's as empty and will-less as a dust bunny. He carries a green plastic pail full of random stuff; maybe he lives on the street. I call him Lowly.

The con notices me studying Lowly. He invites me forward with a sweeping bow, a wad of twenties in his hand. The white man keeps checking the black man's face for a response. When the older speaks a few dry words, the younger laughs with relief. Although the young man is distressed by the loss, he's more distressed by his friend's reticence.

I wonder why they can't locate the bead. They lose again—maybe two hundred dollars by now—yet I know exactly where the bead is hiding. Standing away from the table, I can follow the bead dancing through the con's fingers. So that's why he gathers the players in closer—you can't see from above, but you can easily see from the side. I show this to my father and demonstrate that we can always tell. I propose a counterswindle—"Let's con the con." My dad will bet, and I'll stand behind him and let him know which shell covers the bead by putting a hand on his right shoulder, neck, or left shoulder. My dad is doubtful—"Com'on, dad, let's con the con."

My dad and I have a moment of solidarity. It's my father who always asks how everyone is, how Ed was in his sickness. He is loyal to individuals in recognizable trouble—disease, unemployment. He visits friends in the hospital. When he still had money to give them, he reached for his worn-out wallet with a defeated gesture.

My father's life—I draw the words from a deep well, *The Great Depression.* A brief respite of big bands and fat paychecks. Dissatisfaction at work, chaotic anger at home *where ignorant armies clash by night.* Then grievance and physical pain, and his stories losing value like bad investments. Who can increase their worth now but myself?

So my father reaches for his wallet with that sigh. In his mind, he's betting on me, no sure thing. He puts down a twenty, the Hiring Committee does too. The con's hands fly over the board, the shells jump to life below them. I see the bead clearly as it comes to rest under its shell, and I place my hand on my father's left shoulder. The Hiring Committee goes into a huddle—they choose the center.

Hands rear back, exposing the empty bellies of two shells for all to see; the left shell still covers its secret, a secret no more. My father gets two twenties and a smile, and he looks back at me with a bright face, full of appetite. We play again. The hands fly, I have a clear view, my dad puts forty on the center, the Hiring Committee bets twenty on the right, and my dad is holding eighty dollars.

The con takes us in at a glance. I catch his eye and he nods to me, amused; we share eyes for a moment. There he is, his face and his body. He knows I'm a fag. For a moment he makes me believe that my father stands between us. A man too close to me asks, "Do you have a pencil?" It's Lowly; before I can answer, he cries, "I do, but it's at home!" He looks too expectant, too apologetic. I wonder if he's carrying all his possessions in that pail. If so, why is he so larval? He's dressed in a black suit on such a day. Light sheets off the ocean in a rapture—only the bead sits in darkness.

After a conference, the Hiring Committee decides to bet with us in the next round. The professors lay down three twenties, so I will be helping them recoup their loss. They are success stories, but only that; they don't recognize themselves in loss. I resent them, their wallets packed with bills. I'm proud they're betting on me, I'm a winner, but I want to teach them a lesson. I want to present them with the bitterness in my heart—here's my class anger in the form of my father, and here's my sexuality, a handsome thief, an enemy of the common good. My dad puts down our entire winnings.

My father rocks on his cane, counting on me at last. At this late date, is it possible to turn the tide of discouragement? Do I want to side with such defeated hope? I'm not sure what it means to win.

The con's hands zigzag in front of the inexpressible. One of his nipples slips in and out of his tank top—I wonder if that isn't distracting him. Its tip's erect, chafed by the fabric, gathering itself up to ward off the attention. Or maybe it's perturbed by the salty wind? When he pulls the fabric away from his nipple, the helpless cloth retains its dent.

I'm taking in more and more light, looking away from the game, losing track of the bead, to gather light into me, swallow it with my eyes. Pleasure makes the light go into me as though I were gathering it by the eyeful, closing my eyes, sealing the pleasure inside. Ed died not long ago; maybe that's why I'm seeing the world through his eyes. It's Ed who eats up the light and flirts with the con. And Ed who betrays his father? The father who forced him sexually. The incredible lawlessness of the nuclear family.

I tap my father's right shoulder; my reward is a nod from the con as he scoops up our money. The crowd blurts laughter as though it's a laugh track. The Hiring Committee is solemn, the men's faces drained.

"Wow, Dad," I say, "I guess we struck out." He's naked when he turns to look at me. He shakes his head, incredulous, yet he's also smiling: something has been confirmed, torn down. I feel like a moral curiosity. The con holds his hands up as though to hold back the crowd, though there really isn't one. Now that he has our money, he's full of relation. "Do you come here often? Is this your father? Yes, you have his eyes."

My father has diabetes; he needs to eat right now and it's not a joke. His legs are no good. We go to the nearest café. It resembles an old Chevy with red upholstery and gleaming chrome knobs. For some reason, it smells like sawdust. The hostess's hair swirls in a huge wave around her head, but the restaurant is closing. My father tells the alarmed hostess that he's sick and must have food. She parts like curtains before the manager, who ushers us in with a bow.

We don't talk about my betrayal, but I wonder, Can I describe my life without altering it? Does a dream change anything if you decline to understand its meaning? Is it about money? My father is *from* the Depression; the economic catastrophe is an American ethnicity that Hitler supported by murdering my dad's European relatives. Is it about sex? I recall sighting my father's cock rolling like a sunken log in the tub, flopping in the hallway like a dog's. When

I saw that thing, I hid my own by pulling my scrotum over it—my first and most sincere attempt at drag.

I've said the name Hitler, yet continue to be in the wrong. Our fat waiter takes our order, practically French in his exquisite service. My dad solemnly chews a flap of skin on his cuticle. The con is grit on my skin from the ocean wind. The few diners are finishing up, and who do I see sitting in front of a cup of coffee—it's Lowly. His green pail of belongings sits beside him. He's turned to the next table, enthusing in a stagy voice as though he were part of the diners' conversation, "I do, *too*," and "Actually, I *must* disagree," though no one notices him.

My dad eats slowly and I drift off. He chews till the last fry is gone, but there's still coffee to be sipped. Lowly, my dad and I are the last customers, and it's possible that Lowly is not a paying one. The staff has finished sweeping the restaurant; our fat waiter hangs off the counter, dead on his little feet; the cash register is closed out.

I stare in disbelief when my dad summons the waiter for a refill. The waiter pours with incredible grace. My father slowly drinks. He looks around, daring anyone to complain. The hostess has gone, the music has been turned off, I can hear the dishwashers saying good-bye. Lowly keeps exclaiming, "How very interesting!" He turns to me, urging, "In the bathroom, in the bathroom." I look across the café: there it is. Lowly sneezes loudly and the blast propels me—I'm jumping to orders. I excuse myself with needless formality as though I were going away.

The tacky little room smells flowery as a new magazine. I look around—is there some reason for me to be here? It's cool and quiet. I just rest for a minute. A shell sits on the stainless steel ledge, one of the con's shells. It looks like half of a nut. I pick it up and see it's filled with something, it's filled with sperm. I'm in a dream: the con stops squirming once I jam my tongue into his mouth.

The sperm is still warm. I look around as though he were still here. It's beginning to separate into a plug and clear whey. How did he get past me? The little square window is fastened by a grotty iron handle. The tacky bathroom, my father sipping coffee, the manager waiting by the door with his coat over his arm—it's so unacceptable, so hard to endure, that I lean back against the scuzzy tiles, cover my eyes, and cry a little from lack of relief. I don't have the strength to drag myself forward to the next moment—All bets are off. The shell still carries warmth from his insides. I sniff it: sperm. No way am I going to dip my tongue in, but once I have the idea, I have to swim in that tiny sea of love.

I raise my face to meet veils of sheer awfulness falling from on high. Awfulness on my skin. At the same time, I'm laughing—hah! I laugh at the comedy this makes, as though it celebrates our union like a wedding ring!—a fit end to a day packed with cheap moments. Something happened: the con had an orgasm. That's something. I have no idea how to think about it, except that it's certainly mine, even if it's meant as ridicule—*given* to me, my share of the spoils.

Keith Banner

LILY OF THE VALLEY

IT ISN'T "LOVE" in the dictionary sense of the word, or any sense of the word. It is just this guy, I mean this middle-aged probably whacked-out guy, standing at the cash register at the Goodwill Thriftstore, as I purchase a pair of used but still wearable work pants. I have never seen him here before. At the register I notice his name tag: WARREN. I notice his dead, sad-sack smile. That's a good name for him, I'm thinking, and he is the assistant manager, according to the tag. I'm not saying a word. He has this almost vampire face as he checks out the pants, which are blue and slightly ragged.

Warren looks up at me and says, "One twenty-five, sweetheart."

"Did you just start here?" I ask, not looking at him.

"Last week. Fresh meat," he says, smiling.

I smile. This is the moment of connection. I feel a little scared of him. He must sense this because he folds the pants as carefully as a suburban housewife on speed, to show me something about himself, how careful, how in control he really is, but he isn't. He has the shakes, just enough to make him sexy. I think how pathetic he is, but that's only a defense mechanism: I wonder what he looks like naked, and that is disturbing but sweet, to think of him that way. He is tall and skinny and has outer-space alien eyes, has baldness starting on top, has thick strange sweet lips, almost purple, a nicked chin from sloppy shaving.

He puts the pants into a paper bag and I give him my money and it's over. Outside the air is so muggy my throat closes up, the sun throbbing through haze, glinting off car hoods and white litter. I light up a cigarette, then destroy it, look inside at him again as he takes a pen from behind his ear and marks something up. I'm thinking it's the heat, but then Warren sees me staring at him and suddenly he knows me, he knows my soul, the new guy who manages the Goodwill in Anderson, Indiana, knows my soul.

I take off, but soon return as if by an electromagnetic ray, this time buying a set of jelly glasses.

"Just a shopaholic." Warren's voice is smooth but stylishly gruff.

"I can't stop myself," I say.

"I don't blame you, hon."

He wets his lips, shutting his eyes for a moment of symbolism. I just stand there like an idiot experiencing the genius of a great actor without having any way to appreciate it. Yes: he smells good, too. Unknown cologne, cigarettes, coffee breath. I lean in to him, closer. Two fat ladies at the checkout next to us, run by a tiny black woman, are buying baggy housedresses and record albums, giving us curious and disapproving stares.

"You've got to be kidding," Warren says as I pull back.

"What?"

"You're all of sixteen," he says.

"Twenty."

"Shhhhh," he says. Then he laughs silently. He puts on his glasses to look at my fingernails.

"You keep them clean."

"Yeah."

Someone buys a naked baby doll. Another person buys seven old bowling trophies. I stand next to a basket of coat hangers, then look up at Warren as he turns around.

"This is the life."

"Yup," I say.

Warren stares at me for the longest time. My aunt will say something about my wanting to replace my father. I'll tell her she doesn't know what she's talking about.

"What do you like to eat, my friend?" he whispers.

"Anything," I say.

"I guess I'll need your name." He has a slapdash, movie-star elegance, squeezing out from the orange checkout, toward me.

"Jay," I say.

He stands beside me, inspecting my scalp. I pull back and see Warren seeing me. I can envision myself through his expression, how he thinks I am a little pathetic, too, too tall and gangly to be quote unquote "attractive," with my dumb-ass Greenday T-shirt, my Birkenstocks and faded shorts, my slightly oily hair and, yes, offbeat, doughy complexion: a bookworm, a burgeoning pervert, and maybe he likes that.

"Jay," he pronounces.

"Yeah?"

"I think this could be one of those turning points."

I have no idea what that means, but I smile at him because it sounds hopeful and ominous. He pulls a skinny balloon out of his pants pockets and blows it up into a pink hot dog, and with a few twists and turns it's a dachshund, no shit, sitting there on the counter.

I have to laugh. Warren pops the dog with a safety pin from his shirt pocket.

"I can create and I can destroy," he says in his best Charlton Heston. I figure he must have balloons in his pocket just so he can say that. People standing in the tiny black woman's line are looking at Warren, but then looking away.

"Me, too," is my response.

So I found Warren on the day I bought work pants, on the day I was going to go in to work a little early to make some extra money but instead we went to his apartment at three-thirty and did it, did it till five-thirty. Then I had to call Loretta, the lady who owns Goldenhouse, the Chinese restaurant where I work. I told her I had the flu.

"The flu," however, turned out to be his apartment, the half-lit nausea of his little studio. Dirty clothes were everywhere and there were no pictures on the walls, and I was staring at a plate on his table covered in dried gravy as I told Loretta how sick I was.

"You better be sick," she said. Her accent was almost gone and came out only when she was totally pissed, like when the ex-con who did dishes busted plates or when her ex-husband came into the place wanting to borrow from the register. Then her Chinese fury blasted out of her mouth, and she seemed almost dragonlike, this four-foot lady with a black curly perm, standing in a gold lamé top and polyester pants, wearing dangly earrings and lipstick the color of raw meat.

"Oh, God, Loretta, I feel like shit," I said. "I really do."

I hung up and Warren was in bed still, smoking.

"I don't normally do this," he said.

"Yeah, I know," I said.

Naked, Warren appeared absurd, with his dark flesh sagging a little at the armpits, his chin hitting his chest as he continued to smoke in that awkward position on the bed. Two cats came out of the bathroom and found a place next to him. Warren petted the fluffier one. The light from the blinds made zebra patterns across the blanket. I felt elegant and satiated.

Warren looked up and said, "Do you only tend to drift toward older men?"

"Wait a goddamned minute. Are you older?"

Warren found that amazingly funny. We started to fuck again. I looked at his face as he maneuvered into me. He was the ghost of the Shah of Iran suddenly, regal and debonair and a little terrified of himself, of his power: I was kissing the air around him, smelling him again, the creepy odor of his apartment, the gloomy light in here making it all seem like we were sinking into the ground, into a makeshift cemetery under the Iranian embassy where the corpses did this dance called fucking and everybody, even the people with their heads chopped off, was getting it on.

After, Warren sits up in bed like Nosferatu and tells me to get out.

"I need you to go," he says.

"Why?"

"Issues of space."

He is not joking. He gets out of bed and goes into the bathroom and I hear the shower hiss on. I stand and try to get into the bathroom but he has locked it and then I hear him say through the door, "Do you need a place to stay?"

"Yes," I say, a lie.

"You can stay here as long as you go away when I tell you to."

"Fuck you!"

But I'm laughing.

Rita says, "Why do you want to move in with a total stranger?"

She is an amazing lady, I want to say first off, flabby and tired but still oddly and masculinely glamorous in her postal uniform with a cigarette in her mouth on the patio of her condo, like a character from a short story, her bangs hanging down over her shiny forehead, sunglasses shielding her eyes. She has knee socks, a big mug of coffee, huge, comfortable hiking boots, a wallet on a silver chain.

"Tell me," she says. "Go ahead. Explain this to me."

"Because."

If there is one thing Rita hates, it's when I'm trying to be cute. She backs up and gets ready to go back in, but I stop her by whining. She puts her cigarette out in her coffee mug and puts the mug on the rickety patio table where I sit in a robe and underwear.

"He's so creepy," I say.

"That's why you want to live with him?"

"Yeah."

"Plus, he's an old man."

"Yeah, that, too."

Rita laughs at me, the aunt who took me in after my dad kicked me out. My mom, Rita's sister, died when I was ten, of pneumonia, a nurse who never went to the doctor, and then last year I was suddenly proud of being gay, one year out of high school and with this guy named Brad I had met in Florida. Not a good match, but he was beautiful and willing. I came home and my dad blew up at me, out on the lawn, a fucking TV movie: Brad disappeared in the midst of the turmoil, and I came here to Rita's because she always knew what I was and I always knew what she was and it was nice: it still is. When she brings a friend over, usually a skinny blond lady with hazel or deep-blue eyes, I excuse myself, and then I imagine Rita whispering, "He's my nephew, the best kid in the world."

"You know what I think you ought to do?" Rita asks, retying her left boot.

"What?"

"Quit that shitty job. Quit hanging around downtown like some idiot. Quit burying yourself here and go to school. I'll loan you the money, you know that."

Rita does not look at me as she talks and I love her because she's not being a bitch about the whole thing, just concerned.

"How much can you loan me? A million?"

Rita laughs.

"It's weird," she says suddenly. Changing the subject is her specialty. She stands next to a beige gutter, looking out at the minuscule backyard: "It's weird to think that like three hundred or so people actually depend on me for their mail, you know? Me. Me with my prescription for Prozac and my fully loaded semiautomatic."

She smiles, not allowing herself to laugh at herself, and says, "I don't want you going to live with some strange man who manages a thrift store and who is twice your age and who looks like Count Dracula, but hey, you're all grown up now, aren't you?"

I don't know if she's mad or giving me her blessing or what, but Rita disappears through the tall patio-window curtains, into the condo's kitchen, and I can hear her getting all her gear together, and then she's off to do her duty. I go upstairs and get ready to depart. I don't have much stuff, just uniforms for work, books, clothes. Downstairs I look at myself in the bathroom mirror before leaving and I see the wormy face of a lazy criminal, or the uncle you are afraid of; but also I have youth on my side, and this gives me a menacing glint in the eyes, pouty lips, smooth, shiny skin, a full head of hair.

I want Warren to see me as perfect, the perfect specimen. But then I think that I do need to go on with my life. I remember my dad, who was always miserable doing what he did, a car salesman who turned on the charm on the phone, even when he was about to give my mom the what-for: his skull of a face brightening up as he picked up the receiver, going into an automatic conversation with another car salesman about how much he'd sold, how much he was willing to do, and then hanging up and being totally quiet for a while, looking around at his house and knowing that this was it: his life. You have to insert me somewhere in there, a scrawny little fuck complaining about a bike or a tree house, and then all grown up and coming up to him and saying in his proudest voice, "I'm gay, Dad, and this is Brad."

I hated my dad anyway, so telling him was actually a release of all the manners I thought I was supposed to have. My telling him, though, did something to him, made him fall out of his car-salesman self, made him turn rigid as Pat Robertson. I have to admit I didn't think he had it in him to be righteous, self- or otherwise. I thought he would just ignore it and eventually have us over for dinner, Brad and me bringing over angel-food cake for dessert, with strawberries and fat-free whipped topping.

After all, Dad's has not been a sinless life. But faggotry does something to people. It makes them nervous about what they have, I guess, and there in the front yard with a cantaloupe-colored sky and the humidity at 85 percent and Brad staying in the car until I talked to Dad, and me swinging up to Dad as he came off the porch, almost first thing saying that about my being gay and being with Brad.

"You sick little fuck," Dad whispered. He was flabby, his sleeves rolled up, his tie loose, and I was shocked. I thought my saying that up front would make him break out of his dreary life, not in this hateful way but in the melodramatic self-pitying way of parents with gay children. He would learn to love me and to love Brad my partner (that's what he would end up calling Brad, in his pitiful self-help voice), and then there he would be on *Oprah* talking about loving your kid no matter what and now he thinks of all this as a great big beautiful blessing.

I stood there that day and I did not say anything to my dad and he said, his back turned to me as he walked up the porch steps, "You are not living here, buddy. Get your shit and get out of here. I won't have this."

Dad marched back inside the house. Brad was still in the car, embarrassed, staring away from me. Brad did not want this kind of shit in his life. He was too handsome, too clean for me anyway. I remembered meeting him on a beach, first noticing the back of his neck, the way the hair was trimmed so perfectly at the nape, wanting to taste the edge of his hair, and then I did it, and he had an all-

American laugh, a family with three sisters, a dog who died of diabetes. As I walked back to the car, Brad disintegrated right before my eyes, beamed back to the mother ship. The car was empty except for the sound of some nasal-voiced alternative rock singer singing a song about peaches.

When I arrive at Warren's, Warren is not there. An old lady is cleaning his apartment with the door open.

"Where's Warren?" I ask.

"He's out of here," she says, standing up straight, very pissed. "Got him evicted, finally. That son of a bitch."

"Evicted?"

"Yessir. He does not like to pay his rent. So I had the sheriff come in this morning, and he kicked him out."

"Huh?" I say.

"Yessir."

The old lady has a pasty look, in shorts and a Garth Brooks T-shirt, her hair bobby-pinned into an ornate cap of tiny curls. She is cleaning the sink and stove with gray water.

"You can find him at the track," she says.

"Track?"

"That horse track they just built down by the interstate."

"Oh," I say.

"He goes there and blows his money. He's proud of it. He likes to tell me how much goddamned money he blows and then he asks me for an extension on his rent. Well, them goddamn days are *over*."

She laughs, going back to sticking her head into the oven. From inside the oven, I can hear her voice, "That son of a bitch."

Outside the horse track in Anderson, Indiana, is a huge parking lot and a sign that says YOU'LL HAVE A GOOD TIME YOU CAN BET ON IT. The track is surrounded by newness: Applebee's and TGIF and a shopping mall and new bowling alley and cineplex—a whole new town, really, motels and apartments and housing divisions all looking like a computer-generated backdrop in an expensive blockbuster, about to be blown up by European terrorists in Armani suits. I park for six bucks not knowing what I'm doing, just following the old lady's instructions. As I walk up to the main entrance I can hear bells and an echoed P.A. system. Inside, a race has just begun, satin-saddled horses throwing black dirt behind them on an oblong path. All around me are old people with nothing better to do than drink beer and smoke and throw away money, husbands and wives and lonely widowers and widows.

Suddenly I see Warren walking beside me with a cigarette in his mouth. He does not appear at all nervous. Everything is under control. At first he tries not to recognize me. Then he does and he wants to avoid me. He approaches me finally.

"You into horses, too?"

"Not really."

Warren smiles. "I used to go to Kentucky all the time. Now I can go here. Thank God for convenience. This isn't a great track by any stretch of the imagination, but it does the job. I just bet two hundred on Lily of the Valley. The sweet little names they have here."

The sun is glaring off Warren's black glasses, and we stop beside a trash can. Sweat bees swarm around the can.

I say, "Didn't you just get evicted?"

"Yes, I believe I did."

He smiles again. He seems to be in complete control, killing a sweat bee with the palm of his hand, leading me up to the top deck, where he watches the next race. Lily of the Valley finishes last.

"That was nothing," he says.

"Yeah. So where are you going to live?"

"You got any ideas?" he asks.

"Not really."

Warren wipes sweat off his forehead with a bandanna from his pocket. "I've never been to Las Vegas. You'd think I would want to go to Vegas, but that just seems like a lot of hoo for nothing."

He stands up and stretches. I look at his face and I see something diabolical and innocent, a blend of teenaged boy and fifty-year-old mortician. He sits back in his seat.

"I go to sleep here sometimes. The sounds of the commotion put me to sleep, you know, like the way they say vacuum cleaners do for babies. I just sleep here and I wake up and I go bet. I only work at Goodwill twenty hours a week, so basically I'm here."

The Great Mystery, I think, then I get up, pissed at him, disappointed, thinking I have made my decision finally, that he is even more of a loser than I'd thought and I just don't have room for this kind of bullshit in my little life.

As I turn my back to him, he says, "I'll pick you up tonight."

I turn around, but even before turning around, I feel myself give in automatically.

"What time?" he says, grinning.

"I get off work at eleven."

"Eleven?"

"Yes."

"That's good."

"Pick me up at Goldenhouse, you know where that is?"

"Chinese downtown?"

"Yeah."

"Good."

Another race begins. Warren gets himself situated, lighting a smoke, smoothing back his dark, thinning hair.

It's a slow night at Goldenhouse, so I spend most of it sitting in a booth in back with a black Magic Marker, marking out the name and address of a Muncie Chinese restaurant on decorative paper place mats so that we can use them here on our tables. Loretta got them for free at some restaurant supply store. I've done four stacks before a single customer comes in. After that one customer, I sit down again. Loretta is doing paperwork at the cash register, in a lavender jogging outfit with silver lamé trim and big silver hoop earrings and mint green eye shadow.

"You got nothing to do?" she asks.

"I'm in love, Loretta," I yell back at her, taunting her, bored with blacking out.

Loretta laughs, shaking her head, not saying anything else.

"We'll end up closing early," she says finally.

"His name is Warren." I really do love torturing her sometimes, to see how far I can go before she transforms into Mother Dragon. She does not approve of my gay lifestyle.

"Warren Beatty," I say. "He is the most charming man." (I'm using a Southern-belle accent now.)

Loretta says, "You burn in hell." She laughs a little.

"I thought this *was* hell," I say.

"Close but no cigar," she says.

Finally, I stop marking off the place mats and go outside to sweep. Downtown is completely dead, cocooned in the muggy promise of a storm. There's a huge movie theater from the forties, the State, next to us, the marquee orange and yellow neon, unlit and wordless but still glorious. All the other businesses on the block have also closed down. Everyone has gone out to the suburbs, to where the racetrack is, but Loretta has stayed here stubbornly. Now all that's left is Goldenhouse, the Goodwill, the Section 8 office, a business-machine supply store. It does not fill me with sadness at all, being here with a broom confronted with all that vacancy, because I kind of get off on this solitary glamorous feeling, the only sensitive person left on Earth.

Loretta comes out. She is smoking a long, long cigarette, looking dreamy-eyed.

"It's nice out here," she says.

I lean on the broom. There are no cars, no lights except for the greenish glow of the fluorescent GOLDENHOUSE sign. Loretta gives me one of her cigarettes, as is her custom, and we smoke and talk, she about her shitty ex-husband calling and telling her he owns half the restaurant, something he does every other week when he bounces a bunch of checks, and me about how maybe next year I'll go to college somewhere or buy a new car or buy *something* new. As we smoke, I feel like talking about Warren again, but I keep my mouth shut, and then finally Loretta says, "So, you really in love?"

She's sitting on an old wood bench with FUCK YOU scraped into it.

"Yes. This guy. He just started working at the Goodwill."

"He nice?"

She lights another smoke.

"Very."

"What's gay like?" she asks, her face suddenly serious.

"What do you mean?" I sit down beside her, get another one of her extravagant cigarettes.

"I don't know."

"Shit. It's just something I've always carried around with me."

"I read this article about how it's in your genes."

"Yeah."

"It still makes me sick," she says.

"Whatever," I say.

She lights my cigarette for me, and we sit in silence, watching the street, looking inside at the empty restaurant Loretta owns. It looks sad but comforting, like the way a mental patient might feel about the psych unit, all the tables and maroon booths in a row with the cloth napkins Loretta folds every morning into little tents, the silverware glinting in piles beside the menu board. On one wall is a beautiful painted peacock the size of a Christmas tree, its feathers spread out with little blinking lights embedded in them, a beautiful creation.

"*I* make you sick," I say.

"No," says Loretta. "Forget it. You're a nice boy." She touches my knee then, and I can tell she's trying hard to be my friend so I let her. It starts to rain slowly.

"Let's let it rain on us," she says, with the cigarette in her mouth, her eyes closed.

"Just a little," she whispers.

Warren picks me up in the alley behind the restaurant, after work. His car is a black Monte Carlo, the vinyl roof peeling off in black pieces. He opens the door from the inside, big-band music spilling out.

"This is weird," I say.

"You smell like sauerkraut," he says.

We are on the road to nowhere. I get nervous, looking at him. I wanted to explain how I felt to Loretta, as if by explaining it to someone easily disgusted it might make me see it anew, but now I'm glad it is a secret. This is what my whole life is and will be, a secret from everyone, even though no one really cares to hear the secret anyway.

Warren is tapping his fingers on the steering wheel. I like the smell of Old Spice (I figured out his cologne) and cigarettes and onion breath, I want to tell him. I remember his fucking me. I get all cozy inside, the way his cats must feel around him, and then I ask, "What about your cats? Did they get evicted, too?"

"She kept them," Warren says.

He parks behind the Goodwill and uses his key to get into the storage warehouse. We are assaulted by the musty smell of discarded crap: old beds and clothes and books and records and toys. He flicks a switch, and the whole place, about the size of a movie theater, flickers to life with fluorescence. There is a huge bed at the center, made with a crushed-red-velvet spread and several dirty-looking stuffed animals and elegant pillows at the top. The headboard is garish French Provincial; beside the bed is a nightstand with a bottle of champagne in a cracked ice bucket.

"Our honeymoon suite," Warren says, his voice echoing.

I stare at the bed: it is the center of a huge dusty flower, all the stuff people don't want anymore being the petals. I'm almost shocked. This must be Warren's way of loving me.

Warren turns the lights out after lighting one solitary candle. We walk together to the bed and he pours champagne into jelly glasses. It tastes vinegary and poisonous, but I partake. He gives me the candle.

"Watch me," he says, undressing.

I hold the candle up and watch him. His clothes seem to disappear, pulled into the shadows by little ghost hands. He is an old, sagging angel, or maybe Satan before the face-lift, who the fuck knows? But I do know one thing: I love him in a way I haven't loved anyone before, and maybe since. We scoot all the stuffed animals off the red bed and then I strip, and in the dark warehouse we do whatever comes naturally.

Tomorrow I will awaken sticky and disoriented, will leave very quietly as Warren snores, stretched out like dinosaur bones in a museum. I will enter Aunt Rita's condo and take a shower, will have breakfast with Rita and Lucy, her new girlfriend with a white-blond perm and the crisp suntan of an aging movie star about to do dinner theater, will eat sausage links and wedges of orange and drink coffee with heavy cream, will listen to Rita talk about taking in a boarder and Lucy talk about her two grown sons, and I will feel bright and brand-new, knowing this is going to be my life for a little while, this person here is who I will be.

Matt Bernstein Sycamore

SHITPOKERS

WE DON'T GET OUT of the house until six P.M., rush to the clinic for our seven o'clock appointment. They tell me I have crabs even though a week ago they said I didn't. Gabby's all nerves and a few bumps of coke, waiting for her HIV test results. She turns out negative, we go to Buddha's Delight to celebrate because I'm vegan so we can't go anywhere else.

While we're eating, Gabby sees some van that says Boston Streetworkers, what could that be? I say it must be for street*sweeping*. Gabby says they don't sweep the streets in Chinatown. We leave and the van comes around again, men or boys leaning out, the driver screams you gay *son of* a *shit*. Gabby says, I *am* a son of a shit. I say, me, too, we go to Playland, and Gabby gets an Absolut Cape Cod that's almost colorless, I get water in a Pocahontas cup. Gabby talks to the owner about buying a wig, this queen comes behind the bar to tell me about her forty-fifth birthday: she went out with her friend done up and *no one even blinked*.

We walk to Copley Square, where Jeff Barrows can barely say hello because now he's straight. Gabby calls Lincoln and Randy for her makeup so she can do the eyebrow thing, I call a trick who paged me two hours ago. Over to the Westin Hotel to use the bathroom, which is packed because everyone's moved there to cruise since the Back Bay Station arrests. I get severe back pain in the Westin lobby, and Gabby's strung out or bored.

We go to the White Hen Pantry after sitting on the steps of the library, where I can't paint my nails because it's too dark. And White Hen is definitely the highlight. This boy, seventeen or eighteen, ghetto-style, says why'd you do that shit to your hair, what's up with that shit, that looks fucked up. I say maybe you should put some in *your* hair. He says what, you look fucked up, he's looking me up and down, are you gay? I say of course I am. He says that's fucking disgusting, he's making a big scene all loud, that's fucking disgusting, *you're* fucking disgusting. I say a few things that end in *honey* and he's not too happy, yelling out at me and Gabby as we leave the store, you two are fucking disgusting, God will strike you down, fucking faggots faggot fuckers shitpokers, why you living in *my* world? And of course the butch muscleboy fag behind us in line who looks all scared, doesn't say a word.

On our way to the T we run into our friend from the White Hen again. He's with five or six other boys who look tough and don't speak, look a little uncomfortable but mostly just laugh. Our friend starts making this scene about how he won't get on the train with us, talking to the T worker, saying, they let these faggots on the T? I'm not getting on the train with these faggots. Gabby's scared, I'm filled with anger and adrenaline and scared, too, but mostly just disgusted. We get on the train, and our friend makes a big deal about not using the same door as us but then he stands a few rows away. Gabby says why'd you get on the same car as him?

I'm thinking there's only one car, but maybe she meant the train, I didn't even think of not getting on the train.

Gabby says you're pushing him on, looks like Gabby's about to cry so I decide not to say anything, which is probably the right choice because this guy just goes crazy, screaming and yelling, all glassy-eyed and sweaty—You fuckin' faggot you look like a dog you think that looks good? You look like a fuckin' dog, you dog woof woof both of you—which one's the man and which one's the woman, you both women or you with the purse is the woman? Pink and blue hair—who the fuck gave you that idea?

I'm staring through him for a little while and then reading and trying to look like I don't care. He's imitating RuPaul, saying, *Girlfriend you better work, chantez chantez, what's his name? What's his name?* Your fucking dirty assholes, better wipe them off better fucking clean out those assholes. And everyone on the train is silent of course, or laughing, but I'm not looking up really, we get to Park Street where the train ends and he screams, *faggots,* then goes down to the Red Line.

This woman about our age comes up to us, says I'm really sorry about that, I'm really sorry, I wanted to say something but I couldn't. I think why not? but Gabby says, well, it was too scary. Then another woman comes over, says the same thing, thanks, and they both say I like your hair. And then off of the Lechmere train comes this cute boy who Cookie claims I made out with at the Loft, he gives each of us a soft hard kiss, no idea of what just happened, you girls going out tonight?

We get on the train and everyone's sort of staring. Go to Government Center, I'm painting my nails on the platform and this woman who we've seen here before sits down next to Gabby and starts blabbing about her small paycheck and waitressing and her boyfriend. And she lives on Webster Street where we live, her neighbor complains about the noise they don't make.

The train comes, she says you can't tell how old anyone is these days, how old are you? Gabby says, eighteen, she says I'm twenty-four, well there is that six years I guess but no one knows, we look young and everyone buys their clothes at Macy's now, I moved from New York to Seattle to Wyoming to Seattle to New Haven, thought I'll get a job in Boston, went to school for film but I need a job before I get a *job*. I fight with my boyfriend and we're loud, called the cops on him once and they took him away for the night so the landlord holds that against us. But we're not loud, just look like we should be loud, don't know anyone so we don't have parties, don't even play loud music, walk around in the apartment at three A.M. and the neighbor calls the landlord. Before when I was single I had all these plans, now we like to do nothing and have fun.

Alfred Corn

SEXUAL POLITICS

THINKING BACK to that evening, I'm a little surprised at my reactions, even though feelings of every kind and in all situations have been unpredictable for a long time. I certainly never used to breathe fire or drape myself in the liberation banner. The political person in the family was Joshua, with me more as a supportive spectator. It's true that as the crisis of the epidemic deepened, I felt myself begin to change. Not that there was immediate evidence of that in what I wrote. The ability to say something you care about, while still keeping the crazy balance of form—not to mention an inconvenient commitment to truth—is hindered by a million obstacles; adding one more can sometimes freeze the whole show. Still, I found myself beginning to invent characters and dialogue that had a certain edge to them, riffs that I would have revised out in the old days.

During our first years together, I was always grateful to Joshua for never pressuring me to make my plays fit the mold that his own activist politics might have demanded. In private I would justify myself by saying that having grown up during the pre-1969 Dark Ages, I was glad to have emerged as reasonably sane and productive, someone who didn't conceal that he lived with a person of the same sex, and who allowed liberationist arguments to have whatever effect on him they would. But as for moving to Fire Island, declaring it a gay homeland, and seceding from the Union, I just didn't have it in me.

Joshua was always going to rallies and attending tactical planning meetings—with my approval but without my company. It seemed more appropriate somehow to have him come back and summarize what was being planned. How could it be otherwise, considering we're dealing here with one of the most domestic people in captivity? High-grade inducements have to be dangled in front of me before I stir from my living room and study. One of my most persistent problems was finding subjects for plays outside of Joshua's and my quiet, homelike existence. Theater thrives on agony; we were mostly happy. It may well be that there are more people in our unflamboyant category (which lacks media glamour) than there are drag queens, gay people in prison, or sexual outlaws, but that isn't what theater audiences have been conditioned to buy tickets for. Whose fault is that?

The only thing remotely resembling drama that happened to us came in our second year together. Anyone who stopped to consider the difference in our ages and the fact that Joshua had never lived with a lover before could have seen trouble coming. Like most people in their twenties (of whatever orientation) he'd been used to having short-term relationships with a series of partners. I don't suppose either of us asked ourselves whether the pink-champagne hallucination of that first year would ever end. There were moments (and I'm not a mystic) when I would see Joshua, his darkly tanned skin against the white shower curtain, the faint line of hair that ran from the center of his chest down to his navel and below the bathing-suit line to the powerfully totemic forms there—moments when I would go up to him and hold him very lightly, in our little bathroom sanctuary, among the toothbrushes and bars of soap, feeling a relaxed gratitude, along with an irrational sense that "this had always been and always would be," that in a way it had nothing to do with us in particular—our beleaguered, statistical selves merely an opportunity for some ideal paradigm of love to take bodily form in a specific place during an actual space of numbered minutes (though no one was counting). We were ourselves and more than ourselves. Even an FM news broadcast coming onto the radio in the next room, putting an end to the "Air for G String" or a Louis Armstrong trumpet solo, wouldn't spoil it. For those minutes the fused pair that we were was safe, safe from marauders, safe from the enemy—who often turns out, in fact, to be some grimly judgmental fixture in our own psyches.

The first hint of trouble came one night after dinner, when we were washing the dishes, or rather Joshua was washing and I was drying. I remember that he was wearing a rugby shirt with blue and red stripes. We never performed this joint household chore without getting into involved discussions about sundry subjects, this time, the impending divorce of a married couple we knew. Suddenly Joshua said, "Do you think we're married, in the same way that they are? I mean, is what we have a marriage?"

"Well, as I remember they had a big church wedding. We didn't. Nobody gave us a set of dinner plates or silverware. We can't file joint income tax returns. So I guess we're not actually married."

"But seriously. What would you say we are?"

"What's so great about labels? What do they give you?"

"Just because what we are isn't named doesn't mean it isn't a category. Not naming it actually gives it more control over what happens in the relationship. I mean, I keep thinking that we're trying—unconsciously—to imitate heterosexual marriage, and, meanwhile, what's really at stake is a noncontractual relationship between two men. Which can't possibly be the same as a legally enforced bond between men and women, who will probably produce children."

"No argument there. But you sound like one of those daytime talk shows."

"I just wonder whether we're not in some ways cutting in on our freedom when there's no reason to do so. Given that we're not a married couple."

"Oh." A silence fell. "I don't ever remember telling you not to do anything that you felt you wanted to do." My voice had a funny hoarseness to it, which I tried to harrumph away. I could hear someone's adrenaline-soaked heart beating in my eardrums.

"I didn't say you had. It's more of an atmosphere that's been set up. Don't you ever get the feeling of being hemmed in? Of not doing and saying every important thing you want to?"

I dried the last dish and put it on the rack, noticing that the decorative gold ring around the rim was beginning to wear off, one of those irrelevant details that leap out at you at those moments when your feelings go into overdrive. "Why don't you say what you want to right now?" Of course I knew, in general, what the important thing was going to turn out to be. Which didn't mean that I was prepared to hear that someone had asked him out for that very night and that he wondered whether I would object. If I did, then he wouldn't go. The fact was, at one of his political meetings, he'd met somebody that he was sort of interested in "physically," and he just didn't want to hide anything from me. What I didn't say is, Why don't you hide it from me? That's what wise people do. Haven't you read Colette? Instead, with all the therapist's maturity rap I could muster, I said I was glad he trusted me enough to talk about it because I knew he didn't think having secrets was healthy, and of course I didn't, either. (Fifty percent of me believed that.) I asked if this had been going on for a while. No? Then I didn't have to take it too seriously?

"Only to the extent that it's something I've been thinking about.

I don't want you to feel threatened. It's probably just getting something out of my system."

"Then go ahead and get it out." Inside, I heard "maturity" crack in half. "But if you're worried about being a mere imitation of heterosexual marriage, this imitates it all too well, to judge by current statistics. We may just have to imitate heterosexual divorce while we're at it."

"I was hoping to work through this without anybody getting hurt."

"Hurt? I'm not hurt. I just see this as one of us being a little shortsighted."

"So you really do think of me as a piece of property that you own. Love for you is just a way of putting fences around someone else."

"This is absurd. You're free and twenty-one and have stronger muscles than I do. I don't have any way of putting barbed wire around your—freedom. At the same time, I'm not going to limit myself to the extent of not saying what I think about this."

He suddenly grabbed my shoulders and pulled me close to him. "Look. I love you. Try to love me. Me, not the person you think is me. Maybe I'm not as nice as you want me to be. I'm going now." He walked out of the kitchen, calling back, "Don't wait up. Talk to you tomorrow." Then he was gone.

After the door closed, I realized what an imbecile I'd been. Suppose I had driven him away forever. Why object to some silly instance of sexual curiosity, considering that we were something on another order and were always going to be together? I paced up and down. Come on, he was just trying to maintain the level of honesty that we'd always had by not hiding this from me. That proved he really loved me. Now what was I going to do? If he would just come back once more, I'd behave differently, I would show him how tolerant I could be. I must sit tight until the wave washed over. He said he would talk to me tomorrow. Look, he walked out without taking his jacket. . . .

The "wave" didn't break and wash over for two months, two months during which I felt as though I was drowning. I was never able to appear as accepting and supportive as I tried to be. None of my acting skills came to my aid. We would sit for an interminable half hour together with leaden silences falling, Joshua's head sunk on his chest, mine prickling with questions I didn't dare ask. What's so great about this boyfriend of yours? What's he got that I haven't? Why are you punishing me this way? Of course all my secret self-doubts came roiling to the surface. Joshua was infinitely better-looking than me; how could I expect him to be content with this battered old tank when he could be having fun with a twenty-five-year-old gymnast? And of course he was right about my proprietary attitudes. I didn't want to share what I considered mine with anyone. So, on top of everything else, I wasn't even really a balanced person; instead, I was some sort of creepy miser, trying to hoard up a living, breathing human being in a casket that could only be opened by my key.

To be abandoned by those we love almost always means becoming a self-accuser as well. We come to think that being thrown over is fit punishment, really, and admire the person who left us for his perceptiveness and courage in detaching himself from a substandard partner. I wondered how I had ever imagined I could hold on to Joshua. To complete the lovely picture, I went through with some retaliatory motions, bringing home a pinch-hitter suitable in one way only—but soon realized I'd never be able to follow through with the plan. I wasn't really reassured about my own value and romantic viability; evening the score didn't do for me what it was supposed to. Between being alone in someone's company or alone by myself, I eventually chose the latter.

And yet something animal and stubborn in me refused to give in to the idea that Joshua would never come back. I really had no choice. He was staying at his new interest's apartment now, but he would stop by from time to time to pick up clothes or a book or whatever. I would simply drink him in, fastening on every shaving cut and frayed shirt collar as if they were symbols of some secular sacrament, repeating silently to myself, I will not live in, and will not do dialogue from, a soap opera. I was never able to look at him directly for long. My eyes would settle on a bright gleam reflected from, say, the lip of a stainless-steel ashtray, and that little teardrop of light would become my principle of logic and steadiness.

Later Joshua told me these visits were most often just an excuse to see me and to keep the connection between us alive. I never dared to ask him if he thought he was teaching me a lesson, but, whether he intended it or not, I was learning things. For example, that for me he was worth whatever sacrifice might be required. I know loyalty to oneself comes first, but loyalty in this case demanded that he be part of my life, a life that would be incomplete without him. I also learned not to try to make those idealizing moments we had experienced together any sort of daily standard for taking our measure. "Love," the greatest catchall word ever, was going to have to include much more (and no doubt a bit less) than its whole romantic press would have us believe. After Joshua came back, we made a point of being very much down to earth; from that location we could always sense the presence of the underground river of feeling beneath us, imperturbable and continuous. We had only to dowse for it, it was never not there.

Dennis Cooper

THE FREED WEED

IT WAS MINUTES to closing. A loud, repetitive, dense guitar riff made the store feel unreal and sort of sinister. It could have been old Spacemen 3. Maybe "O. D. Catastrophe," weirdly enough. Chris was leaning on one of the cash registers. He had a pale, impish face, blond, disorganized hair, and a slim, lanky body that drove me insane. When our eyes met he shone, period, for a few seconds there.

"I'm . . . Dennis?" I took a vague step or two in his direction.

"Oh, right." He turned down the music.

"You're Chris. Robert's friend."

"Oh, right." He folded his arms and seemed to blink the store's depths into focus. "Actually, Robert hates me."

I guess I looked confused.

"Robert's trying to kick. So he's against knowing people like me because of . . . you know, his withdrawals and that. But fuck him."

"Yeah, fuck him." Now that Chris mentioned it, there was this junkie-esque weight to his voice. It sort of dragged through his words, like it couldn't be bothered with what he was thinking.

"So you're a junkie."

He gave me a quizzical squint, which he almost immediately wiped. "Off and on," he said. Then his face kind of . . . sturdied, in pride, I think. "I make porns." He sniffled. "Star in them. Or I used to."

"Really?" I'd been inching his way. "Any chance of seeing them?"

From the way his eyes changed, he'd picked up on my interest. They warmed, which sort of normalized his features. I mean, to me he was already perfect. But to most of my friends, he was only OK. I guess you either fetishize fucked-up young guys or you don't. Anyway, he brightened. Really, it was as if someone had just cleaned a century of grime off some masterpiece.

Chris was scanning the store's wildly postered decor. "OK, what are you doing now?" And his eyes flashed at mine. They were definitely warm.

"Now's fine."

"Because I have this idea." He leaned very close. "Check this out." His breath smelled sweet but kind of ugly, like incense. "Give me some money for dope," he said, "and we can watch porn all night, if you want." He grinned sweetly. "I get really, really friendly when I'm high. Sometimes I shock myself."

"Deal." I fished out my wallet and emptied the contents: three twenties. They flapped on the counter.

Chris snickered. "A man on a mission," he said. He picked up the bills and smashed them into one pocket.

I reached for his ass. I mean, all of a sudden, like I was grabbing the wheel of a runaway car. That's not my usual style, but I guess I was really caught up. Junkies are sort of unreal in a way. Every signal's so faint. You could hunt through their features forever and never see one fucking trace of your presence. So you might as well act all self-focused yourself. Because junkies respect other narcissists. Or that's my experience.

Chris laughed, muttered something I couldn't quite hear. "I'll go score," he added. "Meet me at my place in an hour."

"You live in the Fontenoy, right?" Chris's ass was so flimsy it seemed to deflate in my hands. I could feel the small, ornate archway of his hipbones. I might as well have been polishing them with a very soft rag.

Chris stiffened slightly and eased his lower body from the puzzle of my grip. "Yeah. Number eight," he said. I guess my caresses were too complicated or whatever. I've been told that before.

I shoved my hands into my pockets.

"The buzzer doesn't work." Chris backed toward the shelves where the store kept special orders, boxed sets, et cetera. He misjudged the distance and smacked into one of the rows with his ass, knocking things loose. A few CDs clacked to the floor.

"I understand."

"Uh . . . see you soon, then." He made a one-eighty turn and started straightening up.

I left the store and drove around for a while, killing time, dreaming up sex acts. Chris was flotsam, period, every enterable point on his body wide open. When I fantasize about sex, it tends to look like a fire, or like a big pack of shuffling cards, my desires are so furious. Inside that blur, which even I can't completely transgress, it's impossible to tell if I'm worshiping some guy or torturing him. Probably both.

"Hey!" I was squinting down a long, narrow, badly lit hallway with nothing on its walls. "You there?"

Chris materialized. He'd switched into a toddler-size T-shirt and loose jeans that rested so low on his pale, bony hips that an inch of pubes smoked from his belt buckle. "Yeah, hi," he said.

"How's it going?"

"Better." He shook my hand limply. "In the kitchen. Straight ahead."

Two seconds later, things lit up around us. Once upon a time, the room had been fifties-ish cool, with hysterically patterned wallpaper and dozens of knickknack shelves, now spiderwebby and littered with matchbooks. The furniture, counters, dirty dishes, were polka-dotted with roaches, apparently frozen in shock.

"Want a bit of the dope?"

The roaches sprayed into various cracks.

"No, thanks."

Chris opened the fridge, bent way over, and reached deep inside, moving bottles and beer cans around. The back of his T-shirt raised up, exposing a glary patch of skin, much of it ass. Most of my friends are into pumped, boxy asses. But I like them near-nonexistent. Junkies' asses are perfect, partly because they're so scrawny and, at the same time, being so constipated, such weird treasure chests.

I sat at the table and lit a cigarette, pulling a food-caked plate close as my ashtray. Desire was undoing me.

Chris sat down across from me, organizing his dope, works, spoon, bleach, lighter, cotton balls, into a rough semicircle. Cooking his shot, he'd glance up on occasion and smile, gritty-eyed, anticipating the heroin's rush, I guess.

"You know, I'm not that great in bed," he said, hunting a vein. "I'm easy, though. That's the best part. Hey." He found a spot, slid in the needle.

"Don't you tie your arm?" I asked.

"Old wives' tale." Then his eyes batted. "Whoa. Nice." He eased out the emptied syringe. Within seconds, his blank, sort of Swedishy features had morphed into a sunken-eyed, pointy-chinned gargoyle's.

"You all right?"

"Definitely," said his voice.

I spent about a half minute studying him. He looked like a corpse. Like he didn't belong to this world anymore. Calmer and much more together, I mean.

"What are you . . . experiencing?" I tried.

"Oh, it's nice," he mumbled. "Give me a second." He almost smiled, I think.

Chris's kitchen held very few clues about him. It looked sporadically used and smelled very faintly of rotten food, period, which just meant the fucker was semidisorganized—like all youngish guys, basically.

I heard a crash, squeak.

"Uh . . . we should do this." Chris had teetered away from his chair. He entered the hall, staggering, bumping into walls, hunched over like an elderly man.

"Hey, hold on a second."

When we got to the . . . living room, he headed straight for the TV, pushed POWER, and crashed to the floor, nodding out as a beautiful image defogged in its rectangle. "One . . . second," he whispered.

On TV, a slightly too beautiful child—male, I think—eyed the mouth of a cave. The volume was down, but I suspect there was a dangerous sound track. He stepped inside, cocked his head, cringed, then took another few steps. Suddenly there was a shift in perspectives. I was inside the cave, looking back at the child. He was edging my way. Then something humanesque rose up between us and blocked him out.

"Some of these go way back," Chris said. He fed the VCR. "So don't be shocked."

The TV screen held an antique-looking image, two small boys walking hand in hand down a crooked dirt road.

"Jesus, how old were you here?" I squinted through the multi-multi-copied tape's yellowy fog. The boy on the left was unquestionably Chris, albeit blonder, scaled down, and a bit cutesy-wootsy.

"Eleven." He landed midfloor, cross-legged, not far from the TV. "Can you see?" he asked, dragging himself a foot or so to the right.

In the video, Chris and friend stroll for a while. The road is muddy and lined on both sides with scruffy little pines. Chris wears black shorts, a tight yellow T-shirt, knee socks, and white Nikes. He has a rolled-up sleeping bag gripped in one hand. The other boy is wearing a huge purple T-shirt and baggy blue jeans. He's Hispanic, a foot or so taller than Chris, and, oh, twelve, thirteen?

———————

"What's the other boy's story?" I asked, pointing.

"I'm not sure," Chris said. "Some kid. Nice enough and everything."

"Were you into him?"

"Oh, uh . . . I guess."

The Hispanic was cute, but he paled next to Chris, who was totally exquisite, the way some kids are. "Well, you're obviously the star here."

"I was pretty cool, wasn't I?"

"Definitely."

"Yeah, thanks."

The children enter a clearing. Chris unrolls the sleeping bag. The Hispanic boy strips. He has a slim, athletic body, immense genitals, and a violent tan line. Chris is smoothing the bag, oblivious, when the other boy sneaks up behind him and yanks off his T-shirt. They collapse on the bag, kissing furiously, with Chris's pale, ribby back to the camera.

"Were you actually kissing?" I asked.

"Sure, man." Chris looked over his shoulder, studying me, eyes pinched in . . . confusion, I think. "People used to be into me."

"They still are," I said, fixing my eyes on the screen.

"Yeah?" said Chris's voice, almost shyly.

I couldn't risk meeting his gaze for some reason. I sort of hate it when things get too obvious. "Yep." And I cleared my throat.

The children are nude. The Hispanic boy is sprawled on his back. Chris is up on all fours, straddling him in the opposite direction. He's kissing the head of that oversize dick. The Hispanic boy is yanking on Chris's. It's minuscule. Occasionally he raises up slightly and gives it a doggy lick. Whenever this happens, Chris tenses and throws back his head.

"Felt good?"

"What do you think?" Chris's shoulders just slumped. "It's all coming back." He shook his head.

I'd sprung another hard-on. It was cramped painfully within a fold of my jeans. So I unsnapped, unzipped them, and slid it out into the open. But that action made more noise than I had expected.

Chris turned, blinked. "You gonna put that in me?" he asked—jokily, I think. Then his eyes jetted sideways, rejoining the video.

"To say the least."

Chris's face gravitated toward the TV, whose ugly light blasted it. "So what are you into again?" he asked, blinking. "Not that I care."

"Asses," I said, stroking myself to make blatancy easier. "You know, sort of doing your ass in every possible way, if . . . you don't mind. I mean, safely, of course."

Chris shook his head. "Anything's OK if I'm fucked up enough."

The Hispanic boy holds Chris's ass-crack wide open and grins at the camera. Off in the less-focused distance, Chris's bobbing head gives him a blow job. One of the Hispanic boy's fingertips tests the springiness of Chris's asshole, then sinks in to the knuckle. The hand looks gigantic, Chris's ass sort of doll-size in contrast. When the finger withdraws, the hole unfurls.

I could sense my face flushing. "So . . . how did you . . . uh, how did this . . . feel?"

"It felt good," Chris said.

"How . . . experienced were you?" I was beginning to zone. In my daydream, Chris's adolescent ass was an inch from my face.

Chris's head turned again, really twisting his neck. His eyes were slits, like little brush strokes. "Why? Don't I look like I know what I'm doing?"

"Sure, no, that's not what I meant, but—"

On TV, things changed with a bright flash of hazed-over color. The children had shifted locales to a bedroom and were speedily undressing again.

"What's this . . . ?"

"A man's coming in," Chris said. "I think he's supposed to be what's-his-name's father. I never could figure that out."

The children lie on a double bed, kissing. The door opens a crack. A balding Hispanic man, maybe fifty, peers in, spots the children, and grins. He enters, walks straight to the bed, and separates them. The Hispanic boy skitters away. The man grabs Chris's arm, pins him down on the bed, and licks his ass for a while. At one point the man raises up, says a few words, and laughs.

"I'm sure you don't remember what he said."

"No, I do," Chris said. "He said . . . I remember this perfectly . . . he said, 'You're like cream in the shape of a boy.' " Then Chris quarter-turned, eyed me, arched an eyebrow, and cracked up. In so doing, his face just . . . flew open. Teeth, gums, tongue, all completely visible. To be honest, it didn't do his features any favors.

"How'd you respond?"

"Oh . . . I thought it was nice, I think. Didn't I?" He quit laughing and scrunched up his face. That looked better. "Yeah, sure."

"You didn't think he was gross?"

"No, uh . . . I just wanted him to like me."

"Did the camera bug you?"

"Sometimes. Like this shit." He waved at the TV. "Being rimmed was fucked up."

"Were you turned on at all?"

"I don't think so."

"Hm." I squinted at Chris's fuzzy little face, and, yeah, it did look sort of pleased, as opposed to transported.

"It's weird," Chris said, watching his younger self. "With heroin, I'm sort of back in that kid state again. Because you can't come. That's why hustling's OK. It just means that people like you." His eyes glazed a bit. "Do you have a boyfriend?" He turned, studying me, though it didn't appear that he could see very much.

"No." I really must have liked him to say that.

The Hispanic boy is sidelined, calmly smoking a joint. The man, who's in a wild sixty-nine pose with Chris, reaches over and finger-fucks him to be nice or whatever. The man's face is wedged between Chris's splayed legs, which are spasming a little. Chris is blowing the man as best he can given the vastness of the dick and the puniness of his mouth.

"This is intense," I said, stroking myself at a fast yet safe clip.

"Yeah," Chris mumbled. "I can see that. But I was starting to wish it was over. Because the man got too . . . something."

I squinted at the TV. Little Chris seemed "into it," period. "You can't tell," I said.

"I didn't want anyone to know."

The video cut to a new pose. Chris was lying flat on his back. The Hispanic boy had sat down on his face. The man finger-fucked Chris. Chris was holding one of his legs in the air, presumably so future viewers could see where the finger and asshole connected.

"I know this looks hot," Chris said. "I mean, it's exciting me, too." He twisted around, raised one knee, so I could see a dinky hard-on engraved in his jeans leg. "But I was really, really ready for it to be over."

Chris rims the Hispanic boy. His eyes are dilated and blinking. After what he's just said, I can see he is miserable. Still, I'm almost sure that if I'd been watching the porn by myself, sans commentary, I would have been thinking, So this is how ten-year-olds register ecstasy. It's strange how ambiguous everything is, especially children, who just seem like gods when you don't have to deal with them personally.

"Did they pay you?" I asked, trying to sound more concerned than I was. Honestly, I just felt delirious and anxious to fuck him.

"Yeah," he said. "And they gave me some pot."

"So . . . I was thinking that . . . maybe we could . . . sort of . . . go ahead?"

Chris glanced back at me, slightly freaked out, I think. "OK, but there are three videos left." And he made a stupid face that I guess was defensive.

"I mean, during them. If that's not too uncomfortable for you."

"No, I guess not. But I need another shot first. Wait here." Chris rose shakily to his feet and veered out of the room. A few seconds later, he yelled, presumably from the kitchen, "Do you mind if I'm really fucked up? I'll still do what you want."

"Fine," I yelled back.

"Thanks!" I could hear the metallic and scratch-scratching sounds of a shot being readied. "It'll be . . . easier."

The Hispanic boy is gone. Chris is being fucked by the man. The man's eyes are locked on Chris's face, which looks a bit too transported to be on a child. On second thought, maybe he's sort of relieved, since the show's almost over. After thirty, thirty-five seconds, the man yanks out his hard-on. He leans over, fastens his mouth to little Chris's, and comes. Then the visual darkens.

"Hey," I yelled, aiming my voice through the door, down the hall. "You OK?"

Out of the kitchen's slight humming, a very smeared voice, almost unrecognizable, more like a texture, said, "Yeah . . . I'll be . . . there in a . . . minute."

The TV screen blued.

I stood, stretched, and toured the room. Barren walls, thrift-store furniture. By far the most curious, least dusty spot held a smallish bookcase stuffed with kids' storybooks. You know, with those hard, shiny, cartoony covers. I was wondering which one to yank and inspect when a colored light flashed in my peripheral vision.

"Chris!" I listened. "It's starting!"

In the video, Chris, maybe a year or two older, lounges next to a pool wearing small, tight swim trunks. A slightly older boy, around thirteen or so, with a crew cut and skateboarder clothes, tiptoes up with a beer, which he pours over Chris's head. They yell back and forth. Then Chris drags the boy down to the towel and unzips his pants. Chris reaches inside, and they French-kiss.

"Chris," I repeated. "Get your ass in here."

I didn't hear shit. So I took a little trip down the hall. "Oh, Chr-i-i-is."

He was sitting at the table. It was strewn with the same—maybe dirtier—paraphernalia. His eyelids were three-quarters shut, and his mouth was so far ajar that his jaw seemed to swing back and forth in a draft.

"Wake up," I said. "Sex time."

"What?" Chris opened his eyes. He was grimacing, I think. "Then, uh . . . help me, all right?" He held out a very limp, dangly arm. "Because I can't . . . I'm, uh . . . too high."

I raised Chris to his feet and steadied him with a hug. That felt so sweet that I maintained it awhile, absorbing the pokes of his pointy bones, his low body heat, and the long-unwashed smell of his hair. But he kept getting heavier and heavier. So I renegotiated our hug and started walking him back to the living room.

Sometimes, when I'm fucking a guy, I want to wind him up, freak him out, make him writhe. Sometimes I want to do the exact opposite. And with Chris, it was the latter. I wanted him finite, by which I guess I mean dead. But I'm not an evil man, so I did what I do—i.e., hit on a compromise. Chris nodded out, and I explored him as intricately as I could with my tongue, dick, and fingers, and daydreamed insanely until he was gore.

One of my fingers was up Chris's ass. There was this hard rock of shit stuck in there like some horrid antique. I was poking it around. We were lying side by side on the couch. He seemed very far away. Or should I say, I'd just noticed the distance. "What are you thinking about?" I asked.

"I don't know." He'd been staring at . . . what . . . the TV? By that point it was nothing but a frame with some grayish-white snow in the center.

"Tell me," I said, absentmindedly pinching his nipples. They were already flowery from my twists, pokes, et cetera.

Chris's hand fell on the top of my head. "I don't know," he

repeated. He patted me several times. "I'm just so fucked up. I kind of hate it."

"Like how?" And I squeezed a second finger up his asshole. "You mean, the heroin?"

"That," he said. "But not only that. Can I tell you something weird?"

Chris turned onto his side very carefully, then adjusted his head until our eyes were aligned. I've never seen tinier pupils. Still, there was something irregular in them—I mean, apart from his perpetual dazed self-involvement. Whatever it was, it didn't seem to relate to the fingers I'd plugged into his ass, though they must have been affecting his thinking. Technically, I mean.

"I want to die," Chris said. Then his eyes studied mine. "I had this feeling, during the sex, that you knew."

"When?" It sounds strange, but if things get intense in my life, I grow extremely objective, like a journalist.

"I don't remember. You seemed kind of angry."

I'd just worked a third finger into his ass, so most of my thoughts were down there, relaxing in the snugness and heat. "That's so weird," I said. I'd just remembered the moment. We'd been fucking face to face, and a detail from one of my violent fantasies had slipped out of my mouth, and I think I said, "Die," very softly. "Yeah, I was imagining killing you."

"I could tell." He looked up at the ceiling, but he might have been thinking of the sky. "Well, I kind of wish you had."

"You shouldn't say that," I said. "It's too amazing."

Chris looked away, squinted at something, then checked back. "Listen, I just . . . oh, fuck." He shut his eyes. "Please."

"Jesus," I said. "Come on." I slid my unoccupied arm around his back, and we hugged for a while. I was very turned on from exploring his ass, so it felt like love, but in this backhanded way, if that makes any sense. Or it did to me. I mean, I felt totally relaxed, which I almost never feel.

"Think about it," he whispered.

"I did."

"You should kill me."

"I'd get caught." That was sort of a joke.

"I don't care." Chris let out a rough, whistly breath. "Wait here," he added. Then he carefully eased himself off my fingers, struggled to his feet, tottered across the room, and shoved one hand into the bookcase. "Read this." He yanked out a book, turned, and tossed it.

I skimmed the book. It was three quarters cartoony pictures and one quarter gigantic words, very few of them more than one syllable. A little boy who looked vaguely like Chris lost his way in a forest. He noticed a cabin and knocked on the door. A man who looked vaguely like me answered. The man was all friendly at first, but a few pages later he axed the little boy into millions of pieces. The pictures made it look magical.

We sat on the couch, reading books. Chris had grabbed about a dozen and stacked them between us. He was himself again, meaning he looked like an oversize child with unfocused blue eyes.

"They're so violent," I said.

"Mm-hm," he mumbled. He seemed very involved in a story.

The book I was skimming concerned a little boy, maybe Swiss, who gets cooked in an evil dwarf's oven. "How long have you wanted to die, if you don't mind my asking?"

"Oh, God," he said, and put down the book. "Since forever. But it's gotten worse. I think it's the heroin."

"You should quit."

"I know, I know." He reopened the book and tried to bury his eyes in it.

"I'll help you," I said.

Chris wasn't listening. He was back in the book, but he didn't appear to be reading. His eyes looked too starey to take language in. Still, they zigzagged down page after page. "I should have died when I was a kid," he mumbled, and shot me a glance. It was . . . fraught. I don't know how else to describe it. Like he had an idea that was too gargantuan and/or unformulated to pass through such minuscule pupils. "What if it wasn't just you?" he asked.

"Meaning?"

"Because there's this other guy." He put the book aside, took a deep breath, lurched off the couch, and stumbled toward the TV. "I just did a porn with him. Tell me if I'm crazy." He ejected the old tape and slotted in a new one.

In the video, Chris is himself. His costar is a small, flabby boy with a humongous dick—who I slowly realize is a dwarf. Chris is flat on his back, nodding out and in, while the dwarf crawls all over him, licking and nibbling his details. At one point the dwarf takes a seat on Chris's chest, leans way over, gets Chris's neck in a tight stranglehold, meets his eyes, and makes an angry or terrified face.

"That guy totally wanted me dead," Chris said. He smiled serenely and pushed his face into the porn, as if the TV screen were a sunlamp.

"This is creepy," I said. "It's like kiddie porn from hell."

"I don't think it would make any difference," Chris continued, still sunning away. "I'll just get old."

"You can't know that."

"If I'd died as a kid, the world would be totally the same. I haven't done shit in my life. I don't even have any friends."

"We're friends."

"Yeah, maybe." He opened his eyes—technically, anyway. "But wait, watch this. Look at him. Isn't he just . . . ?"

The dwarf continues to choke Chris as murderously as he can, given the babyishness of his hands and the relative girth of Chris's neck. He still looks upset in some manner that's hard to pinpoint. Chris's face is very bloated and purple, but his eyes are just blissed. And without their disapproval, he does make one's mind wander in scary directions. Or my mind, anyway. But then, I'm sick.

"I need another fix." Chris shot to his feet, which made his knees crack explosively. "Do you mind?"

"What? No, no." I was lost in the porn.

The porn had this strange, silly, magical . . . I don't know, charm. I guess it was mostly the fact that I was watching a dwarf, with all his fairy-tale baggage. Anyway, when he finally unhanded Chris, clutched his dick, gave a few whacks, and came, all I could think was, What the fuck?

"Shit," said a voice down the hall.

"You OK?" The porn had just faded to black.

"Yeah." A distant chair creaked. "I have to tell you my fantasy," he yelled. "I keep planning it out in my head." There were some clinks, scrapes. "Sometimes I sit here and think about it and think about it."

"Do tell," I yelled back.

"OK, shit . . . well . . ."

In Chris's fantasy, he's a ten-year-old lost in some forest. He sees a cabin with sweetly lit windows, and knocks. A monster of some sort invites him inside. As soon as the door shuts, the monster tears

Chris's clothes off, ties him down on a bed, and tortures him for hours and hours. Then they fuck, and as the monster comes, he brings out this machete and hacks Chris's head off. That's making a long story short.

"Hey." Chris stumbled through the door and flopped down beside me. He draped one leg over mine. "So what do you think?"

"It sounds like a snuff fairy tale."

"Yeah, of course." He waved at the book pile.

"I mean it's completely unfeasible."

"I guess." Chris yawned, leaned in close, kissed my neck, and laid his head on my shoulder. "But isn't it perfect?" He pecked me again. "Because then the killer and I would be equally happy."

"Maybe for a second or two," I said. "Then you'd just be dead, and he'd be paranoid and guilty for the rest of his life."

"Whatever." Chris's head shifted around on my shoulder. "I'm going to nod for a minute, OK?"

"Sure." I needed some time to reorient anyhow.

It's strange about junkies. I mean, how they smell. The only other place I've ever smelled that particular odor was once, years ago, when a friend of a friend had an epileptic fit in my living room. But in that case the odor exploded right out of him, and with junkies it's more like a radiance.

"Think about . . . about . . ."—Chris swallowed—". . . how you'd want . . . to do it. Because . . . I'm open."

Actually, I'd just gotten the strangest idea.

In my fantasy, Chris's death wish would be the plot of a porn film. I'd write the script, he'd narrate, and the star would be a boy who resembled the much younger him. Essentially, the porn would re-create the fantasy he'd just related. My logic was that maybe if Chris's fantasy could be enacted on film, he'd have it to study, but he would still be alive. And on a purely selfish level, I'd be halfway to literalizing a dream.

"I like mine better," Chris said. He was trying to open his eyes. "That dwarf could play the monster."

"Oh, really?" He sat up, blinked. "So . . . wait. I'd be in a fairy tale, and I'd die, and then . . . the fairy tale would be a film, so I would still be alive but I could watch myself die for the rest of my life?"

"Exactly." I hadn't really thought it out this far.

"Hunh." Chris slid a book from the stack. "I want to be him," he said, cracking the cover. His finger dropped on a page. It showed a little blond boy walking into some scrawl of a forest. "Watch." He turned the page.

The boy walked, it got dark, he saw a cabin, he knocked on the door . . .

Chris's face was getting looser, crazier, lost in the plot. I followed along for a while, then the story's predictable twists and turns lost me, and my eyes trailed off into the wilds of his crotch. It made me want to wander away from the world. So I did.

"That feels nice." Chris patted my hand, snuggled close, and shut the book. "So tell me your fantasy again. You know, slowly."

Those were a pretty few minutes. Chris nodded out, and I day-dreamed aloud. And my fantasy, which put a ten-year-old Chris lookalike through a lyrical nightmare of hot sex and torture, worked its black magic, or became a bizarre fairy tale. It made me feel like a kid. Or maybe I felt like a parent, because it wasn't as if the tale itself became real. But Chris did. Or his story did.

Eric Gabriel Lehman

PASSING THROUGH

I WAS LOOKING at Warren's snapshot when the Plymouth pulled up.

The photo had arrived with a long letter describing all the tests, down to the last bit of bloodwork, the T-cell count, the latest round of protease inhibitors—all that from someone who rarely wrote more than a shopping list. Warren thought I was a wuss, so he loved rubbing my nose in unpleasant things—the details of his father's colostomy, for instance. Then that photo. Warren's head was turned to expose the side of his neck, as though showing off a hickey, except there were those purple spots. I turned the picture over. *See you later, Sucker,* he'd scribbled.

I'd called him to say I was coming out there, but then I hadn't gone. One day his mother picked up the phone and said that if I wasn't on the next plane or two I might not get there in time. Her voice told me that I'd already waited too long. It wasn't until after I hung up that I remembered there were no planes flying out of

Hartsfield because of the airline strike. I got on the night bus and found myself counting mile markers, ominous red eyes flashing in the dark.

I'd made it as far as Dallas by midnight, but when my bus pulled out after its twenty-minute rest stop, I wasn't on it. I'd been smoking a cigarette and drinking a Fanta in the waiting room. I'd been staring at the big clock hanging from the ceiling, watching the little hand jerk from second to second. I don't recommend staring at a clock if you're on your way to visit someone who is dying; it makes you think of how time is passing. When they announced my bus, I wanted to get up, I swear I did. But I didn't. I couldn't. I saw Warren on the face of the clock, spots and all. That second hand kept jerking around. I watched until I realized that I was waiting for the second hand to stop moving. I was waiting for time itself to stop. The next thing I knew, the bus was pulling out. I might have made a run for it, but I didn't. Something held me back, like the safety bar in a roller coaster. I called Warren's mother.

"So you're in Texas," she said, and hung up. She understood what was going on.

I left the station with nothing more than the clothes I wore. I had some money, but the next bus wasn't until the following morning. I decided to hitch.

Warren and I had been together almost three years when he left Atlanta. Leaving Atlanta had been Warren's sole preoccupation for as long as I knew him. It was printed below his picture in the high school yearbook next to "Life Ambitions." He wanted me to go with him. I always found reasons not to. He said I was afraid of making a commitment. He said I was afraid of loving someone. Then one day he was gone, and I felt as if I'd been left hanging in the middle of an argument. Every once in a while he called at five in the morning, ignoring the time difference. I'd just be getting back from my shift at the hotel. *Having fun watching the paint dry?* he'd ask. *Falling in love?*

I was looking at Warren's snapshot when headlights washed over the picture like somebody prying. The Plymouth chugged up to me, looking ready to fall apart. The engine throbbed like a low-flying crop duster.

A guy stuck his head out of the window. He had a mottled face and a receding-hairline ponytail: a drunk or one of those bitter Vietnam vets.

"Can you buy some gas?" he asked.

He didn't ask where I was going, but it was late, so I got in. For the first couple of miles he hardly spoke. The seat sagged low, the floorboards felt ready to give, and a draft sang through the missing glove-compartment door. The back was piled deep in beer cans and Burger King boxes. I didn't see his braces right away; it was too dark. Then I noticed how he went for the dashboard to speed up or brake. I looked closer and saw the metal around his legs and got scared. I was at the mercy of a cripple behind the wheel.

"Polio," he said, watching me. "I was the last one on my block to get it before the vaccine. Ain't that a shit?"

What could I say? The car's noise seemed to get louder.

"Muffler quit on you?" I asked, just to talk.

"No muffler. Mufflers are a waste of money."

"By the way, I'm Leslie," I said.

"Leslie's a girl's name, ain't it?"

I let it pass.

"Is it hard driving with manual controls?"

"No harder than turning on the radio," he said.

That was a good idea—a little music. Except that a black eye stared out from the dash where the radio should have been. I sat back and watched Texas roll by in the dark. It went on forever, a soft, chilly nightmare. We'd passed the last town a couple of miles back, and I felt as if we'd entered a lost dimension, which is how I usually think of Texas anyway. I've hated it ever since the summer my family spent on Matagorda Island, where the local kids made fun of me.

The Plymouth started sounding strange.

"Damn engine," he muttered.

I pointed to the gas gauge. The arrow quivered around empty.

"Gauge is shot. Don't pay any attention to it."

"I thought I saw the needle jump when you started the car before."

He glared at me. He was one of those types who didn't want anyone else telling them about their car. A little while later the car started shuddering and swaying, and he pulled off.

"Before I do a goddamn thing I am going to get out of the car and have me a smoke," he announced.

We'd come to a halt halfway across an overpass. It didn't seem a good place to be. A truck barreled down the highway below. I suggested getting to the other side.

He gave me a look. "There's nothing I hate more than people telling me what to do. That's what Ellen did: played mother. Women can't stop playing mother. They start with dolls and keep right on going."

A car was approaching. The easiest thing in the world would have been for me to stick out my finger and leave this malcontent. But I didn't. The car swept past, it disappeared around a curve, and the road went black.

"I was just trying to be helpful," I said.

"If you want to be helpful, you can hand me those when I ask for them," he said, motioning to the crutches lying below the seat. He opened his door and maneuvered himself out from behind the wheel like a crab climbing over a rock. When he was ready I passed him the crutches, and he heaved himself up with a little grunt. His braced legs clanked up after him, cans tied to a car of newlyweds. He swung over to the shoulder a little too quickly, as if to impress me.

"Smoke?" he said.

I nodded yes without giving a thought to what smoking meant for someone standing on crutches. To get at the pack in his shirt pocket, he pushed his weight off of one crutch for a terrifying second, crooking it against him the way you might a telephone receiver to leave your hands free. Nothing but a low railing separated him from a twenty-foot drop to the road below. Another truck passed, churning up a small tornado, which threatened to yank us up into the air like Dorothy's house, but he held firm.

"Here," he said, shaking a cigarette from the pack. I took it and was about to reach into my pants pocket for matches when I saw him doing the same. A sixteen-wheeler plunged by this time. The overpass buckled, and wind whipped at his shirt. He looked ready to topple like a house of cards but kept right on fishing in his pocket. Why couldn't he have just leaned against the car instead of doing this tightrope act? Why didn't he just ask for a little *help?* He finally pulled out a lighter and began flicking it. It didn't light. He cursed. I couldn't watch.

"How about if I—"

He turned to keep me away and kept on flicking. When the flame stayed alive long enough, he lit his cigarette and let me light mine. The odd car passed, and his braces shone, silver cages jailing his legs. I smoked. I remembered lining up in the school gym for my lump of vaccinated sugar, the bitter splotch stinging my tongue. Had that been for polio? But all the sugar cubes in the world wouldn't help this guy now. Even if something could, he might have just spat it out.

Warren was going to miss the vaccine, too. If they ever got around to making one.

"Ellen was a damn good woman," he said. "The finest I ever knew."

I knew I was supposed to ask who this Ellen was, so I did. He'd just broken up with her, he said. They'd been together almost two years. She was pretty and smart, and he'd loved her more than any other woman he'd known. Two years wasn't two weeks, he said. They'd begun to make plans for the future, too: moving to a bigger place, getting a dog, taking a trip to Hawaii. He'd just bought them a VCR. Every night they'd made love, beautiful love. He looked right at me to make sure I heard. I guess he wanted to make sure I knew that even guys like him could perform.

"Tonight she tells me I have to move out," he said. "I said I wasn't budging. I said it's my house. I popped a video into that VCR and sat back. Then this guy shows up. He's pretty big, mean, and he has a shotgun. I tell him to get out of my house. He tells me that if I don't get my ass the hell out he's going to shoot me straight to hell."

"How could he do that? You said it was your house."

"Well . . . Ellen's name's on the lease."

"So he kicked you out?"

He hurled his cigarette to the ground.

"Hell no. I'm going back there. I'm not going to let some fool break up our happy home, just like that. I'm figuring to let things cool off for a while. Listen. She don't love him. She's just afraid to do anything that might make him mad. And get this straight: he ain't her boyfriend, just some scum that happened to walk into the Kroger's the same time she did. He's got her brainwashed."

"Maybe she likes him," I said.

His eyes widened. "You think she dumped me because cripples can't get it up, right? You think cripples can't hump, right? Is that what you were thinking? Say it, for chrissakes! Well, the answer to your question is, we fucked like bunnies. Ellen never had nothing to complain about. No one needs crutches in bed." He eyed me. "You with someone?"

I thought for a moment. I decided to nod yes.

"Oh yeah? How long?"

"Almost three years."

"What happened? She ditch you, too?"

I didn't know how to go on. Warren couldn't wait to tell total strangers about himself. Not me. But this guy was getting to me, and I was almost ready to pull out the picture of Warren, spots and all, and make him look at it.

I told him I didn't really feel like talking about it.

"If she was that important to you, you'd sure as hell want to talk about it," he said. "You wouldn't be able to talk about anything else."

I took out the picture. "Here, goddammit," I said.

He glanced at it. "So you're a queer?"

I went to take the picture back, but he held on to it. "Looks like my cousin Ernie. Ernie ain't queer, but he got this way about him, so you might think he was. Here." He handed the snapshot back. "How old are you, anyway?" he said.

"Twenty-seven."

"You got a baby face, I thought you were younger. I'm forty-five. Forty-five fucking years old."

A car passed. A man and a woman sat in front, a child in the back, a family. The child—a girl—caught sight of us and leaned forward. I followed the car with my eyes, imagining its warmth, its comfort, and the pleasure of someone taking care of you. It made me think of when I went for rides with my family when I was a kid.

"Life sure is funny," I heard myself say.

"No it *ain't*," he snapped back. "And by the way, you don't have to stick around just for my sake. I can take care of myself."

Another car was coming.

"Go on, stick out your goddamn thumb," he said, ice in his voice.

I almost wanted to. Being with this guy made the world feel crushed and flat. But I let that car pass, too.

"Why didn't you do it?"

I didn't know. "I'm getting cold," I said. "You ready to start pushing the car over to the other side?"

He adjusted his crutches and cranked himself back over to the driver's seat, braced himself beside the open door, and plunked down behind the wheel. The crutches fell away like a rocket's launch pad. He threw them into the backseat. I got ready to push. The car was heavier than I'd expected, maybe because of the special controls or the junk in the backseat. I began to wonder just how long it had been since the guy had been kicked out. The backseat hadn't been cleaned out for days, maybe longer. This guy looked like he hadn't slept in a bed for at least that long. Maybe the whole story about Ellen was make-believe. The wrecked Plymouth might be the only thing he had in the world.

"You got a gas can in the trunk?" I called from the back after we'd made it to the other side of the overpass.

"Used to."

The mess in the backseat was piled too deep to find anything in, and the overhead light was busted.

"You got a flashlight?"

"I've driven this car for five years and I never once needed no flashlight."

"I can't see anything here."

"Open up your goddamn eyes."

I pulled myself out, slammed the door, and walked to the front.

"You know what I think? I think you've got a lot of nerve talking to me like that. Your tank's empty, you're stuck in the middle of nowhere, you got a bum gas gauge, you don't even have a goddamn flashlight to flag someone down, and when someone tries to help you, you give them a hard fucking time."

"I don't have to listen to this from a shit like you—"

"And you're also one of the most pigheaded fools I've ever met. Someone's nice to you, and what do you do? You get on their case. Maybe that's why Ellen left you."

His mouth dropped open. I shouldn't have said that, even if it was probably true. But he'd ticked something off inside me.

"OK, that's it. You get your little queer ass the hell away from my car right now, you hear me?" He gripped the wheel, looking ready to drive off.

"Hey, listen. I didn't mean—"

I'd been leaning into the door, and it fell off. Just like that. I looked down at it, a turtle helpless on its back.

I thought he might start crying. "You fucking shit!" he said.

I tried fitting the door back on its hinges. I didn't think it would work, but I had to do something.

"Get your hands off my car and get the hell out of here!" His voice shook.

I went to the back of the car, tried the trunk. It was locked.

"Open it!" I said. I didn't care what this guy thought. I was going to do what had to be done. "Hey!" I shouted.

I reached under the rim of the hood and started pulling. It gave with a sour clank.

"Goddamn you!" The guy threw himself out of the car and made his way over to me, holding on to the side of the car. I'd already begun rummaging through the trunk. He fell on top of me and swung one arm around my neck. He was strong; it came from using those crutches. I tried to throw him off, but he clung like a frog during mating. His body was rigid and hollow as a cardboard box. He smelled close and oily.

"Know what your problem is?" he said, yelling right into my ear, arms locked across my chest. "You're selfish. Too selfish to love no one else. That's why you don't."

It might have been Warren talking. Maybe being a cripple sharpened his senses, the same way blind people hear so well. I struggled against him, his feet dragged against the asphalt, and we did a kind of dance. I had to get him off me, I had to get him away from me. He knew too much.

"You're crazy," I said. "Get off me."

Headlights appeared, then a souped-up flatbed rose into view, a row of lights over the cab, country music blasting. The chrome grille shone, a jowl of sharp teeth. Its hubcaps reminded me of those killer chariot wheels in *Ben-Hur*.

A young guy leaned out of the window, a can of beer in his hand. "How you guys doing?" he said in a semidrunk drawl. "Hey, look at this," he said to someone next to him. "A bunch of fagolas!"

The guy still held me.

"Get your ugly redneck asses the hell out of here!" he shouted to the guys in the truck.

They looked ready to leap out and bash our heads in, but a car was coming from the other direction, so they went a couple of hundred yards and waited on the shoulder, engine growling like a dog about to snap. The truck looked ready to hang a U-ie and swing back. My heart felt sharp in my chest. Then the truck pulled out and kept going.

"Why in God's name did you say that to him?" I shouted.

" 'Cause that's what he is. Now get the hell out of here. I don't want you messing with my stuff. I don't need your help anymore." He held on to the side of the car and worked his way back to the front seat. "Go on, go!"

Lights appeared down the road, this time from the other direction. I got ready to wave down whoever it was for help. Then I saw: that truck was coming back. I got into the car.

"Roll up the windows," I said. "And don't say anything to them this time." Then I realized the front door was missing. We were trapped. The truck was doing at least fifty and showed no signs of slowing down.

"Get the hell out of here," he said. He gave me a strong push. The truck was coming nearer, looking ready to sideswipe us. Then it switched lanes. It was coming right at us! It was going to smash head-on into us any minute now. The headlights blinded my eyes. An entire planet was coming our way, ready to explode.

"Mother of Jesus," he said.

The truck waited until the very last minute to swerve back into the other lane, brakes screeching like laughter. It roared away, trailing a mocking pedal-steel-guitar twang.

I put my arms around him. He didn't move. We sat there for several minutes.

"Hey," I said. He kept staring ahead. "It's OK. Listen. I'm going to hoof it over to the town up ahead and get gas."

"Don't leave me here alone!"

"I'll be back as soon as I can. What's your name, by the way?"

"Riley," he whispered, sounding afraid that someone might hear him.

I got the trunk open again, found the gas can, and started down the road. I thought of Riley in his sad Plymouth, his house without a front door. Now I was sure: there'd been no Ellen, no VCR, no love. There'd been only Riley and his stiff-legged misery, a kamikaze pilot driving around until he was out of gas.

Moonlight dotted the heads of cabbage stretching out in rows on either side of the road. The night was quiet, mute. No cars came. I looked into the darkness, into a mirror, but I saw nothing. What if Warren and I had stayed together? What if I'd gone out there with him? I began walking faster. I'd missed Warren after he left. I'd kept smelling him in the sheets and towels. But I'd been relieved of having to love someone as intensely as Warren demanded to be loved.

When I first heard that Warren was sick, I panicked. I feared for my own ass. There was no statute of limitations protecting anyone. His bad news could have been mine. Warren had always thrown himself at me, and there hadn't always been time for precautions. Toward the end he'd begun sleeping around to get back at me for not going with him. It was probably around that time that he'd . . . that it'd happened.

I thought back to the summer when my family rented the beach house on Matagorda Island. I was fifteen. The area wasn't popular then; I had whole stretches of shore to myself. One evening I'd stumbled onto a section of beach less trafficked than the others, overgrown with reeds. Figures moved in the shadows behind the dunes. I was frightened and ready to run, but something drew me back; I wanted to know who was there, or else I already knew.

There behind those dunes was the first time I touched a man. I returned the next night, every night, I got to know someone named Drew. He was tall, with a voice as soothing as slumber. He'd pick me up in his arms and carry me to secluded parts of the dunes, and there we'd mess around.

One night I arrived to see men running every which way through the dunes. Beams of light pursued them. The men fleeing past me wore nothing more than underwear or a shirt half on. Some were naked. Their hands masked their faces from the incriminating flashlights. Then I saw who they ran from: kids hardly older than myself, wielding broken bottles. I came upon Drew stumbling through the dunes. He threw his arms around me. My body tensed as I thought of the kids with the broken bottles; I pulled away and fled through the reeds. Seconds later came the dull crack of glass, then a groan. I turned. The skittish beam of a flashlight caught Drew halfway to his knees, face bloodied.

The next day the whole town was talking about the incident. The local paper showed Drew as I'd seen him the night before. The caption read *Galveston Lawyer Caught with His Pants Down.*

I got a ride to the gas station and made a collect call to Warren's apartment. No one answered. I called his neighbor, who told me that Warren had been taken to the hospital the day before. I called there, and Warren's sister said that he was getting some kind of treatment and wasn't in his room. I told her where I was and what had happened.

"He keeps asking about you."

"I'll be there," I said.

"Pray for him," she said.

Just as I hung up, the flatbed truck skidded into the station, music blasting. Two guys jumped out, T-shirts stretched taut over their guts. I kept my back to them and prayed they'd leave without seeing me. I went to the pump and squeezed the gas into the can as quickly as I could. The numbers under "Sale" rolled by a penny at a time, ticking off the seconds before I'd have to pay for the gas. My hand ached from holding up the can. The guys were talking with the station attendant, in no hurry to leave. I went to pay. I kept my head down and motioned with my finger to the flashlights hanging on the wall.

"Hey, you!"

I made like I didn't hear. My hand shook as I pulled out a ten-dollar bill.

One of them came over. "You're with that asshole we passed, aren't you? You tell him he's lucky we didn't ram him off the god-damn road."

The attendant handed me a flashlight and gave me my change. I went to go.

"You look at me when I talk to you!" the other guy said. He shoved two fingers into my shoulder. The wallet fell from my hand. Warren's picture slipped out and landed faceup.

"Hey, look at that!" the first guy said, going to scoop it up.

"That your boyfriend?" said the other.

I got it before he did. "Get the fuck away from me," I told him.

"You little fuck," the first one said, pushing over to me.

The attendant blocked him. "Leave him alone," he said.

I was about to start hitching when I saw them getting back in the truck. I didn't want them running me down, so I waited for them to drive away before heading off. I decided that when I got back to the car I would tell Riley we were returning to Dallas that night. I had an old friend there. I'd call him. Maybe he'd know a place where Riley could stay.

I started walking. What twist of fate had brought us together?

If Riley weren't a cripple, he wouldn't have got stuck out there, he wouldn't have been driving around like a madman, angry at the world, and I wouldn't have wound up with him. All because he hadn't got that lump of sugar. And why hadn't he? Fate? Bad timing? What about Warren? Unless it was because he deserved what he got. There were enough people who believed that. But if that were so, then I should have just as many spots on my neck as Warren. There was no such thing as good or evil, only luck and timing.

Just before I caught sight of the Plymouth, the lights of the truck rounded a curve in the distance. I broke into a run. The gas sloshed inside the can, tugging me every which way. They roared passed me, heading for Riley. When I reached the car, he was gone.

"Riley?" I flicked on my new flashlight and panned the weeds on the side of the road for him in case he'd gone for a leak. (How did he manage that alone?) I listened for any sound of him but heard nothing. My face went hot. What had they done to him? Had they taken him with them? Riley had become important to me. He'd become my responsibility.

"Riley!"

A moan rose from inside the car. There he was, slumped down in front of the seat, crumpled like a piece of cloth.

"What are you doing playing hide-and-seek with me?" I said, trying to shake off my terror. I lifted him up in the seat. His limbs felt held together by cord. I held him by the shoulders.

"They got me," he wheezed. One of the braces had been twisted out of shape. I played the flashlight beam on his torn pants, the bruise on his arm. The crutches weren't in the car. I looked out onto the road and saw one lying on the other shoulder. The moment I let go of Riley, he slumped down in the seat. He was probably hungry, I thought, getting the crutches. Why hadn't I thought to get him something to eat? I didn't know the first thing about crisis. I was a babyface, all right.

Faintly, almost too faintly for me to be sure I'd heard right, strains of country music floated close by. I went around to the back of the car, fumbled with the gas cap, and dumped the gas into the tank. I got behind the wheel and started the ignition. It turned over, but when I went to put my foot on the gas pedal . . .

"Riley, how do you drive this thing?"

He was slumped down into the seat and said nothing. Had he fainted? Was he—

"Riley?"

I grabbed the flashlight and held it to the dash. Where was the gas pedal? Where was the brake? I pulled something, and the car lurched forward into the middle of the road. The lights of the truck seared the rearview mirror. We zipped past a string of houses and a store or two, then plunged back into the void without passing a soul who might have helped us. I prayed for another town to turn up, with people and lights, but there was just more of Texas, large, empty, and hateful.

The truck was moving in closer. I pushed the gas lever all the way forward. The rock and rumble of the car told me we couldn't keep going this fast for too long. The wind through the door opening threatened to suck us out onto the road.

"Riley?"

He still didn't budge. The engine's throb was a death rattle. The truck's rumble was ready to drag us under.

"Where are we going?" Riley mumbled.

I could have cried with relief. "Home," I said, even if I hadn't a clue where that was.

Something skittered across the road right in front of me—an animal, I didn't know what. I squeezed the brake lever. The car shuddered and skidded to a stop. The truck plowed into us from behind and careened off into the darkness. We were catapulted forward. My head hit the windshield. I heard a sound like ice about to crack, felt the glass straining in slow motion. Don't break, don't break, I kept thinking.

When I came to, Riley had rolled out of the car and was lying on the road, a scarecrow without stuffing. The truck lay behind us on its side, its headlights up and down instead of side by side. All was still, except for Tammy Wynette, singing for all she was worth. *Our D-I-V-O-R-C-E became final today . . .*

The next time I came to, I was in a hospital bed, stiff and bandaged.

Later that day the nurse explained that the guy in the gas station had called a state trooper after he saw the truck take off. She said I was all right. I kept asking to see Riley. She said I couldn't, so I was sure that meant he was dead but she didn't want to tell me. Someone on the night shift brought me to him. He was sleeping. They'd put one of his legs into a cast and bandaged his head like mine. The nurse told me that he'd be OK. His leg braces had been propped up in the corner, a pair of skeletons.

Riley was alive.

I was about to leave when something occurred to me.

"What happened to the guys in the truck?" I asked.

She gave me a thumbs-down.

"Both of them?"

She nodded yes.

Warren. I had completely forgotten about him. When I called his hospital room, a stranger picked up the phone. He was no longer there, they said.

I returned to Riley's bed. He was still asleep. He looked peaceful. I sat down beside his bed. Riley, I thought. For God's sake, Riley. Help me.

Jameson Currier

GUIDES

MY FIRST LOVER was a man much older than myself—older, even, than my father was at that time. Will was a college professor, had been my Russian Lit instructor, but I had first met him when some friends of mine introduced us at a disco not far from campus. Will was, the year that I fell in love with him, fifty-five years old. I was barely eighteen, a college sophomore. Will was a tall, thin, elegant-looking man, and before a classroom he was somewhat magnetic, expounding on the gifts of Chekhov, Tolstoy, and Mayakovski; he appealed, at first, to the bookish, academic student within me. The year after I first met him at the gay disco, I enrolled in his class, but when he invited me over to his house one evening, it was clear that his intentions went beyond merely showing me the photographs of Meyerhold's productions that had instigated the invitation. I, of course, had sensed that this would be the case, and I was, in those days, willing to accept him as my guide—*needed* him, in fact, to *be* my guide.

And what a guide he became. He changed the way I cut my hair, the clothes I wore, the courses I took, the books I read, the way I thought and spoke, and, especially, the way I looked upon sex. Our sexual sessions were long and explicit; he would talk to me as he made love to me, describing how he was touching my nipples, what my skin felt like, the way my ass would taste before his lips. And he was full of questions, too, wanting to know what I felt as he rubbed two fingers across the head of my cock, what I was thinking as he kneaded the muscles of my shoulders, if I was scared as he slipped first one finger into my rectum and then another. He did this all with a tenderness he would not admit to, of course; to do so would have been to break one of his private vows, that of never imbuing the sexual act with any sense of love. Will was always cautious about maintaining his distance from me: he would never refer to me as his lover, never, either, admit that he was in love. In fact, he often invited other men—mostly students, but once even another professor—to join us in bed. This was done not only for the pleasure it afforded us but also, purposely, at times, for *my* sake, to make certain I stayed grounded, to keep us at a distance from one another, to ensure I did not fall in love with him, or at least did not fall so hard that when the time came for us to conclude our affair, I would end up feeling hurt or misused—which, of course, I did.

"Imagine what your father must think about all this," Will would say when we were in bed together, before slipping his mouth over my cock. My body would tense, of course; I had told Will all about my father. "Now imagine yourself as a bird in that tree," he would lift his head away from me and say, looking out the window. "First flying into this room, looking at us on the bed, and then soaring back out into the world."

I did just as he suggested, and that was how, in those days, I began to distance myself from the shame my father had instilled in me, through this visualization that I was free of feeling and restriction, liberated, as it were, and I discovered, too, the joy, the physical pleasures of sexuality; it was how I was able, too, months later, when my affair with Will ended, to keep from feeling too abandoned and disheartened.

"Every question in the universe does not have an answer," Will said to me one night while he was cooking dinner, though for every fault or flaw I ever confronted him with, he tried to generate an explanation. What I liked about Will—no, what I *loved* about Will— had a lot to do with the quantity of time we spent together, or rather, with the passage of time that we had together: the longer I spent with him, the more deeply I fell in love with him, despite the fact that the reverse was true for him. For one thing, there was the warmth and security I felt in sleeping with Will every night; two weeks after we started dating each other, I moved out of my dorm and into the house he owned behind the campus library. I spent every night for the next five months with him, even when I realized he had begun seeing someone else in the afternoons.

At first there were the intensely passionate nights; often we could not even make it through dinner before tumbling into bed or, perhaps, beginning to consume each other on the rug or the kitchen floor, a pot or a plate crashing onto the tiles only heightening the brutish physicality of it all as we wrestled our bodies from one position into another. At night, exhausted from lying awake and just holding him in my arms, I would run my fingers lightly through the thick gray hair at his temples or outline the profile of his nose and the cleft of his chin with a fingertip, listening to the rain tap against the black windowpanes or the wind lift and swing the rose bushes that grew outside and brushed up against the bedroom wall nearest the bed; then, finally, I would fall into a light, conscious sleep, only to be aroused by him again nudging me into sex or asking me questions about what I wanted out of my life with him. Lust, I learned in those young days of mine, soon faded into feelings, feelings much deeper than I had ever imagined possible from myself, and I found I could not bear to be out of Will's presence. I showered with him, fixed breakfast with him, memorized the clothes he wore so that when I left the house with him and he went to his office, my mind could follow him throughout his day—sit with him during his appointments with graduate students, know where he was going for lunch, hear what he would say before his classes to someone he was leaning over toward and speaking with in the hall. I wanted to be entirely with him, wanted to know how he felt, how he reacted to everything in his world.

That desire, of course, turned into possessiveness, and that possessiveness turned into an ugly jealousy. But before that happened, before I reached that nasty point, I found a comfortable place with Will and with the way I came to need his body. There was something in the familiarity of his skin, night after night, that continued to arouse me, the way the hair grew sparsely around his navel, for instance, and traveled up his stomach in a thin line and then unfurled like an eagle's spread at his chest, covering two small brown nipples that I could suck on and twist in my mouth like the head of a pin. Some men, of course, find rapture through variety or newness or anonymity of sexual partners, strangers who quicken the pulse, but what I loved about Will was the way I came to know how he felt in my hands—the nubby texture of his back, for instance, or the padded flesh at his shoulders that he had once built up with muscles—and most of all I loved how Will explained to me what he wanted, desired, and needed physically from me, what he let me know felt good for him and to him. Communication was always Will's most admirable asset, even as we were breaking up, a fact that he would announce over and over, even as he drew me more forcibly and more desirably into sex.

I knew how he liked me to sweep my fingers through the hair on his chest, the tips of my fingers running along his shoulders, how he liked me to angle my body through the tweezers of his legs and go down on him, my hands buried beneath his ass, squeezing it forcibly as if kneading dough. I knew that he liked me to graze my fingertips along the length of his body, that he enjoyed as much my massaging his feet as my licking the underside of his balls like a cat.

What came to happen, though, was that he began to keep his body away from me, or rather, he began to remove his mind from the physical act just as mine buried itself profoundly within his skin. In bed, our having sex together came to be my having sex with him, my pleasing him almost selflessly, as if he were an inanimate object whose lust I would have to shake almost violently awake to arouse. It worked, of course; this was the way Will himself had designed it to be, that I would have to knock him into his passion. But the passion was soon hardly ever reciprocal, and it came to feel as if it were a test for me, to see how much it would take before I could make him feel for me. I would find myself hovering over him, straining with an erection, sucking him, rimming him, fucking him, pushing and pushing for him to feel me till my orgasm came like tears of animosity.

It was only when the photographs and magazines began appearing regularly in bed that my feelings really began to be hurt. Not that I had shunned such visual aids before—they had been hot, diverting scenarios at times, especially when Will would create a fantasy that included me within it, with him as a police officer or an army sergeant, for instance, interrogating me on some minor misdemeanor, making the good boy beg before the bad one—but now he began to use them to exclude me: as I leaned over and began to blow him, for instance, he would enter into the fantasy of being with a Colt model, completely shutting my presence out of his head.

How do you keep a man's attention? I wondered in those days. By being distant? By pushing too much? Was there too much sex with Will, or rather, too much emphasis on sex for things to work with Will? Did he desire not to be with me when we were outside the bedroom? Questions came to me in a frenzy in those days, and

I began to miss my classes, began to feel like I was going to jump out of my skin. I would sit in the library, trying to read, staring, fidgeting, able to think of nothing but why Will was purposely hurting me. And then one evening he brought home a young man named Stephen, tall, lanky, with thick brown hair and a beautiful, boyish face marred only by acne scars at his cheeks. When the three of us later ended up in bed, I knew that it was time for me to leave, that things could not be with Will as I wanted them to be in my life. I promised myself I would never let another man hurt me like that. Two months later, at the end of the term, I was on a train to New York City, promising myself I would never let another man have that much power over my life.

"Life is a journey of decisions," Will once said to me after I had shrugged my shoulders and replied, "I don't care, either one," in response to his asking one Saturday night if I wanted to go to a movie or out dancing. I didn't really care which one we did; I was eighteen years old at the time and blindly in love with everything about Will: his tall, slender, runner's build, the bookish eyeglasses he wore, the short, stubbly, graying horseshoe pattern of his hair. All I wanted was to be with him, no matter what we did or where we went. Will, however, thrived on debate and confrontation. "You weren't put into the world to be pampered," he would say to me if he felt things were becoming too comfortable between us—if he felt, for instance, that I was just floating along and en-joying our relationship, which was, well, *just* what I wanted. His intention was neither evil nor devious; what he wanted was for me to be able to stand on my own two feet. He wanted me to decide, for instance, that we should go out dancing, but only so he could convince me that we should go to a movie instead. This was the illogical construct of our relationship, which, in his fashioning, he never wanted termed a *relationship.* "We're falling into a trap," he would say about everything from my socks' invading his underwear drawer to the way gay life seemed to be defined by the late-night disco schedule.

I eventually learned to argue with Will, and a couple of times he even acquiesced to my decisions after some willful pouting on my part, but I have often felt that the best thing he gave me was a knowledge of the subtle things about gay life. I picked up a sense of style from him, everything from the balance of color, fit, and fabric in clothing to why irises are so much more elegant than red roses. Such things were never actually explained to me, of course; at a store, for instance, Will would simply pick out a shirt and tell me to go try it on. When I was standing in front of him again, in a tightly buttoned shirt with my hair all wild and curly and in my eyes, he would tip his chin down so his tiny brown eyes could look over the frames of his glasses. "That's better," he would say, not even adding a smile. And then we would end up at the barber's or the shoe store. And I learned to accept these opinions of Will's as new facts of my life.

Which is why, I think, I found it so upsetting the day I heard about Hank's death; Hank had been Nathan's guide into gay life as Will had been mine, and I knew that the loss of him meant that Nathan must feel as if his past had been lost, too—the creation and history of himself called into question, as it were—as if all those things one wonders about as one stumbles into gay life had never really happened at all.

They had met on the beach in Harwich Port the summer before Nathan was a senior in high school. Nathan's parents had taken a house for a month on Cape Cod; Hank was rehearsing for and then performing in a summer-stock production of the *Comedy of Errors*, which featured a roaming chorus of jugglers and mimes, of which Hank was one. Hank wore only red suspenders and skin-tight black tights in the play; his real costume was his short but magnificent body, all tensed and ribbed and striated and furry about the chest. Nathan never saw that performance, but he did meet Hank on the beach. Hank settled near Nathan's towel one afternoon, though

Nathan did not even notice him, absorbed as he was in reading a book of science-fiction stories by Isaac Asimov.

Like Nathan, Hank had a fascination with things fantastical, and at one point when Nathan looked up from his book, Hank smiled and asked if he had read *Foundation*, which was his own favorite Asimov work. Nathan nodded but said *his* favorite was *The End of Eternity* because it was about time travel, and they fell into a discussion about other authors and books, from Bradbury and *Fahrenheit 451* to Vonnegut and *Slaughterhouse-Five*.

Hank was a restless spirit, never content just to lie on the beach, relax, and talk about science fiction. At first he invited Nathan to join him for long walks along the foamy stretches of sand, but by the end of their first week of friendship, he was teaching him the movements of mime. Their relationship was not consummated sexually that year, though Hank suspected all along that Nathan was gay; their talks would often skirt around potential topics of interest, from bodybuilding to dancing to what was trendy and exciting back in Manhattan, where Hank lived. Nathan, however, was falling in love with Hank, fascinated by him in the same way I was by Will, from Hank's passion for blue Sno-Cones to the smell of his underarms, which wafted through the ocean breeze when they lay side by side on beach towels. Hank aroused the gay man in the young Nathan, but he also charmed that adventurous boyish spirit.

They kept in touch by letter and phone, but their paths did not cross again till two years later, when Nathan moved to the city to begin his freshman year at New York University. Hank, by then, was wildly into the gay life, and his openness both frightened and intrigued Nathan. Hank took Nathan to his first gay bar, Julius's in the West Village, a dark, somber place frequented by a nonthreatening neighborhood crowd, the kind of straight-looking men you would expect to see at ball games or business meetings. But he also walked Nathan to the Hudson River piers and the Rambles in Central Park, where he explained what all the looks and codes and signals between men meant. Hank knew all the stories of the tribe by then, and he passed along gay history like gossip as they walked through the streets of Manhattan and in and out of stores, describing the kind of love they shared with Alexander the Great and the exploits of Oscar Wilde and James Baldwin—all embellished, of course, with his own story, the details of his tricks, from what he did to the guy who lived above the deli on Second Avenue to what type of furniture the man on Seventeenth Street had in his duplex apartment.

And then, one night, he took Nathan back to his apartment on Gramercy Park, dimmed the lights, and gave him enough wine to put him at ease, then undressed him and led him into the bedroom. It is not hard for me to imagine the two of them together, Hank running his hands along Nathan's arms as if to warm a chill and then settling them about his waist; Nathan tensing first his back, then his buttocks, then relaxing as Hank drew him into a kiss, his tongue, warm and ardent, easily parting Nathan's lips. I know how Nathan felt as Hank edged him slowly down onto the mattress: nervous and suspicious, but also wildly eager and thrilled; I felt the same way my first night with Will. Hank was the first man Nathan ever slept with.

For Nathan, this was a combination of mysteries revealed and lust requited. Hank explained, however, after they had been together a couple of times, that he wasn't "into" relationships and didn't intend to get into one with Nathan. He enjoyed the excitement and spontaneity of finding a new trick whenever he was eager for one, and relished, too, the potential danger of anonymous encounters. Still, Hank and Nathan continued to get together occasionally, for dinner or movies, and then began going together to the baths, where Hank would abandon Nathan the moment he had undressed at the lockers, and Nathan would wander around fitfully for hours before ending up in Hank's embrace, long after they had both used and abandoned other strangers.

Hank, eight years older than Nathan, always recognized that Nathan was becoming too attached to him, and so he instead set about opening up the possibilities of Manhattan to an inquisitive college boy—fixing Nathan up on blind dates with friends who were looking for boyfriends, for instance, as Vince had done for me as well, all those years ago. Hank took Nathan to the bookstore in the East Village where Nathan found a part-time job, and went with him to the blood banks and sperm clinic in Midtown, where he showed him how he could earn some extra cash. They went together to the revivals at the Thalia and to the pool at the Mc-Burney Y and in the summers took the ferry out for day trips to Cherry Grove and the Pines. It was Hank's suggestion, too, that Nathan, for a lark, take the anatomy drawing class Hank modeled for at Parsons. Nathan, however, was only angered by Hank's nudity in front of a classroom of artists and strangers, and frequently found himself close to tears because Hank was so insensitive, it seemed, to Nathan's feelings for him. Nathan still held to the belief that one day Hank would realize the error of his ways, and they would settle into a relationship together.

At first Nathan's sketches in the class were wildly cartoonish and full of fury, the body all out of proportion, bulky and muscular, and often attached to a tiny, freakish-looking, shiny bald head. This was before Hank began wearing the inexpensive toupee that Nathan so hated; in those days, Nathan would sometimes help shave Hank's scalp, a process that he found both ironic and erotic. At the end of the twelve weeks of the drawing class, the instructor politely suggested that Nathan try something like graphic arts instead of figure drawing, but Hank noticed in one of Nathan's drawings the way Nathan had exquisitely detailed the contents of the classroom, the small desks and chairs and the concrete blocks of the wall in the background. And so it was Hank who suggested that Nathan try his hand at drawing landscapes.

It was always easy for me to be jealous of Hank. He possessed a part and history of Nathan that I did not know and that, when I glimpsed them, aroused an immense jealousy within me; I always felt so intimately excluded from their friendship. I often heard sto-

ries of things they did together only after the fact; I was never invited
to participate with them, always merely told of the adventure. I felt,
too, that Hank took advantage of Nathan's good nature—by bor-
rowing money, for example, when he couldn't scrape together
enough funds to pay his rent, even though Nathan himself was
struggling to meet his bills. In many ways I always wanted to believe
that Nathan outgrew Hank, the way a child outgrows a toy, but
the truth is that as Nathan drifted further from gay life and deeper
into our relationship through the years, he saw less and less of Hank
because he knew I did not care that much for him. But I knew they
occasionally talked and got together, knew, too, they got together
more often than Nathan told me about, even if it was just Nathan's
showing up for the jazz classes Hank often taught around town.
Hank was also still friendly with Jeff, and I was invariably told
secondhand of his exploits about town. Whenever Hank found
work in an off-Broadway play or showcase, Nathan and I would
always go to see it and visit with Hank backstage.

This, then, is what happened to Hank. Two years ago he was
first hospitalized with pneumonia, then eleven months later he was
back in again, fighting another bout, when a spinal tap showed he
had meningitis. He also had a bacterial infection of his left ear, and
his T-cell count fell below 50. After three weeks in the hospital, he
returned home with a hospital bill of over fifteen thousand dollars.
I knew all of this from phone conversations with Vince and Jeff.
Nathan and I never discussed any of this, we avoided the subject of
Hank like we hoped to avoid the plague, though I know, too, that
Nathan had visited Hank in the hospital several times. The next
year Hank developed an abscess beneath his left armpit that required
surgery; he was treated at the same time for another ear infection.
He had begun, by then, to feel dizzy and lightheaded and had
trouble maintaining his balance. He continued to work part-time
at a card store on Seventh Avenue, occasionally landing a role in a
TV commercial; the residuals he earned from dancing in a thirty-
second spot for a fast-food chain nearly lifted him out of debt.

But his memory began to increasingly fail him, and he became lethargic and confused, till a friend, Tom, finally took him to the emergency room at St. Luke's-Roosevelt. A CT scan revealed an infection similar to *Toxoplasma gondii*, even though that diagnosis could not be confirmed through a blood test ordered by Hank's doctor. After he slipped into a coma, the doctors began treating him for toxoplasmosis. When a brain biopsy still could not detect the specific protozoa that causes toxoplasmosis, another doctor recommended radiation therapy for lymphoma of the brain. At first Hank responded quite well, partially awakening and even reaching a point where he was able to swallow small amounts of baby food fed him by his mother, who had flown in from Iowa. Eventually, however, he slipped back into a coma, and a week later, still unconscious and living off life-support machinery, he developed a bacterial pneumonia. He died two days later.

It was Mrs. Solloway who gave me the news of Hank's death, filling me in on the more gruesome details of his illness when I came home one afternoon from work. I had taken a quick job building a loft bed for an apartment in Chinatown, but the whole time my concentration had been on worrying about Nathan, and I felt I had done a sloppy job with the assignment. Mrs. Solloway had taken the call from Jeff, who had called from Los Angeles and knew Tom, the guy who had been helping Hank at St. Luke's; she had repeated the story to Nathan earlier in the day. Mrs. Solloway had known Hank as long as Nathan had, having met him that first summer on Cape Cod, and had in fact even seen him perform in the *Comedy of Errors*. It had always made me feel guilty that Mrs. Solloway liked Hank where I did not; I felt so small and judgmental.

"He took it well," she said, looking down on me sitting on the sofa where I had landed to absorb all the facts of Hank. "I think he took it well. Don't wake him up just yet, though; he's finally fallen asleep."

I slipped into the bathroom and took a long, steaming shower, though at the end I was still agitated, wanting to wake Nathan and hold him and let him *know* I was holding him. I felt that the only thing I could give him at that moment was the warmth of physical comfort.

He was awake when I entered the bedroom and slipped the towel on the back of the chair and began to dress. We did not speak to each other, but I was conscious of him studying my body as I bent over to put on socks and then a pair of sweat pants and a T-shirt. It was then, I think, that I first recognized a small microbe of hate inside myself, a disgust for the way things had changed for us, really, as if Nathan himself were to blame—but I refused to believe it, pushed the idea of it back down inside me, burying it beneath the skin and tissues and cells of my body, hoping it would never be found again.

"I don't want that to happen to me," he said, his voice cracking the silence of the room like a misfitted floorboard. I looked over at him and met his eyes, which were fixed and determined but reddened by sleep or crying or, perhaps, a little of both.

"Promise me that you'll pull the plug," he said succinctly. It was, I think, the first moment that we had ever together acknowledged the possibility of our own mortality, and I looked determinedly through the top drawer of the dresser for my hairbrush, not wanting to imagine the possibility of Nathan's death.

"And what happens if I go *first?*" I asked, hearing a tone of bitterness creep into my voice.

His eyes narrowed, and he replied, "Don't be cruel."

"I'm sorry about Hank," I said.

"I'm sorry, too."

"We should have"—I heard myself breathe in air—"helped more," I said, and shook my head.

"How?" he asked, and I heard, then, an edge of bitterness in *his* voice. "We can't face our own facts."

"I'm sorry I'm scared," I said, remembering, then, the day I had finally walked away from Will, angry and hurt because I knew he could not give me the irresolute attention I wanted, but scared to find myself a young gay man so vulnerable and lonely within the world. By the time I met Nathan I knew that I could never expect the kind of love I had wanted from Will to happen with any man. I looked at myself in the mirror and tried calmly to brush my hair, noticing, as I did, the creases of tension across my brow. Moments passed between us like years, till I finally heard Nathan say, "I could never give him up, you know."

"I know."

"I can't make those clean breaks like you," he said, referring as much, I believed, to my father as to Will.

"I never expected you to."

And then his demeanor shifted entirely, as if all the tension that held him in place had evaporated. "I didn't want *Hank* to be the reason you left."

"I remember the first night I met you," I said, looking at the image of Nathan sitting up in the bed that was reflected in the mirror. "Christmas night, remember? It was like a gift, you know. I felt so lucky that Hank brought you to that party."

And then I felt myself turning and moving toward the bed, hearing myself say, as if in an echo shouted across a ravine, as I slipped into the bed beside him, "But I always knew it would be a fight to keep you."

Peter Weltner

BUDDY LOVES JO ANN

SWAGGERING, THE COOK LEANED into his newspaper like a man
eager to start an argument. His chef's hat was greasy and torn where
it had been pulled too tight around the back of his head. Every time
he flipped a page, he shifted his weight from one leg to the other.
As he read, he sang along with the radio:

> *Sad bird,*
> *Perching in a cage,*
> *Sings to me*
> *A tune so strange,*
>
> *Sings a song*
> *No wild bird sings:*
> *Unkind love*
> *Has clipped its wings.*

After having observed him closely for the past several hours, Buddy was increasingly astonished at how the cook was always moving even when the man seemed to have nothing to do.

Though all four booths had been empty when he entered, Buddy Birnam had chosen to sit at the diner's counter with his back to the door and to the large wall clock above it, most of whose face, when he strained his neck, he could see in the mirror, its numbers reversed and its second hand ticking backward. The summer before Jo Ann entered first grade, the two of them had played every day, even the cozy rainy ones, in the bushes by the creek behind the toppled fence that marked the divide between the Turner and Birnam properties. From fallen branches, torn vines, and broad leaves, they had built their playhouse. Jo Ann had predicted often that it wouldn't survive the first big storm, but because they enjoyed repairing whatever damage weather and time inflicted upon it, it lasted almost until Buddy's eighth birthday. When Jo Ann determined it was finally beyond any more restoration, they strewed its remains over the woods' floor. Only in recent months had Buddy begun to understand why Jo Ann had insisted they be so meticulous in their work of obliteration.

The fluorescent lights in the diner were as harsh as those in the bus station where sixteen hours ago, in flight from Jo Ann's request for him to do what she had called "one last kindness" for her, he waited to leave for good the town where they had both lived all their lives. Was it wrong for him to refuse her wish? He was certain that it was worse than wrong, that it was damnable, but such conviction had not kept him from running away.

He sipped his coffee, now cooled to a barely palatable lukewarm. When they were children, he and Jo Ann vowed to spend their lives together until death, and they had kept their promise to each other in their own private way. Jo Ann was born on Dogwood Street, Buddy two years later fifty yards around the corner on Stuart Way. Neither of them ever slept a night of their lives farther apart than their two houses or under a roof different from the one under which they took their first breaths.

Buddy glanced at himself in the mirror. How had it happened that a man as seriously old as he was had never spent a night away from home in an unfamiliar bed? Did his asking the question to himself mean he felt regret? Most of his life he had lived, like Jo Ann, alone. Both of Jo Ann's younger sisters had married so long ago, he could barely remember either of them. They'd each moved with their husbands to regions of the country from which it seemed not even mail bothered to travel the great distance back home. Neither returned for the funeral after their mother died from a tumor that had grown to the size of a child in her womb. Less than a year later, Miles Turner was diagnosed with cancer in both lungs. Jo Ann nursed her father for seven months, watching him shrivel and shrink into a voodoo doll's mockery of his former self. Was her own dying more accurately prophesied in his death or her mother's? The truth lay in both, Buddy thought.

The day Miles Turner died, Grover Birnam's bayonet wound from the Great War ripped open again as savagely as if he had run naked into the full swing of an ax. Buddy buried his father less than a month after Jo Ann began wearing black to mourn hers. Complaining about an itch that wouldn't quit, Rosemary Birnam, Buddy's mother, took to scratching her skin all over her body so vigorously with her long, unpainted nails that it bled. After a while, the wounds wouldn't heal. Six months later, he and Jo Ann watched the last of their parents laid to rest beneath a sky as hurtful to the eye as his mother's brightly lit hospital room had been. The row of pine that bordered the town cemetery looked as phony beneath an ash white sun as a dime-store display of plastic Christmas trees. After experiencing so much loss in so short a time, they found in each other not comfort, which neither had ever anticipated, but rest and a little peace.

Each now owned a house, though not one they would attempt

to share as they had the make-believe house in the woods by the creek. Until she retired, Jo Ann was a secretary at an old, respectable, but unprosperous law firm downtown, housed in a mid-nineteenth-century brick building. Only half a block away stood another brick building, nearly as antique, which after the Great War had been converted into a discount clothing store catering mostly to mill workers and tobacco farmers who couldn't afford anything better. Since the month he graduated from high school, Buddy had sold cheap boots, shoes, and hats to these men and their wives and children, earning even less at his job than many of them did at theirs.

Early in his and Jo Ann's working lives, people somewhat better off than they but possessing what they both regarded as much less dignity started to buy up small parcels of the abandoned sheep-grazing land around them and to build on it houses that Jo Ann said resembled trucks or trailers or temporary roadside Dumpsters more than real homes. They couldn't last, she said. When, on a western curve of the creek that flowed eastward between his place and Jo Ann's, colored people began to move in, neither of them knew what to think. But, when pressed, they refused to join the protests organized by their angry neighbors. Thereafter they were frequently shunned, even at the New Hope Methodist Church they attended, as if the wings of virtue they were believed to have worn previously had suddenly dropped off and exposed them as rebellious angels. They acknowledged their ostracism to each other, but claimed not to mind. That the two of them had been correct to shun such rabble-rousing mischief was sufficient justification.

No day would end without their having enjoyed at least one meal together and a game of cards—gin and honeymoon bridge were their favorites. After Buddy relented and bought a TV so they could watch Kennedy debate Nixon, they would sometimes watch it for less high-minded reasons, but for entertainment they still preferred the older music on the radio at Jo Ann's. Every other Saturday, rain or shine, they went to a movie downtown at the Grand, usually after the children had left their matinee and before the teen-agers and younger adults on dates arrived for the evening show. The film over, they ate dinner at the Willow Cafeteria. Buddy invariably selected fried chicken, spoon bread, greens, and either apple pie or, if either was in season, cold watermelon or fresh peaches with syrup. Jo Ann varied her selections more but preferred salads and seldom requested a dessert unless it was cubes of red and yellow Jell-O with a dollop of real whipped cream.

As Jo Ann aged, her buckteeth, bushy eyebrows, and pointed English chin all became more pronounced, as did the translucent clarity of her glass-bottle blue eyes. She started to speak to almost everyone with a frankness she had previously reserved for Buddy, but he knew better than to waste words trying to caution her. For seventy years she had deeply touched his soul. He couldn't tell you why because he didn't understand the reason himself, though he believed her without question when she said he had touched hers as deeply for as long. No one who knew them presumed to ask why they had never married.

How had so many years passed? What had they really done with seven decades, living their lives without event or incident into what astonishingly was now old age? But old age, the always uncanny passage of time, amazed them less than how simple, how easy it had been for them to have been happy for so long. And they had been happy, truly happy, hadn't they? Buddy was sure of it, in part be-cause, unlike their poor parents, not one of whom had ever been blessed with sustained good health, they had been rarely ill or less than sound in mind and body.

Then the winter of his seventieth year, quite by accident it ap-peared, they both began complaining incessantly about this pain or that. One day, Buddy's joints ached worse than his teeth, the next his back hurt worse than his joints, and Jo Ann couldn't seem to stop coughing. Six months ago, on a Sunday evening while they were slicing peaches ripe from Buddy's tree, Jo Ann started to cough so badly she had to excuse herself. When she returned, her face was as white as her handkerchief where it had not been soaked with blood.

The cook refilled his cup. How much coffee had Buddy drunk during the last several hours? When he sipped it, it was hot enough, but sour. Sitting on his stool while he waited for midnight, he had counted only four other customers entering the diner—two women wearing skimpy waitress uniforms, a young mechanic in his greasy coveralls, a checkout clerk from the Winn Dixie up the coast near the bus station, all of whom knew the cook, Leo, by name. Not one of them seemed to notice the old man, but Buddy was relieved that he was invisible to them. He had always wanted to feel invisible to everyone except Jo Ann. We are both, she had remarked years ago, an enigma too uninteresting to try to solve, as boring, thank heaven, as a story without a plot or a point.

For well over forty years he had been called "Mr. Birnam" by everyone who spoke to him. Only Jo Ann still used the little boy's name with which he had been christened. "Buddy," she appealed to him just a few nights ago, speaking with so unfamiliar an emotion that he almost didn't recognize the name as his own. "I know who you really are, Buddy. You're a poet. You see things with a poet's eyes. You experience life with a poet's soul. You're my favorite poet, Buddy." Embarrassed, he demurred politely, reminding her of how little poetry he had read in his life and of how much less he had understood. But with a wicked twinkle in her eye, she refused to withdraw her remark, instead adding, "True poets never deign to write a word."

To his eyes, the lights in the diner seemed to expose the thin bones under his fish-belly white skin. He rolled down his shirt-sleeves and put his suit coat back on. Watching the cook as he worked, he felt his own body shrink into something even smaller than the gawky boy's body into which old age had returned him. Hadn't one adolescence been hardship enough for a lifetime? Burly, big-boned, swarthy yet ruddy-cheeked, the cook was as vibrant as the fire over which he worked. Reluctantly, Buddy glanced at the reflection of the clock as he spooned sugar into his cup. Quarter after eleven. Why he had chosen midnight, so banal a time for such an act, he could not say, but once he had chosen it he knew he could not change it or back out. He had taken enough money from home for the bus trip southeast. No bills were left in his wallet. In his right pocket jiggled some change he would use to pay for the coffee and the tip. On principle, he had never carried a charge card of any kind. Again he checked the clock in the mirror. Was it running fast? "Death before dishonor," his father had declared to him one unforgettable night shortly before his graduation from high school. Buddy listened intently, deeply affected by his father's conviction. Nobody else, not his teachers at school or the preacher at church, had offered him words he could really live by. "Death before dishonor. That's the best and most difficult code a man can accept as his challenge in life. Never dishonor yourself, son." Had he ever really understood what his father meant? Buddy took as deep a breath as his lungs would allow. Amid all the diner's unpleasant odors, was it also the ocean he smelled?

Neither he nor Jo Ann had ever crossed their county's borders, though, especially when he was a boy, he had often yearned to see the beach and ocean. One long weekend each spring, the boys and girls of his town would drive the 357 miles to the coast to party, reckless and free and, he was certain, nearly naked most of the time. Year after year, he had spied them leaving in their cars, returning only a few days later so inalterably changed, their bodies having blossomed as swiftly and beautifully as lilac in the sun, that he could not understand why any rational parent would let them go. Their transformation stunned him. During his own high school years, he hadn't bothered to ask permission from his parents. He understood they were too poor to allow him to indulge in such a folly, and in any case Jo Ann would never have gone with him. To her, girls who wanted such lives were silly. But, especially in the springtime when the pear and cherry trees blossomed, Buddy lamented not having seen the strand alive with young people frisking and basking in the sun while he was also young.

At 11:32 the last customer left the diner. Except of course for himself, the man whom Jo Ann Turner had called over the years the kindest, sweetest, just plain nicest person she had ever known. She had repeated those very words just a little more than twenty-four hours ago. What people did Jo Ann know with whom to compare him? Perhaps enough, he allowed, for him to accept the praise without really knowing what any of it meant.

The cook was scraping the flat grill, his body swaying to the steady rhythm of another rock song on the radio that sat on a corner of the counter. Every time he walked past it, he had to duck under the taut cord that just reached the wall socket over the last booth. Would Jo Ann have called him kind for having let Buddy linger over one cup of coffee, repeatedly refilled, for nearly three hours? Or would she have been repelled, as she often said she had been when she'd observed it in others, by such obvious brawn, grit, and brashness? Even how he flipped a burger was abrupt, almost sullen in that way that never ceased to shock her. "How different you are, Buddy," she would say, grasping his hand in hers.

An announcer on the radio was warning of a big storm. Over the past quarter of a century, hurricanes had washed much of that part of the coast into the sea, but the town of Crescent Beach had vowed not to die. When ruin was irreversible, was it better to accept one's fate or resist? As Buddy strolled the town's remaining board-walk earlier that evening, the cold dense fog obliterated the sky, and the beach seemed to be vanishing before him like snow under a strong sun, melting back into water. Had that vision frightened or comforted him?

Before he could decide, he thought of Jo Ann lying helpless in her bed, alone. Was she accepting her fate or resisting it? Even if he could determine which was the right answer, how could that knowledge advise him? Shivering, he had walked into the diner only because it was the lone building along that strip of the shore with its lights on. Without waiting to be asked, the cook poured him a cup of coffee, piping hot. Soon Buddy felt warm enough to remove his coat and, uncharacteristically, roll up his sleeves.

The cook clicked off the fan over the grill. Had Buddy noticed its whirring before it had been turned off, or how close the surf sounded? In the summers when he was still little, or "littler" as his mother would later say, his father used to call him home for dinner from the porch. Buddy was certain he never heard his voice at all until his father, still crying out his name, approached the bank of the creek, just a few feet away from the green playhouse where Jo Ann's giggling gave them away. How much else during his lifetime had he failed to hear because he didn't want to hear it? "Listen to me," Jo Ann had said to him just before she told him the news he had dreaded for weeks. Had she expected him to put his fingers in his ears? In his own estimation, he'd already heard enough and seen enough of life. Why should he fear more? "Listen to me," Jo Ann repeated, her voice almost savage with insistence.

Wiping his hands on his grease-spattered apron, the cook rested on a stool he'd slid from the other side of the counter, a taller man sitting than Buddy was standing. He scratched behind his ear where patches of his hair were as gray as Buddy's had been twenty years or so ago before it had all turned dirty white and frizzy, like cotton in the boll. "Time to close," he announced. Without risking another glance at the clock, Buddy nodded. "Don't mean to insult you by asking, friend," the cook added, "but you got that look. I've seen it plenty. You found yourself a place to sleep?"

Buddy tried to recall the name of the motel whose sign he'd read as he stepped off the bus, luggageless. "The Seaside Inn," he said, with more of a question in his words than he had intended. "It's very comfortable."

But hadn't the Seaside Inn been boarded up like the two other motels he half-remembered seeing? He decided not to try to correct his mistake since it was his experience that most people expected the old to be confused. Even Jo Ann occasionally expected a certain dottiness from him, excusing his errors to his face as symptoms of his increasing years, though she was his senior by almost twenty-three months. Yet his failure to notice some things, especially important things, had made him increasingly uneasy. "You've been kind to let me linger," he said.

"No problem. Taking a little time away from home, are you?"

"Yes."

"Pretty deserted around here these days. Just a few people on their way elsewhere, like me. Not just because it's off-season. Mother Nature's done her worst. Devastation all up and down this coast for miles."

"It's a shame."

"I like a livelier place myself. Found this joint on my way to sunny Florida." He rubbed the same spot behind his ear. "Stopped here for a meal. I know what a goddamned bowl of chili is supposed to taste like. You know what I'm saying? Cook got so mad, he quit right there and then. I accepted his challenge. Listen, a man complains to me and he's right, I'll try to fix it for him, make it good, you understand? No one's requiring you to pay rent for that stool, are they? You could sit there all night as far as I'm concerned. We all got worries and heartache, am I right? You bet I am."

"Certainly," Buddy acknowledged, slowly backing away and almost stumbling on an empty gumball machine on his way to the door. What had the man been implying? How had his legs gotten so tangled together? He prayed the cook would not think he was a drunk, or worse, infirm. "Good night," he said, waving cheerily. "Thank you so much."

As he left, Buddy opened and closed the door carefully, making certain that he did not trip on one of the steps that led down from the diner to the gravel walkway. In contrast to the warm air of the diner, the outside air was chilly, though nowhere near as cold as the snowstorm he and Jo Ann had played in when they were still in elementary school. Wandering far from their house in delight at the strangeness of it, they had lost their way and almost froze in the unfamiliar woods before their fathers and two neighbor men found them, huddled together beneath the skirt of an old magnolia. Inside the diner, the cook flipped the window sign to CLOSED and pulled down the shades. A few seconds later, the lights inside and above the building went dark.

As Buddy walked north on the sidewalk parallel to the highway, the air smelled brackish and the cloudy night was a spotted greenish gray, like the throat of a frog. Almost every streetlight's globe was broken or lacked a bulb. At one motel, whose road sign optimistically proclaimed CLOSED FOR THE SEASON, grass had pierced the cracked cement drive. So much trash had littered its parking lot that the waste had formed along the motel's south wall an imposing half-pyramid of crumbling debris.

Moving much too fast, a car passed him on the left. As he stopped to watch it zoom through a flashing red light and out of sight, he heard as if for the first time in his life the sound of waves swelling and crashing onto land, a music more compelling to his ears than a church organ's. A few feet farther north, he turned east onto a rickety wooden walkway that zigzagged through the dunes to the ocean. Had the duckboards under his feet felt this way to his father as, crouching, he waited his turn to go over the top? The comparison, though his own, struck him as embarrassing and grandiose.

The wind soughed through the sea oats as it used to through the cane at home before the new people came and cut it down, planting in its place, if anything, clumps of scrub trees and rugged shrubs through which the wind blew silently. The damp cold and wind-carried grit pricked his skin. A sandpiper, foraging late, scurried past. Mournfully Buddy gazed out toward the barely visible horizon where the mottled cloudy sky darkened into the sea. Since rushing, frightened, out of Jo Ann's bedroom the previous night, he had accomplished nothing that did not add to his already great store of self-delusion and folly. Long ago, despite his mother's shrieking protests, he had climbed the same tall pine from which

Jo Ann had fallen the day before and broken her arm in two places. He had not broken his arm, of course. He was only showing off, just as his mother, after scolding him once he had been carried back down, had patiently explained.

Was it high tide? With effort, he slid one foot, then the other into the frigid water. Was this gesture, too, only more showing off? But before he decided to stop himself, he was knee deep, the water creeping up his pants' legs and long johns to his thighs. Death before dishonor, he reminded himself. Duty, honor, the code. His father had said it did not matter what you called it so long as you understood that the poor and unimportant man must obey it as much as the rich and great. But obedience to the moral law, he had warned, was not the same thing as seeking to satisfy the opinions of others. The sole victory anyone ever wins is the battle against himself. That is the meaning of honor, he said, the victory over yourself.

So Buddy had lived honorably. He neither cursed nor swore. He had never cheated anyone out of anything. He had tithed every month of his life. He had kept his body, like his house, spotlessly neat and clean. He neither ate to excess nor drank at all, trying to keep as healthy as he could. Though he did not really care for them, he went out of his way to be polite to children and kind to animals. He made an effort to be always courteous, however sorely he was tried, especially at work. He had hidden from the world only what it required him to hide, had lied to it only when it had insisted that he lie. Since their infancies, he had been faithful to Jo Ann. Above all, he had been faithful to Jo Ann.

Was he being faithful to her still? But what she had asked of him was impossible, dishonorable, wrong. "It would be a kindness," she had said. "Help me end my suffering, please. Please, Buddy. You have always been so kind to me. Be kind again once more, now. Tonight. This pain is more than my soul can stand." But to break the old injunction Thou Shalt Not Kill, above all to break it with Jo Ann, was a horror he could not bear. Death before dishonor, his father had proclaimed. If someone had to be killed, Buddy thought, surely it was better that he kill himself.

The water had reached up to his waist. Was he getting faint? How quickly his lower body had become numb. Waves were beginning to break closer, in swells twice their former size. As irresolute as he was frightened, he slowly began to back out, but as his left foot tested the bottom it found not sand but a hole into which it slipped. Losing his balance. Buddy tumbled backward, sucked beneath the water by an undertow that pushed his face down into the sand and scraped his right cheek across the spines of a shell. A countercurrent dragged him deeper into the ocean. Some force, too huge to be only a wave, broke over him and shoved him across the ocean's floor, over which he rolled like a terrified child somersaulting too fast down a steep, slick hill. If he had no time to ask himself, "Buddy, are you afraid to die?" his flailing body answered for him, fighting against its destruction, though his water-soaked clothes and old man's shoes, even as the current momentarily subsided, held him under like ten-pound weights. Had he blacked out before or after his body went limp, as if in acceptance of its death?

He couldn't remember. Nor could he quite remember being grabbed and dragged back to shore or carried in strong arms the quarter of a mile to Leo's apartment. When he woke up, he found himself in a tiny room, too small to swing a cat in, as Jo Ann would say. It seemed to his watery eyes as bright as the diner, though lit by incandescent bulbs he at first mistook for candles. He was lying naked and swaddled in bedclothes on a couch that hurt every inch of his body the way a monk's bed of rough planks would hurt. Across from him, Leo sat wearing a terrycloth robe and a beach towel wrapped around his neck. He offered Buddy something steaming from a mug. "Here. Drink it," he commanded.

"I can't. I hurt," Buddy mumbled petulantly. "My stomach hurts."

"Drink it anyway."

"I think I'm going to be sick."

"There's a pan on the floor next to you. Use it if you have to."

Against his better judgment, Buddy accepted the mug and sipped from it. "Chicken broth? Jo Ann always fixes me chicken broth when I'm under the weather. Or egg drop soup. She prefers fresh orange juice herself."

"Good for her. Finish it off now."

Buddy did as he was told. "I really don't feel so good. Awful, in fact."

"Who wouldn't when they've just been dragged out of the Atlantic? But you'll be OK. It's just that I waited on that damn dune too long. I should've hooked you before that big wave threw you under. But the next one did us both a favor. Belched you up onto shore like that big fish did Jonah. You sure were heavy to carry for a skinny little old man. Your pulse was so slow and your face so white, I thought we might lose you. But you were breathing good, only a little slow and shallow. You didn't take on much water. Battered and bruised is all. I've seen worse. You'll live."

"You followed me?"

"You were showing all the signs, old man."

Buddy tugged the musty comforter up to his chin. Something in it smelled faintly like hot metal. Or was the odor his own body? Since shame had forced him to quit high school gym, no one had ever looked at him naked. "Where are my clothes?"

"In the tub. I'll take them to the laundry tomorrow." Buddy touched the bandage on his forehead and scalp. "You were bleeding bad. What's your name?"

"Mr. Birnam. Buddy Birnam. I'm sorry, but I really am going to be sick." He rolled onto his side and aimed over the edge of the cushion for the pan.

"That wasn't anything," the man said afterward. "Hardly anything. Just a piddle. Feel better?"

"No." Buddy sighed as sincerely as he had ever sighed in his life. "My manners dictate that I say, 'Thank you.' "

"Don't mention it." Leo carried the pan into the bathroom,

poured the contents into the toilet, flushed, closed the door behind him, and turned out all the lights with the click of two switches. "If you need anything, holler. There's no doctor within thirty miles of this town this time of year, but there's a county hospital half an hour down the road by car. The only thing is that I don't own a car."

Buddy wanted to blow his nose but was embarrassed to have to ask for a tissue. He snuffled and shook his head. "They'd ask questions. All doctors ever do is ask questions."

"Maybe so. Sleep well, old man. I'll be bunking right behind you. We'll talk later about getting you home."

Was he already half asleep the second time Leo, lying on the floor, said good night to him? Had he already fallen completely asleep when he heard the thundercrack of a storm and the rattle and dried gourd sound of rain against the room's one windowpane? He couldn't tell, but surely he was dreaming when he sensed the building sway as if the ocean had reached its foundations and begun to dig beneath them. He felt himself falling.

But nearly all his life, certainly since he was a little boy, he had sensed himself falling as he slept, a continuous plummeting through a dark rabbit hole like Alice's, though his burrow had no bottom to it and no door through which to enter Wonderland on the other side. He'd just keep falling until he woke when he would discover to his shame that, because his body had grown too warm under its covers, he'd thrown them off and exposed himself. Had he actually, as he fell this time, called out the cook's name?

He had dreamed many other dreams, of course, some more frightening, a few more pleasant. But of all his dreams the one where he plunged down an endless silent hole was the most recurrent. His dream, he called it. Had he been dreaming it again that night as he heard the rain still falling, as loud and close as if someone were showering in a room next to him? He clung to the comforter to keep himself covered.

Lumps and buttons from the couch's cushions pressed against

his body. Was he awake then, both the noise of truck tires rolling fast over wet pavement and that of furniture being moved on the floor over his head real? He could taste the metallic cold of ice on his lips, then something warm and salty in the back of his throat. Children were playing, shouting and laughing and throwing leaves, in a yard close by. Trees shimmered in a summer breeze. The dark turned light, then dark again. All his body ached, more than it had ever hurt before, and his right cheek burned hot as steam. Jo Ann lay next to him, her arms crossed over her bosom in that attitude of fake repose that undertakers impose upon the dead. Beneath the odor of talc and rosewater, he could smell flesh as ripe as chicken left too long in the fridge. "Buddy," he heard her complain, "don't you ever throw anything away? But you're usually so tidy, Buddy."

Since he was two years, seven months, and eleven days old, they had never been separated by more than twenty-four hours, not even when either or both of them were sick. As they played in the woods, erecting or improving their various playhouses, other children would sometimes hide in the trees and taunt, "Buddy loves Jo Ann, Buddy loves Jo Ann. Jo Ann and Buddy sitting in a tree, k-i-s-s-i-n-g."

Only Miss Adele Butterfield dared to try to separate them. Because Jo Ann had broken the rules, she'd said, and crossed the line that separated the boys' playground from the girls' at recess. Buddy was in the third grade, Jo Ann in the fifth. He overheard his mother repeating Miss Butterfield's hateful recommendation to his father. "Where's the harm, Rosemary?" he responded. "They're just children. For heaven's sake, where's the harm?" Yet when Buddy was a senior and Jo Ann, her year at business college completed, already working full-time at her job, his father advised him to try dating someone else. "Play the field, Buddy. You're still young. There are plenty of fish in the sea, some lots prettier than Jo Ann Turner." What sense did that make? The two of them had never dated.

"We'll have something finer than a marriage," Jo Ann had asserted when they were still children. And they had had something better, hadn't they? A life chaste and pure, free of anger and rage and jealousy and hatred. Oh, they occasionally bickered or disagreed about trivial things. They'd quarreled. Neither was perfect. Humankind, he had been taught to believe, was not capable of being free of sin. But Buddy loved Jo Ann, Jo Ann loved Buddy. If anyone sought proof, let them examine the path their feet had worn between their two houses, more solid and permanent than any the town or country had built from cement.

He heard Jo Ann's collie, Mimi, barking furiously in the backyard. Jo Ann had named the dog after her favorite character in opera, one she especially loved to listen to on the radio during wintry Saturday afternoons. When the dog Mimi died, put to sleep because she was blind and tormented with pain from old age, Jo Ann refused to listen ever again to Puccini's opera, unable to bear the tears she shed at the poor helpless flowermaker's death. Buddy called again to the dog that was yelping as if at an intruder, but his appeal went as always unanswered.

He opened his eyes. In an alcove, hardly a kitchen, the man stood cooking over a hot plate. Daylight exposed the room's shabby plainness. Years ago, the walls had been painted a glossy pink, now faded into calico patches. Curling squares of brown and rust linoleum covered the rugless floor. On the seat of a straight-backed chair sat a black-and-white television, turned on, but soundless. He wanted to signal to Leo that he was awake, but his consciousness of his nakedness delayed his doing so until he had carefully rearranged the covers over his body.

Leo poured a honey-colored liquid from the pot into a beer mug. "Here," he said. "Drink some more of my miracle brew."

Before he accepted it, Buddy tugged on the covers, drawing them back up to his chin, but in the process exposing his feet and legs, white and shiny as soapstone or a freshly stripped hog bone. "I'm not dressed," he protested.

On the outside of the closet door, an olive drab slicker hung on a hook. When Leo removed the slicker, Buddy saw his clothes, cleaned and placed on hangers, even his long johns neatly folded. "You've been sleeping for," Leo checked his wristwatch, "just about thirty-five hours."

"That's impossible," Buddy responded testily. "I've always been an early riser. I'll want to recompense you for the cleaning of my clothes, of course."

"With what? I checked your wallet. Not much in there, old man. Not even a driver's license."

"I never learned to drive."

Leo brought the four wire hangers draped with clothes to him and lay them across the back of the couch. "Your shoes are there, by the window. Ugliest damn shoes I ever seen. I got them dry pretty good, but they're cracked bad. Wearable. Well, what you waiting for? Me to dress you?"

Buddy grimaced. "Goodness no. Do you think I might have a little privacy?"

"I don't believe you, old man. You're too proud for me," Leo said before he closed the bathroom door behind him. "Holler when you're decent."

His body ached so bad, so much worse than it ordinarily did these days, that it took Buddy even longer than usual to dress, at least twenty minutes, not counting his shoes, which required five more minutes to shove and somehow squeeze on. His back felt as if a knife had slit it from his neck to the crack in his bottom. Had his thighs ever been so sore? But the sweat he was shedding came from neither pain nor fever but shame. What was he going to do now? He hobbled to the john door and tapped on it, then settled into a chintz chair whose faded bluebirds perched on twigs as gnarled as his fingers.

Back in the room, Leo folded the bedclothes that lay piled on the couch, sat them on the floor, and stretched out on the cushions where Buddy still could not believe he had spent the last day and a half. He wished he could see a newspaper to confirm the date. What must Jo Ann be imagining about him and his absence? Was it true, as she once maintained, that there was a natural border between two people, like a river or a mountain range, that neither could cross at death? Then what was the reason for faith? As Leo maneuvered his body to find a comfortable position, the springs squeaked like a swing's chain, yet Buddy had not heard them protest once under his own weight. Leo sat back up. "So, old man," he said. "Tell me. What you want to snuff yourself for?"

"I didn't."

"The truth is powerful."

"Is it?" He had wanted to say "Leo," but couldn't. Why was the man's name so difficult for him to say? He tried it again in his head where it sounded less intimate. "Leo," he said. "I'm not clever, Leo. That's what a teacher once told my parents. Can you imagine? 'Buddy's a very sweet little boy, but we're afraid he's not very clever with the others.' Jo Ann says I'm intelligent. She's even flattered me into thinking I'm quite bright. She said just a few nights ago that I was a poet. I didn't understand. All my life I've had to let Jo Ann be clever for the both of us."

Buddy twisted a loose button on his vest. How had it survived the turbulence at sea when it came off so easily in his fingers? He tucked it into the vest's watch pocket. Out the window, he spotted a section of the boardwalk, a short stretch spared some hurricane's destruction. How slight, how shrunken, how terribly diminished the strand looked when compared with the pictures he had seen of it during its youthful glory days. For the first time Buddy noticed, to his surprise, the ugly pattern of umber scars which crisscrossed Leo's raw face. Once leaving church, Jo Ann had whispered to him that no man's face, not even a preacher's, was as truthful under artificial light as it was under the sun's. He should stop fidgeting with the upholstery. He had always been tempted to fidget when he was upset or nervous, giving himself away.

"Did you ever live in a small town, Leo? Small towns can be very . . . harsh." Buddy took as deep a breath as his sore old dry lungs admitted. "For years now the town's gossips have been saying that Jo Ann and I are really only children who grew old without ever having grown up."

"Jo Ann?"

"How strange. Here I am assuming you know all about it when, of course, you don't know a thing. Jo Ann's my friend, my best and only friend. She's dying, very painfully and slowly. She's been hiding pills so no one would notice beneath silk scarves in a bedside drawer. She's certain that they will work, but she's just as certain that she can't swallow them alone. She'd choke. 'So I need your help, Buddy,' she said. 'I need you to be brave. Just hold my hand. That's all you have to do. Just hold my hand.' " Buddy knew he ought not to cry. It would be weak in front of a strong man like Leo. Yet he wept despite himself, more copiously than he had in weeks.

Leo yanked a handkerchief out of his jeans' pocket and gently patted Buddy's cheek dry, taking particular care around the bandages. "You love her a lot."

"Yes."

"I understand."

"I'm sure you don't. No one ever has. I don't myself, not completely, not anymore."

Leo stood up, then half sat, half leaned against the sofa's broad back. "You sure are a proud old man." He crossed his brawny arms. Why hadn't Buddy noticed the tattoos before, especially the one with the lion? He wished he could read all the letters to see if they spelled a name. "My shift starts soon," Leo said. "You want to stay here for a little while longer or come to work with me?"

"Go with you, I think. I'm afraid of being alone."

"You must be hungry. I'll fix you a real meal."

It started raining again as they walked back to the diner, a cold, deliberate winter's rain without wind. Along one strip of surviving boardwalk, Buddy stumbled and grabbed on to Leo's left arm, holding it for support. Leo slowed the pace, and as they passed a dune alive with sea oats, Buddy began to tell him the story of his life.

Was Leo surprised at its uneventfulness or how quickly it could all be narrated? Never having spoken in this way to anyone before, not even to Jo Ann, who knew it so well already, Buddy had nothing with which to compare Leo's reactions. Was he boring him?

The man had saved his life. But did he want it saved? And did that fact mean he owed Leo some knowledge about the life that he had rescued? What compelled him to continue speaking when clearly there was nothing more to say? Yet he did not stop talking until they reached the sidewalk along the highway, when Leo informed him of how he had bathed him with warm water and a washcloth earlier that morning while Buddy slept. Buddy blushed, his skin hot despite the air's chill, his fingers still clutching Leo's coat.

As they entered the diner, the day cook was already untying his apron. "One lousy customer all morning," he complained, "and all she wanted was coffee and half a Danish. Half a Danish. Why you took this job is beyond me, Leo. If it'd been me in your shoes, I'd have kept hitching down to Florida. Hightail it to where it's sunny and warm all year. But me, I got a wife and a kid and a second job I'm late for now."

"Frank, meet Mr. Buddy Birnam," Leo said. "Mr. Birnam's passing through town on his way back home. Had a little accident a couple of nights ago that slowed him down a little, but he's fine now. Isn't that right, Mr. Birnam?"

"Wish I could go home now," Frank said.

"Give my best to Dorothy and Marlene," Leo said.

"Sure. When I see them," Frank said, slamming the door behind him.

Buddy's head felt hummingbird light in the diner's warm, steam-filled air. At Leo's direction, he slid into a booth, where Leo poured them both a cup of coffee. After their second cup, Leo returned from the grill with two bowls of tomato rice soup and two cheeseburgers with bacon. Buddy ate his burger with the relish of a small boy on his first outing. Between bites, to slow himself down, he found himself talking too much again. "I own a small house.

Not so much a house as a cottage, really. Cozy. But it has two bedrooms, and the yard is lovely, with several fruit trees that still bear the sweetest fruit and a pleasant pond with a little gazebo my father built next to it for shade in the summer. Only the squirrels and the crickets and the frogs make any noise at all. It's where Jo Ann most enjoys reading. I should call Jo Ann. She must be very worried. I have failed her in so many ways. This is excellent soup, Leo. Did you make it yourself? Where did you learn to cook?"

"In the army."

"I was drafted during the Second World War, but to no one's surprise, least of all mine, they refused me. I couldn't have been more grateful."

"I was stationed in Deutschland. Not a bad place, Deutschland, once you get used to all the Krauts. I stayed in six years, then quit. Knocked about for a while over there in Europe, caught a freighter back to the U.S.A., did some short-order cooking in the Big Apple, but New York got stale fast. Tried K.C. and Denver and L.A., then shipped out on the high seas. I've set foot on every continent except Antarctica," he boasted. "I've watched Indian holy men transform straw into spun gold just by capturing the sun's fire in a glass, tasted berries that ripen in the snow, smelled flowers whose perfume was too seductive for any man ever to capture in a bottle, seen birds and beasts no man has ever caged in a zoo. I could write down hundreds of true stories that no one would publish out of disbelief. This here," he said, waving his arm in a dismissive arc, "this crummy joint is just a stopover on my way to the Keys where they say the sea is like flakes of sapphire and the sunsets are red as rubies. Yes sir, Mr. Birnam. I'll be on my way soon, back on the road, free and happy."

Buddy twisted his head to look at the clock. Who was giving Jo Ann her five o'clock medication? Or was she, as she had threatened to do, already refusing it? He set his soupspoon in the empty bowl. "Please lend me one hundred and eight dollars and forty-two cents. I promise to mail you it back with all the rest I owe you as soon as I return home. You have my word."

Leo whistled. "That's a lot of dough, old man. I wish I had that kind of money."

"You don't?"

"I don't. You think I'd be hanging around this dump so long if I did?"

"Couldn't you get it?" Buddy persisted.

"Who from?"

"That man Frank?"

"He's worse off than I am. You heard the man. You never look at me when I'm talking to you, old timer. Why is that?"

"Don't I? I suppose I don't. Please accept my apologies. I imagine I discovered a long time ago that if you really look at someone, even if they are a stranger, they almost always say something to you you don't want to hear. Do you think you might call me 'old' less often, Leo? It's my impression that you're not so young yourself."

"Young as I have to be, Bud. But here's what I'm going to do." He disappeared behind the grill into a small room that might have been a closet. When he returned, he stood next to the table and counted out one hundred and twenty-five dollars. "From the safe," he explained. "But it'll be more than my ass if it's not back in there before the owner checks it next, whenever that is. He's a drunk, but he knows how to count his cash. Do you understand, Buddy? You know what I'm saying? I'm putting my faith in you, old man. I got a record." He pushed the money toward him. "Look at me."

Buddy did as he was told. "But this is theft."

"Damn right."

"I'd be breaking the law."

"There's a higher law here. We have to get you home to your Jo Ann."

"I've never broken the law before. I've never done anything illegal."

"What's taken you so long? Besides, didn't you know that offing yourself was a no-no?"

"Yes. I knew." Buddy stared down at the pile of bills. "Do you suppose you might change that five into coins so I could call Jo Ann?"

When he returned from the corner phone booth, he was hobbling slightly. Wearing a cook's hat, Leo was slicing potatoes behind the counter. "The trick in life is always to keep busy, even when it doesn't make any sense. Who's going to eat these fries? Me, myself, and I, that's who. What did she say?"

"I woke her. But she didn't seem surprised it was me. She had been waiting for my call, she said. She said, 'Don't delay much longer, dear heart, or I'm afraid I'll die cursing God.' Would you like an I.O.U. for the money, Leo?"

"Nope. Never been able to redeem one in my life. Besides, it's not my money, old man. Please don't forget that."

"My bus is due to leave in forty-five minutes."

"You going to be OK?" Leo tossed some potato slices into a wire basket and lowered it into the hot fat. "Look, old man. Buddy. You want me to go with you? All it would take is a nod from you, my hand in that cookie jar again, and the CLOSED sign on the door. Nobody'd ever find me. I leave memories," he bragged, "but not traces."

Buddy gazed at him, dumfounded. "Why would you want to do that?"

"Maybe I like you. Maybe I've got a soft spot for sad, sorry old men. Or maybe it's just because that sounds like a cute little place you have there and I could use a rest. You know what I mean? I never spent any time in a hick backwoods town. Maybe I'd like it. A new experience, worth the try. Whatever. You need some looking after for a while. It's the old story. I help you out, you help me out. A deal?"

Buddy shook his head. "How could I explain it to Jo Ann?"

"Jo Ann, Jo Ann. Jesus, Buddy, she's going to be dead soon."

"You think I'm not fully aware of that fact? How could you say such a hurtful thing to me?"

"You got to face facts. You ever face facts? The truth?"

"I should be leaving, Leo. I'm a slow walker at best, but ever since my . . . accident . . ." He turned toward the door, then shifted his body back so that he could face the counter one last time. "You've been very kind, kinder than I had any reason to expect from anyone. Pray for me, Leo."

"What for? I don't believe in God."

"Don't be ridiculous. Everyone believes in God, even when they don't particularly want to. I've tried very hard not to believe in him lately. But it seems I have no choice."

"You're a strange old bird, Buddy Birnam. It's starting to rain hard again," Leo observed. "There's a spare umbrella leaning over in that corner, left by some dude in a beamer on his way to Savannah. It's yours."

"I accept," Buddy said, picking it up off the floor and waving good-bye.

"Wait a second. Don't leave yet," Leo said. "Just one thing more." He wiped his hands on a towel, put his hat down on the counter, walked over to Buddy, wrapped his arms around him, and kissed him hard on the lips. "There," he said, stepping back.

Buddy wiped the back of his hand across his mouth. "Are you out of your mind?"

"Sure. Give my best to Jo Ann." Leo glanced up at the sky. "Jesus, what crummy weather. Don't forget that dough you owe me," he shouted after Buddy who was halfway down the walk. "You sure as hell aren't going to forget me. Nobody ever does."

As he waited in the tiny, unattended bus station, Buddy watched the door or gazed up at the clock, afraid that Leo would appear at any moment. Could a man take such liberties, should he be allowed to, just because he saved your life? How little he understood the younger generations. What did Leo mean by kissing him, a man who had never been kissed like that in his life? How could he bear such effrontery and presumption along with all else that was horrid in his life, which he was just beginning to admit to himself that he had no choice except to bear?

When, almost an hour late, the bus pulled into the station, Buddy was frantic with worry. What could he tell Jo Ann? She would expect the truth, all of it. She'd intimated as much on the phone. But hadn't they always accepted the necessity of a few secrets between them? Didn't some secrets hold you in their arms and keep you safe and good? He found a seat in an empty section of the bus near the back.

As the bus drove away, he could barely see out because of the condensation that covered the window like frost. He tried to wipe it clean with his coat sleeve before the bus reached the diner, but the driver sped up just as it passed it. Was that Leo's broad back he saw stretching as it bent over the table in the first booth? Was he serving customers?

"Oh, no!" Buddy cried out. "Driver! Driver! Please stop this bus. I must get off. Immediately!" But the bus moved only faster, the driver ignoring him.

Buddy tried to look back, but the diner's sign was no longer in view. He knew neither the restaurant's name nor Leo's last name nor the address of either. How could he mail Leo back his money? Why had he been so careful not to mention the name of the town where he had spent his life? How could he have been so stupid, stupid, stupid?

He would have liked to have blamed his old age, but old habits were as much at fault. Yet other forces seemed to be at work in him, changing him in ways he couldn't name. Would it be better for him to accept or to resist the change? "Poor Jo Ann," he whispered to himself as if speaking in confidence to a stranger.

Nearly as old as himself and wearing a cheap bonnet covered with cotton buttercups, a woman nosily stuck her head over the back of her seat to see what sort of crazy person would be sharing her ride. She shook her head like someone who had seen it all before and settled back into her seat. "Poor man," she remarked to her uninterested companion.

The comment startled him. Was he really a poor man, worthy

of her pity? Had he, in saying "Poor Jo Ann," meant to pity her? But pity could only diminish them both. Undoubtedly the end of life impoverished life. But his life with Jo Ann, his and her life together, had been rich beyond their prayers.

Leo had meant no harm. He was just being brash and vain and vulgar in that way so many people were these days. Yet Leo had been kind. His heart, Buddy was convinced, was generous and kind. Restless, Buddy adjusted his seat so it would recline, though he knew his hurting body would not let him sleep. But he did not really want to sleep. Perhaps he could bring Leo the money afterward. "After Jo Ann's death," he said aloud, trying to persuade himself of its imminent reality. What would happen to him afterward? Whatever became of him in the days soon to come, he owed it to Leo not to forget his obligation. More, kindness must be repaid with kindness. He must think of some appropriate gift.

"Old fool," Buddy said to himself. How dare he have such thoughts at such an hour? Would he betray Jo Ann? Once more he wiped the window clear of fog. But he had to go back. And if he were to delay his return to Crescent Beach, Leo's theft, his theft, might already have been discovered. Yet if he were to rush back. He cupped his hands around his eyes, pressed his nose against the pane, and gazed up into the clearing night sky. The stars in their appalling numbers rolled over him like waves.

Surely Jo Ann would understand. After he told her the whole story, she would respond without a moment's hesitation, "Oh, God's in his heaven, Buddy. He brought you back to me. His angel of mercy sounds a little rough around the edges, not someone I would like to chat with just now. But he sounds kind. You'll need someone kind, Buddy."

Then, ready, she would ask him to fill her glass with water. He would be thinking, as he was thinking now, how strangely like death kindness had come to feel to him. But he would bring the filled glass to Jo Ann anyway, just as she would expect him to do, placed next to her prettiest napkin on her favorite tray.

Thomas Glave

WHOSE SONG?

YES, NOW THEY'RE WAITING to rape her, but how can they know? The girl with strum-vales, entire forests, behind her eyes. Who has already known the touch of moondewed kisses, nightwing sighs, on her teenage skin. Cassandra. Lightskinned, lean. Lovelier to them for the light. How can they know? The darkskinned ones aren't even hardly what they want. They have been taught, have learned well and well. Them black bitches, that's some skank shit, they sing. Give you V.D. on the woody, make your shit fall off. How can they know? Have been taught. Cassandra, fifteen, in the light. On her way to the forests. In the light. Hasn't known a man yet. Hasn't wanted to. How can they know? She prefers Tanya's lips, the skin-touch of silk. Tanya, girlfriend, sixteen and fine, dark glider, schoolmate-lover, large-nippled,-thighed. Tanya. Who makes her come and come again when the mamas are away, when houses settle back into silent time and wrens swoopflutter their wings down into the nightbird's song. Tanya and Cassandra. Kissing. Holding. Climbing and gliding. What the grown girls do, they think, belly-kissing but shy. Holding. She makes me feel my skin, burrowing in. Which one of them thinks that? Which one flies? Who can tell? Climbing and gliding. Coming. Wet. Coming. Laughing. Smelling. Girlsex, she-love, and the nightbird's song. Thrilling and trilling. Smooth bellies, giving face, brushing on and on. Cassandra. Tanya swooping down, brown girls, dusky flesh, and the nightbird's song. How can they know? The boys have been watching them, have begun to know things about them watchers know or guess. The boys, touching themselves in nightly rage, watching them. Wanting more of Cassandra because she doesn't want them. Wanting to set the forests on fire, cockbrush those glens. How can they know? They are there and they are there and they are watching. Now.

Sing this tale, then, of a Sound Hill rape. Sing it, low and mournful, soft, beneath the kneeling trees on either side of the rusty bridge out by Eastchester Creek; where the sun hangs low over the Sound and water meets the sky; where the departed walk along Shore Road and the joggers run; where morning rabbits leap away from the pounding joggers' step. Sing it far and wide, this sorrow song woven into the cresting nightbird's blue. Sing it, in that far-off place, far up away from it all, where the black people live and think they've at last found peace; where there are homes, small homes and large, with modest yards, fruit hedges, taxus, juniper trees; where the silver hoses, coiled, sag and lean; where the withered arms hanging out of second-story windows are the arms of that lingering ghost or aging lonely busybody everybody knows. In that northerly corner of the city where no elevated IRT train yet comes; where the infrequent buses to Orchard Beach and Pelham Bay sigh out spent lives and empty nights when they run; where the Sound pulls watersmell through troubled dreams and midnight pains, the sleeping loneliness and silence of a distant place. Sound Hill, beneath your leaning trees and waterwash, who do you grieve for now?

Sound Hill girl of the trees and the girlflesh, where are you now? Will those waters of the Sound flow beside you now? Caress you with light-kisses and bless you now? The City Island currents and the birds rush by you now? O sing it. Sing it for that yellow girl, dark girl, brown girl homely or fine, everygirl displaced, neither free nor named. Sing it for that girl swinging her ax through the relentless days, suckling a child or selling her ass in the cheap hotels down by the highway truckers' stop for chump change. Sing it for this girl, swishing her skirt and T-shirt, an almost-free thing, instinctual, throwing her head back to the breeze. Her face lifted to the sky. Now, Jesus. Walk here, Lamb. In thy presence there shall be light and light. Grace. Cadence. A witness or a cry. Come, now. All together. And.

How could we know? Three boys in a car, we heard, but couldn't be neighbors of ours. Had to be from some other part of the world, we thought; the projects or the Valley. Not from here. In this place every face knows every eye, we thought, what's up here in the heart always is clear. But they were not kind nor good, neither kin nor known. If they were anything at all besides unseen, they were maimed. Three boys, three boys. In a car. Long legs, lean hands. In a car. Bitter mouths, tight asses, and the fear of fear. Boys or men and hard. In their car. Who did not like it. Did not like the way those forest eyes gazed out at those darker desert ones, at the eyes of that other who had known what it was to be dark and loathed. Yo, darkskinned bitch. So it had been said. Yo, skillet ass. Don't be cutting your eyes at me, bitch, I'll fuck your black ass up. It had been said. Ugly black bitch. You need some dick. Them eyes gone get you killed, rolling them at me like that. It had been said. Had to be, *had* to be from over by Edenwald, we thought. Rowdy, raunchy, no kind of class. Nasty homies on the prowl, not from this 'hood. How could we know? Three boys, fretful, frightened, angry. In a row. The burning rope had come to them long ago in willed and willful dreams, scored mean circles and scars into their once-gorgeous throats. The eyes that had once looked up in wonder from their mother's arms had been beaten, hammered into rings, dark pain-pools that belied their depth. Deeper. Where they lived, named and unnamed. How could they know? Know that those butterflies and orchids of the other world, that ice-green velvet of the other world, those precious stones that got up and wept before the unfeeling sky and bears that slept away entire centuries with memories of that once-warm sweet milk on their lips, were not for them? So beaten, so denied, as they were and as they believed, their own hands had grown to claws over the years; savaged their own skin. Needles? Maybe, we thought. In the reviling at large, who could tell? Pipes, bottles? Vials? So we thought. Of course. Who could know, and who who knew would tell? Who who knew would sing through the veil the words of that song, about the someone-or-thing that had torn out their insides and left them there, far from the velvet and the butterflies and the orchid-time? The knower's voice, if voice it was, only whispered down bitter rains when they howled, and left us only the curve of their skulls beneath the scarred flesh on those nights, bony white, when the moon smiled.

And she, so she: alone that day. Fresh and wet still from Tanya's arms, pajama invitations and TV nights, after-dark giggles and touches, kisses, while belowstairs the mama slept through world news, terrorist bombings, cleansings ethnic and unclean. Alone that day, the day after, yellow girl, walking out by the golden grayswishing Sound, higher up along the Shore Road way and higher, higher up where no one ever walks alone, higher still by where the dead bodies every year turn up (four Puerto Rican girl-things cut up, garbage-bagged, found there last year: bloated hands, swollen knees, and the broken parts); O higher still, Cassandra, where the fat joggers run, higher still past the horse stables and the smell of hay, higher yet getting on to where the whitefolks live and the sundowns die. Higher. Seeking watersmell and sheen for those forests in her eyes; seeking that summer sundown heat on her skin; seeking something away from 'hood catcalls and yo, bitch, let me in. Would you think she doesn't already know what peacefulness means, contains?

She's already learned of the dangers of the too-high skirt, the things some of them say they'd like to put between her knees. The blouse that reveals, the pants that show too much hip. Ropes hers and theirs. Now seeking only a place where she can walk away, across the water if need be, away from the beer cans hurled from cars, the What's up, bitch, yells and the burning circle-scars. Cassandra, Cassandra. Are you a bitch out here? The sun wexing goldsplash across her now says no. The water stretching out to Long Island summerheat on the other side says no, and the birds wheeling overhead, *ok, ok,* they cry, call down the skytone, concurring: the word is no. Peace and freedom, seasmell and free. A dark girl's scent riding on her thighs. Cassandra. Tanya. Sing it.

But they watching. The three. Singing. Listen: A bitch ain't nothing but a ho, sing those three. Have been taught. (But by whom?) Taught and taut. Taught low and harsh, that rhythm. Fierce melody. Melodylessness in mixture, lovelessness in joy. Drunk on flame, and who the fuck that bitch think she is anyway? they say—for they had seen her before, spoken to her and her kind; courted her favor, her attentions, in that car. Can't talk to nobody, bitch, you think you all a that? Can't speak to nobody, bitch, you think your pussy talks and shit? How could they know then?—of her forests, smoldering? Know and feel?—how in that growing silent heat those inner trees had uprooted, hurled stark branches at the outer sky? The firestorm and after-rain remained unseen. Only the lashes fluttered, and the inner earth grew hard. With those ropes choking so many of them in dreams, aware of the circles burnt into their skins, how could they know? How could they not know?

Robbie. Dee. Bernard. Three and three. Young and old. Too old for those jeans sliding down their asses. Too young for the rope and the circle's clutch. Too old to love so much their own wet dreams splashed out onto she they summoned out of that uncentered roiling world. She, summoned, to walk forth before their fire as the bitch or cunt. So they thought, would think and sing: still too young for the nursing of that keening need, the unconscious conscious wish to obliterate through vicious dreams who they were and are, have been, and are not. Blackmenbrothers, lovers, sons of strugglers. Sharecroppers, cocksuckers, black bucks and whores. Have been and are, might still be, and are not. A song. To do away with what they have and have not; what they can be, they think, are told by that outer chorus they can be—black boys, pretty boys, big dicks, tight asses, pretty boys, black scum or funky homie trash—and cannot. Their hearts replaced by gnashing teeth, dirt; the underscraping grinch, an always-howl. Robbie Dee Bernard. Who have names and eyelids, fears, homie-homes. Watching now. Looking out for a replacement for those shredded skins. Cause that bitch think she all a that, they sing. Word, got that lightskin, good hair, think she fly. Got them titties that need some dick up in between. The flavor. Not like them darkskinned bitches, they sing. (But do the words have joy?) Got to cut this bitch down to size, the chorus goes. A tune. Phat pussy. Word, G! Said hey-ho! Said a-hey-ho! Word, my brother. My nigger. Sing it.

So driving. Looking. Watching. Seeing. Their words a blue song, the undercolor of the nightbird's wing. Is it a song you have heard before? Heard it sung sweet and clear to someone you hate before? Listen:—Oh shit, yo, there she go. Right up there. Straight on. Swinging her ass like a high-yellow ho. Said hey-ho! Turn up the volume on my man J Live J. Drive up, yo. Spook the bitch. Gonna get some serious pussy outta this shit.—Driving, slowing, slowing down. Feeling the circles, feeling their own necks. Burning skins, cockheads fullstretched and hard. Will she have a chance, dreaming of girlkisses, against that hard? In the sun. Here. And.

Pulling up.—So, Miss Lightskin, they sing, what you doing out here? Walking by yourself, you ain't scared? Ain't scared somebody gonna try to get some of your skin? Them titties looking kinda fly, girl. Come on, now. Get in.

Was it then that she felt the smoldering in those glens about to break? The sun gleaming down silver whiteheat on her back? *And*

O how she had longed only to walk the walk. To continue on and on and on and through to those copses where, at the feet of that very old and most wise woman-tree of all, she might gaze into those stiller waters of minnow-fishes, minnow-girls, and there yes! quell quell quell quell quell quell the flames. As one of them then broke through her glens, to shout that she wasn't nothing anyway but a yellow bitch with a whole lotta attitude and a skanky cunt. As (oh yes, it was true, rivers and fire, snake daggers and black bitches, she had had enough) she flung back words on what exactly he should do with his mother's cunt, cause your mother, nigger, is the only motherfucking bitch out here. And then? Who could say or know? The 5-0 were nowhere in sight; all passing cars had passed; only the wheeling birds and that drifting sun above were witnesses to what they could not prevent. Cassandra, Cassandra.—Get in the car, bitch.— —Fuck no, I won't. Leave me alone. Leave me—trying to say Fuck off, y'all leave me the fuck alone, but whose hand was that, then, grabbing for her breast? Whose hand *is* that, on her ass, pressing now, right now, up into her flesh?—Stop it, y'all. Get the fuck off before—screaming and crying. Cursing, running. Sneakered feet on asphalt, pursuit, and the laughing loud. An easy catch.—We got you now, bitch.—Who can hear? The sun can only stare, and the sky is gone.

Driving, driving, driving on. Where can they take her? Where will they? They all want some, want to be fair. Fair is fair: three dicks, one cunt. That is their song. Driving on. Pelham Bay Park? they think. But naw, too many people, niggers and Ricans with a whole buncha kids and shit. (The sun going down. Driving on.) How about under the bridge, by Eastchester Creek? That's it, G! Holding her, holding, but can't somebody slap the bitch to make her shut up? Quit crying, bitch. Goddamn. A crying-ass bitch in a little funky-ass car. Now weeping more. Driving on.—Gonna call the police, she says, crying more; choking in that way they like, for then (oh, yes, they know) in that way from smooth head to hairy base will she choke on them. They laugh.—What fucking 5-0 you gonna call, bitch? You lucky we ain't take your yellow ass over to the projects. Fuck your shit in the elevator, throw your ass off the roof. These bitches, they laugh. Just shut up and sit back. Sit back, sit back. Driving on.

Now the one they call Robbie is talking to her.—Open it, he says. Robbie, O Robbie. Eager and edgy, large-eyed and fine. Robbie, who has a name, unspoken hopes; private dreams. How can they know? Will he be dead within a year like so many others? A mirrored image in a mirror that shows them nothing? A wicked knife's slide from a brother's hand to his hidden chewed-up heart? Shattered glass, regret. Feeling now only the circle around his neck that keeps all in thrall. For now he must be a man for them. Must show the steel. Robbie don't be fronting, he prays they think, Robbie be hard. Will they like you better, Robbie, then, if you be hard? Will the big boys finally love you, take you in, Robbie, if you be hard? But it's deep sometimes, isn't it, Robbie, with all that hard? Deep and low. . . . —He knows. Knows the clear tint of that pain. Alone and lonely . . . unknown, trying to be hard. Not like it was back then when *then when he said you was pretty*. Remember? All up in his arms . . . one of your boys, Darrell J. In his arms. Where nobody couldn't see. Didn't have to be hard. Rubbing up, rubbing. Kissing up on you. Licking. Talking shit about lovelove and all a that *But naw man* he said the first time (Darrell J., summertime, 10 P.M., off the court, hotwet, crew gone home, had an extra 40, sweaty chest neck face, big hands, shoulders, smile, was fine), *just chilling whyn't you come on hang out?*—so said Darrell J. with the hands and the yo yo yo yo going on and on with them eyes and *mouth tongue up in his skin* my man—: kissing up on Robbie the second time, pretty Robbie, the third time and the fourth and the *we did and he* kissing licking holding y'all two and O Robbie Robbie Robbie. A homie's song. Feeling then. Underneath him, pretty. In his arms. *Where nobody couldn't see   didn't have to be hard   kissing up on him shy shy and*   himinyou youinhim   Robbie, Robbie. Where has the memory gone? Back then, straddling hips, homie-

kisses and the nightbird's song. But can't go back there, can you?
To feel and feel. Gots to be hard. Can't ever touch him again,
undress him, kiss his thing . . . feel it pressing against the teeth and
the slow-hipped song. Black skin on skin and

*—but he was holding on to me and sliding, sliding way up inside
sucking coming inside me in me in hot naw didn't need no jimmy aw
shit now hold on holding him and I was I was Robbie Robbie Robbie
Darrell J. together we was and I we I we came we hotwet on his belly
my side sliding over him under him holding and we came we* but naw,
man, can't even be *doing* that motherfucking punk shit out here.
You crazy? You bugging? Niggers be getting smoked dusty for that
shit. Y'all ain't never seen *me* do that. Gots to be hard.—So open
it, bitch, he says. Lemme get my fingers on up in there. Awright,
awright. Damn, man, he says, nobody don't got a jimmy? This bitch
stinks, man, he says, know I'ma probably get some V.D. shit on
my hands and shit. They laugh.—He a man, all right. Robbie! Ain't
no faggot, yo. Not like we *heard*. They laugh.—Just put a sock on
it, the one they call Dee says. Chillchill, yo. Everybody gonna get
their chance.

And the sun. Going down, going down. Light ending now, fire
and ice, blue time watersheen and the darkened plunge. Sink,
golden sun. Rest your bronze head in the Sound and the sea beyond.
The birds, going down, going down. Movement of trees, light
swathed in leaves. Going down, going down. And.

Hard to see now, but that's OK, they say. This bitch got enough
for everybody here under the bridge. No one's around now, only
rusty cars and rats. Who cares if they shove that filthy rag into her
mouth and tie it there? It's full of turpentine and shit, but the night
doesn't care. The same night that once covered them in swamps
from fiery light. Will someone come in white robes to save a lightskinned bitch this time?

Hot. Dark. On the backseat. Burning bright. Burning. On the
backseat. Fire and rage.—Naw, man, Robbie, not so hard, man.
You gone wear the shit out fore I get my chance. Who said that?

Which one in the dark? O but can't tell, for all are hidden now, and all are hard. The motherfucking *rig*orous shit, one of them says. Shut up, bitch. Was that you, Bernard? Did you miss your daddy when he went off with the one your mama called a dirty nigger whore, Bernard? Was that where you first learned everything there was to learn, and nothing?—there, Bernard? When he punched you in the face and left you behind, little boy Bernard? You cried. Without. A song unheard. A song like the shadowrain— wasn't it? The shadowrain that's always there so deep, deep down inside your eyes, Bernard. Cold rain inside. Tears and tears. Then fists and kicks on a black shitboy's head. Little punk-looking nigger dumped in a foster home, age ten, named Bernard. Fuckhead faggot ass, the boys there said. The ones who stuck it up in you. Again and again. The second and the third . . . —Don't hurt me, don't!— screamed that one they called the faggot ass pussy bitch. You, Bernard. How could they know? Know that the little bitch punk scrunched up under the bed had seen the whole night and afterward and after alone? Bernard? *Hurts, mama. Daddy*—. Rain. Little faggot ass punk. Break his fucking face, yo. Kick his faggot ass down the stairs. Then he gone suck my dick. Suck it, bitch, fore we put this motherfucking hammer up your ass. The one you trusted most of all in that place, in all those places . . . everywhere? Bernard? The one who said he'd have your back no matter what. Little man, my man, he said. Smiling down. His teeth so white and wide. Smiling down. Smiling when he got you by the throat, sat on your chest and made you swallow it. Swallow it, bitch, he sang. Smiling down. Choking, choked. Deep inside the throat. Where has the memory gone? Something broken, then a hand. A reaching-out howl within the rain. A nightbird's rage. A punk, used up. Leave the nigger there, yo, they said. Til the next time. And the next. On the floor. Under the bed. Under. Bleeding under. You, Bernard.

The words to every song on earth are buried deep somewhere. Songs that must be sung, that must never be sung. That must be released from deep within the chest yet pulled back and held. Plaintive and low, they rail; buried forever beneath the passing flesh, alone and cold, they scream. The singer must clutch them to the heart, where they are sanctified, nurtured, healed. Songs which finally must be released yet recalled, in that place where no one except the singer ever comes, in one hand caressing the keys of life wounded, ravaged, in the other those of the precious skin and life revealed. The three of them and Cassandra know the words. Lying beneath them now and blind, she knows the words. Tasting turpentine and fire, she knows the words.—Hell no, yo, that bitch ain't dead.—A voice.—Fucked up, yo. The rag's in her mouth, how we gone get some mouth action now?— —Aw, man, fuck that shit.— Who says that?—My turn. My turn.—They know the words.

Now comes Dee. Can't even really see her, has to navigate. Wiggles his ass a little, farts softly to let off stress.—Damn, Dee, nasty motherfucker! they laugh. But he is busy, on to something. Sniffs and sniffs. At the bitch's asshole. At her cunt.—Cause yeah, yo, he says, y'all know what's up with this shit. They be saying this bitch done got into some bulldagger shit. Likes to suck pussy, bulldagger shit.—Word?—The phattest bitch around, yo, he says. Bulldagger shit.

Dee. DeeDee. Someone's boy. Has a place that's home. Eastchester, or Mount V. Has a heart that hates his skin and a mind half gone. Is ugly now, got cut up, but smoked the nigger who did it. Can't sleep at night, wanders seas; really wants to die. The lonely bottle might do it if the whiffs up don't. The empty hand might do it if the desire can't. What has been loved and not loved, what seeks still a place. The same hand, pushed by the once-winsome heart, that before painted angels, animals, miraculous creatures. Blank walls leaped into life, lightspeed and light. When (so it seemed) the whole world was light. But was discouraged, led into tunnels, and then of course was cut. The eyes went dim. Miraculous creatures. Where have the visions gone? Look, now, at that circle around his neck. Will he live? Two young ones and a dark girl waiting back there for him, frightened—will he live? Crushed angels drowned in St. Ides—will he live? When he sells the (yes, that) next week to the undercover 5-0 and is set up, will he live? When they shoot him in the back and laugh at the stain that comforts them, will he live?

But now he's happy, has found it!—the hole. The soft little hole, so tight, down there, as he reaches up to squeeze her breasts. Her eyes are closed, but she knows the words. *That bitch ain't dead.* How can they know? When there is time there's time, and the time is now. Time to bang the bulldagger out of her, he sings. Listen to his song:—I'ma give you a baby, bitch. (She knows the words.) Got that lightskin, think you all that, right, bitch? Word, I want me some lightskin on my dick, yo. When I get done this heifer ain't gone be *half* a ho. You know know? Gonna get mines, til you know who you dis and who you don't. Til you know we the ones in *control,* sing it! Got the flavor.—Dim-eyed, banging out his rage. Now, a man. Banging out his fear like the others, ain't even hardly no faggot ass. Def jam and slam, bang bang shebam. On and on as he shoots high, shoots far . . . laughter, but then a sense of falling, careening . . . sudden fear. It doesn't matter. The song goes on.

Night. Hell, no, broods the dim, that bitch ain't dead. Hasn't uttered half a sound since they began; hasn't opened her eyes to let the night look in again; hasn't breathed to the soft beating of the nightbird's wing. The turpentine rag in place. Cassandra, Cassandra. The rag, in place. Cassandra. Is she feeling something now? Cassandra. Will they do anything more to her now? Cassandra, will they leave you there? Focusing on flies, not meeting each other's eyes, will they leave you there? Running back from the burning forests behind their own eyes, the crackling and the shame? Will they leave you there?—Push that bitch out on the ground, the one they call Dee says.—Over there, by them cars and shit.—Rusty cars, a dumping ground. So, Cassandra. Yes. They'll leave you there.

Were they afraid? Happy? Who can tell? Three dark boys, three men, driving away in a battered car. Three boy-men, unseen, flesh, minds, heart. Flame. In their car. O my God, three rapists, the pretty lady in her Volvo thinks, locking her doors at the traffic light. In their car. Blood on the backseat, cum stains, even hair. Who can tell? It's time to get open now. Time to numb the fear.—Get out the whiff, yo.—40s and a blunt.—That bitch got what she deserved.—Those words, whiffs up, retreat, *she deserved it, deserved it*—and they are gone. Mirrored images in shattered glass, desire and longing, chill throbbing, and they are gone. The circles cleaving their necks. Flesh, blood and flame. A whiff and a 40.—We fucked that bitch good, G.—Night. Nightnight. Hush dark silence. Fade. They are gone.

Cassandra. What nightbirds are searching and diving for you now? What plundered forests are waiting for you now? The girl-trees are waiting for you, and so is she. Tanya. The girl-trees. Mama. How can they know? Their eyes are waiting, searching, and will soon be gray. The rats are waiting. They are gray. Cassandra, Cassandra. When the red lights come flashing on you, will they know? Fifteen, ripped open. Will they know? Lightskinned bitch nigger ho, went that song. Will they know? Girl-trees in a burning forest . . . they will know. And the night. . . .

Where is she, they're wondering, why hasn't she come home?

They can't know what the rats and the car-carcasses know.

Cassandra? they are calling. Why don't you answer when night-voices call you home?

Night. . . .

Listen now to the many night voices calling, calling soft, *Cassandra. Come.* Carrying. Up. *Cassandra. Come. Out* and *up.* What remains is what remains. *Out* and *up.* They will carry her. A feeling of hands and light. Then the red lights will come. *Up* and *up.* But will she see? Will she hear? Will she know?

The girl-trees are screaming. That is their song.

It will not appear on tomorrow's morning news.

But then—come now, ask yourself—whose song, finally, shall this be? Of four dark girls, or four hundred, on their way to lasting fire in Sunday school? Of a broken-backed woman, legs bent? Her tune? Of a pair of hands, stitching for—(but they'll never grow). Of four brothers rapping, chugging?—a slapbeat in the chorus? Doing time? Something they should know?

A song of grieving ships, bodies, torch-lit roads?

(—*But then now O yes remember, remember well that time, face, place, or thing: how those ten thousand million billion other ashes eyelids arms uncountable dark ceaseless burnt and even faces once fluttered, fluttered forever, in someone's dream unending, dream of no escape, beneath a blackblueblack sea: fluttered, flutter still and descend, now faces ashes eyelids dark reflection and skin forever flame: descend, descend over laughing crowds.*)

A song of red earth roads. Women crying and men. Red hands, gray mouths, and the circle's clutch. A song, a song. Of sorrowing suns. Of destruction, self-destruction, when eyes lie low. A song—

But whose song is it? Is it yours? Or mine?

Hers?

Or theirs . . . —?

—But a song. A heedless, feckless tune. Here, where the nighttime knows. And, well—

Yes, well—

—So, Cassandra. Now, Cassandra.

Sing it.

Andrew Sean Greer

THE FUTURE OF THE FLYNNS

THIS IS CHRISTMASTIME. The restaurant's air is polished with reflections from bright Italian ornaments—red spindles, wide-mouthed angels, a donkey stamped from tin—but otherwise sits unchanged. To the Amalfi's waiters, the odor of this air is ordinary, sharp with tomato and full of steam. Sometimes when the kitchen door opens, a foul waft comes through over to table 12: the scent of old mussel shells rotting in their juice. Paolo, the maître d', always puts old people at table 12 because they cannot smell anything and cannot taste anything. This evening at 12, an old man sits, folding white napkins into rabbits. Paolo keeps supplying him with the napkins. The ice coating the old man's shoulders is melting into the tweed, and he orders minestrone to warm himself. Table 7 is open for a party of five. A family.

That is the table for the Flynns. How many? Six—they have miscounted somehow. Charlene Flynn has counted her twin sons as one child. So, soon, another chair will have to be hunted up for the extra four-year-old. His name is Danny, and he will order, at the climax of the evening, a plate of "Calamari cooked in its own ink." When the boy orders this simple squid, Paolo will notice a strange horror from the adults at the table. Paolo will wonder about these looks all night, wonder what could be so terrible about a little boy's whim.

The Flynns are getting in the car. The car is still outside their house, surrounded by puffs of snow on either side, the thriftiest kind of snow. In Washington, the mayor has not allotted money for snowplows, so its fallen shapes will remain. The Flynns are all in snow jackets of artificial fibers, clutching themselves and thinking how clear and deadly the night air is—that if it drops one more degree the Flynns will freeze up like eels in a pond, caught in just these self-hugging positions of fear.

But in fact, they aren't all Flynns; two are Hagertons, Charlene's parents visiting from Georgia. Fred Hagerton is talking to Alan Flynn about the car itself, a deep-blue Dodge Dart, a used car. They are discussing the advantages of a new car, and Alan Flynn is thinking that he and his wife cannot afford it, a new car, that his whole life his family has never had a new car. Fred Hagerton drives a new Cadillac. He and his wife also cannot afford it, on his butcher's salary, but they are getting old, and when Fred went to war he promised Leona a new Cadillac one day if he lived, and he lived, and so he drives a new Cadillac.

Where is Leona? Still in the house. A small house, a first house. Mostly living room. A high coffee table sits in the middle, tiled with burnt-yellow squares, and around it are pieces of wooden furniture: a long-legged rocking chair from when the twins were babies, a dining-room chair set out for company, the lusterless leather couch with wings of teak (the great luxury of the room, the new Cadillac of the Flynns). A spider plant hangs above in a beaded macramé cradle. The walls of the room are thin and white. Paintings of abstract orange flowers cheer feebly above the couch.

Leona Hagerton, Charlene's mother, is bent over the coffee table. Her thin hair, dyed a believable red and teased into a dull hot-air balloon of lacquer, catches the fluorescent light. It becomes a glowing nest. She leans over her purse and inserts a letter. It is a letter from soon-to-be-President Jimmy Carter, her boy from Georgia. It is an invitation to his ball in Atlanta. She is bringing it to the restaurant as evidence. It is to be used in her story of why she loves Jimmy Carter so. He invites her, little Leona Hagerton who dresses so poorly that she shivers in her long coat even in the house, Jimmy Carter invites her to parties. Of course, everybody in Georgia gets these invitations.

But that's wrong. Jimmy Carter's election is in November of 1976. But the twins were born in 1970 and cannot be six. Danny cannot order the squid at six and still seem to augur an unexpected, harder life. No, the story is wrong. The twins are four. But let it go. Let her be inserting a letter from Jimmy Carter nonetheless. It doesn't matter.

Charlene is in a gray dress to please her mother, Leona. Leona has always forbidden her girls to wear red. It draws attention; it is the color of a whore. Charlene wears thick glasses and pats the heads of her twin sons. Her hair is barretted above her ears, and she is afraid it makes her nose larger. Her father, Fred, once told her she had a Roman nose: "It roams all over your face!" He always made her sing for guests. I remember that, she thinks to herself. That was how he used to be: lively and brutal.

So Fred and Leona have to be her parents, after all. They could never be Flynns.

Leona wears a pale-green pantsuit she bought at Sears. She is thin as a blade of grass. Her face is made up in pinks from Avon; she sells Avon back in Augusta, Georgia. For Christmas, she will give her daughter Avon perfume and the twins Avon Batman hairbrushes. She is worried, talking furiously about her neighbors to her daughter, though Charlene does not know her neighbors. This loud worrying comforts Leona. She would never speak of this comfort. Sometimes, she asks Fred a question—"Isn't that right, Fred?" or "What was her name, Fred?"—but he doesn't reply and she doesn't expect him to.

Fred doesn't talk, doesn't tell stories anymore, or make his daughters sing, or bring home funny strangers to dinner. In 1960, a man came to the door, holding his hat over his chest, asking to talk to Fred. Charlene overheard the news: two women had died in a car crash in Kentucky. She learned that this was her father's first family, a wife and daughter he'd left for Leona twenty years before. Charlene shouted her rage at him for keeping it a secret, this whole other family he'd abandoned as a young man. Leona left the room, but Fred took his daughter's fury. He stared at her red face and flying ponytail and began to shake. Perhaps he moved, in that moment, from the half of life when you build things to the half of life when they fall apart. Afterward, people would say he seemed "touched," perhaps had come undone. Fred hushed and became this man, this kind, silent, dopey man in the front seat, just smiling without a word.

Fifteen years from now, Charlene will leave her own family, Alan and the grown-up twins. Her father, Fred, will mail her all his butcher knives, dull and half-rusted swords. It will be her old father, the defiant one who died in that car crash, who sends them. Charlene will open the tissue paper, kneeling, put a hand to her mouth, and swallow wordless grief.

But they are all dressed up tonight!

The twins are finally speaking in their secret language, because no one else is talking to them. You would never be able to tell, but they are making up a story. It's about a green boy lost in a house and all the ghosts around him, but there's another little boy there, also green, so it's not so bad, it's never so bad, then. Here's what they sound like:

"Babba bitty boy gitta ghosty house, gitta ghosty babba round . . ."

They sound like babies.

They haven't thought yet about the restaurant, or being hungry, or being cold, or the snot drying on their noses. Danny hasn't planned that he will order the fateful squid.

But wait—why Danny? If they are twins, why shouldn't Marky order the squid? They dress alike, talk the same languages, tell the same stories. At four years old, they are each the focus of the other's world, so why wouldn't they *both* order the squid?

They are becoming different already. Marky, for instance, is very shy. He hides his red nose deep inside the fake-fleece hood of his coat. He lets Danny tell the frame of the ghost story. Marky knows the details and adds them only when necessary: a *green* boy. He likes to run very fast. He despises mushrooms—his father jokes that this is because he dropped Marky on his head as a baby.

Danny is louder, standing in the middle and yelling, *La! La! La!* until a parent notices him or Marky joins in. When he was three, he drew a picture of himself as a girl. Charlene found it. Danny got to see a psychoanalyst at only three. The man said not to worry, that Danny must have looked around him and seen only male-female couples—his parents, partners at day care, his grandparents, Donny and Marie Osmond—and thought that since Marky was obviously male, he must be female. This explanation did not dispel Charlene and Alan's worries. So the psychoanalyst gave them a book called *Growing Up Straight*.

Leona knows about the drawing and the psychoanalyst. Charlene regrets telling her about it in her own, inherited fit of worrying. And Leona is weird about it. She's told Alan that when she was a little girl, all boys of three wore frilly dresses and curled their hair. That is to say, all children did. Boys grew out of it, and girls never did, and the time to worry was later. Alan glared at Charlene during this speech. And Leona has begun on this trip to pay a lot of attention to Danny, which is exactly what *Growing Up Straight* says not to do. Charlene is going to talk to her about it.

So there is already a subtlety to the twins. There is something quiet about Marky and something dangerous about Danny. The twins are quite unaware of all this. Marky does not remember being dropped on his head, and Danny already doesn't remember the psychoanalyst or the drawing, which has been thrown away. Here's all they say: "Babba bother bitty boy bidda ghosty house . . ."

And Leona is still talking. She is telling of her neighbor who puts up green tomatoes so that this time of year all of the cul-de-sac can eat relishes for Christmas. She tells of an Indian family that moved in down the street and gave her a bottle of chutney. Leona did not know what to do with it; it was not relish. She had no interest in it. But her sewing partner, Wilma, got all excited just to see it. So Leona gave it to her, because she seemed to want it, but she feels sorry for Wilma. Wilma gets excitement only out of new and different things. But Wilma is very sad. Leona says she thinks it's fine to be brave, but it's another thing entirely to be brave and never satisfied.

Fred nods and smiles at this story. He's heard it before and likes it this time, too.

And the car turns the corner and stops. The Flynns have arrived at the Amalfi!

Now they have to get out in the cold again. There is a moment of hesitation when Leona has to choose between the cramped back-seat of the Dodge Dart and the frozen air outside. But everyone else is already outside. The twins are dancing around near the bumper, their mittens twirling from their wrists, and they have to be rounded up. Outside, the Amalfi is dark brick with an archway entrance. Dirty yellow lanterns light the side, and the windows are diamond-paned and multicolored. This, Leona thinks, is what a real Italian restaurant should look like.

The boys throw off their coats inside. They, too, are dressed up, both in ruffled shirts. Marky and Danny have wanted ruffled shirts for a whole year now, and Alan had to search all of Washington to find some. Neither parent has any idea where the boys saw them. Marky's shirt is pink; Danny's is light blue. The boys are always color-coded this way: Marky red, Danny blue. Their whole lives, the twins will claim each, respectively, in all honesty, as their favorite color.

Paolo guesses that these are the Flynns. The old man is eating his pear now, after letting the port seep in. Paolo admires the man for his imagination. Paolo walks up, smiling fiercely, with five menus. Coats are being flung onto hooks, and all of the Flynns are red-cheeked, eyebrows high as if surprised by the cold. Charlene explains that they are six. She must have counted the twins as one. Leona pinches Danny's cheek and jokes that they have almost forgot him. Danny stares at his beehived grandmother. Another waiter is sent to get the extra chair for the dangerous twin.

Again, all is Christmas inside the Amalfi. A Christmas tree studded with electric candles, the dented Italian ornaments speckling the walls with light, wicker-bottom bottles of Chianti strung everywhere. The tables spiral out from the tree: two white tablecloths draped at diagonals to each other. Paolo insists on the two cloths when he is maître d'. He saw it once in a magazine.

Leona is mildly flirtatious with Paolo. He smells her Avon perfume and can tell she has dressed up for the Amalfi. She tells him how handsome he is, even touches his cheek with a pink fingernail. And he *is* handsome; he has a Roman nose. Leona clicks her tongue when she notices that he wears no wedding ring. Don't Italian boys get married young? she asks. Paolo blushes, but under his dark skin, so no one can tell. The Anglo Flynns are blushing openly, though, blushing from the cold as if afire. Paolo doesn't answer her question but smiles and gracefully passes out the menus.

Danny and Marky are speaking in their secret language. Alan makes them stop.

Paolo has left to help the old man at table 12 get up to leave. The man says, "Back out into the cold!" and chuckles. Paolo nods.

At table 7, Fred has begun to talk. Everyone else is quiet, watching, their faces pinched with curiosity that he would speak. Even Leona is silent. He is talking about how all his family were musicians. This has come out of nowhere. He is motioning slowly with his red butcher's hands, rowing through the tin-lit air, telling of the ragged South Carolina porch of his old house and how all his brothers would wake up Sunday mornings, polish their instruments, and sit in a row to play for the people going to church. He must have been three or four, and Fred describes himself as being "no bigger than a cricket." He remembers most clearly the cedar crate of instruments and his siblings' reaching in, not for any particular one, but for whatever first touched skin. They worked with whatever they picked up—trombones and little Jew's harps, a concertina and a limberjack. They could play anything in their hands. People always came by to hear them, and Fred remembered how one day a Negro family walked up early in the Sunday morning with a viola in a case. Even Fred could tell that they were poor, poorer even than the Hagertons on their leaning, waterlogged porch. They had been left this viola by a grandfather, and not one of them had ever heard it played. And how his tall brother Furman lifted it from their hands, carefully undid the case, brought out that shining thing, and played it all morning.

Fred fingers the table when he talks. He pushes the words through his sullen lips with concentration. This is not babbling; this is the storytelling of a man who knows his quiet's coming on again. He goes on, though, tells how he was so young then, dizzy on those raucous Sundays, and by the time he was ten all his brothers and sisters had grown up, with porches and dull children of their own, had sold the instruments for flour and sugar and beer. When he tried to speak of that time on the porch with them, that happiest time, they all denied it. They said he'd made it up, made up the whole story. Their frivolous musical youth was an embarrassment, you see, a workingman's embarrassment.

Certainly, no one knows what to say to this. The tin ornaments clink in the silence. Charlene will remember this speech when the butcher knives come in the mail. It will be a time to regret things.

Luckily, Paolo comes back with a little white pad, and chattering indecision commences. Leona finally chooses the spaghetti. Her daughter has the veal scallopini, and so does Alan. Marky gets lots of meatballs, and one can see in his quiet face a joy at the thought of them. Fred is looking down at his empty plate. Leona orders spaghetti for him, too. He doesn't like any other Italian food, she explains to Paolo. Fred says nothing to protest.

And Danny, Danny has the menu propped up in his chubby fingers. He tilts his head right and left, with just the pink tip of his tongue peeking out between his lips. He is concentrating. He sees a line that says, "Calamari cooked in its own ink," and he cannot imagine what it could be. Certainly nothing his grandmother has ever cooked for him, or his mother. Maybe he imagines a fiddler simmering in the broth of his own song. He puts the menu down on the white double cloths.

New silver is sparkling in Paolo's hand. Danny opens his mouth, and Paolo can see there on that pink tongue, rolling like a beveled ruby bead, a prophecy.

William Haywood Henderson

WALKER

WALKER AVARY CROUCHED in the lee of boulders, in the violet bloom of thistles. Through the long cold morning and on past noon, fog reached flat across San Francisco Bay, the water jade in the breeze. He ate wild strawberries. Far below, an acre of tents with their even spacing, their sameness, seemed a plot of graves in the crosshatch of buildings. To the south, in a forest of ruined masts, the old ship Rockwell, with its sides finally given way and its rigging gone, had settled onto the bay's sediment. Four years ago, Captain Avary had abandoned the Rockwell, taken a new ship, and continued west on the Japan route, sailing on from this city with barely a pause, leaving Walker behind.

And through his first winters in the city, when a storm set the waterfront into rhythm, Walker would climb out from one of those ships to the next, find a family in a deckhouse, laundry in the rigging, dark pools in the holds, rank flotsam. On the Rockwell, the farthest ship out from solid ground, he would balance at the stern, above the chop, safe in his oilskin, his face chilled, his ears deafened by the rustle of his hood and the pop of rain. Out there was Yerba Buena Island, the rush of tide mixing salt and less salt, and the far shore, the hills corralling whatever clouds couldn't rise. He knew of desert beyond the hills, of mountains; he knew of the destination of the train he saw moving against the distance, the smoke and steam, the luxurious speed. The train had broken all the way through, east to west to east, and been spiked at Promontory, and now there was nothing to keep the land from filling. He would force his way into the Rockwell's captain's quarters, sit through the evening, and listen for rats in the hold. The glass still kept out the wind, the hull still tight enough, then, to suspend all that dark weight in the swaying storm. Shut in that space, with the silk rotted, with the brass and crystal gone, pried off and carried away, Walker would sleep.

He finished the last of the strawberries, made the descent through the thistles, along the creek, and entered among the buildings. After a long ramble with the buildings rising taller, the ornate shadows of cornices and false fronts swinging slowly with the sun, he turned onto Montgomery Street, to number 121, in through the door. The clerks were all busy muttering and shuffling about in the closing-time doldrums. From a table he picked up a pale blue tourist pamphlet and waved to young Mr. Stanwood, the slick-haired clerk who had chatted him up about graded inclines, chasms and trestles, and the elegance of the Pullman Palace car. *Comfort, Luxury, and Safety Combined. Sleeping on the Pioneer Route.* He stepped back onto the street, sheltered himself in a doorway, and opened the pamphlet, folding out the map to a narrow slice of the continent from Boston to San Francisco, with the web of rails to the east, and to the west the vast squares and angles of open pastel cut only by the single rail line and a few spurs and stage routes and lonely roads. Wyoming Territory, the clean pink square, with hardly a town but along the rail, hardly a road, and the great clusters of mountains, the geysers, Indian country. *Shoshonees and Bannacks. Sweet Water. Heart Mt. Stinking R. Diamond Field. Wind River.* From his back pocket he pulled his old copy of the pamphlet, dropped it on the ground, and replaced it with the new.

He crossed Montgomery, on toward Market, then west to Atkinson Mercantile, around to the alley and the thick metal door. Working his key in the lock, he was into the stockroom, shelves rising with bolts of wool, plates, silk, enamel bowls, powder, bottles of scent. He slipped past a door and its opening toward patrons and windows, moved beyond the light, ran his fingers until he felt a stack of tins—oysters in smoky oil. He palmed three tins and slid them into his pockets.

Along a quick aisle back toward the door, he paused, crouched where he could look through the shelves and into Mr. Atkinson's office. Atkinson was at his desk in his long black suit, his eyes blue in that white untouched face, not a hint of ruddy, the beard black and clipped, the hair black and oiled. Beyond him, pushing her mass of coffee curls back from her brow, Miss Haugen laughed, the lamp warming the side of her face, her shoulder. Walker had met that young woman last week at a party at Atkinson's house, an anniversary celebration—twenty years ago Atkinson had made his first killing, selling ten crates of cookware from the back of a wagon at the wharves, and got himself started from almost nothing, with the city barely settled. And now he'd constructed that house of his, the number etched in glass, and the lamps all lit for the party, hot white overhead and on the walls. The young ladies watched Atkinson talk, watched him tip a couple into the first steps of a waltz. Walker had tried that night to think himself into Atkinson's stance, the bulk of chest and thighs in the black evening wool. A sideboard held platters of great round rolls dusted with flour, pastries glazed with yellow sugar, pink beef, a long fish with its serrated mouth gapped in an almost-grin, its eye blue. Beside the food, Atkinson took Walker by the elbow and drew him round to face the girl, saying, "Miss Teresa Haugen, this is Walker Avary. He is a young man you might want to know someday. Works my merc as if wages were the least of it. For the love of the work? Is that it, Walker?" The girl laughed, her mouth an exquisite crooked rose and delicate teeth, and she reached and pressed fingers to Walker's neck as if testing his tendons, and he said, "I work for you, Mr. Atkinson. Yes, sir," and he moved beyond them, out the glass doors to the terrace, the iron railing, darkness. Turning, he watched the dance slowly gather each guest until only the servants held themselves off the rhythm, and then even the servants were caught by the nearest swirl or grasp and drawn in. The music played on. Walker let himself back in and ate a roll, took a sweet bite of flaky crust, berry, pocketed the fish server, the long-handled sterling like a heavenly trowel, palm fronds hammered along its surface, and he found the front door, out, and down the stone steps.

Walker rose from his crouch in the stockroom, left Mr. Atkinson and Miss Haugen, and was outside, into the alley, the metal door solid again in its jamb. He threw his key high in that gap of brick walls, and the key lost its shape against early evening, rattled on the roof of the laundry behind, slid into the rain gutter, and remained there twenty feet above the muddy drainage.

Gray had blown in. Taking to the deeper streets where the buildings might block the cold, where the horses raised their heads and glared white-eyed, stamped against the tension of the reins, he hurried toward the Mission, finally saw the squat white church ahead in the fog, and entered through those thick walls. It was almost dark but for the votives at the rear, almost silent. He came forward in the narrow space. The beams far above, the design hatched out in fading dye, the Dolores altar with its faces invisible but for the uneasy glint of eyes or a bit of ungrounded gold, a staff raised. The high yellow windows filtered the rush of cloud, leaving him no sense of the floor. He thought he might reel, the building adrift, but he continued, and then he touched the altar, steadied himself. He found the wood cool and almost soft, as if it had dried there a thousand years and lost its core—but it was no older than the country. He remembered the face of the Lord on a locked panel—he made out the eyes, pushed at what he guessed to be the bearded chin, and heard the lock rattle. With his pocket knife, he forced the lock, heard the faintest squeal of hinges, and he placed a tin in that black space and closed the door again, knowing he could not lock it. "Walker Avary," he said, repeated, and then listened for movement, for anyone he might have missed in the dimness. Nothing. Turning, he saw the candles far at the back, their heat trifling with the darkness beneath the choir loft. He came down through the space, found a cache of unlit candles, and took a few. His heart still raced from the ground he'd covered that afternoon, and he hurried from the Mission, accelerating until his pace matched his pulse again.

Beyond open stretches, uneven blocks of housing, he came to a row of storefronts that leaned toward the puddles. He clattered along the sidewalk, in through a door, into a crowd. Forcing himself among the taller men at the bar, he gave his order, felt the heat of them all against the backs of his hands, felt the sudden pain of noise in the curves of his chilled ears, waited in the smell of damp wool.

Even with the railroad, still these men had almost all come round by way of the sea—French, Irish, German, Russian—the whole range, and they all spoke at once. A great Spaniard tossed back a drink, and the drops that escaped his lips ate clean trails through the grime on his chin. Walker knew them all. He had seen these men bathe, nearly bathed with them, in an establishment a few blocks away. In the wood-slat room with the boilers, they each stripped and waited, stepped into the tubs of water gray with soap and heat. One after another. With Walker waiting until the crowd cleared, until no one opened the door to the entry hall, and then he stripped and submerged himself to the neck, the leavings of someone else so close to his mouth—the grime collected in crevices, soil of the city, sweat, flecks of wood and stone and brick, the smear of love. He looked down through the water, slowly ran his fingers over his limbs and under, where the week's work had settled, watched new men come in through the door, watched them so casually drop their shirts, trousers, tatters of long johns, and step through the steam, submerge, laugh, move on. He might wait a long while until he was alone in that room again, and then he slid deeper into the tub, allowed the water to cover him completely, his head back, his hair a loose wavy flow, and he opened his eyes, opened his mouth, swallowed a gulp, came up with his eyes stinging, his mouth sour and intense. He dried himself. He entered back onto the street. For hours, he tasted the ridges and joints of the men, the slab of haunches, heat of straining muscle, direction, precision. For days, he felt the fine coating on his skin, smelled it, knew it kept him safe.

Most evenings, he was with them all in that saloon. The men ate and drank together, might as well have been trapped together on a nighttime voyage for all the time they spent outside those walls. Through the windows onto the street there were never more than specks of light passing. What must the place seem to these men— the plank tables, the yellow walls burnished brown with smoke, the sound of rain on the stovepipe above, plates of hot food, whiskey, a back room with bunks to let. Someone sang, mournful and struggling, words of a vessel, a storm, and finally the voice was lost and someone demanded the proprietor buy a piano. Someone slept in a corner, his coat still buttoned up to his throat. Someone stepped into the darkness of the back hall. They came in from the city, they took their way out into the city again, followed the streets in long looping rambles toward their return. Walker saw a woman come in from the alley, lean there at the door to the back stoop with her skirts up, late at night, and a man had his way, and then another man. As Walker paused before stepping out into the night and across the alley to his own place, he heard from the bunk room, more than once, when there weren't any women, sounds that had little to do with sleep. The building had a strong smell of humid forest, the building was shabby, unsteady, might fall in a few years to be replaced with finer construction, sharper details, the building was completely without foundation, but it locked them together, locked them away from something.

Walker drank his whiskey in tiny sips, holding it beneath his tongue, burning away the day's great tour, the ground he had covered, unfinished yet. The rowdy laughter, held in this box of heat. He spun a coin across the bar, fought his way toward the back, into the kitchen.

"Frank," he said. A tall young Chinese looked up from the stove, from the skillet of eggs. Walker handed him a tin from his pocket, hoisted himself onto the counter near the sizzling fat. "I got time to eat one more of your meals. Make it enough to keep me going."

"Avary," Frank said. "Green River City. I'll tell you again you have the right idea." He slid the tin beneath his apron, handed Walker a cup of coffee, a plate of ham and molasses. "Smart boy. I'll follow you soon, if I got a brain."

"Your brothers expect me, right?"

"I wrote them three times to tell them when you come and what you need."

"Yes. They'll know what I need."

"They know what any man needs in a place like that. All desert, mountains, hostiles. They tell me buffalo and hot stinking springs. Such a big land. They are ready to get you started."

"You didn't tell anyone round here, Frank, that today is it for me?"

"Tell who? I told my girl and she said, Frank, I want us to go, too, and I say tomorrow, or a week, or next year, and then we see my brothers in Green River City."

"Not a week or next year, not for me." Walker finished the meal, slid down from the counter, and gave Frank a sharp sideways hug—the bony angles of the boy, the rich film of cooking, his short black hair bristling against Walker's temple. "Find me if you want, Frank, but I don't know how."

On out the back, he leaped across the alley, beneath an arch, through a brief musty almost-tunnel, and into his room. He'd already swept the bare floor, already cleaned the high window. The evening light was falling west into the ocean. He lit the candle stub on top of the stove. He rolled his mattress off the four crates it lay upon, shifted his shadow around the candlelight, opened a crate, and wedged the last tin and the Mission candles among the other goods, and with a pencil he added them to the list folded on top. He lay down on the crates, watched the sky through the window, the last pink streaks of sun rushing through the clouds.

A long while and someone knocked at the door. He awoke to a square of black sky, a streak of illuminated cloud falling through. The candle had burned away. He opened the door. He saw the darker shapes of two large men against the darkness of the buried walkway. "Here," he said, and they came in past him as if they could see. "Those. There's a manifest for each." They hefted a crate and already they were out the door. He followed. They slid the crate into the back of an enclosed van, returned for the others, loaded them, then stepped up into the van, closed the door behind, and soon a light brightened the tiny side window and Walker heard shuffling and low voices. One of the pine lids dropped.

He left them there, headed beneath the arch and back into his room, stood at the center, listened to the wind rattle the casement. He found his leather case, turned it on its side, and sat on it, waiting. After a while, he thought he heard voices from above, from beyond the walls, the saloon across the alley muffled and shut off from the cold. If he filled his lungs, he could taste the city's fumes—gasses, paint, standing water, and beyond it all, the ocean. He could hear people passing on the street at the head of the alley, he could almost hear bricks stacked, the grass on the hills ready to brown toward summer. And he heard the horse breathing, waiting to lurch that van through the ruts, off into the street.

Unhooking his jacket from the back of the door, he came out, setting the lock. The building was dark above him. No one watching. He stood there at the edge of the alley, gripped his leather case against his chest, waited for the men to emerge from their work.

They were attaching a value to each item. He had no idea what sum they would come out with—there were the new items with nothing but his own touch to mar their clarity, and then the items he had acquired, balanced on his palm, examined to see if the owner had left a trace of oil from the fingertip, a blush of powder, sheen of perfume, a sense of what it had meant, what silhouette its absence would leave in the owner's memory.

Sterling silver fish server, candlesticks, tea tray, sugar bowl. Other odd silver—spoons, butter knives. Pearl necklace. Stack of cook pots. Scarves. Five leather-bound Bibles. Muffin tins. Ivory comb. Black lacquer and mother-of-pearl picture frame with its etching of a fat-faced girl on a lace pillow. Tins and jars of olives, oysters, caviar, snuff, opium. On and on.

Not an easy task, all those four years in the city, to collect four crates of worthy goods, to adjust and discard gradually to improve the value. Some of the merchandise was easy, lifted from a shelf, drawn from a blanket on the beach, but a special item might be a week or more in the getting. The hills were stacked with lit windows, some of them open squares, some draped and shuttered until only obscure patterns of light gave out. It was toward these darker windows that he had made his way. Perhaps he'd first spotted the window from the crest of another hill. He would try to memorize the pattern of buildings that surrounded it, to imagine the view that that window itself opened onto. He shifted slowly through the streets until that view took shape and he knew that through the next alley that world would rise. It did. He was below the window, saw the shuttered pattern illuminated with the light it constrained. He leaned there, ear against the clapboard, and listened. He heard nothing but the sounds of the city—wagon wheels, the hiss of guttered water—until he placed his palm against his outer ear. Then, in the barest increments, the interior emerged.

The men came out from the van. Walker would take whatever they offered—their reputation was too dark for an argument—he hoped they would be fair. "Very good, sir," one of them said, and he handed Walker a roll of bills. "There are many useful beauties in your collection. We thank you." They returned to the van, climbed up front, took the reins, and the wagon rattled into motion.

Walker followed, turned another direction, away through the streets, across the hills. Lights in the windows, lace shadows, flames in glass globes, and the black void of the bay spreading below, beyond, strings of faint light girding the nothing. He came to the waterfront and caught the last ferry to Oakland.

From the stern he watched San Francisco recede. Beneath his feet, through his hands on the rail, the engine's throb increased. The whistle blew, and with the echo the square ranks of windows on the hills seemed to dim for a brief flicker. Already the pathways between those buildings seemed impossible—years of diving through those deepening canyons as if he knew the place, but now it would continue without him, continue toward stranger complexities.

Before the city faded to a faintly glowing strip, he saw the grave of the old boats. Four years since he'd sailed round by the Strait of Magellan, ten months on that ship tarred with age and streaked with the whiteness of salt and sun. The ship had seemed hardly seaworthy, but it had kept on lurching toward the next crest.

Walker could have come round by way of the Isthmus of Panama, could have ridden an oxcart through the jungle, but he'd heard tales of crumbling bungalows lined with the sick. The heat wraps a man till he's ready to peel his skin away. Malarial fever. Cholera. At night, the lushness of the rotting green takes down even the stars in the weight of its noise.

The strait had been a safer risk than Panama, so in his nineteenth year he had come out from the forest to the Boston waterfront and boarded the Rockwell for the ocean voyage round the tip. They made ports in Carolina and Rio, and then on south through open sea. The air seemed to draw ice from their lungs as they neared the strait, the waves took them into their troughs and nearly flipped them back out, the birds seemed high and buffeted in their gray passage. And then they cut in from the open, and the dark green land guided them, protected them as much as any mound of rock could protect a ship from the untold rage of ice to the south.

The Strait of Magellan was cold and incomprehensible—islands, mountains, blind gaps. The dark Fuegians pursued the ship in their canoes, shouting "Yammerschooner" and begging for scraps. At night, by the moon, the ship sailed on through the narrows, no sound of bird or animal. A storm set them to anchor in a cove, and along with the lines of sleet came the occasional arrow from the trees—a stone point, lodged in a plank, was gathered the next morning as a souvenir. A small steamer passed, west to east, rocking and unsteady with its paddle wheels, heading for somewhere, its smoke fogging the channel, its whistle full and clear. The oystercatchers startled from the shore. The otters rolled. The condors hung black against the fast underside of the clouds. And then Cape Pillar and the Pacific. Walker stood in the lee of the deckhouse and watched that rocky end-place recede—the strait was nothing but a scattered puzzle, flooded by sea and storm, a moment of hushed steepness at the end of the world.

The Rockwell went skylarking, the ranks of square sails set straight to the royal, out to the stunsails. The passengers crowded on deck, shifted from sunlight to bellowed shade. Albatross. Driftwood. In the hold, weighing the ship steady, were cheese, shovels, dark bottles of champagne. Even whale oil.

Captain Avary called Walker into his quarters. Whichever way the sun wheeled beyond the glass, the captain's bulk was a shadow against the white walls. He was a tall man, broad and soft, a strong man, his face red and heated. They looked over the charts laid out on the table. Walker pointed to the islands lost in the blue and white, and the captain found a name for each, explained how you aim for a speck a thousand miles away, how you slowly reel that land in until you're in danger of busting your keel on its sharpest edge. "Such a joy when you've arrived," he said. "Such a pleasure of scents. It is what you've anticipated, but you didn't know you'd anticipated it."

"Someone has found each of these places?"

"Wouldn't be on the map otherwise. But some places have been more found than others. That's what makes the journey worth the danger—eventually you'll travel far enough to find yourself alone." He sat Walker on the red pleated-silk settee, said, "You're good company," and rummaged for treats in a cabinet.

Walker accepted the hard maple candies and sardines. "How long you planning to stay in San Francisco, sir?"

"I can't say. I might tighten this ship up, or I might get another. There's value in this cargo. I might keep going to the Orient."

"I could go with you. I could sign on, if you want."

"Oh, I don't know—you're no good in the rigging, and you wouldn't want wages for chores around my cabin or following passengers with a bucket. You're a young man, Walker."

"I guess you'll find a lot of money in the Orient. These quarters won't be nothing next to what you'll have. I'd like to see that."

"Yes, I'll do all right, but you're set for something else. Get some muscle on these skinny bones." He sat beside Walker, pinched his arms. "You'll do better than locking yourself in a little hold like this. I'm sure."

Walker inhaled the captain's brandy breath, held it in his lungs, let it hiss away. He watched the captain's eyes swirl with the window light, those eyes black and without focus, deep beneath the brow, the thatch of graying hair above the sheen of his forehead, nearly sun-stroked.

The captain was right—Walker was almost always unbalanced and aching from the sea. But, still, he wanted the sensation of moving on, of arriving at a sheltered place after months or years of approach through the empty. In the captain's quarters, he found maps of North America, and he folded them, slid them into his shirt, felt them a slight, nearly weightless irritation until he could bring them out, flatten them, trace them under candlelight, alone for a moment or two. The longer he stared, the more clearly the routes emerged, and from where the routes ended he began to guess at the trails, or the lack of trails, and the shape of the horizon, and the number of years it would take for that space to fill, finally.

From an anchorage off a safe, deserted shore, the crew rowed in, landed, and began rolling water barrels up a creek. The ladies stepped into the last foaming edge of the breakers, up toward the dry sand, shook out their hems, and started this way and that, leisurely along the white, looking for shells or a place to sit and watch the men. Walker followed the line of fresh running water across the beach, through the dunes, for a gradual mile of stiff grass and windblown husks of reed, onto the first rocky steepness. The creek carved beneath the lay of the slope, the sound of cool among the flat boulders. He looked for a path but found none. Was this place too hot for men? Not much but cactus, nothing quite green enough to eat. Turning back a moment he saw his shadow stretch far below him, a gray unformed line cut by the black creek. The land reached on toward the ship, the three black masts and yards and booms and furled canvas like a clutch of stanzas afloat in that near blue, a song he'd almost lost in the heat, on solid ground.

He stepped away. The dirt had been packed hard by the sun. Then he was over a lip and faced a wall of rock, water dripping from the seams into a pool as square and stone-lined as if it had been constructed, admired, abandoned a millennium ago, all decoration scoured away by wind and heat. Near the pool was a stretch of tangled green—berry and date. And above, the broken brown hills held the sky from descending and washing the day as white as the white sun.

He undressed and stood at the water's edge, stepped off, submerged, and found the bottom—cobbles of slick round stone. Holding himself beneath the surface, he drifted between earth and air, the sun cooled by the dense water. He kicked, breathed, swam away from his body's salt, the sea's salt. The rock wall sheened with water, channeled by the crevices, dribbling small disturbances. If the water fed this pool, this brief bit of vegetation, it might feed richer hollows farther in. Perhaps this trickle had been a river, its power captured by lakes, by chilled caves, by the windings and dead ends of those sharp hills. That's where men would live—farther in. If he paused long enough, he might find a way to survive here, might find that the cobbles beneath his feet were not stones but turtles. He climbed from the pool. The sun left the hills. The light reflected and waved across his whiteness.

Valuable cargo, he thought. Gain an advantage toward something. He was small, he knew, and not overly strong, but he could get some muscle, get some cargo. He pinched at his shoulders, arms, ankles.

He stepped into the undergrowth. A spine pierced his sole. Gathering blood on a fingertip, he traced the word Avary down his abdomen, painted a stripe down the sunburned limp of his sex and felt it stir a bit, painful. He dove again, left his blood behind, and as he climbed out and started dressing he watched his blood drift on the surface of the water, slowly toward the outlet, over the edge. He followed down the slope. How fast was the water? If the crew was still filling a final barrel, would they take on board a bit of his blood, serve it with the next soup or coffee, swallowed by the captain, held inside?

As the ship moved on with the wind, he found the dark corner of a hold, peeled away his clothes again, and let the cool air soothe his burn. The heat was centered in his gut, in his groin. Leaning against the damp planks, he tried to hold himself still, to see where he was headed. Long after dark, when there was nothing left of the voices from above, he came up through the passages to the captain's door, let himself in, heard the rumble of Avary's breath as he slept in that soft white berth carved and trimmed and ideally placed in the curve of the wall. There was only darkness. He stood at the small thick squares of the window, hoping the glass would magnify the light of the stars, but the white specks swayed and lurched, leaden. If he stared long enough, he might make out the crests of the swells, but they would be unbearably steep, unbearably the same. There—the moon was rising, broad and red—he saw crest after crest cutting across the bark's progress. He turned in that blood light and looked through his own shadow. The room clinked with crystal, richer and tighter than any room he'd known. And the captain—stripped in the heat, his chest heavy, hairy, and the arms like great careless constructions of strength. Walker claimed no surname, so on that day he took the captain's—Avary, of French lineage. He balanced his way across the room, came to the berth's embellished rail, hoisted himself up, and without seeming to stir from his dreams, the captain took him under his arm, let him sleep there without trouble, and then the sun came round again through the waves, and the captain awoke and sent him to fetch breakfast.

They sailed in through the Golden Gate, through a wall of fog that had come up of a sudden and robbed the sight of the headlands and the sunlight beyond. They heard the ocean tear at the rocks, the sea lions cry, and then they were free of those lazy clouds. The hills were green, the settlement scattered across the knobs, hidden away from the endless Pacific.

Scott Heim

DEEP GREEN, PALE PURPLE

HAD GOD STRETCHED his gentle giant's fingers across the dustpaths of our road, across our nighttime porch, to open in one twist of the wrist the entire south front face of our house—walls, windows, and doors out-turned together like a casket or tiny portaled dollhouse— and had God peered into our exposed rooms for inventory, for study of secrets, he would have seen this: the red reclining chair, empty, with the seat, my father's seat, sprung and threadbare; the television, still warm but now silent and dark; sun-starched curtains sleeving windows tinted a paranoid's shade of gray to allow no spies, little light; my father sleeping alone in his room; my mother sleeping, alone and fumy with booze, in hers; money, hidden money, worry and skimp, the rolls of coins and rubber-banded bills stashed in decades-old cigar boxes, in tobacco tins scrubbed shiny long ago by my grandfather, now soiled blackly green with the soil of money; invoices and bills, filed, from the orchard store; the Bible on the bookshelf, for two generations unstudied; the cracked cement square beneath the potbelly woodstove where my brother once constructed and Krazy-Glued a wee warped cabin of Popsicle sticks, then set it ablaze (the ash-black scar remained still, and I doubted he'd forgotten my father's elm-switch punishment); the blue bowl of apples on the table, red skins freckled with hazel, one bitten by my mother during a dead-of-night drunk, her white bite time-tainted to dark umber; the unsmiling wall portraits of my father's parents; the hard water from the faucets, with its acid, eggy smell, never running long enough to be altogether hot; damp socks, most snagged or darned with snarls of thread, filed on the couch and chairs to dry; and last, back there, our bedroom door, shutting Paul in, me in, now closed and quiet and black.

But tonight, if the meddling, gigantic God had opened that door, had overturned and shaken the room to search and search, he could not have found us. Secretly we had escaped. Riled by the heat, my brother and I had outwitted sleep to slip from the house in the calmest hour of night, armed with our pillows, deserters for the forbidden cool of the backyard. It was after two; two-thirty, perhaps. We lay side by side on grass laced lethal with sandburs and chiggers. Somewhere up there hovered stars, mysterious glittering planets, a jet plane sailing much too swiftly with its high, winking, fairy-tale light, but we saw none of it, lulled only by an occluded dark, a threatening storm, a sky flimsy and thrilling as a promise.

Beside me, Paul lay storklike in his sleeper flannels. A scatter of blond hair furled free from the edges of the ragged red stocking cap; I placed my hand there. "It's getting long," I said.

"But I want it longer. In a little bit I'll be able to put the bangs behind my ears. Miriam says only four inches more until I've got enough for a ponytail." Miriam Crowhurst was our neighbor, a stout-set black girl Paul's age, conspicuously outcast in our small-town school, but still his best friend. I knew she had taken to styling his hair, tucking it into his cap to prevent our father from noticing. Paul had told me their fears of some future midnight when the broad-shouldered shadow might slip inside our room: the mouth crooked victorious, the bend toward the bed, the scissors' staccato glint.

We told ourselves we loved him; a son should be mired in love, devoted. Sometimes, though, the love felt proximate to hate, and sometimes further the hate overtook, leaving Paul, me, airless and trembling. Under him like a curse: steering the tractor, rotary-motion, through the orchard; plucking his apples from trees to snuggle them into whichever basket he designated; sidearming the bruised or wormholed to the sky. The coming shutdown of autumn meant enduring his orders and rules. It meant his imminent birth-day, so important: his fiftieth. Older than our mother by a decade and a half—shouldn't this day be important, she'd asked, shouldn't we surprise him real special? Octobers previous, Paul and I had searched racks at corner drugstores, our mother standing patiently with the dollar bill. Cards with photographs of racehorses and stock cars, cartoon drawings of burly policemen, all-star wrestlers, life-guards. But the greetings inside proved misdirected and false. "Daddy," some began, but we'd never called him daddy. Others muted us with "love": disqualified. In the end, our mother chose for us. No sentiment, no singsong poem, best suited this man we flanked at the dinner table, in the apple truck, whose questions bloomed lumps in our throats, whose daily fieldwork had turned his eyes deepset and black, his fingerpads hard as thimbles.

The wind surged and stilled and surged again, smelling of rain, rustling the bowed heads of roland grass and shivering shadows from the trees. I crept one leg closer to Paul, aimed my voice for his ear. "Pretty soon it'll be lots colder," I said. "We can take down the big brown blanket again."

"Nope. The stuffing keeps coming out. If Dad was smart, he'd throw it away."

The blanket was my favorite, and its smell was set permanently in my brain, easily conjured, that fragrant peppery warm of its fleece, early-winter mornings, oozy in-and-out of slumber with my brother beside me, chrysalised, lapsed within a dream, both of us snuffly and dulled with first colds. Its borders wore patches from one of my mother's faded gingham skirts. I couldn't imagine spending January or February nights without it, and to sway Paul's opinion I grasped for something untrue. "Mom fixed it," I said, "last spring. She sewed it up, so we can't get rid of it."

He huddled closer to his pillow. "I'd rather freeze my feet all night than wake up with that fluff all over us."

At that I sat up, leaning even with his knees. "I wouldn't let them get cold." In two quick tugs I shucked the socks from his feet. This was ritual: sometimes, late nights before sleep soothed blackly in, I would gather Paul's feet to my chest and massage them. His body swiveling sideways, head and arms dangling over the bed, Adam's apple pulsing as he swooned. I adored it, slaving for him, so again, in tonight's backyard chill and darkness, I brought his feet to my lap. My fingertips bridging the toes, my palms aligned with arches soft-skinned and curved delicate as a girl's. Kneading and pressing the callused heels. Sometimes Paul made little moans, but tonight, as I began my intricate aggression, he knew to stay silent, careful not to wake our parents.

For a medley of minutes the clouds broke, and between them, nobly, the moon appeared: full, as the kitchen calendar predicted, a knob of bone dragging its white weight across the sky. It shone on the parallel wires of backyard clothesline. On the sheets and pillowcases that quivered there like souls of the orchard's ghosts. On the pair of rusted trash barrels, anchored in the sand, away from the grass, filled with the ashes from past tandem days. And on Paul and me. I resumed rubbing, rubbing. Then the clouds again dressed the light, and from far behind our field came the bark of Dusty, the Crowhursts' pepper-haired German shepherd, faintly lonesome.

"I'm scared," I told Paul. "The other day I was in the orchard and something came after me. Back by the last rows. A ghost. I could hear it breathing."

"Matt," said my brother, using my real name now instead of

"Maggot," the nickname given me by my father. "There's nothing back there. No ghosts." And, softly: "I'll protect you."

Looking down, I noticed that the nails on Paul's toes were clipped perfectly and colored ten colors that under the moon-blazed clouds seemed ten separate hues of purple. I didn't have to ask. Miriam had done this before, had streaked Paul's hair with wash-off dye, had painted his lips and nails in stripes and glitters and swirls. When our father traveled, Miriam sometimes visited, and after she left I would find remnants of dress-up clothes she'd brought, a trashcan of tissues smudged with mascara. I knew if our father discovered these secrets he would brand Paul a sissy, and Miriam a filthy nigger. But Paul kept his games confidential, and I, Maggot, didn't mind: my knowledge was a thirteen-year-old's knowledge, without upshot or bias, and I was nowhere near our father, not even close, caring less what my brother created and daydreamed behind bolted doors with his silly chubby dark-skinned girl.

"That's enough," Paul said, moving his feet away, retrieving his socks. "Much obliged, sir." As I eased back beside him, a wet flicker brushed my face. The first hint of rain. Wind hit the tree limbs to launch their pinnate leaves, scattering, swooping upon our make-shift bed like bats. Soon the rain would fall fully upon us. But we would never surrender: we would brave the hot or cold, the dry or unsufferably wet. We had no mother or father; we were nomads, drifters from town to purgatorial town, sleuthlike, rash, needing no one.

Paul put one arm between his pillow and the grass and turned to face the house. The hair shook from his shoulder and revealed, at the height of his spine, a pimple, beaded exquisitely white. Soon silence reigned, but I longed to stay awake, wanted Paul to keep speaking, to unravel one of his hundreds of late-night stories. No, he wasn't sleeping. I sensed an unease, a concern, in the curved tension of his body. As I whispered "Paul," I slid closer, toeing the back of his knee with the softness of a moth.

"It might not matter soon," Paul said, returning to the discussion of the blanket, our parents. "I might not always be there in that stupid crowded bed with you anyway."

His words frightened me a little: slow words, apprehensive, and I almost heard, inside them, his shivery heartbeat. At last I asked, "Why not?"

"Can't you tell things are changing? Mom's with Crowhurst all the time. Can't say I blame her, either, because he pays her ten times the attention Dad ever has. And how do you think she gets her booze?" In the pause I pictured Mr. Crowhurst, his dark liquid eyes and pressed white shirts, father to Miriam and husband to the freakish shut-in wife I'd never seen. So out of place on his land; his race, his easy nature, his ignorance of farming. I thought of his embarrassed smiles when our father, in the orchard with Paul and me, caught him tending to his boxes of bees, his hobby, in his back stretch of pasture. I'd heard Paul's stories about the affair but couldn't believe them, not quite; couldn't envision my mother together with him in some top-secret motel.

Paul continued. "Don't be mad at her, though. It's rough for her with Dad. At least now she's found someone who pays attention."

"I'm not mad," I said. "But what's that got to do with you? How's that mean you won't always be here?"

He turned now to face me, a mark from his charcoal pencils on the side of his chin. "Dad's going to find out about Mom," Paul said. "If he doesn't know already. Because he knows a lot of things. He knows about me, too. You know what I'm saying? He's taking me along Saturday so it can be us, just us two, alone. He wants to *talk* to me."

For the weekend Paul would join our father in the fruit truck, another journey delivering apples across the state. Suddenly I understood Paul's meaning, the weight and danger, and I protested. "No. Don't tell him. Wait."

"Until when? Someday you may have to get by without me. On

your own." He hesitated, and my terror swelled, palpable in the drizzly air. Finally, he smiled. "But not for good. I'd never leave you for good." Still, his smile made a weak bandage. Already I felt our father's fury; already, my brother slipping. Above, leaves trembled like pennants, spraying us. "It's them," Paul said. "They're the reason I'd go, not you."

And in this darkest part of night the drizzle stopped its tease and began dropping heavy from above. Half-speed, it seemed, this rain we'd needed for weeks, swirling down—yet we would not go inside, we refused to think of our father's ire, the money it would waste to launder our flannels, our muddied pillowcases. I couldn't form other questions for Paul; panicked still at his imminent standoff with our father, I merely waited out the night and watched the rain, blinking only when it sprinkled my eyes.

Minutes and hours. I hovered a hand above Paul's face to prove his sleep; indeed he was gone, long gone, and again I touched the hair around the stocking cap. Wet, his curls went silky in my hands, oily, too, like the sweet filaments of yellow inside a pod of corn. By now the rain was so thick we could have punctured it. It had to penetrate the trees to get to us, the overhanging drapery of leaves, and by the time the water hit our bodies it had turned a bubbly green. Our clothes and skin were smeared with it, leaf-bled rainshade, and though anticipating my father's wrath, I cared nothing nonetheless and let the stains deepen. In retrospect, this green, this specific night, seems so fleeting, it may never have existed at all. I wish I could have savored it, wish I could have held my brother closer, turned a deeper, a durable and darkly indelible, shade of green.

But I fell asleep. Paul fell asleep. On waking, the rain had tapered, and bunches of those wet leaves lay along our bodies. Even in predawn I saw their heraldry, mostly greens, but also coppers, also tea-shade tans; in my fingers they tingled, waxy and firm. Touching them was like touching money. I heard a noise behind us, far behind, in the orchard, perhaps, and mindful of the ghosts

I pulled tight to my brother. Fear fluttered through me; I placed my head against his rail-boned chest. I couldn't imagine him leaving, ever. The solace, the security. Paul had tumbled deep-sleep so my burden, against him, mattered nil, lodged now in his commencing dream. I listened for his heart, tuning out the shudder and hiss of drizzle, the surrounding night. At last, its velvet thrum. My eyes closed for what seemed seconds, and when I opened them again the rain, the deep-green rain, had whirled conclusively away, a far-off bird was trying first notes, and the sky had gone pale as paper, meaning morning.

Work, postdinner, loading the truck for tomorrow: all around us the late-fall apples, a shallow sea of yellow, of reds both deep-dark and pinkish, overflowing and bumping from baskets. We moved gently, cautiously, about them. If the sky outside had set afire, had fallen in shards to the earth, we wouldn't have noticed, stuck as we were inside the fruit trailer, dark rectangular box behind our father's truck, with nothing to see or smell but apples. Pectin and pulp in our hair, our ears. Sweat dripping beads from our temples, spreading bibs at our shirtfronts. Our footheels and backbones would ache at school—first semester only three days away—but we couldn't stop. By the time I followed Paul inside the house, a dark-of-night drape had lowered, and we were tired, too tired for anything but sleep.

The house was dangerously quiet. In the kitchen, we discovered he had joined her in drink: fifth of gin on the table, orbited by her stolen, dwarfish bottles; twin glistening hoops of sweat from glasses they had carried to his room. Although we couldn't hear them, we knew. She went to his bed only when he, too, drank, forced there by some threat behind his eyes. Having learned about Owen Crowhurst, I realized my mother's imperative; perhaps now, as I stood with Paul at the sink, she was tricking my father, further erasing suspicion, closing her eyes and forcing soft fraudulent sighs. I could smell my father's cheap cologne, dabbed to his neck for her, for this. I imagined his hands on her, cold as guns. And her hands, too, the raw scratched skin, the knuckles pearling white as she clutched at the mattress, endure, endure, surrender.

Paul worked his palms over the pink cake of soap. Tomorrow he would leave with our father, off to the smaller towns, Halstead, Medicine Lodge, and the larger, Derby, Wellington, Coffeyville. Overnight, returning on Sunday for school the next morning. Along the way they would supply fruitstands, the merchants of each city, our antonyms: whites whole levels above our trash; blacks nothing like the crazy Crowhursts; dads and sons who would steal snickers and winks as my father and brother drove away. I had traveled cross-state with my father before. Sometimes I rode with Paul, and some-times, before Halloween, I cramped in the truck with both Paul and my mother, the trailer stocked with pumpkins, with cobwebbed fall-colored husks of Indian corn. On these special October trips, she would costume us, romance our faces with rouges, paints, to surprise the town-by-town sellers. Past years, Paul and I had been transformed to long-haired apemen, crackerjack clowns, dime-store vampires or ghouls. But now, in September, Halloween waited weeks away. I couldn't guess what it held. Between now and then: what secrets Paul could reveal, what risks my mother could let slip.

We stayed at the kitchen table until they emerged. My father fixed two new drinks; neither looked into our faces, yet both seemed acutely aware, the way they'd treat two dying boys. She had tissued the lipstick from her mouth. Its red smudged neither my father's cheeks nor his chin, but a stain showed on the inner crease of his fingers as he poured his bourbon and her gin. His hand had kept her quiet. "Pop for you two," he told us, stepping into the adjoining room. "Keeping it cold in the freezer." He shut the light and clicked the television's silver knob; the glass went between his knees as he eased into his chair.

So we would drink with them. Mine was regular cola, but he had remembered Paul's favorite, grape, the dull-labeled generic brand, but still grape. We sat at the table, our backs to him, the television's nimbus teetering about the rooms. "Thank you," I said, because I knew I should. Quickly Paul gave thanks as well. My mother smiled and sat with us. Her sweatshirt, gray with dimmed penny-orange tiger, seemed too warm for the weather; when she exhaled, the kitchen air went flammable from her evening of drink.

Our flannels lay rain-stained and green in the pile of dirty laundry, waiting for my mother's patient scrubbing. As I thumbed the top of the can I sensed my father's anger still, his silence throwing its dense blanket across us. We should give more thank-yous, I thought; should show extra satisfaction for his mercy, these little unexpected gifts. Try harder, yes, I would. I tipped the can to my lips and swallowed, and then, equally quiet, Paul opened his. But the grape must have been jostled, must have overturned or shaken in the freezer, and with the release of pressure came a firecracker hiss. Paul out-thrust the can, far from his clothes, trying to shield its top with his hand; the pop came gushing free regardless, a fuss of violet fizz, sparkling the table, dripping foam to the kitchen floor.

Paul's eyes widened to our mother. When she drank, we could always easily gauge her: her face would flush, and we knew she felt strangely secure, lodged within some shifted city we wouldn't discover for several years, a place where the sounds slurred and the ceilings and walls went calm, wobbling and loosely drifting. A few drinks and my mother would relax, often pull us toward her, and her hugs felt good, warm, a warm like dipping gently into limitless summer water. Yet my father was the opposite. His drunks, infrequent as they were, bore no resemblance to hers: sullen, squinting at us, he stammered orders and stomped through rooms, a knife-blade, shimmery with violence. And so we felt this father rising for us. Felt the blade opening. The grape made pools at Paul's feet, and suddenly my father stood there, over the mess with him, triggered by my brother's clumsiness. "Just like a girl," he said. Only in his rage did the stuttering vanish, and he continued, flawlessly taunting. "Stupid. I buy you something, you spill it. Can't steer the tractor right, can't get the fence fixed, can't even open a goddamn can."

My mother straightened in her chair. "Now, Robert," she whispered.

"Keep shut," he told her. He reached for the can, not taking it, just waiting until Paul moved his arm to lift it fatherward. The sides were trickled with purple, but my father squeezed it in his left grip, took Paul's arm with his right. "Little faggot," he said. "That's what we got here. A maggot and a faggot." From my place at the table I sensed the pride rising in my father's chest, the laughter at his own joke, his rhyme. "Maggot and Faggot, Faggot and Maggot."

"Stop," my mother said, threading the word between her clenched teeth. As the sound hit the air, his hand curled tighter around Paul's arm, and he looked at her, furious. She nodded. "Cease fire, right now."

He laughed then, not really a laugh but more a growl, the can held out before him like a beacon, its purple dribbling to the table. Within the achy motionless silence I couldn't guess what he would do. Maybe he had planned it all, had shaken the can himself before lodging it skewed in the freezer. Maybe he would leave now, walk outside, as he'd done before, to stay away for hours. The quiet continued. He stared her down. Finally my mother opened her mouth, nodding again at his hand on Paul's skin. "I said stop it."

In a single white-blurred instant he flung his arm forward, the arm with the can, and turning to my mother I saw what he'd done: her face now damp with it, the pale bubbled grape, bubbling and dropping and lining parallel streams down her shirtfront. He pistoned his arm again, a second aim to douse her face with the rest, but even on its splash she made no sound. My father dropped the can. It knocked the table with a soft click and rolled, emptied, in one weak arc toward my chair. As he left the room he mumbled, his gaze at his feet, "Teach you yet." He paused at the door; before it slammed, the rest of his words: "Like a goddamn corpse in bed and still takes *their* side."

Gone, gone; only his cologne left, the hum of him, only the print of a fingernail on Paul's arm, a slit I could have fitted a dime through, now seeping a crescent of blood. Without warning the kitchen had become a cell; we were a trio of prisoners, trapped and taunted by the warden. I could hear the echoey racket of his billy club against the bars. Could feel the air shattering apart, the shatter of a window as the victim's body crashes through. There were shotguns in the house, there were pocketknives and pills and snake-coiled rope. And three of us, waiting to be ripped, turned inside out.

We began to clean the kitchen. No one spoke, not her, not him or me. And as we cleaned, I remembered a story I'd heard from Paul: when he was younger, just a little boy, and me only a baby, there had been an accident in the orchard. Strong winds, fallen ladder, firepower lightning-bolt: what its source was, Paul didn't know, but an outsized peach-tree branch had broken and fallen on him. The branch was sturdy and thick and knobbed like knuckle-bone, and Paul lay pinned beneath it, helpless, his leg nearly fractured. He recalled the scratch of leaves against his face, the sand in his mouth as he writhed against the earth. He could not remember the pain or the blood. But he did know the smell of the rescuing father, the man's sudden miracle of arm as it hugged the branch, lifted it, and bandied it to his side. He pressed his son close to his chest and patted his head, gently touched the wound and whispered *OK, you're OK.*

Paul had told this story many times, often late at night when we stretched pre-slumber in our beds and murmured to each other, cautiously, face to flashlit face. Yet I couldn't imagine that man, saint and superhero who had saved my brother, the identical man as this. *Maggot and Faggot.* Surely some change had happened, some diminution or sorcery. The man in Paul's memory had carried the boy back, all dense orchard lanes and pasture scrub, to the house; the man had laid him warm in blankets, had taken the blue bandanna from his overall pocket and after a gentle rib-tickling tied it bandit-style around Paul's head. Had patted his forehead and soothed his voice into his ear. *Sweetheart,* the voice said. Not *Stupid.* Not *Faggot.* Much, much later, after Paul had left home and I was older, I would think of this accident—the slender leg curved crooked in the sand, the wreck of peaches and leaves—and, missing Paul and wanting to know more, request details from my mother. But she would only stare, her eyes deadwater-blank, the story unknown and missing from her mind. "I'm sorry, Matthew . . . nothing like that ever happened." Maybe Paul had resurrected the wrong man. Maybe he had stretched the truth. But it was how he wanted to picture our father, the rescuer, the intrepid, the strongman saying *Sweetheart.* For years I went along with this hero, Paul's hero. For years I remembered him that way, too.

Justin Chin

CHINESE RESTAURANT

I THOUGHT YOU'D LIKE to know what really goes on in the kitchens of Chinese restaurants.

Well, when they say, "No M.S.G.," they're lying. When they say, "Tell us how hot and spicy," they really don't give a flying lizard fuck what you tell them—there's only one recipe, and you're going to eat it. And yes, they do spit into the food of the idiot— you know, the one whom everybody in the restaurant can hear: "How hot and spicy is that? Is it hot hot, or spicy hot, or chili hot, or garlic hot? It's not peppers, is it? 'Cos if it's too hot, I get a burning in my asshole when I shit." (Order the fucking steamed vegetables, buddy.) And yes, they do laugh quite unmercifully at the fool who actually tries to follow the pictorial instructions about how to use chopsticks that're printed on the back of the chopsticks wrapper. And just what the hell is Kung Pao, anyway?

In the kitchen of a Chinese restaurant they don't wash their hands much, but you already knew that. In the kitchen of a Chinese restaurant, someone is working way too hard for minimum wage, but hey—it's a family thing, so it's OK, and hey—it's America, where you make it if you work twelve hours a day, seven days a week, so you can dream that American Dream, you know the one: where Diane Parkinson of *The Price Is Right* or Bob Barker of *The Price Is Right* spreads it just for you. (Which one depends on your sexual orientation, No Substitutions Please. Unless, of course, you're bi, then it's your lucky day.) Come On Down!

In the kitchen of a Chinese restaurant, the waiter lives in fear of deportation, the dishwasher lives in fear of being bashed for stealing some stinking job nobody wants, the kitchen helper is scared to death of participating in the democratic political process, and the chef knows someone who has AIDS at home or abroad.

From the kitchen of a Chinese restaurant I look for some semblance of the familiar. I look for home in every bite. In the dead spit of morning, after equal hours of "Silence = Death," "ACT-UP FIGHT BACK," and "What Do We Want? A Cure! When Do We Want It? Now!" I want some friendly solace & all I find is a lousy jerk-off, interrupted only by the three-hundred-pound clerk who sticks his head through the door every ten minutes to yell, "Buy your tokens. Get into a booth or get out of here!"

I find no simple gesture can erase it all. I find a border that I cross each day for a decent wage of self-deception: call it optimism, call it a punch-fuck, fist-fucking the ass of the quality of life (and it's a tight one, too, baby).

I find a pissant pleasure, a memoir of failure, cancer for brains. & I want to go, got to go, got to find this thing called home.

In the kitchen of a Chinese restaurant, I am queer for queer & I refuse to pass my ugliness for roses. I refuse to trade my queer for your queer.

At this point you're probably thinking, Wait a minute, all of this wasn't in *The Joy Luck Club;* all this wasn't in the PBS special presentation *A Thousand Pieces of Gold,* & all of this probably isn't in that stage production of *The Woman Warrior,* either.

But I just thought that you should know what goes on in the kitchens of Chinese restaurants.

Now go eat.

Allan Gurganus

Preservation News

Being the journal of THE SOCIETY FOR THE SALVATION
OF HISTORIC NORTH CAROLINA ARCHITECTURE

Funded by Grants from the National Endowment for the Humanities and Generous Donors Like You

ISSUE NUMBER 14

AVAILABLE FOR RESTORATION
ELKTON GREEN
(2.4 acres, located downtown Falls, N.C., Person County)

Elkton Green is the preeminent bracketed Victorian gingerbread mansion in northeastern North Carolina. It will be leveled by wreckers if some fairy-god-purchaser is not found by April 1. Help us, please?

Preferably somebody with plenty of good sense, mad about history, alive to the finer nuances of strong-armed social pretense, and with a discretionary income to sort of match. Pretty please? Little family foundations are always nice. We just know you're out there.

Fact is, we have got two extensions from the very cooperative Falls Town Zoning Board. But even with a treasure like Elkton

Green, this, my friends, is our literal last chance. Already bids have come in for the pearwood-and-mahogany parqueted spiral staircase, for all the stained glass; but these are bids from a chain restaurant that will perform a mastectomy, that will then wedge bits of the mansion's exquisite features into separate franchises where people order their quite bad beef awfully overcooked. Large portions of too-buttered "garlic bread" are intended to distract them. It makes us swoon, the thought. Perish it.

Built in 1856 for the Penner-Coker Family, this high Victorian "pile" seems to have been inspired by the minarets of the Prince's "Folly" Pavilion at Brighton. Elkton Green retains its Tudor rose medallions and endearingly redundant cornices. Even its brackets are bracketed. A gracious, indeed showoff, home in the downtown Historic Summit District, we are talking twenty-four rooms; we're talking porches enough to accommodate every banished smoker left alive in Falls, N.C. Lavish plantings survive, including a mature box maze (needs work, as mazes, alas, tend to).

The lawn, rolling clear down to the River Tar, is a fine acre-and-a-half. We speak now of a lawn so suitable for croquet, I'll throw in my own best 1920s Wilson set, and just leave it up for you to look at, and get vague credit for.

Elkton Green's West Wing features a faux Romanesque capital set directly beside one that might be called "Adirondack Carnival Ecclesiastical Ecstatic." Our "right-hand person," the inimitable Mary Ellen Broadfield, said, "This home is like some lady from a very good family who's had entirely too much coffee and feels forced to try on every hat in a third-rate shop, all at once." There are sane people who consider the house overornamented. But for us, the mansion's gingerbread detailing represents Elegance pushed—testing—clear to the edge of Comedy. (Which is just where some of us most long to live!)

Elkton Green's fourteen-foot ceilings boast heavy, indeed, luscious moldings; there are faux marbled baseboards and grained doors and a dining-room mural (oil on leather, ten by twenty-one feet). Its subject seems to have been suggested by Judge J. V. Coker's extensive collection of American Indian artifacts. Coker's brilliant early acquisitions—however dubiously gained from those rough-hewn grave-robbing bounty hunters known even then as "New York art dealers"—formed the cornerstone gift of what is now the Smithsonian's impressive horde.

The mural shows a band of fruit-carrying Indians, generically bare if genitally unspecified. They greet one paunchy Quaker-looking gent smiling from beneath a probably-hurtful black tricorn hat. (There is an eerie similarity to Edward Hicks's later Peaceable Kingdom series.) The fat white guy is said to resemble the great-great-grandfather of Elkton Green's builder, one Judge Josiah Vestry Coker (1670–1749). He remained on fine terms with his Native American neighbors even through the Tuscarora War of 1711. He negotiated the release of certain English lady settlers taken as hostages. They were freed through his personal diplomacy and an anonymous donation of "many sovereigne of the King's coinage, meetly dispatched by His Own horses." The mural is of museum quality and unique in our state.

Some people have complained that I tell too much about the history of each house. That is not possible.

For the record, the man who built Elkton Green inherited a goodly fortune via this very judge and arts collector. But plump Caleb Coker soon handsomely supplanted his patrimony through naval stores, pitch and rope and turpentine, sold along the state's then-bustling steamship coast. Coker's own King Cotton holdings—taken collectively—equaled half the landmass of Rhode Island. It was he, Caleb Hunstable Coker (1812–1891), who conceived of Elkton Green as the site for his beautiful daughter's wedding. This prior to his actually having a daughter. (Such is the energy and optimism of our America!) The mansion's stained-glass skylight-lit staircase was designed to make stunning the choreography of one girl's white-veiled descent.

Concord, Coker's only child, was born just three years after the home's completion. Her mother died in childbirth. Fortunately for herself and her father (and his architects!), Concord proved to be the beauty a fifty-one-step staircase preordained.

It was Concord, at age eighteen, who founded the first Falls Public Lending Library for Ladies. She furnished it with her cast-off novels. (She is said to have read two a day since age ten. Her father saw this as proof of her refinement [and incidentally his own].) When Concord finally wed at the age of thirty-one, she chose a future chief justice of the state supreme court. By her day's standards, Concord Coker was already middle-aged. This last-minute reprieve from spinsterhood and a threatened end to the Coker line further piqued her father's extravagance. It had already been expressed, perhaps too malely, in this house that, for all its feminizing frontal gingery lace, remains blessed with a Grover Cleveland girth of solemnity, not to mix metaphors or, worse, periods. Elkton Green's builder swore it must now fulfill its destjny, must now become the stage for what Caleb Coker announced, in print alas, would be "the wedding of the century."

The bride's proud poppa, nine-term mayor of Falls, imported a sixty-piece string orchestra from (not Richmond but) Philadelphia. Through his naval connections, he chartered one of the last for-lease four-masted schooners, *Reliance*. It brought all instruments, the three requested extra harps, and distinguished Yankee visitors south to Wilmington's harbor.

But Mr. Coker was too ambitious and too rich to stop there. He soon stage-managed a single decorative touch that even now gives him an ongoing life in local Falls legend. (Who could ask for anything more?) With help from a railroad-owning friend and later business partner of the Barnum and Bailey Circus, Caleb Coker imported spiders, yes, specialty spiders, from South America. I don't pretend to understand all this, but the eight news clippings here—long since turned brown as cigars—all vouch for the insects' unlikely presence. The exact species has been lost to us, despite our tireless research. It grieves us, this lapse; my fondest hope was to offer the species' exact Latin name. I fear there's no time left before our present Issue #14 must be "put to bed." However, I HAVE discovered that these creatures were brought to Falls by rail.

Thanks to a bibliophilic fellow preservationist, I own the somewhat comic shipping invoice. Under "Descrp. Laden Goods," some shaky hand has written, "Spiders, large, South American, keeper was well-spoken & aware of poss. passenger discomfort. Paid first class fare for each cage. Kept crates draped excllnt. All steps taken." Spiders arrived in steel containers described by one witness as "little metal safes with wire-mesh-covered breathing holes." The insects' trainer released them at night into Elkton Green's water oaks, camellias, and over its then-young box maze on the south lawn. Spiders soon spun gossamer at a rate almost unseemly and till-now locally unknown. Two dawns later, they had overshot even Christo, wrapping Elkton Green entire. Silver webbing was said to cover every shrub and bracketed spindle. According to a newspaper account, "one wheelbarrow, a tall ladder left in the wrong place, and glassy results of the milkman's visit soon needed freeing from sudden gauze." Mounting even taller ladders, slaves now sprinkled real gold dust over all the webs. The whole place then got strung with six thousand, yes, white Chinese lanterns. For an evening wedding, the grounds were lit with "over twenty thousand white tapers, of the finest."

At six A.M. the Coker retainers began lighting the white lanterns. Now, to our jaded eyes, this lightshow might seem a pleasing sight. But for Falls, of the period, where one oil lamp per kitchen table was considered a luxury, such display shone without parallel. It took twenty-one servants twelve hours to light and relight every wick, avoiding the still-busy spiders, by now themselves turned gold. Come sunset, two counties' fire departments stood by, so stoked with rum toddies that their utility was undercut, but happily never needed. It was reported how by evening the glow could be seen fully one and a half miles away.

A chronicle of the day inevitably mentions Midas. The *Falls Herald Traveler* called the nighttime sight of Elkton Green "locked within the powdered gold candleglow casts over finest webbing, a spectacle from pre-Christian myth, in its excess both offputting and yet wondrous as some children's book's occurrence. A strange idea, so perfectly implemented that it shall not be soon forgot by any of the over 1,000 uninvited guests allowed and even encouraged to stand outside Elkton Green's castiron gates and stare. Each onlooker was provided a gilt packet of rice to shower upon the handsome escaping bridal couple. It must be noted that, while the bride appeared almost starkly beautiful, Elkton Green itself, a home easily accommodating the exceptional string orchestra of 60, plus unnumbered guests, glowed with a fond pride that seemed cordial, aware, and all but human in its outward-looking joy. Many onlookers remarked the impression of a house come utterly, as it were, sentiently and watchfully alive."

Elkton Green now stands, somewhat startled it must be admitted, in downtown commercial Falls, N.C. It is within easy take-out distance of both a Hardee's and a Colonel Sanders, alas. Three years back, we personally planted fast-growing Leyland cypresses to screen such blight. The mansion rests on 2.4 acres of its original 880. It is just around the corner from the White-Rooker-designed Gothic Revival Courthouse. (Would it be immodest to mention our organization's having saved this masterwork in January 1983?) Elkton Green still holds a place of honor along Summit Avenue, a street lined with other Victorian mastodons and the magnolias planted by Falls's "Betterment Committee" in 1891. Why the four-car garages, aluminum outbuildings, and easy parking for five hundred (count 'em) cars? Genteelly put, . . . Elkton Green was, during the late 1950s, transformed into Falls's finest white funeral establishment. I say, there must be life after embalming for Elkton Green! Pul-lease?

Falls is located just off I-95 and I-40, the main byways linking Miami and New York. This certainly helps give Elkton Green, with its extensive leaded windows, arched interior doorways, Vermont marble rose-and-lotus-carved hearth facings, its commodious rooms and ingenious still-working system of dumbwaiters, great potential as a going bed-and-breakfast. (If that is what it takes to save it.) Anyone who has seen and loved Orson Welles's *The Magnificent Ambersons,* anyone who has ever nursed a fantasy of issuing one's own white-draped daughter from the head of a great staircase featuring the period's requisite bronze of bare-bottomed Mercury (he's there), needs to see (then save) this brave survivor.

It's a very big house built to edify, impress, and perhaps slightly terrify this little town. For a moot $210,000, it's yours to use—as gently or as bullingly—as you see fit.

Square feet: 6,899. Lot: 2.4 acres. Zoning: B1 (central business). Revolving funds available immediately. Plus ample parking for your next garden party of 650 guests, for your own (second or third?) wedding or, if need be, hygenic facilities befitting your (first) funeral! Everything's ready. We know you're out there. It's yours, please.

The history (& the croquet) come free.

A COMMEMORATIVE ISSUE

Celebrating the Life of Thedore Hunstable Worth

volunteer interim editor: MARY ELLEN BROADFIELD

You have just read the last "Available for Restoration" note actually written by our much-missed leader, gadfly, and inspiration, Theodore "Tad" Worth. I was just one of the many people touched by him. I am but one of the countless fortunates now living in a house Tad saved from the bulldozer. I feel I must make a few remarks. Some will be statesmanlike and formal (as is our wont, we preservationists!). Others will, no doubt, prove utterly uncalled-for, and therefore of a sort I think he'd like.

I.

A PERHAPS TOO PERSONAL REFLECTION

First I knew Tad Worth only socially, as everybody did. But I can't say I counted Tad a close friend.

Our deeper contact commenced six years ago. It was just after my husband died. I was sitting in my Hillsborough kitchen, feeling more than a little sorry for myself. My children had flown the coop for college, perpetual grad school, and, at long last, jobs. The game of bridge, eventful and statistically challenging though it can be, had begun to let me feel a bit abandoned, too. Nothing seemed enough. Nothing actually meant anything. Tad had a curious way of being at the right place at the right time. Or as someone later put it, "At the right time, for the right place . . ." Right for the salvation of noble houses and their sometimes mopey occupants.

This gift of timing secured for our grandchildren and for theirs the continuing presence of churches, two of them African Methodist Episcopal, one major nineteenth-century courthouse, the German-carved carousel at High Point, and an entire downtown district slated for destruction only ten days after Tad's first inquiries to save it. (Few of us will forget a twenty-four-hour vigil that felt like getting the heroine untied from the railroad tracks!)

I was not the only old "widow woman" in Tad Worth's Morocco-bound, paint-splattered address book. There is a natural law that allows us, the ladies, I mean, to have an extra decade or three. There is some justice in that, I believe. Even so, many of these widows confess to feeling like ramshackle old "historic" home-places themselves. I felt myself to be some house suddenly emptied of all its occupants and, despite possessing fairly decent dentil moldings, fallen into disrepair beyond the help of Elizabeth Arden, the National Trust, or the Holy Spirit!

The moment my husband died, I became such a crumbling "prestige property." Well, imagine the pleasure of this old home-place upon being turned, half against her will, into an office, then upgraded into Action Central till, through being an unsalaried "bed-and-breakfast," I finally found myself having become, to quote my Trekkie children, "The Mother Ship."

All on behalf of Historic Preservation, and all on account of this extraordinary very down-to-earth type of person who gave me "the call." Like that Caravaggio depicting the tax collector's being summoned from his counting table to Duty, to Care, and to, at last, A Cause.

This "number" of our periodical must be different from any other. We must all reflect some of what we've lost in a person of Tad's moral and artistic talents. This issue will offer you, our loyal donors and supporters and readers, Tad's fellow carpenters and archivists, snobs and friends, something like his own last will and testament.

Tad's housemate, Dan Trevor, can tell you how much willpower Tad, as the strength lessened, gave to writing his parts of this, Issue #14. There were several new properties he planned to describe more fully, hoping to intrigue a latent buyer. (He was at work on a love poem to Shadowlawn Plantation when he died. But Elkton Green was the only home Tad managed, from his bed, to fully "portray.") It must be admitted, in his hospital room on March 28 we told Tad that we'd found the long-awaited "fairy god-purchaser" for Elkton Green. We invented certain details—a family foundation based on a carpeting concern—the newly retired Connecticut couple looking for a getaway, etc. We told Tad that Elkton Green had been saved, thanks to a faxed copy of his seductive history! We lied to him. What good, by then, to let him know we'd lost the place?

It was just one of the properties Tad had worked years to "wrestle" onto the registry. (He had bought and planted those cypresses three years before the place was even listed with us. It took a whole Saturday, and the lad did it all "on spec.") If we sacrifice any more of these exquisite plantation and small-town homes to the wrecking crew, so much remaining beauty will be taken from our state. It meant everything to Tad, sketching out these farms and houses as only Tad Worth could. His room at Duke Hospital was stacked with deeds and court records, with wills in Xerox, slave rosters, an antique leather "elephant" folio marked "Characteristic Non-Poisonous Spiders of Central and South America, depicted in native circumstances," architectural and decorating sourcebooks from the eighteenth century to the present. There were six potted orchids. Somebody had thrown an old paisley shawl over the curtain rod circling his bed. A new nurse walked in one day and said, "So, who lives here? Merlin?" We all laughed and, though weak by then, Tad, never one to miss a comic opportunity, spoke up, "More like Merlin's maid, honey."

Tad died on the night of April 1. (He'd once stated he was aiming for that date, intending some final confession of foolishness.) He perished believing Elkton Green had been spared. With some difficulty, he told us just where his prized croquet set was stored, ready. We found the mallet stand already tied with a grass-green satin bow.

May I, as editor emeritus (that is, the only local person "tetched" enough to even try and edit this thing), permit myself the luxury of trying to set down a few memories of Tad? "For the record," as he would put it. Tad Worth was a great believer in "the record." No one ever did more to keep our dear state's record legible or longer "in print."

Though he's a person sure to be remembered vividly by those who knew him, Tad is someone oddly apt to disappear. He planned that, you see. He was very quick at giving others credit, perhaps too quick. Tad seemed eager to blend into the heaps of deeds of his library research, into the lives of his "lieutenants," into the very timbers and planks of those properties he saved. I cannot bear anonymity for this boy of ours—and though he'd reached his early forties, "a boy" is what he'll always seem to me, to someone my age. You will find his name on no plaque at any of the more than fifty-seven homes and public edifices he helped us spare. Just the names of original builders, of founding farmers, mayors, owners, and, of course, the time-tested family names of those prosperous bored "widow women" who became Tad Worth's funding and phoning army. But on what marble tablet do we find Theodore Hunstable Worth's moniker engraved?

Let that start here. Call this "a personal indulgence," but telling Tad's particular truth also presents a chore of excruciating difficulty. I was once asked to speak—extemporaneously!—at the funeral of a woman who had worked for my family for fifty-three years. All I know is that I managed to say something. That in itself seemed feat aplenty. Here, at least, I have the blessing of silence, shelter, and revision. So I am going to take my jolly good time, if that's all right. It's odd but I feel my whole life has been a preparation for doing just this. Which is maybe why I feel so nervous about overstaying, overstating. Tad inspires overstatement, and perhaps demands it! If only I could find a prose style as modest, upright, and human in scale as the Federal architecture Tad loved best. That's what I intend here: to make one little Doric temple on a hill for him.

For the record, Tad gave me the first job I ever had, apart from wife and mother and friend, and all that those massive duties entail. Such tasks were precisely what women of my generation expected. But certain energies always went untapped. Precisely in not being asked after, many skills remained undescribed, and therefore went unknown. Tad believed in my "structural integrity" at a time when this rickety old structure sorely doubted she would stand for one more day.

He walked into my house without knocking. I had not been able or willing to even answer my front door. I was so out of sorts and thought so poorly of myself after George died. I felt responsible for that, I guess (the way we poor WASPs will). Until Tad's helpful revision, St. Sebastian had always somehow been my idea of a life, a search for further sharper arrows! Yikes, but it's true. So, actually saying, "Knock knock," into my kitchen walks this chunky, agreeable young man with high color, long blondish red hair, a blue Oxford-cloth buttondown, and chinos whose knees proved he'd been down on all fours checking some ancient building's footings (not that I would've used that term back then). From his alligator belt, a jingling eight-inch key ring. He wore Topsiders, at least they had the outline of Topsiders, but they seemed created by Mr. Jackson Pollock, so paint-and-plaster-swirled were they. In one hand, he held a little note that I myself had scribbled to him after some recent party. I'd mailed it six days prior to George's being found in his fishing boat. It was a thank-you note for something or other, a joking little teasing little letter I'd jotted, nothing really.

"You can write, Mary Ellen." So Tad said. "You slipped up and showed us that. This thing had us all doubled over, laughing. And it cracked us up three hours prior to drink time. I don't know if you understand what a rare and negotiable skill writing simply and persuasively is! No? I thought not. A skill useful for my purposes, of course. But now you've tipped your hand, you simply have to come onboard. You owe it to the rest of us. I'm going to have to hold you to your word. You are a person of your word, aren't you, Mary Ellen Broadfield?" I had not the foggiest idea what young Tad Worth was talking about. I expressed this aloud.

From a deep pocket of his nasty chinos, he pulled out a folded wad of papers, blueprints, statistics. They concerned a certain property he believed he could get his hands on for the Register. Scraps of inspectors' reports, Polaroids of glum interior details, and, I believe, a matchbook from Sanitary Seafood with room measurements jotted there among traces of Tabasco sauce. He told me: First, this home needs saving from the razing crews that have been real instrumental in making so much of our state look like Ohio or anywhere dull else on Earth. Then this home must be put up for sale, Tad explained. That particular day, he wisely assumed nothing (given my grieving state and probable witchlike appearance). He spelled it out: The house, once sold at subsidized prices, would be restored. "Not just pickled and 'museumified' but inhabited, returned to its function. Providing shelter, comfort, and incidental joy." That's a direct quote. Still, peeved, I sat there blinking.

Tad settled beside me at my own kitchen table. From his country doctor's bag of a briefcase, he eased forth the sheaf of photographs he'd taken with his similarly paint-scarred Pentax. He said the house was called Sandover. Toward me, he then pushed a jotted list of people in the town where this ignored domestic masterpiece had stood since 1803. People who could help. "I just know you must know about three-quarters of the hard-drinking gentry down Little Washington way." He tried flattering me back into life. I knew that trick well enough.

I told him I didn't maintain contact with all that many people really. I also told Tad I'd just had kind of a shock, with George dying alone on the Neuse River, right after I had pronounced such fishing trips "a big fat bore." I had made my husband go by himself to drift around alone in a deceased condition. It took the Coast Guard five long days to find our boat. I swear the wait nearly killed me. I said I needed time.

My own address book was buried under some Erle Stanley Gardners and the answering machine I'd just installed to fend off universal sympathy and gossipy well-wishers. There was a grand total of twenty-one unreturned phone calls blinking on the thing. One rumor I'd been allowed to overhear claimed that my late husband had been discovered faceup in our boat, features half consumed by seagulls (not true). Such tittletattle can challenge a person's sense of dignity and value, not to mention shaking her accustomed social standing.

Three of those waiting calls would turn out to be from Tad Worth here. He now said, "You need a martini is what you need, girl, and then you need to go get your address book over there out from under those cheap paperback mysteries. I assume that Gutenbergy Biblely humongous-looking thing is your address book? And then we need to compare the names on this list to the names in yonder tome-ette, and then you need to get your excellent sinewy ass in gear, girl. I hear you don't even answer your phone no mo'. You've already quit coming to the door. I know what that means, Mary Ellen. I've been there, gir'friend, and I'm telling you, Get with the program. And while you're up, I could use a martini too. But, look, just show the gin a vermouth bottle, just scare it by maybe whispering the word 'Vermont'—that's vermouth enough—and then you need to come back here and focus on something past the tip of your fine Hollingsworth nose. I don't reckon you have any 'snack items' or cheese or anything around, do you? Not that my Gothick saddlebags need it, Heaven presarve 'em." I stared at him as if he were speaking Serbo-Croat. I finally said, "Does the phrase 'over-the-top' mean anything to you, young man?"

"Mean anything? It's my goddamn credo!"

So, before Tad would even consider leaving, he made me, after two goodly drinks, no more, telephone three girls I'd known at St. Catherine's. One of them was married, as it happened, to the longtime mayor of Little Washington. If I had ever known that, I'd forgot. Everybody in Washington, N.C., will tell you their town is years older than our nation's copycat capital; and therefore should be called "The Original Washington." That's where Sandover, the Meade-Ulrich mansion, was located, a twenty-room late Georgian palace about to be done away with—so that public servants at City Hall would have better parking opportunities each morning. I ask you! Tad left me with this list and other homework, plus he scheduled a return appointment, said he'd come back in three days, no later. To see how I'd done. I believe three days has certain precedents as an ideal Resurrection time. He knew I'd need that long to get out of a green chenille—yes, chenille—robe I'd taken to sulking around in. (I still don't know how that got into my closet or where it's got to since.)

Reached a point where I did not remember actually formally vol-
unteering. He'd left behind the spooky photos of water-stained
heart-pine Adam-panelled parlors, of fanlights shaped like yard-
wide scallop shells, of English boxwoods about the size of the planet
Pluto (his line not yours truly's). Here I was, not even a dues-paying
member. All the paperwork was disfiguring my kitchen table. I felt
put upon. And yet somehow, by the following Thursday, I had
talked the mayor's wife (Deedee Pruden, darling girl, always so good
in art class at "catching likenesses") into heading a task force that
would make the Meade-Ulrich mansion a hospitality center for the
city of Little Washington. In other words, I felt like I had somewhat
helped to start to save an antebellum jewel that'd taken three years
and forty thousand 1803 dollars and untold day laborers—slaves
and Boston brick masons—to build.

By the following week, Tad and Dan were right here cooking
softshell crabs at my own till-lately seldom-used (except for coffee) stove. And it was only when I heard myself say, by phone
(while they eavesdropped as planned), heard myself say flirtatiously to a boy from Shelby that I used to date, "Honey? Reeve?
Are you listening? Because if you and the other so-called pillars of
Shelby sit around there sipping your 'Jacks and water' while some
nouveau Atlanta yahoo takes his tractor to that Osage House's
bracketed cornices given an Italianate flavor by the square porch
posts and those heavy corn-patterned pilasters in our beloved re-
gion's finest Greek Revival idiom, why, the ghost of your sainted
Grandmother Spruill (who always liked me, God rest her soul),
she's going to put a serious hex on your golf game, Reeve. Now,
THINK."

And it was only when Tad and Dan laughed, then covered their
mouths (afraid to mess up a hard deal I was driving with a little of
my late husband's serious financial flair, if I do say so myself!)—it
was only then that your Mary Ellen Broadfield here understood
how preservation might, if approached correctly, prove . . . well . . .
preservative.

II.

I mention that last part only because, this now being my newsletter (ha ha!), I simply chose to mention it. But in the above incident, I represent just one of hundreds, or maybe a thousand or two other people he is forever rescuing. You see? I keep falling into the present tense when speaking of Tad. I expect we all will for a long time yet. I must say, it's unbelievable he's dead. My husband perished of natural causes at age seventy-one (is this too personal? I'll leave that to my closest friends and second-readers to later decide). When my husband died, I felt I could not go on. George had provided such a definition of my life. I was suddenly a single-owner home with no history but his. It seemed so unfair, his perishing at seventy-one. Then Tad died at a bit more than half George's age, died of causes I cannot call natural (though nature, I reckon, contains them). And "unfair" took on a whole new kind of meaning. Fact is, I simply cannot believe Tad Worth is dead. You keep waiting for the voice, then you keep waiting for its echo. This must be what it's like to lose your own child. Downtown, you keep seeing resemblances in perfect strangers glimpsed from behind. You actually go up to them. They turn around and their faces look hideous, only because the faces are not his. But you all know all this already.

Well . . . Tad was, as we can attest, a jack-of-all-trades. Having been so philanthropic with his smallish trust fund so early on, he fairly well had to be. During his forty-three years, he worked in various unlikely roles to support his overriding concern for preservation and supporting, only incidentally, himself. He would've cringed on hearing our lieutenant governor's graveside mention of how Tad spent his own inheritance saving houses he then practically gave away to others, homes he never really lived in except to work on them. Tad was briefly a garden designer, specializing in period herbal and knot gardens (before they became a fad, so cutesied up). Then he owned a profitable business that recast old sundials, garden statuary, and obelisques. But daily management was something he mostly left to others. This allowed Tad time to drive his pickup on secondary Carolina roads, seeking vine-covered subjects for "mere salvation," his dachshund always in back, barking at all chickens and most trees. Tad was also a sought-after caterer (though that sounds too menial for somebody who came in and cooked for his friends and later sort of permitted them to slip him a little something oblique if princely). His softshells, sautéed in lime juice, then battered with crumbled pecans, were truly not to be missed. He acted as a paint contractor and period consultant for Tryon Palace and other such sites. But never Historic Williamsburg, a bête noire he never tired of "dishing." Tad didn't consider their scholarship serious and called them "the Walt Dig-nys." Forever strong in his likes and dislikes, our Tad. He did a lot of things quietly well. Tad always assumed that everybody could, too. Well, everybody else can't, actually. But young Mr. Worth never ceded his amateur standing. Jefferson remained his god. The eighteenth-century's farmer-statesman-gourmand-classicist-architect was Tad's long-range ideal and therefore his daily yardstick and reality. And though half the world still genuflects to Jefferson's undoubted genius, Tad was something that Mr. Jefferson never ever thought to try to be: I mean that our plumpish rosy Theodore Worth stayed, to the end, a very very funny person. And even Tad admitted, "Marse Jefferson was, if not all things, then most. But nobody ever did accuse him of being exactly a laugh riot."

It is important to stay realistic about one's mentors.

Can you hear me trying?

I saw Tad sit down and play brilliant backgammon and then lose on purpose, if that was required. Say there was a resistant elder citizen, some old gal very unlikely to hand over a group of "important" farm-building dependencies; say an incoming mall was already waving bushel baskets of cash at her for that same tract. And here was Tad "throwing" a backgammon game for preservation. "There are many ways to win," he grew quite snippish when I teased him about this later. I've also seen Tad go right up onto the fourth story of a slate roof just after rain and say only, "Whoo, I gots them Hitchcock vertigos," after he'd spied whatever mountain goats go up that high to see, and then (like a kitten I once owned) he needed aid and ladders in getting down, almost needed smelling salts. From the ground, a martini was often held aloft and sloshed around for inspiration.

And none of us shall ever forget watching Tad veer into action at Zoning Board meetings statewide. I went to school on how he managed those.

The local boards would know only that some outsider had requested an extra session. Like all of us, the poor things were already "meetinged" to death. Their arms were crossed, their shoes already tapping, their watches exposed for easy consulting. In Tad would sweep, plump and therefore somewhat more trustworthy. He wore his one dark conservative suit and was looking fairly neat for a change. No paint on the pair of brown wingtips he called his MBA drag. For once he left his pesky dog in the truck. I'd begged him to.

Since his family was an old one ("Old and rotten," he liked to quote William Carlos Williams), he had a sense of other towns and who their leading families were. He'd always arrive at Town Hall a bit early. There, he could mill around out front and chat up farmers about crop allotments and outlawed pesticides, he could talk to housewives about the mahi-mahi being sold at Piggly-Wiggly since March and how rare you dared to serve it, and he was not above mentioning his other vice: *All My Children.* Tad once told me after an especially successful meeting (in which he saved the 1873 Conger-Halsey Girls' Academy outside Rocky Mount), "I swear, Mary Ellen, keeping up with a good soap, it's the next-best thing to being a Mason."

Meeting was called to order; first thing, he'd get up and say his usual grinning "hi," then tell a joke about some boy hick getting the better of a society woman trying to cheat him out of his sainted mother's pie-safe at a flea market over in Swan Quarter. His accent was one kind of icebreaker, the seeming irreverence another.

Tad would then begin his slide presentation about some local building these folks had been driving past their whole lives, one they had assumed to be merest shack eyesore, one held up mostly by its own Virginia creeper and poison ivy old enough to grow berries big as scuppernong grapes. Tad Worth's talks never lasted more than twenty-two minutes. I checked. Others, watches readied, forgot to. He congratulated locals on the important period piece they'd all helped keep standing till this very hour. He presented stories about who'd built it and why; he specialized in the early builders' faults, erotic peccadilloes, and hobbies and, always a plus, the deaths of any of their young children. Not a dry eye in the house. Right up to the wainscoting ledge of the shameless, young Squire Worth oftimes went. He used to quote his beloved Jane Austen, "One does not love a place the less for having suffered in it." He told what church the homebuilders had attended, and which of that sanctuary's rose windows they donated in 1814, and by the end, our Mr. Worth had mentioned the family name—legitimately mentioned—of most people present, including the security guards.

Tad never scheduled anything after. He knew that if his pitch to save a structure worked, he'd be instantly invited to one, if not three, homes of the competitive local hostesses. (Here in Society N. Carolina at least, each town is going to have either two or three "leader art patrons." There's never only one.) Many's the night we arrived back home in Hillsborough after two A.M. Tad understood how this was all part of it, making himself available (to each jealous hostess in turn, if need be).

I don't know when he caught the missionary fervor about old houses. He'd grown up in one that had been lost. Maybe that set him on his course. Or maybe, during college, at Charlottesville? I once asked him why he matriculated there. "For the real estate?" he laughed. I'm not sure if such long local midnight parties bored

him as they sometimes did me. (I shall hold my own tongue here.)
But if so, Tad certainly never showed it. He never condescended;
he had his loves and his strong dislikes, but he did not fail to look
all kinds of people in the eye. "Never met a stranger." We now
claim 110 city chapters in this state, and each represents dozens of
not-that-riveting two A.M.s, much Triscuit-eating by our Tad. Two-
thirty and he still sat there, overanimating some creweled wing
chair, discussing the recent tuition increase at Ravenscroft School
and the best way to make your new garden statuary look ancient:
pour half a gallon of buttermilk on it and watch the setting in of
what Tad called "the blue-chip greenies."

You will remember that young Mr. Worth was accompanied most
everywhere by his brown low-stomached dachshund bitch, Circa.
He said he called her that because, whenever you thought of her,
she was "always around then." She was the bad dog you often find
near your most accommodating people. (It seems they let their dogs
take it out in trade.) Some people complained Tad Worth's zeal for
saving broken houses was overshadowed by one dog he never house-
broke.

   I recall how the construction fellows at Sandover, the hired
workers (not us volunteers), always got a kick out of Circa, her
carrying on in that intelligent if indolent manner. But, you see, they
heard her name as "Circus." And Tad was much too gentlemanly—
meaning too smart, kind, or efficient—to try explaining the joke.
. . . ("No, boys, 'Circa,' you recall, is an art historical term," etc.)
"Tad bud, you got her name right," one fellow called from the
gable roof, " 'At dog's a pure-tee circus." Just then she was running
around the big house, and Tad, that quick, pointed as she wheezed
around the corner a third time, said, "Yeah, Bobby Ray. A three-
ring circus." Roofers, laughing, shook their heads. I saw again how
good Tad was at taking others' mistakes, period mistakes, class mistakes, even our failures of nerve or character, and setting some pe-

riod pediment atop them. A true Jeffersonian. He did that during this particular widow woman's Chapter Eleven of life; walked in, "Knock knock," and placed a finial or crown upon the head of one old lady wearing an extremely unattractive pistachio-green chenille robe.

Tad himself was also always around, always talkative, and his shirttail forever seemed to be coming out, and he kept threatening to do sit-ups when he someday got around to it, "just as soon as Burleigh Hall is finally secure." He did have faults. If I've already presumed to point out Jefferson's, I don't think Tad would mind my adding a few of his own. I never quite trust eulogies that make out anyone to be angelic. No one utterly is. Such saccharine gush would, to employ one of Tad's own oversalty phrases, "absolutely gag a maggot." (I am trusting his own brand of luridness to call me back from my inherent sentiment about him. Maybe that is a form of immortality—giving one's survivors tools to avert their being overmaudlin in recalling oneself? I don't know.) We all understood this much:

Tad could really get his feelings hurt. He could become overly silly at times, and you couldn't pull him out of it, not even for emergencies. Once people crossed him or played dirty pool to cheat him out of some church he was trying to save, well, Tad never forgot. "They, my dear, are off Mother's" (he sometimes comically referred to himself as "Mother") "list, for good." He either loved you or he really just didn't.

Once you were off "Mother's list," special pleading—be it presidential, papal, or from on high—couldn't reinstate you, oh dear me, no. All his own considerable skills (what a diplomat he would have made!) had long since been lined up and pressed toward one end—preserving what was old and beautiful and in jeopardy. He'd given everything he owned away to save the beautiful and local.

There, plain obstinate selfishness baffled him. (There is, I hate to tell you, a lot of that around just now.) But every time Tad bumped into it, he seemed to find it brand new. It could be a bore.

He literally did not understand greed. "Why wouldn't she give it away rather than see it torn down?" He sometimes made me feel guilty for how people I despised behaved!

More than once, in our legal wrangling, we came up against some old person who would literally prefer to see their own family homeplace burn; better that than allow one Yankeefied stranger to set foot in it. This, Tad puzzled over, as if he had heard wrong. "What?" he asked and, at times, seemed to be blaming us, chastising the messengers. In the face of such meanness, Tad himself grew obstinate and childlike; you saw he didn't really want to know that part of people. How lucky that he saw as little of it as he did.

There are about six Republican families, major landholders in our fine state, tribes he couldn't abide; these were groups (nameless here, please) who could—with one phone call, or a signature—have spared the places he tried daily to preserve. They did not. They let treasure after treasure go. And they assumed nobody knew. Well, listen, if they'd half-guessed the social damage their own stinginess had done them and their climbing grandkids forever, they'd have handed Mr. Worth a stack of blank checks and just run.

Like all people who're obsessed, every turn of conversation led Tad back to the house he was just then trying to spare. He used to joke that perfect happiness would be to save the Shadowlawn Plantation down near Edenton ("my possible all-time fave") and to lose that fifteenth midriff pound of his, and on the same day. He was always almost going on a diet, but only once he had sampled whatever it was that we were cooking. People did love feeding him. There was never a more appreciative eater of one's work. Our leader claimed that his mother must've been a Jewish mom switched at birth and uneasily disguised as a bony Episcopalian "who inherited only the garnets." Tad claimed the first word he learned from her was "eat." And the second two were "Duncan Phyfe." And it is a sad note to admit that though he did finally gather contributors and grants enough to begin Shadowlawn's "mere salvation," he also lost more pounds than the anticipated fifteen.

If I'd been told that at my present age, I would feel fully at ease with computers, I would simply not have believed it. But here I am, facing a blue screen, writing this. I now possess copies of all the disks left in Tad's laptop when he died. I scan through documents with a Peeping Tom's guilty joy. It is a holy trust. It feels like still getting notes and mail from him. I cannot help—even if out of sequence—saving two things found there.

First, he'd noted George MacDonald's observation "Home is the only place where you can go out and in. There are places you can go into, and places you can go out of, but the one place, if you do but find it, where you may go out and in both, is home."

In one file I found what Tad had left out of the "Elkton Green" description with which I opened. Coming on it filled me with such dread. I recalled the day I first understood that something was terribly wrong with Tad's health, he who seemed a sort of Friar Tuck, invincible.

Not two hours after the wedding ceased, newspaper accounts of the day tell how a young man carried his drowned bride one step at a time up onto the porch, moving slowly, bent across her, weeping like a child, moving toward the silenced father of Concord. The same mansion was still glowing golden, set there within spiders' webbing that now ceased seeming whimsical, that now looked only, and ever after, sinister. As if inviting spiders to a wedding had meant, from the start, to court disaster.

Pressing the Midas image forward to its usual end: Tragedy struck as it so often does when any person makes so spendthrift a display as had Caleb Coker. He felt he'd finally achieved exactly his fondest wish, to build a house meant to contain the "wedding of the century." Whenever anything we do drives us to say it is the whatever "of the century," perhaps we really should back off a bit. Our dearest wishes we must never utter quite aloud. The golden rice tossed, Concord's trousseau had been loaded onto the roof of an enclosed carriage. Said conveyance was swagged, of course, in white satin ribbons and the gardenias she loved. The horses were matched and extremely white. The travel to the train station would be but the shortest of jaunts. Not two miles from the spun-gold mansion—at what is still a difficult juncture of what's even now a poorly planned twist where U.S. 40 meets U.S. 98 over the still-too-narrow Melius Bridge—the married couple's coach driver, having imbibed many a celebratory rum toddy, misjudged that hairpin curve. The great weight of twelve steamer trunks strapped atop the vehicle caused it to tilt starboard and then wobble four inches off the Melius Bridge. Just one wheel slipped past its siding. But such was the weight of one father's gifts, Concord's new novels, unworn fineries, furs, the silver hairbrushes and mirror, the whole wagon fell into what, just there, was but a shallow brook. Four white horses naturally followed. Concord had been seated on the side of the vehicle, which struck rocks first, and she was either drowned or crushed by the bulk of her unasked-for fineries. Her young husband survived. Contemporary accounts never fail to sketch—with that day's love of melodrama and stagey tableaux—the inevitable final scene. Caleb Coker was now supervising the exquisite comedy of his slaves, twenty, armed with butterfly nets trying to recapture the rental spiders, themselves powdered gold. (You can survive that and even safely eat gold dust in small amounts, as a recent vulgar 1980s party-food vogue in Japan and Manhattan makes clear.) Contemporary accounts insist that the bridegroom, himself unscratched during the dreadful mishap, caught a ride on the first vehicle to chance upon the broken bridge railing. And while the country crowd yet waded in the shallows to fish out silks and the drunken coachman—one black farmer, guiding his mule cart, deposited the groom at the curb of a brilliant home still-festive. The orchestra played even better now that most guests were gone. Up

*there on Elkton Green's great gallery porch, Caleb Coker was
yet visible, continuing to offer and accept champagne toasts, now
laughing, flipping a gold piece to the slave who'd caught the
largest spider fastest. When up the carpet toward Elkton Green,
his wet shoes leaving traces, came the bridegroom, bearing in
his arms the body of Concord.*

　　*Imagining the moment when the girl's doting and ecstatic
father first caught sight of his only child, dead . . . it remains
unimaginable. No, not quite unimaginable . . .*

I'm struck again by what a religious nature young Mr. Worth had.
I simply mean he wasn't simply anecdotal; he believed in more than
experience, far more than mortal brick and mortal mortar and English boxwoods that grow only a half inch a year, which simply
makes your big ones mean more. It all implied a sort of "belief
system," as my son who did divinity school might say.

　Maybe this explained why, as an adult, Tad lived in that comfortable but perfectly ordinary little cottage built in the forties, the
1940s. It was really fairly spare, the way he lived. Tad never acted
happier than when he was in one of the properties that he himself,
with all his wiles and charms, had saved. But he didn't yet feel quite
entitled to occupy one himself. Maybe that's why the older houses
were so free in revealing their secrets to him. Safe to fess up their
former family problems—safe, their offered news, preserved with
him. He saved face, for real estate, a sort of go-between for occupants living and dead, as I shall demonstrate in a bit.

As I stated, he attended the University of Virginia. He worked each
summer as a day-labor gardener on the grounds of Monticello.

　Tad claimed that in the household's former vegetable patch, they
were forever tilling up weather gauges or oxidized iron yardsticks,
eighteenth-century glass beakers drilled with holes. Science was a
cottage industry there. It reached Tad so clearly and daily that Jef-

ferson's whole enterprise had been an experiment, a tester's way-station. And, in later talks, Tad would mention this vision of democracy as a series of go-for-broke if scientifically observed risk-takings. Pushed far enough, these make democracy theological, not just coolly rational. Jefferson's quest to understand some divine master scheme presupposes one. It assumes some ferocious Palladian blueprint, a golden mean of absolute proportion underwriting all our messy doings and our failed designs. Just such striving and good faith shaped the Federal buildings Tad loved best, their symmetry and modesty, the frontal almost virginal candor.

Tad Worth's relation to Jefferson became immediate for many of us locals: There is a handsome illustrated volume called *Mr. Jefferson in Motion, a Documentary Biography in His Own Words*. I'm told that the book is still in print; it is by one Jean Garth Randolph. One photo's caption reads: "Contemporary Model wears a favorite red under-waistcoat owned by Jefferson from circa 1800–1820. Silk crepe with brown velvet collar, woolen sleeves, and a lining consisting of cut-apart knotted cotton and wool fleece stockings, upper back embroidered 'TJ. Monticello.'" And there, in three-quarters profile, his long auburnish hair tied back with a black grosgrain ribbon in the simplest eighteenth-century manner, stands Tad. Nineteen if unsmiling, he's still recognizable, but he looks like some overpretty Renaissance page of about twelve. Of course, he was shorter than Jefferson's six three or, some claim, four. Still, there is our boy, on record.

"Puttin' on Marse Tom's gear, that's my Tidewater idea of real high cotton." But Tad always refused to look at his own printed image. For a while, that big book was on absolutely everybody's end table.

Tad once confessed to me, while half tipsy, that he had—as an undergrad history major—overstepped traditional respectfulness at Monticello. He'd been helping to catalog Jefferson's remaining clothes. "I knew that traces of his DNA (not to mention plain ole man-sweat) must still be soaked into one of those outsized white linen nightshirts he wore most when he was around thirty-five, and incidentally writing the Declaration. So one rainy afternoon, once all the nice docent ladies tripped upstairs for tea, I stayed on. First I sniffed Jefferson's white shirt. Eyes closed, I admitted I could smell mainly only basement—just time. So, it was then, Mary Ellen? well, I decided I'd better taste it. Just to make sure. I soon pressed my li'l mouth to the underarm of that fine linen, and before you could say '1776,' I was just suckling like a kitten." He grew oddly bashful; he hushed. And that made me come right out and ask, "What did? . . ." (I knew how far I'd come, when I allowed myself to articulate this. . . . I feared I was about to learn more than someone of my age, upbringing, and conventional beliefs strictly needed know. But I had asked, hadn't I?)

"What did it . . . he taste like? you were wondering aloud, were you, darlin' M.E.?" Tad actually made me nod then; nothing would do but that I become his Compleat Conspirator! Finally, a sly smile, and Tad's lips smacked, recalling. I saw a dreamy lit-up carnal Cheshire Cat grin begin as our friend bent nearer my good ear. He whispered, "I'd say . . . the great one's flavor was funky if semi-steely—busy, a bit overly Scottish, but ver' ver' salty. Naturally athletic. All too mortal, all too real. I mean, of course, all too male. But mainly, Jefferson tasted . . . mmm . . . preoccupied."

"You don't say" was the little I managed to remark.

Our five senses, I suppose, each practice a different sort of preservation. And I'd just met one novel way of gaining knowledge. My upright innocent mother had once stated that she hoped her little Mary Ellen might "someday develop a taste for American history."

I had, literally. He was such a literalist, Tad. Chewing Jefferson's laundry! Preservationists are literal. That's what makes them necessary. That's what lets them know so completely what they know. And once you know those things, ceremony or good manners cannot force you to unlearn them. I just mentioned my mother. She was born during Victoria's reign and a dearer if more orthodox lady you never met. She is long dead, Mother. But it just struck me that, were she to read what you've just done, her only child writing about one man gnawing on another man's article of clothing (most especially if the chewee proved to be Mr. Jefferson), well, Mother would quite simply have a small stroke, Mother would. And if she further understood I planned to let my written account "out of the house," placing it before the eyes of dozens, possibly even a few hundred, perfectly respectable people like yourself, Mother would then haul off and have herself a second, far more massive, stroke. It would, in fact, have killed her, this. And yet, I am doing it, aren't I? Because I was taught to. Because it feels right. I know what I know, now.

I later told a lifelong woman friend about Tad's wonderful imagination in sucking the Signer among Signer's shirt armpits; and it was only upon seeing the dear woman's face go fairly haywire that I understood. Some lucky people keep growing, while others happily sign off on doing that ever again. I was, at seventy-eight, still having my assumptions enlarged. I can thank one young fellow for keeping me perpetually off-guard and, perhaps, occasionally, even off-color. (Oh, but, my dears, I wasted so much of my life being needlessly embarrassed!)

Tad dropped out of the architectural school after an argument over period authenticity, and I am sure that he was right in both his scholarship and his assessment of his enemy's flawed character. He never shied away from the concept of a worthy opponent. He was a voluble "Yellow Dog Democrat"—which means that he'd have voted against a Republican even if a yellow dog—meaning some farmdog of no distinction—were running as the Democrat. His politics lost us certain big-time funders. "We don't want that kind of money, anyway. They're always expecting you'll let them throw their granddaughter's debut ball in the eighteenth-century Lutheran church they helped pay to save. I had a woman tell me she could just picture her little Courtney and Courtney's dad doing a waltz on the altar of a sanctified church; this dizzy dame would then have Courtney and her young marshal whisked away in a white carriage with matching white horses. Caterers there even for the horses. They've learned nothing from their lives."

We all heard his favorite toast, inherited from a late great-grandfather, Major A. B. Worth, who fought so gallantly in the War, "Confusion to the Enemy!"

When Tad got a grant from the state of North Carolina, an objection was made by an oldtime far-right-wing walleyed senator who mentioned Tad by name, in Raleigh's *News and Observer,* as "a gay rights activist leeching taxes from the life's blood of decent normal family people." Tad had this letter framed, a central relic and badge of honor in his crowded fascinating basement "office."

His friend Dan was, even more than some of us, changed by Tad's strong influence. Dan could calm him down as no one else could, and Dan's unbelievable know-how got us out of many a jam. Dan Trevor winched our big cars out of many a horrid red-clay ditch. Dan's kindness shored up more than a few sagging roofs. There are contractors interested only in building new structures, and ones who're in love with saving old ones. We were lucky Dan belonged to the latter group. It was, through helping Tad save the old Conger-Halsey Academy for Girls outside Rocky Mount, Dan came to know him first. By the end, they'd become inseparable as foxhole survivors. But it did surprise us when they moved in together. (Dan said it shocked him, too!)

After Dan left Carolyn, his wife, the gifted potter, once Dan started living with Tad, those three became models for us. Dan's wife and Tad managed to remain close friends. I must say it really was sort of unbelievable to somebody of my years and expectations. Carolyn has worked wonders as our major brochure designer and volunteer bookkeeper. Tad became the loving unofficial godfather to young Taylor, Dan and Carolyn's son. It was Taylor who spoke with such beautiful simplicity at the funeral service last month at All Saints' Episcopal and who played a tearful yet perfect recorder

solo that fairly well destroyed some of us. Tad always said that
Taylor was not to be trifled with, as he had the soul of a clear-eyed
naturalist eighteenth-century cleric, and all at age nine. This, young
Master Trevor proved at last Sunday's wrenching service. "Not a
dry eye in the apse, hunh, kiddo?" as our Tad might have put it.

Maybe I should say, along with Tad's idol of a generalist, Mr.
Jefferson, "If I'd had more time, I'd have written you a shorter
letter." Like all of us who knew Tad Worth, I benefited from quite
a good teacher. He was forever leaving me scraps of good things
he'd found. I'd step out for my mail and find these slips of paper
clothespinned to our battered box. There was never a signature,
only very careful noting of where he'd found what. I put them up
on our household altar of the present day, the refrigerator door.

I quote just one, the most recent. He must've sent it over via
Dan because Tad was by then too weak for walking, even the short
distance from his place to mine. The passage is out of Rilke's *Note-
books of Malte Laurids Brigge* and serves as epigraph from a book of
photographs Tad loved, a book about a beautiful decrepit Georgian
house in the Irish countryside. "It isn't a complete building; it has
been broken into pieces inside me; a room here, a room there, and
then a piece of a hallway that doesn't connect these two rooms, but
is preserved as a fragment, by itself. In this way, it is all dispersed
inside me—the rooms, the staircases that descend so gracefully and
ceremoniously, and other narrow, spiral stairs, where you moved
through the darkness as blood moves in the veins . . . all this is still
inside me and will never cease to be there. It is as if the image of
this house had fallen into me from an infinite height and shattered
upon my ground."

III.

This is the story I've been getting to.

Once, not that many months ago, though it seems about half a decade, Tad urgently summoned our little architecture discussion group to quickly gather, to meet him at Shadowlawn on the coast. This meant a three-and-a-half-hour drive. He phoned from the pay phone down there, insisted he needed us there and today and he knew it was very short notice, but that we must arrive by a certain time of evening. To the minute, we must be there.

Well, we're all very busy people—self-defensively so, I sometimes think, but he rarely gave us any direct orders. Tad never actually asked much of anything for himself. He let you offer whatever you felt able to provide the Cause. He had forty immensely capable but very different major people doing this, which is why our organization has been, I believe, in the end, so successful. Tad Worth didn't just praise the idea of the individual contribution and then get quickly bureaucratic and lord it over us minions from his too-new mahogany desk in some high-rent headquarters. The power was always out there in the community. As our lieutenant governor said at Tad's funeral (in a short but fine address), "Education was behind it all." We'd been schooled by him, our eyes had. (And as he said, "Once your eyes know, the heart follows; it's a matter of zoning.") But, oddly, Lt. Gov. Whitt Coventry might have been speaking of Tad's own far-ranging education. His pickup truck was a book-mobile. He read at red lights. Tad taught us by always teaching himself to keep learning. Then we personally applied the lesson.

So we said, "It must be important if he insists that we turn up by six-o-seven sharp." I do think that was the actual time, six-o-seven. He was on the drug AZT by then (now proved, as some of us suspected, to do more harm than good). Tad's T-cell count was at its lowest so far. (Though back in those earliest days we didn't know what "low" meant.)

He'd finally got hold of one of our state's most beautiful of domestic masterpieces. The message he left on my answering machine was just, "Girlfriend? Shadowlawn—home-free!" Tad only got it after years of honest legal chess and much backgammon dishonestly inept.

———————

Having got his hands at last on Shadowlawn, he wanted to spend his own last energies restoring this house of houses. He wanted to live right there on the coast, alone in the big house. It was still an absolute wreck at the time (this was March). I insisted he stay at a motel nearby. I set up an account by phone with them, I made them call me when he didn't turn up for a night. Dan would spend every weekend down there with him, chipping paint and hauling things. But, like most people, Dan had a child, a job and house payments that kept him inland on weekdays. We all worried not just about Tad's diminishing health but about his falling in a house that'd never had a phone. But Tad was like that, when he'd finally acquired a property, this one especially. He felt exempt from harm once he was on the grounds, once Tad knew the acreage had finally been saved. There had been vandals swarming all through Shadowlawn for years, and to imagine him, in that barn of a place, with its exterior doors too weather-bowed to lock, all alone there on a cot! Circa would be his only lowslung if snippish guardian. And by then Tad was not so strong as he thought. As he pretended.

It's odd, in thinking back, he was very cautious about getting from historic property to property, an almost wrecklessly safe driver. Bad at it but at least aware of that. "Better he shouldn't know he's such a menace on the highway," as our dear friend Mimi Goldberg might say, "The Divine Miss Mimi," as Tad called her. But once there, on the saved grounds, Tad acted fearless in crawling under houses or clambering straight up on the beams, and then somebody had to run get the ladders again to help lead him down. And with a drink, as reward.

I rode to the coast with our hurriedly assembled group in somebody's Volvo wagon. I think it was Mimi's car, because there were several thermoses of libation, as I recall. The Reverend Sapp had brought one of his famous goose pâtés. I confess to feeling scared that Tad had hurt himself, that he'd half-slid into delusions thanks to all the toxic contradictory medicines they had him on. I'd let my husband go to the coast unsupervised, and I vowed none of that would happen again.

Well, we arrived down there quite close to the assigned hour. It looks extremely presentable now, thanks to Tad's day labor and many volunteer Saturdays by a devoted core "salvation" group down Edenton way. The approach to the plantation house had been slyly planned in 1810. A good idea has simply gotten better. You follow twin rows of now-enormous magnolias interspersed with apple trees, long since past their bearing years. And when you make the turn, you see the Federal house, a white Greek temple built to some goddess or no, more surprising, like the severe young goddess herself, upright as a dare against the bright green water of the Albemarle Sound, and you literally gasp. Despite the leaks and years and teenaged pyromaniacs, "it is," Tad would say of the columned place, "like some old lady come into a party, and who can still make a hell of an entrance. Even on two canes."

Still, at the time I am discussing, Shadowlawn's Doric plantation house was as yet a firetrap and a total mess. Only somebody with a certain amount of nerve would attempt to even set foot inside the big house, much less sleep there. Every fourth floorboard was spongy with "blue-chip greenies," and you'd fall right through. Vandals had seen fit to build fires in the middle of fourteen-inch-planked-heartpine floors. They didn't use the fireplaces which, weirdly enough, proved perfectly functional when somebody (Tad, I think) finally thought to try them. Day-Glo swastikas disfigured the walls up and down the spiral staircase, whatever of its hand-turned balusters had not been burned to make the midfloor bonfires. Skulls and hate-crime obscenities were painted on the walls, misspelled. These racial cursewords looked pornographic in rooms so graceful and, in many ways, despite their age, as yet so innocent.

It's awful how a beautiful old house, abandoned, draws to itself the worst element, satanists and Hell's Angels, "drifters" and the Klan. It becomes a blank screen onto which such riffraff projects the world's wickedest emotions. Saving such a house means calling back the world's best again, to balance out such awful ugliness. I am told that the word *religion* means to physically literally "bind up again," to repair something pre-existing, to "restore." And in our modern world, even with so darn much "available for restoration," the rejuvenation of a fallen temple is, quite literally, a mission doubly religious. I know that now.

I remember Tad greeting us from the portico, waving, cutting up, calling "a big hi hi hi!" As we walked nearer, we saw he was smiling and looked absolutely filthy. Tad was happiest dirtiest. He was, I can say, the least claustrophobic person I have ever met in my life, and the cellars and crawlspaces he jumped right into, those make me . . . well, I started to say, make me feel that he's safer, wherever he's got off to. Basement-wise, underground-wise. There. I will stop all that. He would scold me terribly for that. He loved true feeling, but hated sentiment—except in grand opera, Mad Ludwig's castles, or in fifties melodramas. . . . (Susan Hayward's electric-chair weeper, *I Want to Live!*, was oftimes quoted.)

He stood there filthy, with green mold on one cheek and smiling, looking even thinner than ten days ago. But absolutely beaming.

"What've you found?" somebody asked. Then Circa came charging us, growling, protecting him. She went for the Reverend Sapp's ankle. He kicked her a pretty good one. Tad had told us that any self-defense must be judged legal around Circa's testiness. I can show you marks on my left ankles that prove how often liberalism fails.

It was Tad Worth himself, contrary to what he told the papers, who turned up the heavy silver service for sixty buried behind the collapsed well-housing at Pilgrim's Respite out past Belhaven. It was the sale of those thirty-pound silver punchbowls, shaped like a group of plunging dolphins reined and ridden by putti, that helped us fund most of our restoration of the grounds there. We assumed he'd come across some major booty here, too.

So, Tad now crooked his finger at us, led us around toward the back of the Big House. I remember how he idly touched one side of a massive column, he acted like someone taking an inventory of its crackled fluted surface. I knew he did this for support, I knew by now the house was there to keep Tad standing. I remember the way a few of his oldest friends looked at one another, immediately recognizing his greater frailty, but doing so behind him, saving face. This was in early March, I'm sure now, because some of those immense forsythia bushes nearest the sound were just popping out their first brave yellow. The whole mansion smelled of wood rot, a scent we have all learned to recognize and loathe. (Just as new-cut lumber, especially cypress and cedar, now outranks yours truly's old standby Shalimar as my new all-time favorite scent!) Tad, thinned to looking somewhat perfect if pale was becoming honeycomb-candlewax, translucent.

He stationed himself in the crook of Shadowlawn's major chimney. It stands fully three stories tall (three if you count the overseer's parapet). Its outward brick is inset with pale oyster shells that form the founding family's initials a yard high and all vined together with Chippendale high spirits. As usual, Tad wore on his belt a ring clinching three full pounds of keys—old "blue-chip greeny" skeleton ones fitted to many of the good eighteenth-century homes surviving along our Carolina coast. Though the day was chill, Tad leaned there without a sweater in this brick-heated little natural alcove. I think there were two large English boxwood screening and enclosing half of it, making it seem even more a secret resting place. The sort of place that children find and love and where they hide first. The crenellated chimney's orangish bricks (probably fired on the site, but said to be ballast from an English ship, *Plenitude*) retained the warmth from whatever sun there'd been that day.

"I want us to have a little seminar, my folks. About occupants of historic homes. The people that get left behind. . . ." We had already

talked at length about which kind of independently wealthy, professional, and very rare young couples are likely to put up with the
headaches of dripping roofs, custom-cut joists, and 1790s termite
damage, with tourists knocking on their doors and grad students an-
nouncing they did a dissertation concerning your stairwell and so
must be let in. I believed that by saying "the people that get left behind," Tad meant such potential buyers for Shadowlawn proper.

"I've held off doing this till you all got your dear carcasses on
down here. Can't start to hint how ver' much I 'preciate youall's
coming so doggone fast." Then Tad pulled from the torn back
pocket of his spill-art chinos a favorite Smith and Hawken trowel.
He kissed its blade, as if for luck. Next, in this little spot of late
light filtered and glimmering across the inlet, Tad bent painfully
down. It was like watching someone eighty, eighty-five. But, once
on all fours, he starting digging as if he were about eight, and possessed.

Circa soon got into the act, scratchy and snappish. She tried to
claw the dirt right alongside his. Defending him, the dog acted jealous for all Tad's attention. I guess each of us wanted that. Come to
think of it, so did all "his" houses. They were competitive for Tad's
fullest energies, ready to monopolize his talent at concentrating.
And the mansions used opera divas' pet tricks; when Tad spent too
much time with one grand dame, the others had breakdowns,
sprung leaks, threw material tantrums. Possessive, the great homes.
"They're childish as brilliant singers are," he once told us, "that are
pitifully in need of our constant reassurance. You'd think that the
greater the voice, the less hand-holding they'd require. Oh but 'au
contraire.' Never get enough, these ole gals—coquettes, geniuses."

If we'd been watching anybody but Tad, we might have asked
why this fellow had dragged us down here on a weekday afternoon,
a three-and-a-half- or four-hour drive one way, and just to study
him scooting around in clay for some stray tulip bulb or minié ball
or something. It certainly took him quite a while, hacking down
there. It did seem maybe . . . delusional, this digging. Skinny as he'd

got, I found it hard to watch him strain. Even his back looked narrower, which made the shoulder blades poke out like starter kits for wings. His dog was going even crazier than usual, poor overbred creature. She behaved as if he were about to uncover some dinosaur egg in the act of hatching. He laughed over at her, "Good Circa. I know, I know. You smell them, right?" I remember watching perspiration darken the back of his blue shirt. Digging this hard used up about one full week of Tad's waning energy. But we would not have dreamed of saying, "Here, let me." Still, the long wait was almost dentally painful.

About the time that even we, of his faithful inner cadre, were starting to picture the one remaining half-full thermos, the Saran Wrapped pâté in Mimi's old wagon, Tad's blade struck something stone or metal. He shouted, "They're right. I knew. They never have lied to me."

We stepped closer, we saw he'd dug a trench about a foot or eighteen inches deep, cut right up against the foundation's powdery brick footing. By laboriously leaning on the chimney, Tad stood. I worried, I saw that he was light-headed, rising too fast and him embattled by so many competing primitive drugs. You learn to hate these stopgap "cures" as much as you respectfully despise the gin-clear antipreservationist disease itself.

From the hole, our Tad lifted a dark tin box with a latch on it, two feet long, filthy it was; he dragged it free of pinkish tree roots and up into sight. Grinning, he held it off to one side the way my husband displayed the fish he'd caught, as if to use his own body as a yardstick, scale of reference. Once Tad had tugged the thing to better light, he flopped down beside it, panting with transparent pleasure and exhaustion. I remember the look of his long hand touching the tin. How blue-veined and aristocratic his wasting hand looked, stroking the black prize. All of us, no matter how old and creaky we were (chronologically in most of our cases) managed to drop right onto the grass in a rough circle close up around and against him. His hands shook so, prying it open. Somebody finally tried helping, but Tad, uncharacteristic, snapped, "No!" setting Circa off. And we all grew more still, more withdrawn, afraid to even glance at one another. I can't explain the tension. Expectation mixed with social embarrassment. Dread, and something a bit ghoulish, this caffeinated kind of curiosity.

Once opened, the tin casket proved stuffed with what'd been yellow straw but a very long time back. Then some cloth, home-spun, even I could tell that (I, who seem to have no knack for historical fabrics—one of my own sundry blind spots). It was sewn into a cloth valise, joined shut with big childlike stitches, faded red thread. This packet had then been sealed, crusted over, with what appeared to be about twenty candles' worth of wax. The Reverend Sapp, who claimed some archaeological experience in the Middle East from his Virginia Episcopal Seminary days, frowned a bit at Tad's utter lack of methodical scientific technique. Tad was ripping into this item like some Christmas present meant only for himself. But that didn't bother me one bit. None of us ever found the things he did. Hadn't we piled into the car to come and see exactly this, this thingum, whatever it was?

I knew how sick he already was (though he could still hide it cleverly well). I knew how much work he felt he must yet do down here. (Some of us would later labor alongside him here, at Shadow-lawn, as he scraped ninety years of varnish off the carved ivy pan-eling he'd found under beaverboard upstairs. By then Tad worked while hooked to his IV pole on a rolling tripod. He wore an oxygen tank, clear tubes in his nose. "Lorgnettes for nostrils" Tad called these tubes, with a whimsy that came to seem more and more cou-rageous—more of a buttress, somehow more "architectural"—as we watched him all but evaporate before our eyes. He was doing restoration "against doctors' orders." Somebody'd made a joke of the IV pole by taping cardboard Chippendale claw-and-ball feet onto its tripod castor legs. By then, we understood a thing or two about Tad's glorying enslavement to the work of "binding up again," his will to make this last house perfect.)

But that early evening, with us bunched all around him, as he tore open the shroud cloth, Tad gave off a little howl. It's that I remember best. Every quality we loved in him was in that sound. It was a kid's cowboy-and-Indian war whoop but contained his knack that managed, in the worst of circumstances, to find something funny and pleasurable waiting. It's the quality that let him proselytize so effectively for our cause; he showed people the pleasure of old houses, the pleasure of letting the places yield up their separate secrets to you. Allowing them to confide in you as you, trusting, dwelt in them. One detail at a time. As your human friends will, "Oh, and did I ever mention how, once, here? . . ." People were soon hooked, they became utterly addicted to old houses. He was actually a sort of marriage broker. And people thanked our Tad Worth here, for hooking them to the one whose lies, pretensions, secrets, whose own looks, best matched theirs.

From the box he lifted two joined dolls. One was a dark wooden effigy, almost a totem. It was obviously home-carved, maybe ten inches long. The other had a porcelain head, a stuffed bodice, two simplified bisque hands attached to cloth tube arms. Sawdust was sifting from her torso at the narrow waist. She had hair painted in a buttermilky brown and with delft blue eyes and you didn't need carbon dating to know the thing was eighteenth century. Oddly enough, the arms of this porcelain doll were literally wired around the black carved wooden figure. That one's hair was, or had been, knotted rope. If the porcelain doll was obviously English, the gumwood one was African or African-inspired in its angularity. But however stylized, it seemed strangely more human than the costly porcelain one. The dark form's only facial features were two red bone buttons set deep into wood, representing her eyes. This wooden one's arms had also been rope, square knotted at their ends to signify as hands. Both rope arms were trussed around the bodice of the porcelain doll. Embracing, the pair was still bound to each other, face to face, further joined by loops of circling wire long since rusted red-brown and staining the yellowed muslin.

Tad held up the clinging two of them, a unit. We considered the joined pair from all angles. Circa kept snarling, competitive-sounding, guarding, in the quince. Of course we looked from the effigies back up to Tad's face. Ready to be told what they meant. We were always expecting it from him and Tad certainly usually gave at least an educated guess. Sometimes his intuitive faking turned out to be truer than the gathered experts' mustiest certainty. His going directly to that silver, buried by the stone well-housing out back of Pilgrim's Respite, being but one profitable example among dozens, hundreds.

I saw he had done right, to get us here just at dusk. Since all this happened on the westerly facing of the Shadowlawn plantation house, the sun gave off this wintry red but full of gold. The light had moved far higher up the chimneys. Our being so in blue shadow made us feel a little underwater and unreal here, squatting on the ground. The inlet's reflection threw moving highlight lines, wavering across the uncertain faces of our little group. I remember looking hard at Tad and he gave me this open stare that was confused and awed yet pleased at once. I could see his cheekbone's sweeping edge, so suddenly elegant, you knew it would be terminal.

I worried he had been feverish down here and without phoning me or telling any of us, sick in that grim little motel he loved "because it looks like the one in *Psycho*" and had a blue neon star blinking on its front. But before he explained this twin effigy, I guessed he'd first have to say something silly, wry or indirect, the way he did. "I know you've got a toddy or two hidden out in Mimi's car, and I can't believe you've made me get down on my dingy knees and fetch this thang up and that I still have to beg you all for one li'l ole drink." Somebody ran for the thermos, and I mean they ran. Because we were waiting. We sensed it, you see. We already did.

He started crying then. Or laughing. I think it was the only time

I'd ever seen Tad Worth actually shaking with emotion—though his eyes were forever tearing up over seemingly small things. He leaned against the Flemish-bond brick chimney, he touched the shell initials of the founders. It was odd to find him, of all people, abruptly speechless. For the first time.

Usually, talking off the cuff, Tad could populate any front porch's Windsor chairs, could describe the familiar (if long-dead) occupants right into them. Call it fund-raising via hackle-raising. At some meeting, he'd say, "Imagine it's the notoriously cool summer of 1840, no bird song much, the doomed young consumptive Annabella Cameron's journal noted . . . ," and you'd see the most hard-hearted of city managers gaze back, eyes narrowed, as if resisting a sudden interior draft, necks stiffening, a bit defiant and even furious, but already cooperating despite themselves.

"Well, what?" I asked him. We were seated scattered all around him and somebody touched his shoulder, and he was smiling but eyes running water. I had hoped that the disease would spare him possible blindness. I'd read everything on the subject. I knew that for Tad, blindness would be just one zoning district shy of death. The smell, that close to the dirt in March, spoke about our many chances at finally thawing out; and with spring rushing in from the inlet and up from underground, we waited there. We sat in the sad smoky smell of the beautiful crumbling house.

"About six-oh-seven yesterday, I saw the girls who buried this." He looked from face to trusted face. We glanced at one another. Faux-casual. First it seemed he meant that some local children had dug this box up and then maybe they'd reburied it, maybe he had caught them. But the dirt he'd been hacking at was good packed red clay, weathered-baked nearly bricklike on the surface and unbroken for centuries, it seemed. Rev. Sapp now scurried back with martinis sloshing in a red thermos lid. He hadn't brought one of the leaded crystal tumblers we unregenerate drinkers travel with (a bit ostentatiously) and that we sometimes broke, but never our best tumblers. Rev. Sapp said, "What?" like some kid who hates missing something by going for refreshments and is bitter at seeing how just that has happened. We shook our heads to show we didn't know, not yet.

Tad downed his drink all at once and choked, then laughed at doing so, which helped. He said for the record that he had been stooping over, right there, not four feet off, at the corner of the portico the afternoon before. It had been exactly this time of day with light reflected from the sound, moving curved lines over the brick, much as it did now. Tad said he had been cleaning out some of the giant honeysuckle that'd claimed the lattice lathing under the broad front porch. There was a clump of mint (for juleps) and he was doing battle with honeysuckle vines in hopes of saving the mint, "which I admit has held its own since 1810 but it's never too late to give a thing a break finally, right?" He said he heard a chiming knock, like some shovel striking the chimney, just three times.

"I was squatting over yonder, there, just there near Circa's quince.—Hush, darling, please do hush now, girl.—And, you know, me as usual, sweating like a pig. And when I wiped my forehead with the back of my hand and looked toward the sound, and when I took my hand down? I saw two little girls. They were charming, one black, one white. About eight to ten years old. They were holding on to each other, standing there and just facing me, looking me over. They had an expression that seemed to hint as how I was the one out of place, and they—of all the people on the farm—were at least glad to be the first to notice me. I said something like 'hi,' something witty like 'hi,' right? At first they only stared at me, each keeping very very still. But extremely there, you know, and conscious and seeming amused that I was such a mess and down on my knees. They both seemed to be wondering what was I doing on their farm. I could see plainly enough that the white girl had light brown hair chopped off just at the shoulders and was in a sort of gingham dress, checked, brown and red, floorlength, groundlength out here, but it could've been some sixties hippie-child's 'granny dress.' And the black girl—blue-black African black—wore a homespun almost burlapy thing, very simple with long sleeves and a boat neck and she had pierced ears with small star-shaped pewter bits, pewter, I was sure of it, pewter stars in her ears. For some reason, that seemed a tipoff, like, you know, 'pewter,' tin mixed with lead, get it? But no, I was just as dumb as before. They were standing there arm-in-arm and not quite smiling but very pleased looking, very much together, as if about to laugh but scared to hurt my feelings. Behaving as if . . . how to explain this? . . . as if there were many other people all over the plantation, working the place, and like they had strolled off into one quiet corner—a favorite place, I felt—for a nice moment alone together and had found me. (I sensed how crowded the farm really was, busy and productive but sort of hostile to children, something in their sense of secrecy, the bond between them, suggested that.) And it was only then I noticed they were pointing down, they both were. Toward the same spot. I just hadn't seen that, not at first. Or maybe when they guessed they could trust me, they indicated the one spot. I was here by myself. Circa, excepted. I mean, the volunteers had left about four-thirty, and I was just doing a few last clean-up chores. Needed a quick nap on the cot in the foyer. Then, and only then— and by the way, all this is just taking maybe just, oh, eight to twelve seconds, this whole loaded glance—very quick, very matter-of-fact— it was only then I noticed the texture of the bricks behind them, and only then, like a dolt, does it occur to me that I can see the goddam bricks, like, THROUGH them, right? Well, here's the really dopey part, I smile at them, as if they live here, as if I'm the slave gardener and know so, and yet to prove I also have a reason for being here, too, right? I go back to the vine I've been yanking on, and I actually lift my gigantic vat of Round-Up I've been spraying at the honeysuckle, like I'm bored, like I'm just going on with my work, and only then, having turned my entire back on them, do I do this incredible Three Stooges eye-popping doubletake. *Boing,* hair up—eyes out to here—and of course they're gone.

"You know the phrase 'disappeared into thin air'? Well that's what I had seen happen. I'd never felt that phrase meant much— isn't all air thin? Well, air so recently evacuated does, believe me, feel damn 'thin.' Who says air can nevah be too rich or too thin, hunh? But I kept thinking 'thin air,' 'thin,' like snatching at that phrase, because I so wanted to touch them, to hold on to them. Mainly to ask them things. I didn't run to phone anybody, didn't tell a soul. Not at first. Didn't even ring Dan, I mean nobody. And then about two o'clock this morning, at the Norman Bates motel, I wake and sit up and say aloud, setting poor Circa to barking, 'They buried something. They were burying something. And I caught them at it and so then, they went ahead and showed me where they'd hidden it.' I was that sure of it, I called you up.

"Now you're all here, and here is this cask, these dollthings. I mean I wanted you to see the progress on the house generally. But I felt I had to have my sanctum sanctorum nearest-dearests here for this. I figured that if I didn't hit anything, I would stop digging, as if suddenly even more than usually absentminded lately—then I'd maybe stand up and just show you the handpainted horse-and-river French mural paper we're beginning to uncover in the foyer, and then I'd take you all to the Fish House over near Edenton for dinner, but I'd not say nothin' and jes' keep rollin' along. But to find these things, the one a slave toy and the other something porcelain and plainly English import. I believe it was a pact between them, the girls, to go ahead and wire their arms around each other, the dolls. Like they knew their friendship couldn't stand whatever tests were coming—a saleable slave child and the owner's daughter, or the overseer's—but to plant these here. As a sign, near the house, a sign they loved each other. To show they knew that, and to save it some."

By now the light was mostly gone. Only the tips of the four

chimneys held a charged kind of sandpapery red, like the heads of matches. The shadow where we stopped felt privileged but too permanent. It'd gotten some colder. We could see the scallop boats, their lights blinking way out there, coming home, nets hoisted after the long day's catch. Two bats kept diving near the house. And Tad lifted his effigies, Tad moved to pass these into the hands of the person nearest him, everything, that tin box, the wax-sealed bag and those odd dolls, still bound together . . . he handed it to somebody who instinctively drew back, acting almost comically repulsed. She . . . actually, it was I, alas . . . pulled away as if fearing that this thing had come direct and scalding from some infernal oven. Would it burn, or freeze? Maybe it was how quick and saturated the darkness had just got. I felt he was placing some image of himself dead into hands not willing to accept that yet. (Still not.) I steeled myself . . . hating this squeamishness that seemed so unlike me, at least the "me" I could admire even a bit. But then Mimi, God love her, laughed and said, "What is this, hoodoo voodoo? Gi' me it!" and reached past me, grabbed the thing. Out of order. Then we each took hold of his find, all of us, me going right after Mimi. I think it was something about my husband's death, and being so near the water. Made me hesitate, then feel that I had let Tad down. I felt like St. Peter, denying on the crucial night. It's odd, but we all held on to the dolls, and even the box, and for quite a while. As if greeting them, a cordial welcome, to above ground. It seemed we'd expected even these to melt into the same thin air where the girls had gone. We expected the dolls to vanish when they left Tad's hands as he tried to fit them into ours. We knew then, that "thin air" was already welcoming him. But the object(s) remained, object, solid, like his legacy—like Tad himself till then—so reassuringly material. These figures had lasted the way inanimate things get to (lucky for us, as our compass points and referents). Lord knows, we don't.

Then our group drove over to Edenton for shrimp and oysters and scallops, which were excellent and right off the boat, everything's so fresh down there. At dinner, no one really mentioned what he'd dug up. I remember how quiet was the long car ride home without Tad. I begged him to come back home to Hillsborough just for tonight. He'd have none of it, of course. On the long trip back, it wasn't so much that we were spooked . . . though we were, and in some new way. I'd always felt a little scared for him, bodily, I mean. Worried for his fragile bones, a fall, thing like that. Now something else took over.

I'd heard him joke about certain young lady ghosts that hived around/inside the stone privy yet standing at an old girl's academy, the Burwell School, right in Hillsborough. "The Haunted Outhouse," Tad called it. I asked him what if felt like, his freely moving around this particular ghost nest; his knowing that they knew that he was there, observing, enjoying. "Oh, M.E., I'd say like 'walking through a rain of talcum powder too fine to notice but it still gets your hair feeling whitish and you can sort of smell it, dusty humany basementish almost rose-smelling' sorta"; but he grinned as if only teasing. Even so, it stopped me, how certainly (I mean how lightly) he'd said all that.

In the car, I sat shoulder to shoulder with my friends riding west. I recalled his "They never have lied to me."

Well, you need not be Sherlock to deduce as how this means a critical mass, of earlier sightings, or promptings, promises. In the car bound home, I think we kept so hushed and a little glum, because we knew—if we hadn't before—who he was. We knew that Tad wouldn't make up such things—he'd never ever lied to me, or to anybody, except out of white-lie kindness, or during something like losing at backgammon for preservation's sake. I chastised myself for that three-second delay in taking what he'd handed me first. But, even so, we all suddenly unwillingly knew he was going to die. Soon. Somehow his seeing the occupants of this last great house he'd saved showed us just how soon (four weeks). He'd made us start to see the bricks through him. Come to think of it, we'd always seen the bricks through Tad!

Tad's mission (and I can use that word in good conscience here)

his mission was about so much more than just saving certain pretentious properties for a few more generations of socially ambitious
Carolinians who could afford to replace octagonal slate roofing tiles
than can cost, as we all know, up to thirty-nine dollars per. The
houses whom he'd saved were suddenly extravagantly giving
groundbreaking housewarming gifts back to him. Presents from
presences! Farewells. They meant "Well done, ye good and faithful
servant."

That's just one story about him. But it's the one that came to me.
I know there are people in historic preservation who are only interested in the architecture, in the pediments, the lemon-oiled perfectible period detail. I fear I've met a few. I fear I myself have been
wedged into more than a few mullioned window seats with Laura
Ashley floral prints and peppermint stripe piping on the cushions
tucked under my increasingly historical whatever (and there till after
two A.M.). These experts consider the people who actually live (or
lived) in these fine places as being something like the furniture . . .
you maybe need them there to make the house seem finished, but
they're incidental to the structure's superior claims. With Tad, the
living, the livingness of the place and what went on there and what
might go on there next, that was the definition of his passion, boxwood by old rose, slate by slate, mantel to passing mantel.

Then Tad died. At noon, March 31, Dan left a message on my
machine; he said that during the night, Tad had typed in caps on
his computer notebook, HERE GOES. Dan suggested maybe I
should get to the hospital. "It's started," Tad told me in his quiet
way. By the time I found the message and rushed in there, it was
almost over and I held one hand and Dan was on the other, as at
some birth. He was spared nothing, Tad, but he presided over it,
"inhabited" his dying. Our boy half-hosted it as he'd done every-

thing else. With one of his final breaths, by then so far past language that had been a great ally of his, he blew a sort of kiss.

Dan Trevor—after contacting Tad's parents (who were, for various reasons, unable to be with him at the end), Dan, after signing the coroner's papers, after speaking to doctors and nurses and the many close friends who'd gathered—bent toward Tad's computer. (It was still glowing in one corner of the unlit room.) At 1:04 A.M., Dan withdrew the disk containing Tad's final "Available for Restoration." I had agreed to take over this newsletter, so Dan handed it to me.

Back home, and right after the funeral, soon as I saw the pages printed out, I understood that despite Tad's determination to finish Issue #14, despite Tad's victory in staying one room ahead of the dementia, certain lapses had occurred. Confusions about sequence and details beset him at the end. Because of a final throat infection, Tad was sometimes unable to speak ("the worst indignity, dammit"), so he'd commenced typing notes to Dan and others, using the screen of his Toshiba notebook. These were interspersed with hard-sell raves about some condemned home's architectural niceties. The computer's amber screen was often his hospital room's only night-light.

Tad's notes and personal asides found their way into what, without such personal interjections, might have been a more official, if less original, text.

With Dan's permission and after my having misgivings about it, I want to offer a sample of this final document. I do this, being sure that Tad Worth, always able to see beauty latent under surface rust and seeming ruin, would approve.

In the final hospital stay, during his first clear weeks, Tad wrote the portrait of Elkton Green with which this issue started. (Despite that, I thought, irresistible come-on, we lost that great house to the insatiable yellow bulldozers.)

After describing Elkton Green so well, after thinking his portrait had sold the house but now unable to talk effectively, Tad still tried to interest some new buyer in Shadowlawn, too. He would work on this document during his stray good ten-minute patches. By then the plantation house had been largely restored by Tad and the crew. And I'm glad to say that we have now sold Shadowlawn to Pam and Joseph Coventry, who know exactly what they have and are willing to do even more to pull it back from the edge. So, Tad, it is saved.

This, the end of his Shadowlawn entry, was the last thing he typed. It's what I choose to print of all his final rambling pages:

The carriage house retains its frilled facing and a small family chapel, close by the water, still have traces of an ebonized Maltese cross atop its modified cupula. . . . The records show that slave and master worshiped here as one and

The same tired Restoration was paintaking and needs further expetise regarding modern plumbing. Still suitable fr. occupancy. Somebody is out there, sure of that . . . needs.

New systems required throughout, oh true. . By now there are hookups for natural gas heat and air, the evenings especially, and the sense of others who;'ve been near and can be . . . Mint, mention mint . . .

Abvout how close to water, mention. Noble approach mention noble approach, and english boxes. Many, big as Pluto, planet Pluto, not dog. Joke. How the fires could have been set in middle of floors don't know, we found the fireplaces to still draw perfectly perhaps a hundered years since fullest use, birds nests and old squirrels nests went up like tinders but the thrill to run outdoors at night and see smoke coming curling, like a thing relearning to breathe really, most beautiful though feared for stray sparks, must get screens, Dan. . . . screens to prevent cinders setting everything me saved afire.

Dan, hi, will leave the machine on . . . rougher today . . . if miss you, sorry. Must sleep more, The shakes bigtime. Drenchola. Tell Taylor hi, and to practice. Any word from parents?

Pain is bracketed now. One does not love a place less for having suffered in it, right? Rite? How can I sleep when nurses keep comin in waking me & waking me? Their good cheer wears one dow..y Extensive remodel needed. Priotico nearly complete. Big family could be so happy there, house has many treasure to yeield. Fish from dock. Smoke house sutible for guesshouse, aroma mild but pleasant,. can be shown daily, key at store . . . house dedc to comfort, Mint nearby mention drinks . . The parlor facing south, original glass throws shapes thoughtful human on wall and mofvews . . . tireder, language going, structre goiim ss-Ncup[e Confusion to the emeynesNeeds work but for immediate occupancy. . . . . . . Keep thinking we didn't pay phonebill again. Is it on? A life spent in non-profit okay! Confusion, the enemy. Hi hon, wkae me anyway? What the name the scrolling at corners, supports? Begins w.C. Look up later. My books. Around here somewhere. The right book. Find what type spiders web would best take gold dust? Dr Fscher glmmy. Last rose summer, pure gloss? Miss you, will

Sq ft: 6,8888844 ik rooms, zned for living.. . . .Where is my father and where is my m.. Aint no sech thang as bluechip-greenies—its all just greenies . . , Dan Dan why you so kind me? iBoy, talk about AVAIL For resoration! loans availbe, save this one pls. . Any word yet? Circa exema ok? Somthng nr chimney esp. signs & wondrs Waake me anyway ok? have M.E. correct this, fake it, will make press time, fine, sure . . . I hear water. There's bad break, leak, flor below, chk on rushingf water damage close ;;;I see certai of Its columns, all Ionic! I knew that. So Dry mouth./ Most of this must go but which of these is the bearing wall? Pme jakbaa. 777kkkkkkkkkkkkkkkkkkkkkkk-66#33 can restore to suit any new owner. Fix. I know you'r out there.

I buried something. They dug it up for me.

Am mostly beyond all tired. mst. ctch winx . . . Treated

2X6s^ I"Smokehouse roof leaki. Fix first. Always fix roof first, I keep . . . I forget. All keys, hall drwer.
    hi
    HERE GOES

IV.

I end by remembering a meal we had together. (One thing I must blame him for is how readily he knocked me off my diet. He'd show up with two bags of stray ingredients from the Wellspring Market in Chapel Hill, asking, "But whatever shall we DO with all these perishables? As Marse Wilde said, 'Simple pleasures are the last refuge for the complex.' ")

We were seated at my back table, finishing some raw oysters. This was when you could still eat those raw without worrying so. We'd only just acquired Shadowlawn, work had just started. But already, when he got up to fetch something, Tad was forced to reach out for the counter to support himself. Of course, he made it look quite natural, you know. Regal. Like, oh, he was solemnly recalling something.

Tad had been worrying over some legal issue involving right-of-way, easement to the entrance of the Shadowlawn big house, and he was frustrated and weak, a combination new to him. He said, "I really don't know nothin' bout rebirthin no houses, Mizz Scarlet." He stopped, head drooping and knuckles going white along my counter's ledge. I'd never seen him conventionally depressed before. Then I understood just how enraged he was at all the details, all the work left undone, and with only us amateurs trying to fake it in our way. However earnest, we all lacked his genius for vamping, guessing, making it LOOK right and therefore FEEL right, and in that order of zoning.

"I know it must be frustrating," I said, clumsy but well meaning.

"And yet, do think of everything you've saved, fifty-six or -seven masterpieces that were headed only for the wrecking ball, Tad. Do remember whatall you have achieved, m'dear." "Well, it's true we've set aside a single-family dwelling or two. But that's such a fraction. Of what's lost, M.E. Plus, I is so tired of keeping house, keeping on keeping on sweeping them flo's. Turns out, I do do windows after all."

"You are a window, honey." I was about to get started. "You are a window in a door." But he stopped me from saying something even more sappy and far too comforting. Too easy, I mean.

Then he pointed out the kitchen window to his truck. Circa, yappy, was guarding it. I saw all these clothes piled in the back. "Everything I've never been able to fit into, till today. And I feel some runway turns coming on. Point me toward your nearest changing room, prego, Coco?"

Tad had brought everything he'd ever purchased just in case he ever lost the weight. Today and today precisely, he'd got down to the very size he'd always imagined being (is this too much? he always told me there was no such thing as too much entertaining truth). He carried many armfuls into my front parlor. I set up a chair in the foyer, between those big flanking Victorian peerglasses, fifteen feet of beveled mirrors admiring mostly each other. I built a fire in either adjoining parlor, I put on a stack of Bix and Billie, and turned them way up. I even let poor Circa in, despite the half-idolatrous way I love my rugs. Needless to say, we treated ourselves to a few stiff drinks. Then he came out in one ensemble after another. First it was very funny, then it got unbearably sad, so sad, it turned hilarious. He was not a stranger to overdoing, as he'd told me that first day.

Tad wore every outfit, in high dudgeon with that comic-brave business he did so much during the last four years (a little *Dark Victory* in there, as he admitted). Tad staged the privatest of fashion shows for me. All the clean good clothes he'd never once squeezed into. "I've kept these in a separate closet forever called, 'Someday My Prints Will Come, in Handy . . .' " He brought more in from his green Ford pickup. Heaped, were all horizontal stripes, the pleated pants and tartan plaids. Circa was almost comically underfoot, yapping, entering into the spirit, running up to the mirror, considering herself, playing tag with her own reflection. She seemed weirdly smart today and almost charming.

Tad had visibly become exactly the splendid-looking person we'd all always seen, the one that Tad himself had never quite believed was under there. Perfect finally, and startled by it, Tad kept changing outfits, he was soon looping up and down my staircase, cutting through my good steep rooms in this house he'd saved, doing dips and turns and by the end, and after several more than our usual drier-than-the-Sahara martinis, we were both laughing and crying at once. Soon I was putting on every tweed overcoat left over from my George, and all the houseguests' orphaned raingear and whatever clothes my missing children yet stash upstairs. Hysterical, we were. Ah, but it was wonderful.

It felt like a perfect weekend house party, but it lasted only six hours. Just the two of us, taking all the parts. We were playing the way hard-disciplined schoolkids will when given, by accident, the run of the big house. It was a time as fine as ones I recalled from the mid to late thirties. For me, the very pinnacle of fun. House parties at Nag's Head just before the second war with all my girlfriends from St. Catherine's and many of the freckled courteous lovesick boys whose planes would soon have to get shot down.

As he finally walked past me, exhausted and practically croupy from the serious laughs we'd had and how it tested his failing lungs, I noticed something. Tad was by then wearing only a wool vest and Bermuda shorts, he was barefoot. I saw how thin his legs had gotten. How brown, how beautiful they were that scale. If his frontal padding always made him seem a Victorian edifice with furbelows and curly notches and overgenerous ornamentation, that joyful bulk had now changed. He was reverting, in period, at least. He'd slid back down from a too-prosperous 1870, to severer civic 1840 back to strict, pure, personal 1810. Today, Tad was exactly 1810!

I saw, being a beneficiary of his own architectural discussion group, that Tad had shrunk down to exactly his own favorite moment in American domestic design. His former happy corpulence had, in ending, finally achieved what he'd once called "the chaste, Greek proportions of the Federal." Tad had always explained to us: The Federal period was the last moment when, believing mankind (at least of the American sort) to be perfectible, architecture proved that possible. Proved that perfection, too, can become a self-fulfilling prophecy.

I just wanted to say something nice to him, is all. But, stupidly, I chose to talk about his weight, which also meant of course how much of it he'd lost. I said, "Your legs . . . ," and stopped, just hating myself, you know.

"Why? Are they finally fairly 'good'? Think so, M.E.? Well then, back kick, shuffle ball-change. All they needed was one serious pencil-sharpener apiece. Quit while you're ahead, hmmm? I seem to have gotten everything I wanted, for the wrong reasons. *Too Much Too Soon.* But, can you imagine me one day actually walking up onto the portico at Shadowlawn, when most of it is done, and me feeling great for one whole week, with a northwest breeze and no mosquitoes and just to be up on that porch, and me wearing khaki Bermudas with hardly any paint on them, and upright at last on legs this thin? Ooh, all I need is a couple more bronzer sticks and another NEH grant, gir'friend. Can I grate some extra horseradish for your ersters, honey? I'm right here at it. I am up."

"Your legs are Federal now."

At last, I managed to say it.

He glanced down, studied them, and looked right back up at me, "My God, they are. Quelle achievement!" Then, oh, how he smiled at me. It was almost worth it, just for that one smile.

I cannot explain the look of happiness Tad gave me then.

I cannot explain how I go on seeing all the bricks through him. Can't start to tell you the joy he yet gives me, day by day, room to room.

If—(here I am going to go ahead and do this)—if, as we are promised, "In my Father's house are many mansions . . . ," then there is a little justice after all.

He's occupied.

EDITOR'S NOTE

The year 1997 was filled with surpassingly fine novels by gay men. Edmund White, D. Travers Scott, Scott Heim, Kevin Killian, Allan Gurganus, Chris Bram, Richard House, and Aryeh Lev Stollman are all remarkable writers with remarkable novels, and I recommend them, though they are not conveniently excerptable in this anthology.

There are stories that should also be remarked upon here that did not appear in this volume on "technicalities." Peter Weltner, represented by the fine story "Buddy Loves Jo Ann," also received an O. Henry for his story "Movietone: Detour," published in *Fourteen Hills.* I let it go, but reluctantly. I urge readers to look at stories about gay men that are not by gay men—Annie Proulx's *New Yorker* story "Brokeback Mountain" and Lorrie Moore's "Lucky Ducks" in *Harper's* are two fine examples.

Note also that while the excerpt from Alfred Corn's novel *Part of His Story* is attributed to the publisher, it also appeared in the *Evergreen Review,* another strong literary venture for queer writing.

There are several excellent gay literary magazines available in better bookstores across the country. Look for them and enjoy the stories firsthand. I am especially thrilled with the consistently high quality of fiction appearing in the pages of Garland Richard Kyle's *modern words,* Kevin Killian's and Dodie Bellamy's *Mirage (#4)/Period(ical),* and Aldo Alvarez's on-line journal *Blithe House Quarterly.* The *James White Review,* until recently edited by the pioneering Phil Wilkie, is now in the capable hands of Jim Marks and will continue to provide the best gay fiction to be offered. In addition, while it is not a gay journal by definition, *Fourteen Hills,* a literary magazine published by San Francisco State University, is one of the most enjoyable publications and has become the forum for any number of excellent works by and about gay writers.

For solace and shelter, my thanks to Michael Nava and Paul Reidinger, charter members of the HGMS dining club. A very special thanks to Hugh Rowland, Anthony Veerkamp, Michael Kaye, Peter Ginsberg, Felice Newman, Richard LaBonte, Terry Adams, Kevin Killian, David Ebershoff, and Michael Lowenthal. You all know why.

CONTRIBUTORS

Keith Banner lives in Cincinnati, Ohio, with Bill Ross, his boyfriend. He is a social worker (soon going to part-time) who helps out people who are mentally retarded. His writing has appeared in *Christopher Street, James White Review,* and the *Minnesota Review,* and he has stories forthcoming in the *Kenyon Review, Men On Men 7,* and *James White Review.* His first novel is coming out next year from Alfred A. Knopf, titled *The Life I Lead.*

Justin Chin is a writer and performance artist. He is the author of "Bite Hard" and "Mongrel: Essays, Diatribes & Pranks."

Dennis Cooper is the author of the novels *Closer, Frisk, Try,* and *Guide,* the short fiction collection *Wrong,* and *The Dream Police: Selected Poems 1969–1993* (all Grove Press). He has published two books in collaboration with visual artists—*Horror Hospital Unplugged* (with Keith Mayerson) and *Jerk* (with Nayland Blake). He is a contributing editor of *Spin* magazine and has written for *Artforum, George, Grand Street, Interview,* and other publications. *Weird Little Boy,* his multimedia collaboration with composer John Zorn, musicians Mike Patton and Chris Cochrane, and artist Nayland Blake, was released this spring on Avant Records (Japan). He lives in Los Angeles, where he is completing his fifth novel.

Alfred Corn has published seven collections of poetry, his most recent being *Present.* He has been awarded fellowships from the Guggenheim, the National Endowment for the Arts, the Academy and Institute of Arts and Letters, and the Academy of American Poets. A frequent contributor to the *New York Times Book Review, Washington Post Book World,* and *The Nation,* he also writes art criticism for *Art in America* and *ARTNews* magazine. Corn lives in New York City and is at work on a second novel.

Jameson Currier is the author of *Dancing on the Moon: Short Stories About AIDS* and the documentary film *Living Proof: HIV and the Pursuit of Happiness.* His novel, *Where the Rainbow Ends,* to be published by Overlook in the fall of 1998, is a continuation of the characters depicted in "Guides" and was awarded a fiction grant from the Arch and Bruce Brown Foundation. His short fiction has appeared in *Certain Voices; Ex-Lover Weird Shit; Men on Men 5; Our Mothers, Our Selves; Man of My Dreams; All the Ways Home; The Mammoth Book of Gay Erotica;* and *Best Gay Erotica.* A member of the National Book Critics Circle, Mr. Currier resides in Manhattan.

J Eigo's short fiction has appeared in anthologies, little magazines, and art tabloids. An early AIDS activist, he drafted the federal policy that expanded access to experimental AIDS drugs. His theater and dance writing has appeared in such publications as *Theatrical Gamut* and *Dance Ink.* An occasional model, he has appeared on gallery walls and in the pages of *Honcho.* His erotic fiction has been published in the anthologies *Stallions, Best Gay Erotica 1997,* and *Butch Boys.* Recent essays on sexual rights appear in publications from the groups Sex Panic and GMHC.

Thomas Glave, a Bronx native, has recently completed graduate studies at Brown University and a collection, *Whose Song? And Other Stories.* A

1997 O. Henry Award recipient, he is an assistant professor of English at SUNY/Binghamton and has work forthcoming in *Callaloo* and the *Kenyon Review*. He is a 1998–99 Fulbright Recipient.

Robert Glück is the author of two novels, *Margery Kempe* and *Jack the Modernist*, both from High Risk Books/Serpent's Tail. Other books include *Reader*, poems and short prose; *Elements of a Coffee Service*; as well as a number of poetry chapbooks. Glück's work has appeared in the *Faber Book of Gay Short Fiction, Discontents, Poetics Journal, Men on Men 1* and *4, Zyzzyva, Flesh and the Word 4*, and elsewhere. The *1994 Dictionary of Literary Biography* lists Glück as one of the ten best postmodern writers in North America. He lives in San Francisco with his lover, Chris Komater.

Andrew Sean Greer is the recipient of the *Ploughshares'* 1996 Cohen Award for Best Short Story, for a piece that appeared in a volume of the journal edited by Richard Ford. Most recently, his work has appeared in the August 1997 edition of *Esquire,* and he has a work of short fiction forthcoming in *Story* magazine. He is a graduate of the University of Montana Writing Program and currently lives in San Francisco.

Jim Grimsley is the author of *My Drowning, Dream Boy,* nominated for the Lambda Award for Fiction and awarded the GLBTF Book Award for Fiction from the American Library Association, and *Winter Birds*, a finalist for the PEN/Hemingway Award. He is the recipient of the Sue Kaufman Prize from the American Academy of Arts and Letters. He is an award-winning playwright in residence at Atlanta's 7Stages Theatre.

Allan Gurganus is the author of *Oldest Living Confederate Widow Tells All, White People,* and *Plays Well with Others*. His fiction appears regularly in places like the *New Yorker, Paris Review, Men on Men, Harper's,* and *GRANTA*. He lives in New York City and North Carolina.

Scott Heim is the author of two novels, *Mysterious Skin* and *In Awe;* a book of poetry, *Saved from Drowning;* and the adapted script for the forthcoming *Mysterious Skin* film. He holds master's degrees from the University of Kansas and Columbia University. Originally from a farm in Kansas, he currently lives on the top floor of a brownstone in Brooklyn. In the works are a horror-film script, a second book of poems, and a new novel, *We Disappear.*

William Haywood Henderson has taught creative writing at Harvard and Brown and is a former Wallace Stegner Fellow in Creative Writing at Stanford. He grew up in Colorado and Wyoming and now lives in San Francisco. He is the author of *Native* and *The Rest of the Earth.*

Tom House divides his weeks between New York City and East Hampton, where he bartends part-time. His stories have appeared in such publications as the *Gettysburg Review, Harper's, Chicago Review, Best American Gay Fiction 2, North American Review,* and the *Literary Review.* He welcomes comments or queries at TomHouse1@aol.com.

Eric Gabriel Lehman has published novels, short stories, and essays. He received the 1998 New Letters Prize for Fiction and lives in New York City.

Matt Bernstein Sycamore has been published in *Flesh and the Word 4, Queer View Mirror 1* and *2, Women and Performance, Quickies,* and other publications. He is currently editing a nonfiction anthology, *Tricks and Treats: Sex Workers Write About Their Clients,* to be published by Haworth in 1999. He is also working on a collection of short stories. He publishes the zine *Mattilda's Purse* and lives in New York.

Peter Weltner has published four books: *Beachside Entries/Specific Ghosts* (stories with drawings by Gerald Coble), *Identity and Difference* (a novel), *In a Time of Combat for the Angel* (three short novels), and *The Risk of His Music* (seven long stories). He has recently completed a new novel, *Lay Aside Fear.* His work has appeared in *Men on Men 4* and the O. Henry Prize Story anthologies of 1993 and 1998. His new novel will appear in spring 1999 from Graywolf. He teaches modern and contemporary American poetry and fiction at San Francisco State University and lives in San Francisco with his partner, Atticus Carr, a medical social worker.

ALSO RECOMMENDED

"ephemera," Aldo Alverez, from *Amelia*

"Beauty, I Think," Shawn Behlen, from *modern words*

"Old World Manners," Bruce Benderson, from *Brothers of the Night*

"Deeper Inside the Valley of Kings," Kevin Bentley, from *Flesh and the Word* 4

"Sister Marvelous," Thomas Burke, from *The Great Lawn*

"Up with the Devil," C. Bard Cole, from *Dirty*

"After Van," David Ebershoff, from *Genre*

"Exile," Kevin Esser, from *RFD*

"Burial," Drew Ferguson, from *Blithe House Quarterly*

"Weightlines," Drew Limsky, from *HIS2*

"The Acuteness of Desire," Michael Lowenthal, from *Other Voices*

"Je T'Aime, Batman, Je T'Adore," Kelly McQuain, from *Best Gay Erotica 1997*

"Washing Up," James Morrison, from the *Crescent Review*

"I was living in the gay rodeo . . . ," Jacques Servin, from *Blithe House Quarterly*

"The Passenger," Jim Tushinski, from *Pen & Sword*

COPYRIGHT ACKNOWLEDGMENTS

ALSO AVAILABLE

BEST AMERICAN GAY FICTION 1
Edited by Brian Bouldrey

"An annual series that promises to take gay belles lettres out of its literary ghetto. . . . The fiction gathered here is united more by its quality than its queerness. . . . The word *best* is entirely accurate."—*Out* magazine

Contributors:

Aldo Alvarez
Rick Barrett
Stephen Beachy
Christopher Bram
Bernard Cooper
Michael Cunningham
Jason K. Friedman

Robert Glück
Jim Grimsley
Scott Heim
R. S. Jones
Kevin Killian
Adam Klein
Michael Lowenthal
Ernesto Mestre
Jim Provenzano
Dick Scanlan
JL Schneider
Matthew Stadler
Joe Westmoreland
Edmund White

BEST AMERICAN GAY FICTION 2
Edited by Brian Bouldrey
Foreword by Bernard Cooper

"A highly readable collection. . . . From the elations of first love to the emptiness of a partnerless old age, *Best American Gay Fiction 2* explores the full range of human emotion."—*Swing*

Contributors:

Stephen Beachy
Mitchell Cullin
David Ebershoff
Gary Fisher
Andrew Holleran
Tom House
Ishmael Houston-Jones
John R. Keene
Kevin Killian
Russell Leong

R. Zamora Linmark
Paul Lisicky
Michael Nava
Kolin J. M. Ohi
Dale Peck
D. Travers Scott
Scott Thomas
William Sterling Walker
Donald Windham
Karl Woelz
David Wojnarowicz

Published by Back Bay Books